The Big Book Of Classic Fairy Stories

'The Fairy Book'

THE BIG BOOK ❧ OF CLASSIC ❧ FAIRY STORIES

'THE FAIRY BOOK'

BY THE AUTHOR OF

'JOHN HALIFAX, GENTLEMAN'

WITH 32 ILLUSTRATIONS IN COLOR
BY WARWICK GOBLE

PORTLAND HOUSE
NEW YORK

This edition published 1987 by Portland House
Distributed by Crown Publishers, Inc.
225 Park Avenue South
New York, New York 10003

ISBN 0-517-63792-8

Printed and bound in Hungary
h g f e d c b a

PREFACE

A PREFACE is usually an excrescence on a good book, and a vain apology for a worthless one ; but in the present instance a few explanatory words seem necessary.

This is meant to be the best collection attainable of that delight of all children, and of many grown people who retain the child-heart still—the old-fashioned, time-honoured classic Fairy-tale. It has been compiled from all sources—far-off and familiar ; when familiar, the stories have been traced with care to their original form, which, if foreign, has been re-translated, condensed, and in any other needful way made suitable for modern British children. Perrault, Madame d'Aulnois, and Grimm have thus been laid under contribution. Where it was not possible to get at the original of a tale, its various versions have been collated, compared, and combined ; and in some instances, where this still proved unsatisfactory, the whole story has been written afresh. The few real old English fairy tales, such as *Jack the Giant-Killer*, *Tom Thumb*, etc., whose authorship is lost in obscurity, but whose charming Saxon simplicity of style, and intense realism of narration, make for them an ever-green immortality—these have been left intact ; for no later touch would improve them. All modern stories have been excluded.

Of course, in fairy tales instruction is not expected—we find there only the rude moral of virtue rewarded and vice punished. But children will soon discover for themselves that in real life all beautiful people are not good, nor all ugly ones wicked ; that every elder sister is not ungenerous, nor every stepmother cruel. The tender young heart is often reached as soon by the imagination as by the intellect : and without attempting any direct appeal to either reason or conscience, the Editor of this Collection has been especially careful that it should contain nothing which could really harm a child.

She therefore trusts that, whatever its defects, this Fairy Book will not deserve a criticism, almost the sharpest that can be given to any work—"that it would have been better if the author had taken more pains."

CONTENTS

THE FAIRY BOOK

LIST OF ILLUSTRATIONS

By WARWICK GOBLE

THE FAIRY BOOK

ILLUSTRATIONS

THE SLEEPING BEAUTY IN THE WOOD

ONCE there was a royal couple who grieved excessively because they had no children. When at last, after long waiting, the queen presented her husband with a little daughter, his majesty showed his joy by giving a christening feast, so grand that the like of it was never known. He invited all the fairies in the land—there were seven altogether—to stand godmothers to the little princess ; hoping that each might bestow on her some good gift, as was the custom of good fairies in those days.

After the ceremony, all the guests returned to the palace, where there was set before each fairy-godmother a magnificent covered dish, with an embroidered table-napkin, and a knife and fork of pure gold, studded with diamonds and rubies. But alas ! as they placed themselves at table, there entered an old fairy who had never been invited, because more than fifty years since she had left the king's dominion on a tour of pleasure, and had not been heard of until this day. His majesty, much troubled, desired a cover to be placed for her, but it was of common delf, for he had ordered from his jeweller only seven gold dishes for the seven fairies aforesaid. The elderly fairy thought herself neglected, and muttered angry menaces, which were overheard by one of the younger fairies, who chanced to sit beside her. This good godmother, afraid of harm to the pretty baby, hastened to hide herself behind the tapestry in the hall. She did this, because she wished all the others to speak first—so that if any ill gift were bestowed on the child, she might be able to counteract it.

The six now offered their good wishes—which, unlike most wishes, were sure to come true. The fortunate little princess was to grow up the fairest woman in the world; to have a temper sweet as an angel; to be perfectly graceful and gracious; to sing like a nightingale; to dance like a leaf on a tree; and to possess every accomplishment under the sun. Then the old fairy's turn came. Shaking her head spitefully, she uttered the wish that when the baby grew up into a young lady, and learned to spin, she might prick her finger with the spindle and die of the wound.

At this terrible prophecy, all the guests shuddered; and some of the more tender-hearted began to weep. The lately happy parents were almost out of their wits with grief. Upon which the wise young fairy appeared from behind the tapestry, saying cheerfully, "Your majesties may comfort yourselves; the princess shall not die. I have no power to alter the ill-fortune just wished her by my ancient sister—her finger must be pierced; and she shall then sink, not into the sleep of death, but into a sleep that will last a hundred years. After that time is ended, the son of a king will find her, awaken her, and marry her."

Immediately all the fairies vanished.

The king, in the hope of avoiding his daughter's doom, issued an edict, forbidding all persons to spin, and even to have spinning-wheels in their houses, on pain of instant death. But it was in vain. One day, when she was just fifteen years of age, the king and queen left their daughter alone in one of their castles, when, wandering about at her will, she came to an ancient donjon tower, climbed to the top of it, and there found a very old woman—so old and deaf that she had never heard of the king's edict—busy with her wheel.

2

" What are you doing, good old woman ? " said the princess.

" I'm spinning, my pretty child."

" Ah, how charming !   Let me try if I can spin also."

She had no sooner taken up the spindle than, being lively and obstinate, she handled it so awkwardly and carelessly that the point pierced her finger.   Though it was so small a wound, she fainted away at once, and dropped silently down on the floor.   The poor frightened old woman called for help ; shortly came the ladies in waiting, who tried every means to restore their young mistress, but all their care was useless.   She lay, beautiful as an angel, the colour still lingering in her lips and cheeks ; her fair bosom softly stirred with her breath : only her eyes were fast closed.   When the king her father and the queen her mother beheld her thus, they knew regret was idle—all had happened as the cruel fairy meant.   But they also knew that their daughter would not sleep for ever, though after one hundred years it was not likely they would either of them behold her awakening.   Until that happy hour should arrive, they determined to leave her in repose.   They sent away all the physicians and attendants, and themselves sorrowfully laid her upon a bed of embroidery, in the most elegant apartment of the palace.   There she slept and looked like a sleeping angel still.

When this misfortune happened, the kindly young fairy who had saved the princess by changing her sleep of death into this sleep of a hundred years, was twelve thousand leagues away in the kingdom of Mataquin. But being informed of everything, she arrived speedily, in a chariot of fire drawn by dragons.   The king was somewhat startled by the sight, but nevertheless went to the door of his palace, and, with a mournful countenance, presented her his hand to descend.

The fairy condoled with his majesty, and approved

of all he had done. Then, being a fairy of great common sense and foresight, she suggested that the princess, awakening after a hundred years in this ancient castle, might be a good deal embarrassed, especially with a young prince by her side, to find herself alone. Accordingly, without asking any one's leave, she touched with her magic wand the entire population of the palace—except the king and queen; governesses, ladies of honour, waiting-maids, gentlemen ushers, cooks, kitchen-girls, pages, footmen—down to the horses that were in the stables, and the grooms that attended them, she touched each and all. Nay, with kind consideration for the feelings of the princess, she even touched the little fat lap-dog, Puffy, who had laid himself down beside his mistress on her splendid bed. He, like all the rest, fell fast asleep in a moment. The very spits that were before the kitchen-fire ceased turning, and the fire itself went out, and everything became as silent as if it were the middle of the night, or as if the palace were a palace of the dead.

The king and queen—having kissed their daughter and wept over her a little, but not much, she looked so sweet and content—departed from the castle, giving orders that it was to be approached no more. The command was unnecessary; for in one quarter of an hour there sprung up around it a wood so thick and thorny that neither beasts nor men could attempt to penetrate there. Above this dense mass of forest could only be perceived the top of the high tower where the lovely princess slept.

A great many changes happen in a hundred years. The king, who never had a second child, died, and his throne passed into another royal family. So entirely was the story of the poor princess forgotten, that when the reigning king's son, being one day out hunting and stopped in the chase by this formidable wood, inquired what wood it was and what were those towers which he

"'Is it very far from hence?' asked the wolf . . ." *(Page 225)*

"A young girl of wonderful beauty lay asleep on an embroidered bed." (*Page 6*)

saw appearing out of the midst of it, no one could answer him.   At length an old peasant was found who remembered having heard his grandfather say to his father, that in this tower was a princess, beautiful as the day, who was doomed to sleep there for one hundred years, until awakened by a king's son, her destined bridegroom.

At this, the young prince, who had the spirit of a hero, determined to find out the truth for himself. Spurred on by both generosity and curiosity, he leaped from his horse and began to force his way through the thick wood.   To his amazement the stiff branches all gave way, and the ugly thorns sheathed themselves of their own accord, and the brambles buried themselves in the earth to let him pass.   This done, they closed behind him, allowing none of his suite to follow : but, ardent and young, he went boldly on alone.

The first thing he saw was enough to smite him with fear.   Bodies of men and horses lay extended on the ground ; but the men had faces, not death-white, but red as peonies, and beside them were glasses half filled with wine, showing that they had gone to sleep drinking. Next he entered a large court, paved with marble, where stood rows of guards presenting arms, but motionless as if cut out of stone ; then he passed through many chambers where gentlemen and ladies, all in the costume of the past century, slept at their ease, some standing, some sitting. The pages were lurking in corners, the ladies of honour were stooping over their embroidery frames, or listening apparently with polite attention to the gentlemen of the court, but all were as silent as statues and as immovable. Their clothes, strange to say, were fresh and new as ever : and not a particle of dust or spider-web had gathered over the furniture, though it had not known a broom for a hundred years.   Finally the astonished prince came to an inner chamber, where was the fairest sight his eyes had ever beheld.

A young girl of wonderful beauty lay asleep on an embroidered bed, and she looked as if she had only just closed her eyes. Trembling, the prince approached and knelt beside her. Some say he kissed her, but as nobody saw it, and she never told, we cannot be quite sure of the fact. However, as the end of the enchantment had come, the princess awakened at once, and looking at him with eyes of the tenderest regard, said drowsily, " Is it you, my prince ? I have waited for you very long."

Charmed with these words, and still more with the tone in which they were uttered, the prince assured her that he loved her more than his life. Nevertheless, he was the most embarrassed of the two ; for, thanks to the kind fairy, the princess had plenty of time to dream of him during her century of slumber, while he had never even heard of her till an hour before. For a long time did they sit conversing, and yet had not said half enough. Their only interruption was the little dog Puffy, who had awakened with his mistress, and now began to be exceedingly jealous that the princess did not notice him as much as she was wont to do.

Meantime all the attendants, whose enchantment was also broken, not being in love, were ready to die of hunger after their fast of a hundred years. A lady of honour ventured to intimate that dinner was served ; whereupon the prince handed his beloved princess at once to the great hall. She did not wait to dress for dinner, being already perfectly and magnificently attired, though in a fashion somewhat out of date. However, her lover had the politeness not to notice this, nor to remind her that she was dressed exactly like her royal grandmother, whose portrait still hung on the palace walls.

During the banquet a concert took place by the attendant musicians, and considering they had not touched their instruments for a century, they played extremely well. They ended with a wedding march : for that very evening the marriage of the prince and princess was celebrated, and though the bride was nearly one hundred years older than the bridegroom, it is remarkable that the fact would never have been discovered by any one unacquainted therewith.

After a few days they went together out of the castle and enchanted wood, both of which immediately vanished, and were never more beheld by mortal eyes. The princess was restored to her ancestral kingdom, but it was not generally declared who she was, as during a hundred years people had grown so very much cleverer that nobody then living would ever have believed the story. So nothing was explained, and nobody presumed to ask any questions about her, for ought not a prince to be able to marry whomsoever he pleases?

Nor—whether or not the day of fairies was over—did the princess ever see anything further of her seven godmothers. She lived a long and happy life, like any other ordinary woman, and died at length, beloved, regretted, but, the prince being already no more, perfectly contented.

HOP-O'-MY-THUMB

THERE once lived in a village a faggot-maker and his wife, who had seven children, all boys ; the eldest was no more than ten years old, and the youngest was only seven. It was odd enough, to be sure, that they should have so many children in such a short time ; but the truth is, the wife always brought him two and once three at a time. This made him very poor, for not one of these boys was old enough to get a living : and what was still worse, the youngest was a puny little fellow who hardly ever spoke a word. Now this, indeed, was a mark of his good sense, but it made his father and mother suppose him to be silly, and they thought that at last he would turn out quite a fool. This boy was the least size ever seen ; for when he was born he was no bigger than a man's thumb, which made him be christened by the name of Hop-o'-my-thumb. The poor child was the drudge of the whole house, and always bore the blame of everything that was done wrong. For all this, Hop-o'-my-thumb was far more clever than any of his brothers; and though he spoke but little, he heard and knew more than people thought. It happened just at this time, that for want of rain the fields had grown but half as much corn and potatoes as they used to grow ; so that the faggot-maker and his wife could not give the boys the food they had before, which was always either bread or potatoes.

After the father and mother had grieved some time, they thought that as they could contrive no other way to live, they must somehow get rid of their children. One night when the boys were gone to bed, and the faggot-maker and his wife were sitting over a few lighted sticks, to warm themselves, the husband sighed deeply, and said, "You see, my dear, we cannot maintain our children any longer, and to see them die of hunger before my eyes is what I could never bear. I will, therefore, to-morrow morning take them to the forest, and leave them in the thickest part of it, so that they will not be able to find their way back : this will be very easy ; for while they amuse themselves with tying up the faggots, we need only slip away when they are looking some other way."

"Ah ! husband," cried the poor wife, "you cannot, no, you never can consent to be the death of your own children."

The husband in vain told her to think how very poor they were.

The wife replied "that this was true, to be sure ; but if she was poor, she was still their mother"; and then she cried as if her heart would break. At last she thought how shocking it would be to see them starved to death before their eyes ; so she agreed to what her husband had said, and then went sobbing to bed.

Hop-o'-my-thumb had been awake all the time ; and when he heard his father talk very seriously, he slipped away from his brothers' side, and crept under his father's bed, to hear all that was said without being seen.

When his father and mother had left off talking, he got back to his own place, and passed the night in thinking what he should do the next morning.

He rose early, and ran to the river's side, where he filled his pockets with small white pebbles, and then went back home. In the morning they all set out, as their father and mother had agreed on; and Hop-o'-my-thumb did not say a word to any of his brothers about what he had heard. They came to a forest that was so very thick, that they could not see each other a few yards off. The faggot-maker set to work cutting down wood ; and the children began to gather the twigs, to make faggots of them.

When the father and mother saw that the young ones were all very busy, they slipped away without being seen. The children soon found themselves alone, and began to cry as loud as they could. Hop-o'-my-thumb let them cry on, for he knew well enough how to lead them safe home, as he had taken care to drop the white pebbles he had in his pocket along all the way he had come. He only said to them, " Never mind it, my lads ; father and mother have left us here by ourselves, but only take care to follow me, and I will lead you back again."

When they heard this, they left off crying, and followed Hop-o'-my-thumb, who soon brought them to their father's house by the very same path which they had come along. At first they had not the courage to go in ; but stood at the door to hear what their parents were talking about. Just as the faggot-maker and his wife had come home without their children, a great gentleman of the village sent to pay them two guineas, for work they had done for him, which he had owed them so long that they never thought of getting a farthing of it. This money made them quite happy ; for the poor creatures were very hungry, and had no other way of getting anything to eat.

The faggot-maker sent his wife out immediately to buy some meat ; and as it was a long time since she had made a hearty meal, she bought as much meat as would have been enough for six or eight persons. The truth was, when she was thinking what would be enough for dinner, she forgot that her children were not at home ; but as soon as she and her husband had done eating, she cried out, " Alas ! where are our poor children ? how they would feast on what we have left ! It was all your fault, husband ! I told you we should repent leaving them to starve in the forest !—Oh mercy ! perhaps they have already been eaten by the hungry wolves ! " The poor woman shed plenty of tears : " Alas ! alas ! " said she, over and over again, "what is become of my dear children?"

The children, who were all at the door, cried out together, " Here we are, mother, here we are ! "

She flew like lightning to let them in, and kissed every one of them.

The faggot-maker and his wife were charmed at having their children once more with them, and their joy for this lasted till their money was all spent ; but then they found themselves quite as ill off as before. So by degrees they again thought of leaving them in the forest : and that the young ones might not come back a second time, they said they would take them a great deal farther than they did at first. They could not talk this matter so slily but that Hop-o'-my-thumb found means to hear all that passed between them ; but he cared very little about it, for he thought it would be easy for him to do just the same as he had done before. But though he got up very early the next morning to go to the river's side to get the pebbles, a thing which he had not thought of hindered him ; for he found that the house door was double-locked. Hop-o'-my-thumb was now quite at a loss what to do ; but soon after this, his mother gave each of the children a piece of bread for breakfast, and then it came into his head that he could make his share do as well as the pebbles, by dropping crumbs of it all the way as he went. So he did not eat his piece, but put it into his pocket.

It was not long before they all set out, and their parents took care to lead them into the very thickest and darkest part of the forest. They then slipped away by a by-path as before, and left the children by themselves again. All this did not give Hop-o'-my-thumb any concern, for he thought himself quite sure of getting back by means of the crumbs that he had dropped by the way; but when he came to look for them he found that not a crumb was left, for the birds had eaten them all up.

The poor children were now sadly off, for the farther they went, the harder it was for them to get out of the forest. At last, night came on, and the noise of the wind among the trees seemed to them like the howling of wolves, so that every moment they thought they should be eaten up. They hardly dared to speak a word, or to move a limb, for fear. Soon after there came a heavy rain, which wetted them to the very skin, and made the ground so slippery, that they fell down almost at every step, and got dirty all over.

Before it was quite dark, Hop-o'-my-thumb climbed up to the top of a tree, and looked round on all sides to see if he could find any way of getting help. He saw a small light, like that of a candle, but it was a very great way off, and beyond the forest. He then came down from the tree, to try to find the way to it; but he could not see it when he was on the ground, and he was in the utmost trouble what to do next. They walked on towards the place where he had seen the light, and at last reached the end of the forest, and got sight of it again. They now walked faster; and after being much tired and vexed (for every time they got into lower ground they lost sight of the light), came to the house it was in. They knocked at the door, which was opened by a very good-natured-looking lady, who asked what brought them there. Hop-o'-my-thumb told her that they were poor children, who had lost their way in the forest, and begged that she would give them a bed till morning. When the lady saw that they had such pretty faces, she began to shed tears and said, "Ah! my poor children, you do not know what place you are come to. This is the house of an Ogre, who eats up little boys and girls."

"Alas! madam," replied Hop-o'-my-thumb, who trembled from head to foot, "what shall we do? If we go back to the forest, we are sure of being torn to pieces by the wolves; we would rather, therefore, be eaten by the gentleman : besides, when he sees us, perhaps he may take pity on us and spare our lives."

The Ogre's wife thought she could contrive to hide them from her husband till morning ; so she let them go in and warm themselves by a good fire, before which there was a whole sheep roasting for the Ogre's supper. When they had stood a short time by the fire, there came a loud knocking at the door : this was the Ogre come home. His wife hurried the children under the bed, and told them to lie still, and she then let her husband in.

The Ogre asked if supper were ready, and if the wine were fetched from the cellar; and then he sat down at the table. The sheep was not quite done, but he liked it much better half raw. In a minute or two the Ogre began to snuff to his right and left, and said he smelt child's flesh.

"It must be this calf which has just been killed," said his wife.

"I smell child's flesh, I tell thee once more," cried the Ogre, looking all about the room ; "I smell child's flesh ; there is something going on that I do not know of."

As soon as he had spoken these words, he rose from his chair and went towards the bed.

"Ah! madam," said he, "you thought to cheat me, did you? Wretch! thou art old and tough thyself, or else I would eat thee up too! But come, come, this is lucky enough ; for the brats will make a nice dish for three Ogres, who are my particular friends, and who are to dine with me to-morrow."

He then drew them out one by one from under the bed. The poor children fell on their knees and begged his pardon as humbly as they could; but this Ogre was the most cruel of all Ogres, and instead of feeling any pity, he only began to think how sweet and tender their flesh would be; so he told his wife they would be nice morsels, if she served them up with plenty of sauce. He then fetched a large knife, and began to sharpen it on a long whetstone that he held in his left hand; and all the while he came nearer and nearer to the bed. The Ogre took up one of the children, and was going to set about cutting him to pieces; but his wife said to him, "What in the world makes you take the trouble of killing them to-night? Will it not be time enough to-morrow morning?"

"Hold your prating," replied the Ogre; "they will grow tender by being kept a little while after they are killed."

"But," said his wife, "you have got so much meat in the house already; here is a calf, two sheep, and half a pig."

"True," said the Ogre, "so give them all a good supper, that they may not get lean, and then send them to bed."

The good creature was quite glad at this. She gave them plenty for their supper, but the poor children were so terrified that they could not eat a bit.

The Ogre sat down to his wine, very much pleased with the thought of giving his friends such a dainty dish: this made him drink rather more than common, and he was soon obliged to go to bed himself. Now the Ogre had seven daughters, who were all very young like Hop-o'-my-thumb and his brothers. These young Ogresses had fair skins, because they fed on raw meat like their father; but they had small grey eyes, quite round, and sunk in their heads, hooked noses, wide mouths, and very long sharp teeth standing a great way off each other. They were too young as yet to do much mischief; but they showed that if they lived to be as old as their father, they would grow quite as cruel as he was, for they took pleasure already in biting young children, and sucking their blood. The Ogresses had been put to bed very early that night : they were all in one bed, which was very large, and every one of them had a crown of gold on her head. There was another bed of the same size in the room, and in this the Ogre's wife put the seven little boys, and then went to bed herself along with her husband.

Now Hop-o'-my-thumb was afraid that the Ogre would wake in the night and kill him and his brothers while they were asleep. So he got out of bed in the middle of the night as softly as he could, took off all his brothers' nightcaps and his own, and crept with them to the bed that the Ogre's daughters were in : he then took off their crowns, and put the night-caps on their heads instead : next he put the crowns on his brothers' heads and his own, and got into bed again ; expecting, after this, that, if the Ogre should come, he would take him and his brothers for his own children. Everything turned out as he wished. The Ogre waked soon after mid-night, and began to be very sorry that he had put off killing the boys till the morning : so he jumped out of bed, and took hold of his large knife. "Let us see," said he, "what the young rogues are about, and do the business at once!" He then walked softly to the room where they all slept, and went up to the bed the boys were in, who were all asleep except Hop-o'-my-thumb. He touched their heads one at a time, and feeling the crowns of gold, said to himself, "Oh, oh! I had like to have made such a mistake. I must have drunk too much wine last night."

He went next to the bed that his own little Ogresses were in, and when he felt the night-caps, he said, "Ah! here you are, my lads" : and so in a moment he cut the throats of all his daughters.

He was very much pleased when he had done this, and then went back to his own bed. As soon as Hop-o'-my-thumb heard him snore, he awoke his brothers, and told them to put on their clothes quickly, and follow him. They stole down softly into the garden, and then jumped from the wall into the road : they ran as fast as their legs could carry them, but were so much afraid all the while, that they hardly knew which way to take. When the Ogre waked in the morning, he said to his wife, grinning, " My dear, go and dress the young rogues I saw last night."

The wife was quite surprised at hearing her husband speak so kindly, and did not dream of the real meaning of his words. She supposed he wanted her to help them to put on their clothes ; so she went upstairs, and the first thing she saw was her seven daughters with their throats cut, and all over blood. This threw her into a fainting fit. The Ogre was afraid his wife might be too long in doing what he had set her about, so he went himself to help her ; but he was as much shocked as she had been at the dreadful sight of his bleeding children. " Ah ! what have I done? " he cried ; " but the little rascals shall pay for it, I warrant them."

He first threw some water on his wife's face ; and, as soon as she came to herself, he said to her : " Bring me quickly my seven-league boots, that I may go and catch the little vipers."

The Ogre then put on these boots, and set out with all speed. He strided over many parts of the country, and at last turned into the very road in which the poor children were. For they had set off towards the faggot-maker's cottage, which they had almost reached. They watched the Ogre stepping from mountain to mountain at one step, and crossing rivers as if they had been tiny brooks. At this Hop-o'-my-thumb thought a little what was to be done ; and spying a hollow place under a large rock, he made his brothers get into it. He then crept in himself, but kept his eye fixed on the Ogre, to see what he would do next.

The Ogre found himself quite weary with the journey he had gone, for seven-league boots are very tiresome to the person who wears them ; so he now began to think of resting, and happened to sit down on the very rock where the poor children were hid. As he was so tired, and it was a very hot day, he fell fast asleep, and soon began to snore so loud, that the little fellows were terrified.

When Hop-o'-my-thumb saw this he said to his brothers, "Courage, my lads! never fear! you have nothing to do but to steal away and get home while the Ogre is fast asleep, and leave me to shift for myself."

The brothers now were very glad to do whatever he told them, and so they soon came to their father's house. In the meantime Hop-o'-my-thumb went up to the Ogre softly, pulled off his seven-league boots very gently, and put them on his own legs : for though the boots were very large, yet being fairy-boots, they could make themselves small enough to fit any leg they pleased.

As soon as ever Hop-o'-my-thumb had made sure of the Ogre's seven-league boots, he went at once to the palace, and offered his services to carry orders from the king to his army, which was a great way off, and to bring back the quickest accounts of the battle they were just at that time fighting with the enemy. In short, he thought he could be of more use to the king than all his mail coaches, and so should make his fortune in this manner. He succeeded so well, that in a short time he made money enough to keep himself, his father, mother, and six brothers, without the trouble of working, for the rest of their lives. Having done this, he went back to his father's cottage, where all the family were delighted to see him again. As the great fame of his boots had been talked of at court in this time, the king sent for him, and indeed employed him very often in the greatest affairs of the state, so that he became one of the richest men in the kingdom.

And now let us see what became of the wicked Ogre. He slept so soundly that he never discovered the loss of his boots ; but having an evil conscience and bad dreams, he fell in his sleep from the corner of the rock where Hop-o'-my-thumb and his brothers had left him, and bruised himself so much from head to foot, that he could not stir : so he was forced to stretch himself out at full length, and wait for some one to come and help him.

Now a good many faggot-makers passed near the place where the Ogre lay ; and, when they heard him groan, they went up to ask him what was the matter. But the Ogre had eaten such a great number of children in his life-time, that he had grown so very big and fat that these men could not even have carried one of his legs ; so they were forced to leave him there. At last night came on, and then a large serpent came out of a wood just by and stung him, so that he died in great pain.

By and by, Hop-o'-my-thumb, who had become the king's first favourite, heard of the Ogre's death ; and the first thing he did was to tell his majesty all that the good-natured Ogress had done to save the lives of himself and brothers. The king was so much pleased at what he heard, that he asked Hop-o'-my-thumb if there was any favour he could bestow upon her. Hop-o'-my-thumb thanked the king, and desired that the Ogress might have the noble title of Duchess of Draggletail given to her ; which was no sooner asked than granted. The Ogress then came to court, and lived very happily for many years, enjoying the vast fortune she had found in the Ogre's chests. As for Hop-o'-my-thumb, he every day grew more witty and brave ; till at last the king made him the greatest lord in the kingdom, and set him over all his affairs.

CINDERELLA

OR

THE LITTLE GLASS SLIPPER

THERE was once an honest gentleman who took for his second wife a lady, the proudest and most disagreeable in the whole country. She had two daughters exactly like herself in all things. He also had one little girl, who resembled her dead mother, the best woman in all the world. Scarcely had the second marriage taken place, than the step-mother became jealous of the good qualities of the little girl, who was so great a contrast to her own two daughters. She gave her all the menial occupations of the house; compelled her to wash the floors and staircases to dust the bedrooms, and clean the grates; and while her sisters occupied carpeted chambers hung with mirrors, where they could see themselves from head to foot, this poor little damsel was sent to sleep in an attic, on an old straw mattress, with only one chair and not a looking-glass in the room.

She suffered all in silence, not daring to complain to her father, who was entirely ruled by his new wife. When her daily work was done, she used to sit down in the chimney-corner among the ashes; from which the two sisters gave her the nick-name of *Cinderella*. But Cinderella, however shabbily clad, was handsomer than they were with all their fine clothes.

It happened that the king's son gave a series of balls,

19

to which were invited all the rank and fashion of the city, and among the rest the two elder sisters. They were very proud and happy, and occupied their whole time in deciding what they should wear ; a source of new trouble to Cinderella, whose duty it was to get up their fine linen and laces, and who never could please them however much she tried. They talked of nothing but their clothes.

"I," said the elder, "shall wear my velvet gown and my trimmings of English lace."

"And I," added the younger, "will have but my ordinary silk petticoat, but I shall adorn it with an upper skirt of flowered brocade, and shall put on my diamond tiara, which is a great deal finer than anything of yours."

Here the elder sister grew angry, and the dispute began to run so high, that Cinderella, who was known to have excellent taste, was called upon to decide between them. She gave them the best advice she could, and gently and submissively offered to dress them herself, and especially to arrange their hair, an accomplishment in which she excelled many a noted coiffeur. The important evening came, and she exercised all her skill to adorn the two young ladies. While she was combing out the elder's hair, this ill-natured girl said sharply, "Cinderella, do you not wish you were going to the ball?"

"Ah, madam" (they obliged her always to say madam), "you are only mocking me ; it is not my fortune to have any such pleasure."

"You are right ; people would only laugh to see a little cinder-wench at a ball."

Any other than Cinderella would have dressed the hair all awry, but she was good, and dressed it perfectly even and smooth, and as prettily as she could.

The sisters had scarcely eaten for two days, and had broken a dozen stay-laces a-day in trying to make themselves slender ; but to-night they broke a dozen

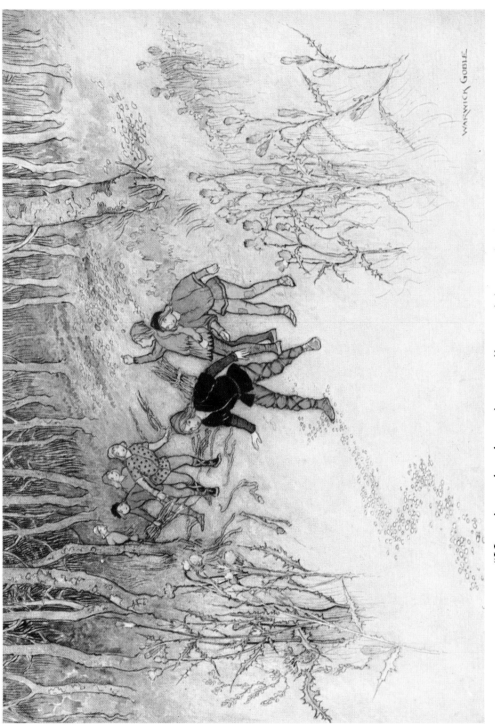

WARWICK GOBLE

"Hop-o'-my-thumb . . . knew well enough how to lead them safe
home, as he had taken care to drop the white pebbles he had in
his pocket along all the way he had come." (*Page 10*)

"The only remnant of her past magnificence being one of her little glass slippers." *(Page 24)*

more, and lost their tempers over and over again before they had completed their toilette. When at last the happy moment arrived, Cinderella followed them to the coach ; after it had whirled them away, she sat down by the kitchen fire and cried.

Immediately her godmother, who was a fairy, appeared beside her. " What are you crying for, my little maid ? "

" Oh, I wish—I wish——" Her sobs stopped her.

" You wish to go to the ball ; isn't it so ? "

Cinderella nodded.

" Well, then, be a good girl, and you shall go. First run into the garden and fetch me the largest pumpkin you can find."

Cinderella did not comprehend what this had to do with her going to the ball, but being obedient and obliging, she went. Her godmother took the pumpkin, and having scooped out all its inside, struck it with her wand ; it became a splendid gilt coach, lined with rose-coloured satin.

" Now fetch me the mouse-trap out of the pantry, my dear."

Cinderella brought it ; it contained six of the fattest, sleekest mice. The fairy lifted up the wire door, and as each mouse ran out, she struck it and changed it into a beautiful black horse.

" But what shall I do for your coachman, Cinderella ? "

Cinderella suggested that she had seen a large black rat in the rat-trap, and he might do for want of better.

" You are right ; go and look again for him."

He was found, and the fairy made him into a most respectable coachman, with the finest whiskers imaginable. She afterwards took six lizards from behind the pumpkin frame, and changed them into six footmen, all in splendid livery, who immediately jumped up behind the carriage, as if they had been footmen all their days. " Well, Cinderella, now you can go to the ball."

"What, in these clothes?" said Cinderella piteously, looking down on her ragged frock.

Her godmother laughed, and touched her also with the wand; at which her wretched threadbare jacket became stiff with gold, and sparkling with jewels; her woollen petticoat lengthened into a gown of sweeping satin, from underneath which peeped out her little feet, no longer bare, but covered with silk stockings and the prettiest glass slippers in the world. "Now, Cinderella, depart; but remember, if you stay one instant after midnight, your carriage will become a pumpkin, your coachman a rat, your horses mice, and your footmen lizards; while you yourself will be the little cinder-wench you were an hour ago."

Cinderella promised without fear, her heart was so full of joy.

Arrived at the palace, the king's son, whom some one, probably the fairy, had told to await the coming of an uninvited princess whom nobody knew, was standing at the entrance, ready to receive her. He offered her his hand and led her with the utmost courtesy through the assembled guests, who stood aside to let her pass, whispering to one another, "Oh, how beautiful she is!" It might have turned the head of any one but poor Cinderella, who was so used to be despised, that she took it all as if it were something happening in a dream.

Her triumph was complete; even the old king said to the queen, that never since her majesty's young days had he seen so charming and elegant a person. All the court ladies scanned her eagerly, clothes and all, determining to have theirs made next day of exactly the same pattern. The king's son himself led her out to dance, and she danced so gracefully that he admired her more and more. Indeed, at supper, which was fortunately early, his admiration quite took away his appetite. For Cinderella herself, with an involuntary shyness she sought out her sisters ; placed herself beside them and offered them all sorts of civil attentions, which, coming as they supposed from a stranger, and so magnificent a lady, almost overwhelmed them with delight.

While she was talking with them, she heard the clock strike a quarter to twelve, and making a courteous adieu to the royal family, she re-entered her carriage, escorted tenderly by the king's son, and arrived in safety at her own door. There she found her godmother, who smiled approval ; and of whom she begged permission to go to a second ball, the following night, to which the queen had earnestly invited her.

While she was talking, the two sisters were heard knocking at the gate, and the fairy godmother vanished, leaving Cinderella sitting in the chimney-corner, rubbing her eyes and pretending to be very sleepy.

"Ah," cried the eldest sister maliciously, "it has been the most delightful ball, and there was present the most beautiful princess I ever saw, who was so exceedingly polite to us both."

"Was she ?" said Cinderella indifferently ; "and who might she be ?"

"Nobody knows, though everybody would give their eyes to know, especially the king's son."

"Indeed !" replied Cinderella, a little more interested ; "I should like to see her. Miss Javotte "—that was the elder sister's name—"will you not let me go to-morrow, and lend me your yellow gown that you wear on Sundays?"

"What, lend my yellow gown to a cinder-wench ! I am not so mad as that " ; at which refusal Cinderella did not complain, for if her sister really had lent her the gown she would have been considerably embarrassed.

The next night came, and the two young ladies, richly dressed in different toilettes, went to the ball. Cinderella, more splendidly attired and beautiful than ever, followed them shortly after. "Now remember twelve o'clock," was her godmother's parting speech ; and she thought she certainly should. But the prince's attentions to her were greater even than the first evening, and in the delight of listening to his pleasant conversation, time slipped by unperceived. While she was sitting beside him in a lovely alcove, and looking at the moon from under a bower of orange blossoms, she heard a clock strike the first stroke of twelve. She started up, and fled away as lightly as a deer.

Amazed, the prince followed, but could not catch her. Indeed he missed his lovely princess altogether, and only saw running out of the palace doors a little dirty lass whom he had never beheld before, and of whom he certainly would never have taken the least notice. Cinderella arrived at home breathless and weary, ragged and cold, without carriage, or footmen, or coachmen ; the only remnant of her past magnificence being one of her little glass slippers ;—the other she had dropped in the ball-room as she ran away.

When the two sisters returned they were full of this strange adventure, how the beautiful lady had appeared at the ball more beautiful than ever, and enchanted every one who looked at her ; and how as the clock was striking twelve she had suddenly risen up and fled through the ball-room, disappearing no one knew how or where, and dropping one of her glass slippers behind her in her flight. How the king's son had remained inconsolable until he chanced to pick up the little glass slipper, which he carried away in his pocket, and was seen to take it out continually, and look at it affectionately, with the air of a man very much in love ; in fact, from his behaviour during the remainder of the evening, all the court and royal family were convinced that he had become desperately enamoured of the wearer of the little glass slipper.

Cinderella listened in silence, turning her face to the

kitchen fire, and perhaps it was that which made her look so rosy ; but nobody ever noticed or admired her at home, so it did not signify, and the next morning she went to her weary work again just as before.

A few days after, the whole city was attracted by the sight of a herald going round with a little glass slipper in his hand, publishing, with a flourish of trumpets, that the king's son ordered this to be fitted on the foot of every lady in the kingdom, and that he wished to marry the lady whom it fitted best, or to whom it and the fellow slipper belonged. Princesses, duchesses, countesses, and simple gentlewomen all tried it on, but being a fairy slipper, it fitted nobody ; and beside, nobody could produce its fellow slipper, which lay all the time safely in the pocket of Cinderella's old linsey gown.

At last the herald came to the house of the two sisters, and though they well knew neither of themselves was the beautiful lady, they made every attempt to get their clumsy feet into the glass slipper, but in vain.

" Let me try it on," said Cinderella from the chimney corner.

" What, you ? " cried the others, bursting into shouts of laughter ; but Cinderella only smiled, and held out her hand.

Her sisters could not prevent her, since the command was that every young maiden in the city should try on the slipper, in order that no chance might be left untried, for the prince was nearly breaking his heart ; and his father and mother were afraid that though a prince, he would actually die for love of the beautiful unknown lady.

So the herald bade Cinderella sit down on a three-legged stool in the kitchen, and himself put the slipper on her pretty little foot, which it fitted exactly ; she then drew from her pocket the fellow slipper, which she also put on, and stood up—for with the touch of the magic shoes all her dress was changed likewise—no longer the poor despised cinder-wench, but the beautiful lady whom the king's son loved.

Her sisters recognised her at once. Filled with astonishment, mingled with no little alarm, they threw themselves at her feet, begging her pardon for all their former unkindness. She raised and embraced them; told them she forgave them with all her heart, and only hoped they would love her always. Then she departed with the herald to the king's palace, and told her whole story to his majesty and the royal family, who were not in the least surprised, for everybody believed in fairies, and everybody longed to have a fairy godmother.

For the young prince, he found her more lovely and lovable than ever, and insisted upon marrying her immediately. Cinderella never went home again, but she sent for her two sisters to the palace, and with the consent of all parties married them shortly after to two rich gentlemen of the court.

ADVENTURES OF JOHN DIETRICH

There once lived in Rambin, a town near the Baltic Sea, an honest, industrious man named James Dietrich. He had several children, all of a good disposition, especially the youngest, whose name was John. John Dietrich was a handsome, smart boy, diligent at school, and obedient at home. His great passion was for hearing stories, and whenever he met any one who was well stored with such, he never let him go till he had heard them all.

When John was about eight years old he was sent to spend a summer with his uncle, a farmer in Rodenkirchen. Here he had to keep cows with other boys, and they used to drive them to graze about the Nine-hills, where an old cowherd, one Klas Starkwolt, frequently came to join the lads, and then they would sit down all together and tell stories. Consequently Klas became John's best friend, for he knew stories without end. He could tell all about the Nine-hills, and the underground folk who inhabited them; how the giants disappeared from the country, and the dwarfs or little people came in their stead. These tales John swallowed so eagerly that he thought of nothing else, and was for ever talking of golden cups, and crowns, and glass shoes, and pockets full of ducats, and gold rings, and diamond coronets, and snow-white brides, and the like. Old Klas used often to shake his head at him and say, " John! John! what are you about? The spade and scythe will be your sceptre

27

and crown, and your bride will wear a garland of rosemary and a gown of striped drill."

Still John almost longed to get into the Nine-hills, for Klas had told him that any one who by luck or cunning should get the cap of one of the little people might go down with safety, and instead of becoming their slave, he would be their master. The fairy whose cap he got would be his servant, and obey all his commands.

Midsummer-eve, when the days are longest and the nights shortest, was now come. In the village of Rambin old and young kept the holiday, had all sorts of plays, and told all kinds of stories. John, who knew that this season was the time for all fairy-people to come abroad, could now no longer contain himself, but the day after the festival he slipped away to the Nine-hills, and when it grew dark laid himself down on the top of the highest of them, which Klas had told him was the principal dancing-ground of the underground people. John lay there quite still from ten till twelve at night. At last it struck twelve. Immediately there was a ringing and a singing in the hills, and then a whispering and a lisping and a whiz and a buzz all about him, for the little people were now come out, some whirling round and round in the dance, and others sporting and tumbling about in the moonshine, and playing a thousand merry pranks. He felt a secret dread creep over him at this whispering and buzzing, for he could see nothing of them, as the caps they wore made them invisible ; but he lay quite still, with his face in the grass and his eyes fast shut, snoring a little just as if he was asleep. Yet now and then he ventured to open his eyes a little and peep out, but not the slightest trace of them could he see, though it was bright moon-light.

It was not long before three of the underground people came jumping up to where he was lying ; but they took no heed of him, and flung their brown caps up into the air, and caught them from one another. At length one snatched the cap out of the hand of another and flung it away. It flew direct, and fell upon John's head. He could feel, though he could not see it; and the moment he did feel it, he caught hold of it. Starting up, he swung it about for joy, and made the little silver bell of it tingle, then set it upon his head, and—O wonderful to relate!—that instant he saw the countless and merry swarm of the little people.

The three little men came slily up to him, and thought by their nimbleness to get back the cap, but he held his prize fast, and they saw clearly that nothing was to be done in this way with him, for in size and strength John was a giant in comparison of these little fellows, who hardly reached his knee. The owner of the cap now came up very humbly to the finder, and begged, in as supplicating a tone as if his life depended upon it, that he would give him back his cap. "No," said John, "you sly little rogue, you'll get the cap no more. That's not the sort of thing: I should be in a nice perplexity if I had not something of yours; now you have no power over me, but must do what I please. And I will go down with you, and see how you live below, and you shall be my servant.—Nay, no grumbling, you know you must. And I know it too, just as well as you do, for Klas Starkwolt told it to me often and often."

The little man made as if he had not heard or understood one word of all this; he began all his crying and whining over again, and wept, and screamed, and howled most piteously for his little cap. But John cut the matter short by saying to him, "Have done; you are my servant, and I intend to take a trip with you." So the underground man gave up the point; especially as he well knew there was no remedy.

John now flung away his old hat and put on the cap, and set it firmly on his head, lest it should slip off or fly away, for all his power lay in it. He lost no time in trying its virtues, but commanded his new servant to fetch him food and drink. The servant ran away like the wind, and in a second was there again with bottles of wine, and bread, and rich fruits. So John ate and drank, and looked on at the sports and the dancing of the little people, and it pleased him right well, and he behaved himself stoutly and wisely, as if he was a born master.

When the cock had now crowed for the third time, and the little larks had made their first flutter in the sky, and the daybreak appeared in slender white streaks in the east, then there went a whisper, hush, hush, hush, through the bushes, and flowers, and trees ; and the hills rang again, and opened up, and the little men stole down and disappeared. John gave close attention to everything, and found that it was exactly as he had been told. And behold ! on the top of the hill where they had just been dancing, and which was now full of grass and flowers, as people see it by day, there rose, of a sudden, a small glass door. Whosoever wanted to go in stepped upon this ; it opened, and he glided gently in, the glass closing again after him ; and when they had all entered it vanished, and there was no further trace of it to be seen. Those who descended through the glass door sank quite gently into a wide silver tun or barrel, which held them all, and could easily have harboured a thousand such little people. John and his man went down also, along with several others, all of whom screamed out and prayed him not to tread on them, for if his weight came on them, they were dead men. He was, however, careful, and acted in a very friendly way towards them. Several barrels of this kind went up and down after each other, until all were in. They hung by long silver chains, which were drawn and guided from below.

In his descent John was amazed at the wonderful brilliancy of the walls between which the tun glided down.

They seemed all studded with pearls and diamonds, glittering and sparkling brightly, while below him he heard the most beautiful music tinkling at a distance, so that he did not know what he was about, and from excess of pleasure he fell fast asleep.

He slept a long time, and when he awoke he found himself in the most beautiful bed that could be, such as he had never seen in his father's or any other house. It was also the prettiest little chamber in the world, and his servant was beside him with a fan to keep away the flies and gnats. He had hardly opened his eyes when his little servant brought him a basin and towel, and held ready for him to put on the nicest new clothes of brown silk, most beautifully made; with these was a pair of new black shoes with red ribbons, such as John had never beheld in Rambin or in Rodenkirchen either. There were also there several pairs of glittering glass shoes, such as are only used on great occasions. John was, we may well suppose, delighted to have such clothes to wear, and he put them on joyfully. His servant then flew like lightning and returned with a fine breakfast of wine and milk, and delicate white bread and fruits, and such other things as little boys are fond of. He now perceived, every moment, more and more, that Klas Starkwolt, the old cowherd, knew what he was talking about, for the splendour and magnificence here surpassed anything John had ever dreamt of. His servant, too, was the most obedient one possible; a nod or a sign was enough for him, for he was as wise as a bee, as all these little people are by nature.

John's bedroom was all covered with emeralds and other precious stones, and in the ceiling was a diamond as big as a nine-pin bowl, that gave light to the whole chamber. In this place they have neither sun, nor moon, nor stars to give them light; neither do they use lamps or candles of any kind; but they live in the midst of precious stones, and have the purest of gold and silver in abundance, from which they manage to obtain light both by day and by night, though indeed, properly speaking, as there is no sun here, there is no distinction of day and night, and they reckon only by weeks. They set the brightest and clearest precious stones in their dwellings, and in the ways and passages leading under the ground, and in the places where they have their large halls, and their dances and feasts; and the sparkle of these jewels makes a sort of silvery twilight which is far more beautiful than common day.

When John had finished his breakfast, his servant opened a little door in the wall, where was a closet with silver and gold cups and dishes and other vessels, and baskets filled with ducats, and boxes of jewels and precious stones. There were also charming pictures, and the most delightful story-books he had seen in the whole course of his life.

John spent the morning looking at these things; and, when it was mid-day, a bell rung, and his servant said, " Will you dine alone, sir, or with the large company ? "

" With the large company, to be sure," replied John. So his servant led him out. John, however, saw nothing but solitary halls, lighted up with precious stones, and here and there little men and women, who appeared to him to glide out of the clefts and fissures of the rocks. Wondering what it was the bells rang for, he said to his servant— " But where is the company ? " And scarcely had he spoken when the hall they were in opened out to a great extent, and a canopy set with diamonds and precious stones was drawn over it. At the same moment he saw an immense throng of nicely dressed little men and women pouring in through several open doors; the floor opened in several places, and tables, covered with the most beautiful ware, and the most luscious meats, and fruits, and wines, arranged themselves in rows, and the chairs arranged themselves along beside the tables, and then the men and women took their seats.

The principal persons now came forward, bowed to John, and led him to their table, where they placed him among their most beautiful maidens, a distinction which pleased John well. The party too was very merry, for the underground people are extremely lively and cheerful, and can never stay long quiet. Then the most charming music sounded over their heads ; and beautiful birds, flying about, sang sweetly : these were not real but artificial birds, which the little men make so ingeniously that they can fly about and sing like natural ones.

The servants of both sexes, who waited at table, and handed about the gold cups, and the silver and crystal baskets with fruit, were mortal children, whom some misfortune had thrown among the underground people, and who, having come down without securing any pledge, such as John's cap, had fallen into their power. These were differently clad from their masters. The boys and girls were dressed in snow-white coats and jackets, and wore glass shoes, so thin that their steps could never be heard, with blue caps on their heads, and silver belts round their waists.

John at first pitied them, seeing how they were forced to run about and wait on the little people ; but as they looked cheerful and happy, and were handsomely dressed, and had such rosy cheeks, he said to himself, "After all, they are not so badly off, and I was myself much worse when I had to be running after the cows and bullocks. To be sure, I am now a master here, and they are servants ; but there is no help for it : why were they so foolish as to let themselves be taken and not get some pledge before-hand ? At any rate, the time must come when they shall be set at liberty, and they will certainly not be longer than fifty years here." With these thoughts he consoled himself, and sported and played away with his little playfellows, and ate, and drank, and made his servant and the others tell him stories, for he always liked to hear something strange, and to get to the bottom of everything.

They sat at table about two hours : the principal person then rang a little bell, and the tables and chairs all vanished in a whiff, leaving the company standing on their feet. The birds now struck up a most lively air, and the little people began to dance, jumping and leaping and whirling round and round, as if the world were grown dizzy. And the pretty little girls that sat next John caught hold of him and whirled him about ; and, without making any resistance, he danced with them for two good hours. Every afternoon while he remained there he used to do the same ; and, to the last hour of his life, he always spoke of it with the greatest glee.

When the music and dancing were over it might be about four o'clock. The little people then disappeared, and went each about their work or their pleasure. After supper they sported and danced in the same way ; and at midnight, especially on starlight nights, they slipped out of their hills to dance in the open air. John used then, like a good boy, to say his prayers and go to sleep, a duty he never neglected either in the evening or in the morning.

For the first week that John was in the glass-hill he only went from his chamber to the great hall and back again. After then, however, he began to walk about, making his servant show and explain everything to him. He found that there were here most beautiful walks, in which he might ramble along for miles, in all directions, without ever finding an end of them, so immensely large was the hill that the little people lived in, and yet outwardly it seemed but a little hill, with a few bushes and trees growing on it.

He found also meadows and lanes, islands and lakes where the birds sang sweeter, and the flowers were more brilliant and fragrant than anything he had ever seen on earth. There was a breeze, and yet one did not feel the wind ; it was quite clear and bright, but there was no heat ; the waves were dashing, still there was no danger ; and the most beautiful little barks and canoes came, like white swans, when one wanted to cross the water, and went backwards and forwards of their own accord. Whence all this came nobody knew, nor could his servant tell anything about it.

These lovely meads and plains were, for the most part, all solitary. Few of the underground people were to be seen upon them, and those that were just glided across them, as if in the greatest hurry. It very rarely happened that any of them danced out here in the open air ; sometimes about three of them did so ; at the most half a dozen : John never saw a greater number together. The meadows never seemed cheerful, except when the earth-children, who were kept as servants, were let out to walk. This, however, happened but twice a week, for they were mostly kept employed in the great hall and adjoining apartments, or at school.

For John soon found they had schools there also ; he had been there about ten months, when one day he saw something snow-white gliding into a rock, and disappearing. "What!" said he to his servant, "are there some of you too that wear white, like the servants?" He was informed that there were ; but they were few in number, and never appeared at the large tables or the dances, except once a year, on the birthday of the great Hill-king, who dwelt many thousand miles below in the great deep. These were the oldest men among them, some being many thousand years old ; they knew all things, and could tell of the beginning of the world, and were called the Wise. They lived all alone, and only left their chambers to instruct the underground children and the attendants of both sexes.

John was greatly interested by this news, and he determined to take advantage of it ; so next morning he made his servant conduct him to the school, and was so well pleased with it that he never missed a day. The scholars were taught reading, writing, and accounts, to compose and relate histories and stories, and many elegant kinds of work ; so that many came out of the hills very prudent and learned. The biggest, and those of best capacity, received instruction in natural science and astronomy, and in poetry and riddle-making, arts highly esteemed by the little people. John was very diligent, and soon became a clever painter ; he wrought, too, most ingeniously in gold, and silver, and stones ; and in verse and riddle-making he had no fellow.

John had spent many a happy year here without ever thinking of the upper world, or of those he had left behind, so pleasantly passed the time—so many an agreeable playfellow had he among the children.

Of all his playfellows there was none of whom he was so fond as of a little fair-haired girl, named Elizabeth Krabbin. She was from his own village, and was the daughter of Frederick Krabbe, the minister of Rambin. She was but four years old when she was taken away, and John had often heard tell of her. She was not, however, stolen by the little people, but came into their power in this manner. One day in summer, she, with other children, ran out into the fields : in their rambles they went to the Nine-hills, where little Elizabeth fell asleep, and was forgotten by the rest. At night, when she awoke, she found herself under the ground among the little people. It was not merely because she was from his own village that John was so fond of Elizabeth, but she was a most beautiful child, with clear blue eyes and ringlets of fair hair, and a most angelic smile.

Time flew away unperceived : John was now eighteen, and Elizabeth sixteen. Their childish fondness was now

36

"When the cock had now crowed for the third time, . . . the little
men stole down and disappeared." *(Page 30)*

"At last she remembered her dream, rushed to the grass-plot, and there saw him lying apparently dead." (*Page 59*)

become love, and the little people were pleased to see it, thinking that by means of her they might get John to renounce his power, and become their servant ; for they were fond of him, and would willingly have had him to wait upon them ; the love of dominion is their vice. But they were mistaken ; John had learned too much from his servant to be caught in that way.

John's chief delight was walking about alone with Elizabeth ; for he now knew every place so well that he could dispense with the attendance of his servant. In these rambles he was always gay and lively, but his companion was frequently sad and melancholy, thinking of the land above, where men lived, and where the sun, moon, and stars shine. Now it happened in one of their walks, that as they talked of their love, and it was after midnight, they passed under the place where the tops of the glass hills used to open and let the underground people in and out. As they went along they heard of a sudden the crowing of several cocks above. At this sound, which she had not heard for twelve years, little Elizabeth felt her heart so affected that she could contain herself no longer, but throwing her arms about John's neck, she bathed his cheeks with her tears. At length she spake :

" Dearest John," said she, " everything down here is very beautiful, and the little people are kind, and do nothing to injure me, but still I have always been uneasy, nor ever felt any pleasure till I began to love you ; and yet that is not pure pleasure, for this is not a right way of living, such as it should be for human beings. Every night I dream of my dear father and mother, and of our churchyard, where the people stand so piously at the church-door waiting for my father, and I could weep tears of blood that I cannot go into the church with them, and worship God as a human being should ; for this is no Christian life we lead down here, but a delusive half heathen one. And only think, dear John, that we can

37

never marry, as there is no priest to join us. Do, then, plan some way for us to leave this place ; for I cannot tell you how I long to get once more to my father, and among pious Christians."

John too had not been unaffected by the crowing of the cocks, and he felt what he had never felt here before, a longing after the land where the sun shines. He replied :

" Dear Elizabeth, all you say is true, and I now feel that it is a sin for Christians to stay here ; and it seems to me as if our Lord said to us in that cry of the cocks, ' Come up, ye Christian children, out of those abodes of illusion and magic ; come to the light of the stars, and act as children of light.' I now feel that it was a great sin for me to come down here, but I trust I shall be forgiven on account of my youth ; for I was a child and knew not what I did. But now I will not stay a day longer. They cannot keep *me* here."

At these last words, Elizabeth turned pale, for she recollected that she was a servant, and must serve her fifty years. "And what will it avail me," cried she, " that I shall continue young and be but as twenty years old when I go out, for my father and mother will be dead, and all my companions old and gray ; and you, dearest John, will be old and gray also," cried she, throwing herself on his bosom.

John was thunderstruck at this, for it had never before occurred to him ; he, however, comforted her as well as he could, and declared he would never leave the place without her. He spent the whole night in forming various plans ; at last he fixed on one, and in the morning he despatched his servant to summon to his apartment six of the principal of the little people. When they came, John thus mildly addressed them :

" My friends, you know how I came here, not as a prisoner or servant, but as a lord and master over one of you, and consequently, over all. You have now for the ten years I have been with you treated me with respect and attention, and for that I am your debtor. But you are still more my debtors, for I might have given you every sort of annoyance and vexation, and you must have submitted to it. I have, however, not done so, but have behaved as your equal, and have sported and played with you rather than ruled over you. I now have one request to make. There is a girl among your servants whom I love, Elizabeth Krabbin, of Rambin, where I was born. Give her to me, and let us depart. For I will return to where the sun shines and the plough goes through the land. I ask to take nothing with me but her, and the ornaments and furniture of my chamber."

He spoke in a determined tone, and they hesitated and cast their eyes to the ground ; at last the eldest of them replied :

" Sir, you ask what we cannot grant. It is a fixed law that no servant should leave this place before the appointed time. Were we to break through this law, our whole subterranean empire would fall. Anything else you desire, for we love and respect you, but we cannot give up Elizabeth."

" You can and you shall give her up," cried John in a rage ; " go think of it till to-morrow. Return here at this hour. I will show you whether or no I can triumph over your hypocritical and cunning stratagems."

The six retired. Next morning, on their return, John addressed them in the kindest manner, but to no purpose ; they persisted in their refusal. He gave them till the following day, threatening them severely in case of their still proving refractory.

Next day, when the six little people appeared before him, John looked at them sternly, and made no reply to their salutations, but said to them shortly, "Yes or No?" And they answered with one voice, "No." He then ordered his servant to summon twenty-four more of the principal persons, with their wives and children. When they came, they were in all five hundred, men, women, and children. John ordered them forthwith to go and fetch pickaxes, spades, and bars, which they did in a second.

He now led them out to a rock in one of the fields, and ordered them to fall to work at blasting, hewing, and dragging stones. They toiled patiently, and made as if it was only sport to them. From morning till night their taskmaster made them labour without ceasing, standing over them constantly, to prevent their resting. Still their obstinacy was inflexible ; and at the end of some weeks his pity for them was so great that he was obliged to give over.

He now thought of a new species of punishment for them. He ordered them to appear before him next morning, each provided with a new whip. They obeyed, and John commanded them to strip and lash one another till the blood should run down on the ground, while he stood looking on as grim and cruel as an Eastern tyrant. Still the little people cut and slashed themselves, and mocked at John, and refused to comply with his wishes. This he did for three or four days.

Several other courses did he try, but all in vain ; his temper was too gentle to struggle with their obstinacy, and he began now to despair of ever accomplishing his dearest wish. He began to hate the little people whom he was before so fond of ; he kept away from their banquets and dances, associated only with Elizabeth, and ate and drank quite solitary in his chamber. In short, he became almost a perfect hermit, and sank into moodiness and melancholy.

While in this temper, as he was taking a solitary walk in the evening, and, to divert his melancholy, was flinging the stones that lay in his path against each other, he happened to break a tolerably large one, and out of it jumped a toad. The moment John saw the ugly animal, he caught him up in ecstasy, and put him into his pocket and ran home, crying, "Now I have her! I have my Elizabeth! Now you shall catch it, you little mischievous rascals!" And on getting home he put the toad into a costly silver casket, as if it was the greatest treasure.

To account for John's joy you must know Klas Starkwolt had often told him that the underground people could not endure any ill odour, and that the sight or even the smell of a toad made them faint and suffer the most dreadful tortures, so that, by means of these animals, one could compel them to anything. Hence there are no bad smells to be found in the whole glass empire, and a toad is a thing unheard of there ; this toad must therefore have been enclosed in the stone from the Creation, as it were for the sake of John and Elizabeth.

Resolved to try the effect of his toad, John took the casket under his arm and went out, and on the way he met two of the little people in a lonesome place. The moment he approached them they fell to the ground, and whimpered and howled most lamentably, as long as he was near them.

Satisfied now of his power, he next morning summoned the fifty principal persons, with their wives and children, to his apartment. When they came, he addressed them, reminding them once again of his kindness and gentleness towards them, and of the good terms on which they had hitherto lived together. He reproached them with their ingratitude in refusing him the only favour he had ever asked of them, but firmly declared he would not give way to their obstinacy. "Wherefore," said he, "for the last time, I warn you ;—think for a minute, and if you then say No, you shall feel that pain which is to you and your children the most terrible of all sufferings."

They did not take long to deliberate, but unanimously

replied " No " ; for they thought to themselves, What new scheme has the youth hit on, with which he thinks to frighten wise ones like us? and they smiled when they said No. Their smiling enraged John above all, and he ran back to where he had laid the casket with the toad, under a bush.

He was hardly come within a hundred paces of them when they all fell to the ground as if struck with a thunderbolt, and began to howl and whimper, and to writhe, as if suffering the most excruciating pain. They stretched out their hands, and cried, " Have mercy ! have mercy ! we feel you have a toad, and there is no escape for us. Take the odious beast away, and we will do all you require." He let them kick a few seconds longer, and then took the toad away. They then stood up and felt no more pain. John let all depart but the six chief persons, to whom he said—

" This night, between twelve and one, Elizabeth and I will depart. Load then for me three waggons, with gold, and silver, and precious stones. I might, you know, take all that is in the hill, and you deserve it, but I will be merciful. Further, you must put all the furniture of my chamber in two waggons, and get ready for me the handsomest travelling-carriage that is in the hill, with six black horses. Moreover, you must set at liberty all the servants who have been so long here that on earth they would be twenty years old and upwards, and you must give them as much silver and gold as will make them rich for life, and make a law that no one shall be detained here longer than his twentieth year."

The six took the oath, and went away quite melancholy, and John buried his toad deep in the ground. The little people laboured hard according to his bidding. At midnight everything was out of the hill, and John and Elizabeth got into the silver tun and were drawn up.

It was then one o'clock, and midsummer-eve, the

very time that twelve years before John had gone down into the hill. Music sounded around them, and they saw the glass hill open, and the rays of the light of heaven shine on them for the first time after so many years ; and when they got out they saw the streaks of dawn already in the east. Crowds of the underground people were around them busied about the waggons. John bade them a last farewell, waved his brown cap three times in the air, and then flung it among them. And at the same moment he ceased to see them ; he beheld nothing but a green hill, and the well-known bushes and fields, and heard the church-clock of Rambin strike two. When all was still, save a few larks who were tuning their morning songs, they both fell on their knees and worshipped God, resolving henceforth to lead a pious and a Christian life.

When the sun rose, John and his Elizabeth, with the children whom they had saved from the underground people, set out for Rambin. Every well-known object that they saw awakened pleasing recollections ; and as they passed by Rodenkirchen, John recognised, among the people that gazed at and followed them, his old friend Klas Starkwolt, the cowherd, and his dog Speed. It was four in the morning when they entered Rambin, and they halted in the middle of the village, about twenty paces from the house where John was born. The whole village poured out to gaze on these Asiatic princes ; for such the old sexton, who had in his youth been at Moscow and Constantinople, said they were. There John saw his father and mother, and his brother Andrew, and his sister Trine. The old minister, Krabbe, stood there too, in his black slippers and white nightcap, gaping and staring with the rest.

John discovered himself to his parents, and Elizabeth to hers, and the wedding-day was soon fixed, and such a wedding was never seen before or since in the island of Rugen ; for John sent to Stralsund and Greifswald for whole boat-loads of wine and sugar and coffee, and whole herds of oxen, sheep, and pigs. The quantity of harts and roes and hares that were shot on the occasion it were vain to attempt to tell, or to count the fish that were caught. There was not a musician in Rugen and Pomerania that was not engaged, for John was immensely rich, and he wished to display his wealth.

John did not neglect his old friend Klas Starkwolt, the cowherd. He gave him enough to make him comfortable for the rest of his days, and insisted on his coming and staying with him as often and as long as he wished.

After his marriage, John made a progress through the country with his beautiful Elizabeth, and they purchased towns and villages and lands until he became master of nearly half Rugen, and a very considerable portion of the country. His father, old James Dietrich, was made a nobleman, and his brothers and sisters gentlemen and ladies—for what cannot money do?

John and his wife spent their days in acts of piety and charity. They built several churches, they had the blessings of every one that knew them, and died universally lamented. It was Count John Dietrich who built and richly endowed the present church of Rambin. He built it on the site of his father's house, and presented to it several of the cups and plates made by the underground people, and his own and Elizabeth's glass shoes, in memory of what had befallen them in their youth. But they were all taken away in the time of the great Charles the Twelfth of Sweden, when the Russians came on the island, and the Cossacks plundered even the churches, and took away everything.

BEAUTY AND THE BEAST

THERE was once a very rich merchant who had six children, three boys and three girls. As he was himself a man of great sense, he spared no expense for their education. The three daughters were all handsome, but particularly the youngest; indeed she was so very beautiful, that in her childhood every one called her the Little Beauty; and being equally lovely when she was grown up, nobody called her by any other name, which made her sisters very jealous of her. This youngest daughter was not only more handsome than her sisters, but also was better tempered. The two eldest were vain of their wealth and position. They gave themselves a thousand airs, and refused to visit other merchants' daughters; nor would they condescend to be seen except with persons of quality. They went every day to balls, plays, and public walks, and always made game of their youngest sister for spending her time in reading or other useful employments. As it was well known that these young ladies would have large fortunes, many great merchants wished to get them for wives; but the two eldest always answered, that, for their parts, they had no thoughts of marrying any one below a duke or an earl at least. Beauty had quite as many offers as her sisters, but she always answered, with the greatest civility, that though she was much obliged to her lovers, she would rather live some years longer with her father, as she thought herself too young to marry.

It happened that, by some unlucky accident, the

merchant suddenly lost all his fortune, and had nothing left but a small cottage in the country. Upon this he said to his daughters, while the tears ran down his cheeks, " My children, we must now go and dwell in the cottage, and try to get a living by labour, for we have no other means of support." The two eldest replied that they did not know how to work, and would not leave town ; for they had lovers enough who would be glad to marry them, though they had no longer any fortune. But in this they were mistaken ; for when the lovers heard what had happened, they said, " The girls were so proud and ill-tempered, that all we wanted was their fortune : we are not sorry at all to see their pride brought down : let them show off their airs to their cows and sheep." But everybody pitied poor Beauty, because she was so sweet-tempered and kind to all, and several gentlemen offered to marry her, though she had not a penny ; but Beauty still refused, and said she could not think of leaving her poor father in this trouble. At first Beauty could not help sometimes crying in secret for the hardships she was now obliged to suffer ; but in a very short time she said to herself, " All the crying in the world will do me no good, so I will try to be happy without a fortune."

When they had removed to their cottage, the merchant and his three sons employed themselves in ploughing and sowing the fields, and working in the garden. Beauty also did her part, for she rose by four o'clock every morning, lighted the fires, cleaned the house, and got ready the breakfast for the whole family. At first she found all this very hard ; but she soon grew quite used to it, and thought it no hardship ; indeed, the work greatly benefited her health. When she had done, she used to amuse herself with reading, playing her music, or singing while she spun. But her two sisters were at a loss what to do to pass the time away : they had their breakfast in bed, and did not rise till ten o'clock. Then they commonly walked out, but always found themselves very soon tired ; when they would often sit down under a shady tree, and grieve for the loss of their carriage and fine clothes, and say to each other, " What a mean-spirited poor stupid creature our young sister is, to be so content with this low way of life !" But their father thought differently, and loved and admired his youngest child more than ever.

After they had lived in this manner about a year, the merchant received a letter, which informed him that one of his richest ships, which he thought was lost, had just come into port. This news made the two eldest sisters almost mad with joy ; for they thought they should now leave the cottage, and have all their finery again. When they found that their father must take a journey to the ship, the two eldest begged he would not fail to bring them back some new gowns, caps, rings, and all sorts of trinkets. But Beauty asked for nothing ; for she thought in herself that all the ship was worth would hardly buy everything her sisters wished for. "Beauty," said the merchant, " how comes it that you ask for nothing : what can I bring you, my child ? "

"Since you are so kind as to think of me, dear father," she answered, " I should be glad if you would bring me a rose, for we have none in our garden." Now Beauty did not indeed wish for a rose, nor anything else, but she only said this that she might not affront her sisters ; otherwise they would have said she wanted her father to praise her for desiring nothing. The merchant took his leave of them, and set out on his journey ; but when he got to the ship, some persons went to law with him about the cargo, and after a deal of trouble he came back to his cottage as poor as he had left it. When he was within thirty miles of his home, and thinking of the joy of again meeting his children, he lost his way in the midst of a dense forest. It rained and snowed very hard, and, besides, the wind was so high as to throw him twice from his horse. Night came on, and he feared he should die of cold and hunger, or be torn to pieces by the wolves that he heard howling round him. All at once, he cast his eyes towards a long avenue, and saw at the end a light, but it seemed a great way off. He made the best of his way towards it, and found that it came from a splendid palace, the windows of which were all blazing with light. It had great bronze gates, standing wide open, and fine courtyards, through which the merchant passed ; but not a living soul was to be seen. There were stables too, which his poor starved horse, less scrupulous than himself, entered at once, and took a good meal of oats and hay. His master then tied him up, and walked towards the entrance hall, but still without seeing a single creature. He went on to a large dining-parlour, where he found a good fire, and a table covered with some very nice dishes, but only one plate with a knife and fork. As the snow and rain had wetted him to the skin, he went up to the fire to dry himself. "I hope," said he, "the master of the house or his servants will excuse me, for it surely will not be long now before I see them." He waited some time, but still nobody came : at last the clock struck eleven, and the merchant, being quite faint for the want of food, helped himself to a chicken, and to a few glasses of wine, yet all the time trembling with fear. He sat till the clock struck twelve, and then, taking courage, began to think he might as well look about him : so he opened a door at the end of the hall, and went through it into a very grand room, in which there was a fine bed ; and as he was feeling very weary, he shut the door, took off his clothes, and got into it.

It was ten o'clock in the morning before he awoke, when he was amazed to see a handsome new suit of clothes laid ready for him, instead of his own, which were all torn and spoiled. "To be sure," said he to himself, "this place belongs to some good fairy, who has taken pity on my ill luck." He looked out of the window, and instead of the snow-covered wood, where he had lost himself the previous night, he saw the most charming arbours covered with all kinds of flowers. Returning to the hall where he had supped, he found a breakfast table, ready prepared. "Indeed, my good fairy," said the merchant aloud, "I am vastly obliged to you for your kind care of me." He then made a hearty breakfast, took his hat, and was going to the stable to pay his horse a visit; but as he passed under one of the arbours, which was loaded with roses, he thought of what Beauty had asked him to bring back to her, and so he took a bunch of roses to carry home. At the same moment he heard a loud noise, and saw coming towards him a beast, so frightful to look at that he was ready to faint with fear. "Ungrateful man!" said the beast in a terrible voice, "I have saved your life by admitting you into my palace, and in return you steal my roses, which I value more than anything I possess. But you shall atone for your fault: you shall die in a quarter of an hour."

The merchant fell on his knees, and clasping his hands, said, "Sir, I humbly beg your pardon: I did not think it would offend you to gather a rose for one of my daughters, who had entreated me to bring her one home. Do not kill me, my lord!"

"I am not a lord, but a beast," replied the monster: "I hate false compliments: so do not fancy that you can coax me by any such ways. You tell me that you have daughters; now I will suffer you to escape, if one of them will come and die in your stead. If not, promise that you will yourself return in three months, to be dealt with as I may choose."

The tender-hearted merchant had no thoughts of letting any one of his daughters die for his sake; but he knew that if he seemed to accept the beast's terms, he should at least have the pleasure of seeing them once again. So he gave his promise, and was told he might then set off as soon as he liked. "But," said the beast, "I do not wish you to go back empty-handed. Go to the room you slept in, and you will find a chest there ; fill it with whatsoever you like best, and I will have it taken to your own house for you."

When the beast had said this, he went away. The good merchant, left to himself, began to consider that as he must die—for he had no thought of breaking a promise, made even to a beast—he might as well have the comfort of leaving his children provided for. He returned to the room he had slept in, and found there heaps of gold pieces lying about. He filled the chest with them to the very brim, locked it, and, mounting his horse, left the palace as sorrowful as he had been glad when he first beheld it. The horse took a path across the forest of his own accord, and in a few hours they reached the merchant's house. His children came running round him, but, instead of kissing them with joy, he could not help weeping as he looked at them. He held in his hand the bunch of roses, which he gave to Beauty, saying, "Take these roses, Beauty ; but little do you think how dear they have cost your poor father" ; and then he gave them an account of all that he had seen or heard in the palace of the beast.

The two eldest sisters now began to shed tears, and to lay the blame upon Beauty, who, they said, would be the cause of her father's death. "See," said they, "what happens from the pride of the little wretch : why did not she ask for such things as we did? But, to be sure, Miss must not be like other people ; and though she will be the cause of her father's death, yet she does not shed a tear."

"It would be useless," replied Beauty, "for my father shall not die. As the beast will accept of one of his daughters, I will give myself up, and be only too happy to prove my love for the best of fathers."

"No, sister," said the three brothers with one voice, "that cannot be; we will go in search of this monster, and either he or we will perish."

"Do not hope to kill him," said the merchant, "his power is far too great. But Beauty's young life shall not be sacrificed: I am old, and cannot expect to live much longer; so I shall but give up a few years of my life, and shall only grieve for the sake of my children."

"Never, father!" cried Beauty. "If you go back to the palace, you cannot hinder my going after you: though young, I am not over-fond of life; and I would much rather be eaten up by the monster, than die of grief for your loss."

The merchant in vain tried to reason with Beauty, who still obstinately kept to her purpose; which, in truth, made her two sisters glad, for they were jealous of her, because everybody loved her.

The merchant was so grieved at the thoughts of losing his child, that he never once thought of the chest filled with gold; but at night, to his great surprise, he found it standing by his bedside. He said nothing about his riches to his eldest daughters, for he knew very well it would at once make them want to return to town: but he told Beauty his secret, and she then said, that while he was away, two gentlemen had been on a visit at their cottage, who had fallen in love with her two sisters. She entreated her father to marry them without delay, for she was so sweet-natured, she only wished them to be happy.

Three months went by, only too fast, and then the merchant and Beauty got ready to set out for the palace of the beast. Upon this, the two sisters rubbed their eyes with an onion, to make believe they were crying; both the merchant and his sons cried in earnest. Only Beauty shed no tears. They reached the palace in a very few hours, and the horse, without bidding, went into the same stable as before. The merchant and Beauty walked towards the large hall, where they found a table covered with every dainty, and two plates laid ready. The merchant had very little appetite; but Beauty, that she might the better hide her grief, placed herself at the table, and helped her father; she then began to eat herself, and thought all the time that to be sure the beast had a mind to fatten her before he ate her up, since he had provided such good cheer for her. When they had done their supper, they heard a great noise, and the good old man began to bid his poor child farewell, for he knew it was the beast coming to them. When Beauty first saw that frightful form, she was very much terrified, but tried to hide her fear. The creature walked up to her, and eyed her all over—then asked her in a dreadful voice if she had come quite of her own accord.

"Yes," said Beauty.

"Then you are a good girl, and I am very much obliged to you."

This was such an astonishingly civil answer that Beauty's courage rose: but it sank again when the beast, addressing the merchant, desired him to leave the palace next morning, and never return to it again. "And so good-night, merchant. And good-night, Beauty."

"Good-night, beast," she answered, as the monster shuffled out of the room.

"Ah! my dear child," said the merchant, kissing his daughter, "I am half dead already, at the thought of leaving you with this dreadful beast; you shall go back and let me stay in your place."

"No," said Beauty boldly, "I will never agree to that; you must go home to-morrow morning."

They then wished each other good-night, and went to bed, both of them thinking they should not be able to close their eyes; but as soon as ever they had lain down, they fell into a deep sleep, and did not awake till morning. Beauty dreamed that a lady came up to her, who said, "I

"And she climbed up and easily broke off a branch, with its silver
leaves and golden fruit, and handed it to the knight." *(Page 67)*

"When the lady came she gave the handkerchief to the magician."
(Page 76)

am very much pleased, Beauty, with the goodness you have shown, in being willing to give your life to save that of your father. Do not be afraid of anything ; you shall not go without a reward."

As soon as Beauty awoke, she told her father this dream ; but though it gave him some comfort, he was a long time before he could be persuaded to leave the palace. At last Beauty succeeded in getting him safely away.

When her father was out of sight, poor Beauty began to weep sorely ; still, having naturally a courageous spirit, she soon resolved not to make her sad case still worse by sorrow, which she knew was vain, but to wait and be patient. She walked about to take a view of all the palace, and the elegance of every part of it much charmed her.

But what was her surprise, when she came to a door on which was written, BEAUTY'S ROOM ! She opened it in haste, and her eyes were dazzled by the splendour and taste of the apartment. What made her wonder more than all the rest, was a large library filled with books, a harpsichord, and many pieces of music. "The beast surely does not mean to eat me up immediately," said she, "since he takes care I shall not be at a loss how to amuse myself." She opened the library, and saw these verses written in letters of gold on the back of one of the books :

> Beauteous lady, dry your tears, ·
> Here's no cause for sighs or fears ;
> Command as freely as you may,
> For you command and I obey.

"Alas !" said she, sighing, "I wish I could only command a sight of my poor father, and to know what he is doing at this moment." Just then, by chance, she cast her eyes on a looking-glass that stood near her, and in it she saw a picture of her old home, and her father riding mournfully up to the door. Her sisters came out to meet him, and although they tried to look sorry, it was easy to see that in their hearts they were very glad. In a short time all this picture disappeared, but it caused Beauty to think that the beast, besides being very powerful, was also very kind. About the middle of the day she found a table laid ready for her, and a sweet concert of music played all the time she was dining, without her seeing anybody. But at supper, when she was going to seat herself at table, she heard the noise of the beast, and could not help trembling with fear.

"Beauty," said he, "will you give me leave to see you sup?"

"That is as you please," answered she, very much afraid.

"Not in the least," said the beast; "you alone command in this place. If you should not like my company, you need only say so, and I will leave you that moment. But tell me, Beauty, do you not think me very ugly?"

"Why, yes," said she, "for I cannot tell a falsehood; but then I think you are very good."

"Am I?" sadly replied the beast; "yet, besides being ugly, I am also very stupid : I know well enough that I am but a beast."

"Very stupid people," said Beauty, "are never aware of it themselves."

At which kindly speech the beast looked pleased, and replied, not without an awkward sort of politeness, "Pray do not let me detain you from supper, and be sure that you are well served. All you see is your own, and I should be deeply grieved if you wanted for anything."

"You are very kind—so kind that I almost forgot you are so ugly," said Beauty earnestly.

"Ah, yes!" answered the beast with a great sigh; "I hope I am good-tempered, but still I am only a monster."

"There is many a monster who wears the form of a man ; it is better of the two to have the heart of a man and the form of a monster."

"I would thank you, Beauty, for this speech, but I am too senseless to say anything that would please you," returned the beast in a melancholy voice ; and altogether he seemed so gentle and so unhappy, that Beauty, who had the tenderest heart in the world, felt her fear of him gradually vanish.

She ate her supper with a good appetite, and conversed in her own sensible and charming way, till at last, when the beast rose to depart, he terrified her more than ever by saying abruptly, in his gruff voice, "Beauty, will you marry me ? "

Now Beauty, frightened as she was, would speak only the exact truth ; besides, her father had told her that the beast liked only to have the truth spoken to him. So she answered, in a very firm tone, "No, beast."

He did not go into a passion, or do anything but sigh deeply, and depart.

When Beauty found herself alone, she began to feel pity for the poor beast. "Oh!" said she, "what a sad thing it is that he should be so very frightful, since he is so good-tempered ! "

Beauty lived three months in this palace very well pleased. The beast came to see her every night, and talked with her while she supped ; and though what he said was not very clever, yet, as she saw in him every day some new goodness, instead of dreading the time of his coming, she soon began continually looking at her watch to see if it were nine o'clock ; for that was the hour when he never failed to visit her. One thing only vexed her, which was that every night, before he went away, he always made it a rule to ask her if she would be his wife, and seemed very much grieved at her steadfastly replying "No." At last, one night, she said to him, "You wound me greatly, beast, by forcing me to refuse you so often; I wish I could take such a liking to you as to agree to marry you: but I must tell you plainly that I do not think it will ever happen. I shall always be your friend; so try to let that content you."

"I must," sighed the beast, "for I know well enough how frightful I am; but I love you better than myself. Yet I think I am very lucky in your being pleased to stay with me: now promise me, Beauty, that you will never leave me."

Beauty would almost have agreed to this, so sorry was she for him, but she had that day seen in her magic glass, which she looked at constantly, that her father was dying of grief for her sake.

"Alas!" she said, "I long so much to see my father, that if you do not give me leave to visit him, I shall break my heart."

"I would rather break mine, Beauty," answered the beast; "I will send you to your father's cottage: you shall stay there, and your poor beast shall die of sorrow."

"No," said Beauty, crying, "I love you too well to be the cause of your death; I promise to return in a week. You have shown me that my sisters are married, and my brothers are gone for soldiers, so that my father is left all alone. Let me stay a week with him."

"You shall find yourself with him to-morrow morning," replied the beast; "but mind, do not forget your promise. When you wish to return, you have nothing to do but to put your ring on a table when you go to bed. Good-bye, Beauty!" The beast sighed as he said these words, and Beauty went to bed very sorry to see him so much grieved. When she awoke in the morning, she found herself in her father's cottage. She rang a bell that was at her bedside, and a servant entered;

but as soon as she saw Beauty, the woman gave a loud shriek ; upon which the merchant ran upstairs, and when he beheld his daughter he ran to her, and kissed her a hundred times. At last Beauty began to remember that she had brought no clothes with her to put on ; but the servant told her she had just found in the next room a large chest full of dresses, trimmed all over with gold, and adorned with pearls and diamonds.

Beauty, in her own mind, thanked the beast for his kindness, and put on the plainest gown she could find among them all. She then desired the servant to lay the rest aside, for she intended to give them to her sisters ; but, as soon as she had spoken these words, the chest was gone out of sight in a moment. Her father then suggested, perhaps the beast chose for her to keep them all for herself : and as soon as he had said this, they saw the chest standing again in the same place. While Beauty was dressing herself, a servant brought word to her that her sisters were come with their husbands to pay her a visit. They both lived unhappily with the gentlemen they had married. The husband of the eldest was very handsome, but was so proud of this, that he thought of nothing else from morning till night, and did not care a pin for the beauty of his wife. The second had married a man of great learning ; but he made no use of it, except to torment and affront all his friends, and his wife more than any of them. The two sisters were ready to burst with spite when they saw Beauty dressed like a princess, and looking so very charming. All the kindness that she showed them was of no use ; for they were vexed more than ever when she told them how happy she lived at the palace of the beast. The spiteful creatures went by themselves into the garden, where they cried to think of her good fortune.

" Why should the little wretch be better off than we ? " said they. " We are much handsomer than she is."

"Sister!" said the eldest, "a thought has just come into my head : let us try to keep her here longer than the week for which the beast gave her leave ; and then he will be so angry, that perhaps when she goes back to him he will eat her up in a moment."

"That is well thought of," answered the other : "but to do this, we must pretend to be very kind."

They then went to join her in the cottage, where they showed her so much false love, that Beauty could not help crying for joy.

When the week was ended, the two sisters began to pretend such grief at the thought of her leaving them, that she agreed to stay a week more : but all that time Beauty could not help fretting for the sorrow that she knew her absence would give her poor beast ; for she tenderly loved him, and much wished for his company again. Among all the grand and clever people she saw, she found nobody who was half so sensible, so affectionate, so thoughtful, or so kind. The tenth night of her being at the cottage, she dreamed she was in the garden of the palace, that the beast lay dying on a grass-plot, and with his last breath put her in mind of her promise, and laid his death to her forsaking him. Beauty awoke in a great fright, and burst into tears : "Am not I wicked," said she, "to behave so ill to a beast who has shown me so much kindness? Why will not I marry him ? I am sure I should be more happy with him than my sisters are with their husbands. He shall not be wretched any longer on my account ; for I should do nothing but blame myself all the rest of my life."

She then rose, put her ring on the table, got into bed again, and soon fell asleep. In the morning she with joy found herself in the palace of the beast. She dressed herself very carefully, that she might please him the better, and thought she had never known a day pass away so slowly. At last the clock struck nine, but the beast did not come. Beauty, dreading lest she might truly have caused his death, ran from room to room, calling out, " Beast, dear beast " ; but there was no answer. At last she remembered her dream, rushed to the grass - plot, and there saw him lying apparently dead beside the fountain. Forgetting all his ugliness, she threw herself upon his body, and, finding his heart still beat, she fetched some water and sprinkled it over him, weeping and sobbing the while.

The beast opened his eyes : " You forgot your promise, Beauty, and so I determined to die ; for I could not live without you. I have starved myself to death, but I shall die content since I have seen your face once more."

" No, dear beast," cried Beauty passionately, " you shall not die ; you shall live to be my husband. I thought it was only friendship I felt for you, but now I know it was love."

The moment Beauty had spoken these words, the palace was suddenly lighted up, and all kinds of rejoicings were heard around them, none which she noticed, but hung over her dear beast with the utmost tenderness. At last, unable to restrain herself, she dropped her head over her hands, covered her eyes, and cried for joy ; and, when she looked up again, the beast was gone. In his stead she saw at her feet a handsome, graceful young prince, who thanked her with the tenderest expressions for having freed him from enchantment.

" But where is my poor beast ? I only want him and nobody else," sobbed Beauty.

" I am he," replied the prince. " A wicked fairy condemned me to this form, and forbade me to show that I had any wit or sense, till a beautiful lady should consent to marry me. You alone, dearest Beauty, judged me neither by my looks nor by my talents, but by my heart alone. Take it then, and all that I have besides, for all is yours."

Beauty, full of surprise, but very happy, suffered the prince to lead her to his palace, where she found her father and sisters, who had been brought there by the fairy-lady whom she had seen in a dream the first night she came.

"Beauty," said the fairy, "you have chosen well, and you have your reward, for a true heart is better than either good looks or clever brains. As for you, ladies," and she turned to the two elder sisters, "I know all your ill deeds, but I have no worse punishment for you than to see your sister happy. You shall stand as statues at the door of her palace, and when you repent of and have amended your faults, you shall become women again. But, to tell you the truth, I very much fear you will remain statues for ever."

LITTLE ONE EYE, LITTLE TWO EYES, AND LITTLE THREE EYES

THERE was a woman who had three daughters, the eldest of whom was called Little One Eye, because she had only one eye in the middle of her forehead ; the second, Little Two Eyes, because she had two eyes like other people ; and the youngest, Little Three Eyes, because she had three eyes, one of them being also in the middle of the forehead. But because Little Two Eyes looked no different from other people, her sisters and mother could not bear her. They said, "You with your two eyes are no better than anybody else ; you do not belong to us." They knocked her about, and gave her shabby clothes, and food which was left over from their own meals ; in short, they vexed her whenever they could.

It happened that Little Two Eyes had to go out into the fields to look after the goat ; but she was still quite hungry, because her sisters had given her so little to eat. She sat down on a hillock and began to cry, and cried so much that two little streams ran down out of each eye. And as she looked up once in her sorrow, a woman stood near her, who asked, "Little Two Eyes, why do you cry ?"

Little Two Eyes answered, "Have I not need to cry ? Because I have two eyes, like other people, my sisters and my mother cannot bear me ; they push me out of one corner into the other, give me shabby clothes, and nothing

61

to eat but what they leave. To-day they have given me so little that I am still quite hungry."

The wise woman said, "Little Two Eyes, dry your eyes, and I will tell you something which will keep you from ever being hungry more. Only say to your goat, 'Little goat, bleat; little table, rise,' and a neatly-laid table will stand before you with the most delicious food on it, so that you can eat as much as you like. And when you are satisfied and do not want the table any more, only say, 'Little goat, bleat; little table, away,' and it will all disappear before your eyes." Then the wise woman went out of sight.

Little Two Eyes thought, "I must try directly if it is true what she has said, for I am much too hungry to wait." So she said, "Little goat, bleat; little table, rise"; and scarcely had she uttered the words, when there stood before her a little table, covered with a white cloth, on which was laid a plate, knife and fork, and silver spoon. The most delicious food was there also, and smoking hot, as if just come from the kitchen. Then Little Two Eyes said the shortest grace that she knew, "Lord God, be our Guest at all times.—Amen," began to eat, and found it very good. And when she had had enough, she said as the wise woman had taught her—"Little goat, bleat; little table, away." In an instant the little table, and all that stood on it, had disappeared again. "That is a beautiful, easy way of housekeeping," thought Little Two Eyes, and was quite happy and merry.

In the evening, when she came home with her goat, she found a little earthen dish with food, which her sisters had put aside for her, but she did not touch anything— she had no need. On the next day she went out again with her goat, and let the few crusts that were given her remain uneaten. The first time and the second time the sisters took no notice; but when the same thing happened every day, they remarked it, and said, "All is not right with little Two Eyes; she always leaves her food, and she used formerly to eat up everything that was given her ; she must have found other ways of dining."

In order to discover the truth, they resolved that Little One Eye should go with Little Two Eyes when she drove the goat into the meadow, and see what she did there, and whether anybody brought her anything to eat and drink. So when Little Two Eyes set out again, Little One Eye came to her and said, " I will go with you into the field, and see that the goat is taken proper care of, and driven to good pasture."

But Little Two Eyes saw what Little One Eye had in her mind, and drove the goat into long grass, saying, " Come, Little One Eye, we will sit down ; I will sing you something." Little One Eye sat down, being tired from the unusual walk and from the heat of the sun, and Little Two Eyes kept on singing, " Are you awake, Little One Eye ? Are you asleep, Little One Eye ? " Then Little One Eye shut her one eye, and fell asleep. And when Little Two Eyes saw that Little One Eye was fast asleep, and could not betray anything, she said, " Little goat, bleat ; little table, rise," and sat herself at her table, and ate and drank till she was satisfied ; then she called out again, " Little goat, bleat ; little table, away," and instantly everything disappeared.

Little Two Eyes now woke Little One Eye, and said, " Little One Eye, you pretend to watch, and fall asleep over it, and in the meantime the goat could have run all over the world ; come, we will go home." Then they went home, and Little Two Eyes let her little dish again stand untouched ; and Little One Eye, who could not tell the mother why her sister would not eat, said, as an excuse, " Oh, I fell asleep out there."

The next day the mother said to Little Three Eyes, " This time you shall go and see if Little Two Eyes eats out of doors, and if any one brings her food and drink, for she must eat and drink secretly."

Then Little Three Eyes went to Little Two Eyes, and said, " I will go with you and see whether the goat is taken proper care of, and driven to good pasture." But Little Two Eyes saw what Little Three Eyes had in her mind, and drove the goat into long grass, and said as before, " We will sit down here, Little Three Eyes ; I will sing you something." Little Three Eyes seated herself, being tired from the walk and the heat of the sun, and Little Two Eyes began the same song again, and sang, " Are you awake, Little Three Eyes ? " But instead of singing then as she should, " Are you asleep, Little *Three* Eyes ? " she sang, through carelessness, " Are you asleep, Little *Two* Eyes ? " and went on singing, " Are you awake, Little Three Eyes ? Are you asleep, Little *Two* Eyes ? " So the two eyes of Little Three Eyes fell asleep, but the third did not go to sleep, because it was not spoken to by the verse. Little Three Eyes, to be sure, shut it and made believe to go to sleep, but only through slyness ; for she winked with it, and could see everything quite well. And when Little Two Eyes thought that Little Three Eyes was fast asleep, she said her little sentence, " Little goat, bleat ; little table, rise," ate and drank heartily, and then told the little table to go away again, " Little goat, bleat ; little table, away." But Little Three Eyes had seen everything. Then Little Two Eyes came to her, woke her, and said, " Ah ! Little Three Eyes, have you been asleep ? you keep watch well ! come, we will go home." And when they got home, Little Two Eyes again did not eat, and Little Three Eyes said to the mother, " I know why the proud thing does not eat : when she says to the goat out there, ' Little goat, bleat ; little table, rise,' there stands a table before her, which is covered with the very best food, much better than we have here ; and when she is satisfied, she says, ' Little goat, bleat ; little table, away,' and everything is gone again ; I have seen it all exactly. She put two of my eyes to sleep with her little verse, but the one on my forehead luckily remained awake."

Then the envious mother cried out, "Shall she be better off than we are?" fetched a butcher's knife and stuck it into the goat's heart, so that it fell down dead.

When Little Two Eyes saw that, she went out full of grief, seated herself on a hillock, and wept bitter tears. All at once the wise woman stood near her again, and said, "Little Two Eyes, why do you cry?"

"Shall I not cry?" answered she. "The goat who every day, when I said your little verse, laid the table so beautifully, has been killed by my mother; now I must suffer hunger and thirst again."

The wise woman said, "Little Two Eyes, I will give you some good advice; beg your sisters to give you the heart of the murdered goat, and bury it in the ground before the house-door, and it will turn out lucky for you." Then she disappeared, and Little Two Eyes went home and said to her sisters, "Dear sisters, give me some part of my goat; I don't ask for anything good, only give me the heart."

Then they laughed, and said, "You can have that, if you do not want anything else." Little Two Eyes took the heart, and buried it quietly in the evening before the house-door, after the advice of the wise woman.

Next morning, when the sisters woke, and went to the house-door together, there stood a most wonderful splendid tree, with leaves of silver, and fruit of gold hanging between them. Nothing more beautiful or charming could be seen in the wide world. But they did not know how the tree had come there in the night. Little Two Eyes alone noticed that it had grown out of the heart of the goat, for it stood just where she had buried it in the ground.

Then the mother said to Little One Eye, "Climb up, my child, and gather us some fruit from the tree."

Little One Eye climbed up, but when she wanted to seize a golden apple, the branch sprang out of her hand : this happened every time, so that she could not gather a single apple, though she tried as much as she could.

Then the mother said, "Little Three Eyes, do you climb up ; you can see better about you with your three eyes than Little One Eye can."

Little One Eye scrambled down, and Little Three Eyes climbed up. But Little Three Eyes was no cleverer, and might look about her as much as she liked—the golden apples always sprang back from her grasp. At last the mother became impatient, and climbed up herself, but could touch the fruit just as little as Little One Eye or Little Three Eyes ; she always grasped the empty air.

Then Little Two Eyes said, "I will go up myself ; perhaps I shall prosper better."

"You ! " cried the sisters. "With your two eyes, what can you do ? "

But Little Two Eyes climbed up, and the golden apples did not spring away from her, but dropped of themselves into her hand, so that she could gather one after the other, and brought down a whole apron full. Her mother took them from her, and instead of her sisters, Little One Eye and Little Three Eyes, behaving better to poor Little Two Eyes for it, they were only envious because she alone could get the fruit, and behaved still more cruelly to her.

It happened, as they stood together by the tree, one day, that a young knight came by.

"Quick, Little Two Eyes," cried the two sisters, " creep under, so that we may not be ashamed of you" ; and threw over poor Little Two Eyes, in a great hurry, an empty cask that stood just by the tree, and pushed also beside her the golden apples which she had broken off.

Now, as the knight came nearer, he proved to be a

handsome prince, who stood still, admired the beautiful tree of gold and silver, and said to the two sisters :

"To whom does this beautiful tree belong ? She who gives me a branch of it shall have whatever she wishes."

Then Little One Eye and Little Three Eyes answered that the tree was theirs, and they would break off a branch for him. They both of them gave themselves a great deal of trouble, but it was no use, for the branches and fruit sprang back from them every time. Then the knight said :

"It is very wonderful that the tree belongs to you, and yet you have not the power of gathering anything from it."

They insisted, however, that the tree was their own property. But as they spoke, Little Two Eyes rolled a few golden apples from under the cask, so that they ran to the feet of the knight ; for Little Two Eyes was angry that Little One Eye and Little Three Eyes did not tell the truth.

When the knight saw the apples he was astonished, and asked where they came from. Little One Eye and Little Three Eyes answered that they had another sister, who might not, however, show herself, because she had only two eyes, like other common people. But the knight desired to see her, and called out, "Little Two Eyes, come out." Then Little Two Eyes came out of the cask quite comforted, and the knight was astonished at her great beauty, and said :

"You, Little Two Eyes, can certainly gather me a branch from the tree ?"

"Yes," answered Little Two Eyes, "I can do that, for the tree belongs to me." And she climbed up and easily broke off a branch, with its silver leaves and golden fruit, and handed it to the knight.

Then the knight said, "Little Two Eyes, what shall I give you for it ?"

"Oh," answered Little Two Eyes, "I suffer hunger and thirst, sorrow and want, from early morning till late evening ; if you would take me with you and free me, I should be happy."

Then the knight lifted Little Two Eyes on to his horse, and took her home to his paternal castle ; there he gave her beautiful clothes, food, and drink as much as she wanted, and because he loved her so much he married her, and the marriage was celebrated with great joy.

Now, when Little Two Eyes was taken away by the handsome knight, the two sisters envied her very much her happiness. "The wonderful tree remains for us, though," thought they ; "and even though we cannot gather any fruit off it, every one will stand still before it, come to us, and praise it." But the next morning the tree had disappeared, and all their hopes with it.

Little Two Eyes lived happy a long time. Once two poor women came to her at the castle and begged alms. Then Little Two Eyes looked in their faces and recognised her sisters, Little One Eye and Little Three Eyes, who had fallen into such poverty that they had to wander about, and seek their bread from door to door. Little Two Eyes, however, bade them welcome, and was very good to them, and took care of them ; for they both repented from their hearts the evil they had done to their sister in their youth.

JACK THE GIANT-KILLER

In the reign of the famous King Arthur there lived, near the Land's End of England, in the county of Cornwall, a worthy farmer, who had an only son named Jack. Jack was a boy of a bold temper; he took pleasure in hearing or reading stories of wizards, conjurors, giants, and fairies; and used to listen eagerly while his father talked of the great deeds of the brave knights of King Arthur's Round Table. When Jack was sent to take care of the sheep and oxen in the fields, he used to amuse himself with planning battles, sieges, and the means to conquer or surprise a foe. He was above the common sports of children, but hardly any one could equal him at wrestling; or, if he met with a match for himself in strength, his skill and address always made him the victor. In those days there lived on St. Michael's Mount, of Cornwall, which rises out of the sea at some distance from the mainland, a huge giant. He was eighteen feet high, and three yards round; and his fierce and savage looks were the terror of all his neighbours. He dwelt in a gloomy cavern on the very top of the mountain, and used to wade over to the mainland in search of his prey. When he came near, the people left their houses; and, after he had glutted his appetite upon their cattle, he would throw half-a-dozen oxen upon his back, and tie three times as many sheep and hogs round his waist, and so march back to his own abode. The giant had done this for many years, and the coast of Cornwall was greatly hurt by his thefts, when Jack boldly resolved to destroy him. He therefore took a horn, a shovel, a pickaxe, and a dark lantern, and, early in a long winter's evening, he swam to the Mount. There he fell to work at once, and before morning he had dug a pit twenty-two feet deep, and almost as many broad. He covered it over with sticks and straw, and strewed some of the earth over them, to make it look just like solid ground. He then put his horn to his mouth, and blew such a loud and long tantivy, that the giant awoke, and came towards Jack, roaring like thunder : "You saucy villain, you shall pay dearly for breaking my rest ; I will broil you for my breakfast." He had scarcely spoken these words, when he came advancing one step further ; but then he tumbled headlong into the pit, and his fall shook the very mountain.

"O ho, Mr. Giant ! " said Jack, looking into the pit, "have you found your way so soon to the bottom ? How is your appetite now ? Will nothing serve you for breakfast this cold morning but broiling poor Jack ? "

The giant now tried to rise, but Jack struck him a blow on the crown of the head with his pickaxe, which killed him at once. Jack then made haste back, to rejoice his friends with the news of the giant's death. When the justices of Cornwall heard of this valiant action, they sent for Jack, and declared that he should always be called Jack the Giant-Killer ; and they also gave him a sword and belt, upon which was written, in letters of gold :

> This is the valiant Cornishman
> Who slew the giant Cormoran.

The news of Jack's exploits soon spread over the western parts of England : and another giant, called Old Blunderbore, vowed to have revenge on Jack, if it should ever be his fortune to get him into his power. The giant kept an enchanted castle in the midst of a lonely wood. About four months after the death of Cormoran, as Jack was taking a journey into Wales, he passed through this wood; and, as he was very weary, he sat down to rest by the side of a pleasant fountain, and there he fell into a deep sleep. The giant came to the fountain for water just at this time, and found Jack there; and as the lines on Jack's belt showed who he was, the giant lifted him up and laid him gently upon his shoulder, to carry him to his castle; but, as he passed through the thicket, the rustling of the leaves waked Jack; and he was sadly afraid when he found himself in the clutches of Blunderbore. Yet this was nothing to his fright soon after; for, when they reached the castle, he beheld the floor covered all over with the skulls and bones of men and women. The giant took him into a large room, where lay the hearts and limbs of persons who had been lately killed; and he told Jack, with a horrid grin, that men's hearts, eaten with pepper and vinegar, were his nicest food, and, also, that he thought he should make a dainty meal on his heart. When he had said this, he locked Jack up in that room, while he went to fetch another giant, who lived in the same wood, to enjoy a dinner off Jack's flesh with him. While he was away, Jack heard dreadful shrieks, groans, and cries from many parts of the castle; and soon after he heard a mournful voice repeat these lines:

"Haste, valiant stranger, haste away,
Lest you become the giant's prey.
On his return he'll bring another,
Still more savage than his brother;
A horrid, cruel monster, who,
Before he kills, will torture you.
Oh valiant stranger! haste away,
Or you'll become these giants' prey."

This warning was so shocking to poor Jack, that he was ready to go mad. He ran to the window, and saw the two giants coming along arm in arm. This window was right over the gates of the castle. "Now," thought Jack, "either my death or freedom is at hand."

There were two strong cords in the room. Jack made a large noose, with a slip-knot at the ends of both these, and, as the giants were coming through the gates, he threw the ropes over their heads. He then made the other ends fast to a beam in the ceiling, and pulled with all his might, till he had almost strangled them. When he saw that they were both quite black in the face, and had not the least strength left, he drew his sword, and slid down the ropes; he then killed the giants, and thus saved himself from a cruel death. Jack next took a great bunch of keys from the pocket of Blunderbore, and went into the castle again. He made a strict search through all the rooms, and in them found three ladies tied up by the hair of their heads, and almost starved to death. They told him that their husbands had been killed by the giants, who had then condemned them to be starved to death, because they would not eat the flesh of their own dead husbands.

"Ladies," said Jack, "I have put an end to the monster and his wicked brother; and I give you this castle and all the riches it contains, to make you some amends for the dreadful pains you have felt." He then very politely gave them the keys of the castle, and went farther on his journey to Wales.

As Jack had not taken any of the giant's riches for himself, and had very little money of his own, he thought it best to travel as fast as he could. At length he lost his way; and, when night came on, he was in a lonely valley between two lofty mountains. There he walked about for some hours, without seeing any dwelling-place, so he thought himself very lucky at last in finding a large and handsome house. He went up to it boldly, and knocked loudly at the gate; when, to his great terror and surprise, there came forth a monstrous giant with two heads. He spoke to Jack very civilly, for he was a Welsh giant, and all the mischief he did was by private and secret malice, under the show of friendship and kindness. Jack told him that he was a traveller who had lost his way, on which the huge monster made him welcome, and led him into a room, where there was a good bed in which to pass the night. Jack took off his clothes quickly ; but though he was so weary, he could not go to sleep. Soon after this, he heard the giant walking backward and forward in the next room, and saying to himself :

> "Though here you lodge with me this night,
> You shall not see the morning light ;
> My club shall dash your brains out quite."

"Say you so?" thought Jack. "Are these your tricks upon travellers? But I hope to prove as cunning as you." Then, getting out of bed, he groped about the room, and at last found a large thick billet of wood ; he laid it in his own place in the bed, and hid himself in a dark corner of the room. In the middle of the night the giant came with his great club, and struck many heavy blows on the bed, in the very place where Jack had laid the billet, and then he went back to his own room, thinking he had broken all his bones. Early in the morning, Jack put a bold face upon the matter, and walked into the giant's room to thank him for his lodging.

The giant started when he saw him, and he began to stammer out, "Oh, dear me! is it you? Pray how did you sleep last night? Did you hear or see anything in the dead of the night?"

"Nothing worth speaking of," said Jack carelessly ; "a rat, I believe, gave me three or four slaps with his tail, and disturbed me a little, but I soon went to sleep again."

The giant wondered more and more at this ; yet he

did not answer a word, and went to bring two great bowls of hasty-pudding for their breakfast.

Jack wished to make the giant believe that he could eat as much as himself; so he contrived to button a leathern bag inside his coat, and slipped the hasty-pudding into this bag, while he seemed to put it into his mouth. When breakfast was over, he said to the giant, "Now I will show you a fine trick; I can cure all wounds with a touch; I could cut off my head one minute, and the next put it sound again on my shoulders: you shall see an example." He then took hold of the knife, ripped up the leathern bag, and all the hasty-pudding tumbled out upon the floor.

"Ods splutter hur nails," cried the Welsh giant, who was ashamed to be outdone by such a little fellow as Jack; "hur can do that hurself." So he snatched up the knife, plunged it into his stomach, and in a moment dropped down dead.

As soon as Jack had thus tricked the Welsh monster, he went farther on his journey; and, a few days after, he met with King Arthur's only son, who had got his father's leave to travel into Wales, to deliver a beautiful lady from the power of a wicked magician, by whom she was held in enchantment. When Jack found that the young prince had no servants with him, he begged leave to attend him; and the prince at once agreed to this, and gave Jack many thanks for his kindness.

King Arthur's son was a handsome, polite, and brave knight, and so good-natured, that he gave money to everybody he met. At length he gave his last penny to an old woman, and then turned to Jack, "How shall we be able to get food for ourselves the rest of our journey?"

"Leave that to me, sir," replied Jack; "I will provide for my prince."

Night now came on, and the prince began to grow uneasy at thinking where they should lodge.

"Sir," said Jack, "be of good heart; two miles farther there lives a large giant, whom I know well; he has three heads, and will fight five hundred men, and make them fly before him."

"Alas!" cried the king's son, "we had better never have been born than meet with such a monster."

"My lord, leave me to manage him, and wait here in quiet till I return."

The prince now stayed behind, while Jack rode on at full speed; and when he came to the gates of the castle, he gave a loud knock. The giant, with a voice like thunder, roared out, "Who is there?"

Jack made answer, and said, "No one but your poor cousin Jack."

"Well," said the giant, "what news, cousin Jack?"

"Dear uncle," said Jack, "I have heavy news."

"Pooh!" said the giant, "what heavy news can come to me? I am a giant with three heads, and can fight five hundred men, and make them fly before me."

"Alas!" said Jack, "here is the king's son coming with two thousand men to kill you, and to destroy the castle and all that you have."

"Oh, cousin Jack," said the giant, "this is heavy news indeed! But I have a large cellar underground, where I will hide myself, and you shall lock, bolt, and bar me in, and keep the keys till the king's son is gone."

Now, when Jack had barred the giant fast in the vault, he went back and fetched the prince to the castle; they both made themselves merry with the wine and other dainties that were in the house. So that night they rested very pleasantly, while the poor giant lay trembling and shaking with fear in the cellar underground. Early in the morning, Jack gave the king's son gold and silver out of the giant's treasure, and accompanied him three miles forward on his journey. The prince then sent Jack to let his uncle out of the hole, who asked him what he should give him as a reward for saving his castle.

"Why, good uncle," said Jack, "I desire nothing but the old coat and cap, with the old rusty sword and slippers, which are hanging at your bed's head."

"Then," said the giant, "you shall have them ; and pray keep them for my sake, for they are things of great use. The coat will keep you invisible, the cap will give you knowledge, the sword will cut through anything, and the shoes are of vast swiftness ; they may be useful to you in all times of danger, so take them with all my heart."

Jack gave many thanks to the giant, and then set off to the prince. When he had come up with the king's son, they soon arrived at the dwelling of the beautiful lady, who was under the power of a wicked magician. She received the prince very politely, and made a noble feast for him : when it was ended, she rose, and, wiping her mouth with a fine handkerchief, said, "My lord, you must submit to the custom of my palace ; to-morrow morning I command you to tell me on whom I bestow this handkerchief, or lose your head." She then left the room.

The young prince went to bed very mournful, but Jack put on his cap of knowledge, which told him that the lady was forced, by the power of enchantment, to meet the wicked magician every night in the middle of the forest. Jack now put on his coat of darkness, and his shoes of swiftness, and was there before her. When the lady came she gave the handkerchief to the magician. Jack, with his sword of sharpness, at one blow cut off his head ; the enchantment was then ended in a moment, and the lady was restored to her former virtue and goodness. She was married to the prince on the next day, and soon after went back, with her royal husband and a great company, to the court of King Arthur, where they were received with loud and joyful welcomes; and the valiant hero Jack, for the many great exploits he had done for the good of his country, was made one of the Knights of the Round Table.

As Jack had been so lucky in all his adventures, he resolved not to be idle for the future, but still to do what services he could for the honour of the king and the nation. He therefore humbly begged his majesty to furnish him with a horse and money, that he might travel in search of new and strange exploits. "For," said he to the king, "there are many giants yet living in the remote parts of Wales, to the great terror and distress of your majesty's subjects; therefore, if it please you, sire, to favour me in my design, I will soon rid your kingdom of these giants and monsters in human shape."

Now when the king heard this offer, and began to think of the cruel deeds of these bloodthirsty giants and savage monsters, he gave Jack everything proper for such a journey. After this, Jack took leave of the king, the prince, and all the knights, and set off, taking with him his cap of knowledge, his sword of sharpness, his shoes of swiftness, and his invisible coat, the better to perform the great exploits that might fall in his way. He went along over hills and mountains; and on the third day he came to a wide forest. He had hardly entered it, when on a sudden he heard dreadful shrieks and cries; and forcing his way through the trees, saw a monstrous giant dragging along, by the hair of their heads, a handsome knight and a beautiful lady. Their tears and cries melted the heart of honest Jack; he alighted from his horse, and, tying him to an oak-tree, put on his invisible coat, under which he carried his sword of sharpness.

When he came up to the giant he made several strokes at him, but could not reach his body, on account of the enormous height of the terrible creature; but he wounded his thighs in several places; and at length, putting both hands to his sword, and aiming with all his might, he cut off both the giant's legs just below the garter ; and the trunk of his body, tumbling to the ground, made not only the trees shake, but the earth itself tremble with the force of his fall. Then Jack, setting his foot upon his neck, exclaimed, "Thou barbarous and savage wretch, behold, I come to execute upon thee the just reward for all thy crimes" ; and instantly plunged his sword into the giant's body. The huge monster gave a groan, and yielded up his life into the hands of the victorious Jack the Giant-Killer, whilst the noble knight and the virtuous lady were both joyful spectators of his sudden death. They not only returned Jack hearty thanks for their deliverance, but also invited him to their house, to refresh himself after his dreadful encounter, as likewise to receive a reward for his good services.

"No," said Jack, "I cannot be at ease till I find out the den that was the monster's habitation."

The knight, on hearing this, grew very sorrowful, and replied, "Noble stranger, it is too much to run a second hazard ; this monster lived in a den under yonder mountain, with a brother of his, more fierce and cruel than himself ; therefore, if you should go thither, and perish in the attempt, it would be a heart-breaking thing to me and my lady ; so let me persuade you to go back with us, and desist from any farther pursuit."

"Nay," answered Jack, "if there be another, even if there were twenty, I would shed the last drop of blood in my body before one of them should escape. When I have finished this task, I will come and pay my respects to you."

So when they had told him where to find them again, he got on his horse and went after the dead giant's brother.

Jack had not ridden a mile and a half before he came

in sight of the mouth of the cavern ; and, nigh the entrance of it, he saw the other giant sitting on a huge block of timber, with a knotted iron club lying by his side, waiting for his brother. His eyes looked like flames of fire, his face was grim and ugly, and his cheeks were like two flitches of bacon ; the bristles of his beard seemed to be thick rods of iron wire ; and his long locks of hair hung down upon his broad shoulders like curling snakes. Jack got down from his horse, and turned him into a thicket ; then he put on his coat of darkness, and drew a little nearer to behold this figure, and said softly, "Oh, monster ! are you there ? It will not be long before I shall take you fast by the beard."

The giant all this while could not see him, by reason of his invisible coat ; so Jack came quite close to him, and struck a blow at his head with his sword of sharpness ; but he missed his aim, and only cut off his nose, which made him roar like loud claps of thunder. He rolled his glaring eyes round on every side, but could not see who had given him the blow ; so he took up his iron club, and began to lay about him like one that was mad with pain and fury.

"Nay," said Jack, "if this be the case, I will kill you at once." So saying, he slipped nimbly behind him, and jumping upon the block of timber, as the giant rose from it, he stabbed him in the back ; when, after a few howls, he dropped down dead. Jack cut off his head, and sent it, with the head of his brother, to King Arthur, by a waggon which he had hired for that purpose. When Jack had thus killed these two monsters, he went into their cave in search of their treasure. He passed through many turnings and windings, which led him to a room paved with freestone ; at the end of it was a boiling cauldron, and on the right hand stood a large table, where the giants used to dine. He then came to a window that was secured with iron bars, through which he saw a number of wretched captives, who cried out when they saw Jack, " Alas! alas! young man, you are come to be one among us in this horrid den."

" I hope," said Jack, " you will not stay here long ; but pray tell me what is the meaning of your being here at all ? "

" Alas!" said one poor old man, " I will tell you, sir. We are persons that have been taken by the giants who hold this cave, and are kept till they choose to have a feast ; then one of us is to be killed, and cooked to please their taste. It is not long since they took three for the same purpose."

" Well," said Jack, " I have given them such a dinner, that it will be long enough before they have any more."

The captives were amazed at his words.

" You may believe me," said Jack, " for I have killed them both with the edge of this sword, and have sent their large heads to the court of King Arthur, as marks of my great success."

To show that what he said was true, he unlocked the gate, and set the captives all free. Then he led them to the great room, placed them round the table, and placed before them two quarters of beef, with bread and wine ; upon which they feasted their fill. When supper was over, they searched the giant's coffers, and Jack divided among them all the treasures. The next morning they set off to their homes, and Jack to the knight's house, whom he had left with his lady not long before.

He was received with the greatest joy by the thankful knight and his lady, who, in honour of Jack's exploits, gave a grand feast, to which all the nobles and gentry were invited. When the company were assembled, the knight declared to them the great actions of Jack, and gave him, as a mark of respect, a fine ring, on which was engraved the picture of the giant dragging the knight and the lady by the hair, with this motto round it :

JACK THE GIANT-KILLER

Behold in dire distress were we,
   Under a giant's fierce command ;
But gain'd our lives and liberty
   From valiant Jack's victorious hand.

Among the guests then present were five aged gentlemen, who were fathers to some of those captives who had been freed by Jack from the dungeon of the giants. As soon as they heard that he was the person who had done such wonders, they pressed round him with tears of joy, to return him thanks for the happiness he had caused them. After this the bowl went round, and every one drank the health and long life of the gallant hero. Mirth increased, and the hall was filled with peals of laughter. But, on a sudden, a herald, pale and breathless, rushed into the midst of the company, and told them that Thundel, a savage giant with two heads, had heard of the death of his two kinsmen, and was come to take his revenge on Jack ; and that he was now within a mile of the house, the people flying before him like chaff before the wind. At this news the very boldest of the guests trembled ; but Jack drew his sword, and said, " Let him come, I have a rod for him also. Pray, ladies and gentlemen, do me the favour to walk into the garden, and you shall soon behold the giant's defeat and death."

To this they all agreed, and heartily wished him success in his dangerous attempt.

The knight's house stood in the middle of a moat, thirty feet deep and twenty wide, over which lay a draw-bridge. Jack set men to work, to cut the bridge on both sides, almost to the middle, and then dressed himself in his coat of darkness, and went against the giant with his sword of sharpness. As he came close to him, though the giant could not see him for his invisible coat, yet he found some danger was near, which made him cry out :

" Fa, fe, fi, fo, fum,
I smell the blood of an Englishman ;
Let him be alive, or let him be dead, .
I'll grind his bones to make me bread."

"Say you so, my friend?" said Jack; "you are a monstrous miller, indeed!"

"Art thou," cried the giant, "the villain that killed my kinsmen? Then I will tear thee with my teeth, and grind thy bones to powder."

"You must catch me first," said Jack; and throwing off his coat of darkness, and putting on his shoes of swiftness, he began to run, the giant following him like a walking castle, making the earth shake at every step.

Jack led him round and round the walls of the house, that the company might see the monster; then, to finish the work, he ran over the drawbridge, the giant going after him with his club; but when he came to the middle, where the bridge had been cut on both sides, the great weight of his body made it break, and he tumbled into the water, where he rolled about like a large whale. Jack now stood by the side of the moat, and laughed and jeered at him, saying, "I think you told me you would grind my bones to powder; when will you begin?"

The giant foamed at both his horrid mouths with fury, and plunged from side to side of the moat; but he could not get out to have revenge on his little foe. At last Jack ordered a cart-rope to be brought to him; he then drew it over his two heads, and by the help of a team of horses, dragged him to the edge of the moat, where he cut off his heads, and before he either ate or drank, sent them both to the court of King Arthur. He then went back to the table with the company, and the rest of the day was spent in mirth and good cheer.

After staying with the knight for some time, Jack grew weary of such an idle life, and set out again in search of new adventures. He went over hills and dales without meeting any, till he came to the foot of a very high mountain. Here he knocked at the door of a small and lonely house, and an old man, with a head as white as snow, let him in.

"Good father," said Jack, "can you lodge a traveller who has lost his way?"

"Yes," said the hermit, "I can, if you will accept such fare as my poor house affords."

Jack entered, and the old man set before him some bread and fruit for his supper. When Jack had eaten as much as he chose, the hermit said, "My son, I know you are the famous conqueror of giants; now, at the top of this mountain is an enchanted castle, kept by a giant named Galligantus, who, by the help of a vile magician, gets many knights into his castle, where he changes them into the shape of beasts. Above all, I lament the hard fate of a duke's daughter, whom they seized as she was walking in her father's garden, and brought hither through the air in a chariot drawn by two fiery dragons, and turned her into the shape of a deer. Many knights have tried to destroy the enchantment and deliver her, yet none have been able to do it, by reason of two fiery griffins, who guard the gate of the castle, and destroy all who come nigh; but as you, my son, have an invisible coat, you may pass by them without being seen; and on the gates of the castle you will find engraved by what means the enchantment may be broken."

Jack promised that in the morning, at the risk of his life, he would break the enchantment; and after a sound sleep, he arose early, put on his invisible coat, and got ready for the attempt. When he had climbed to the top of the mountain, he saw the two fiery griffins; but he passed between them without the least fear of danger, for they could not see him because of his invisible coat. On the castle-gate he found a golden trumpet, under which were written these lines:

Whoever can this trumpet blow
Shall cause the giant's overthrow.

As soon as Jack had read this, he seized the trumpet, and blew a shrill blast, which made the gates fly open, and the very castle itself tremble. The giant and the conjuror now knew that their wicked course was at an end, and they stood biting their thumbs and shaking with fear. Jack, with his sword of sharpness, soon killed the giant, and the magician was then carried away by a whirlwind. All the knights and beautiful ladies, who had been changed into birds and beasts, returned to their proper shapes. The castle vanished away like smoke, and the head of the giant Galligantus was sent to King Arthur. The knights and ladies rested that night at the old man's hermitage, and next day they set out for the court. Jack then went up to the king, and gave his majesty an account of all his fierce battles. Jack's fame had spread through the whole country; and at the king's desire, the duke gave him his daughter in marriage, to the joy of all the kingdom. After this, the king gave him a large estate, on which he and his lady lived the rest of their days in joy and content.

TOM THUMB

In the days of King Arthur, Merlin, the most learned enchanter of his time, was on a journey ; and being very weary, stopped one day at the cottage of an honest ploughman to ask for refreshment. The ploughman's wife, with great civility, immediately brought him some milk in a wooden bowl, and some brown bread on a wooden platter. Merlin could not help observing, that although everything within the cottage was particularly neat and clean, and in good order, the ploughman and his wife had the most sorrowful air imaginable ; so he questioned them on the cause of their melancholy, and learned that they were very miserable because they had no children. The poor woman declared, with tears in her eyes, that she should be the happiest creature in the world, if she had a son, although he were no bigger than his father's thumb. Merlin was much amused with the notion of a boy no bigger than a man's thumb ; and as soon as he returned home, he sent for the queen of the fairies (with whom he was very intimate), and related to her the desire of the ploughman and his wife to have a son the size of his father's thumb. She liked the plan exceedingly, and declared their wish should be speedily granted. Accordingly, the ploughman's wife had a son, who in a few minutes grew as tall as his father's thumb. The queen of the fairies came in at the window as the mother was sitting up in bed admiring the child. Her majesty kissed the infant, and, giving it the name of

Tom Thumb, immediately summoned several fairies from Fairyland, to clothe her new little favourite :

> An oak-leaf hat he had for his crown,
> His shirt it was by spiders spun :
> With doublet wove of thistledown,
> His trousers up with points were done :
> His stockings, of apple-rind, they tie
> With eye-lash pluck'd from his mother's eye :
> His shoes were made of a mouse's skin,
> Nicely tann'd with hair within.

Tom was never any bigger than his father's thumb, which was not a large thumb either ; but as he grew older, he became very cunning, for which his mother did not sufficiently correct him ; and by this ill quality he was often brought into difficulties. For instance, when he had learned to play with other boys for cherry-stones, and had lost all his own, he used to creep into the boys' bags, fill his pockets, and come out again to play. But one day as he was getting out of a bag of cherry-stones, the boy to whom it belonged chanced to see him.

"Ah, ha, my little Tom Thumb!" said he, "have I caught you at your bad tricks at last ? Now I will reward you for thieving." Then drawing the string tight round his neck, and shaking the bag, the cherry-stones bruised Tom's legs, thighs, and body sadly ; which made him beg to be let out, and promise never to be guilty of such things any more.

Shortly afterwards, Tom's mother was making a batter-pudding, and that he might see how she mixed it, he climbed on the edge of the bowl ; but his foot happening to slip, he fell over head and ears into the batter, and his mother, not observing him, stirred him into the pudding, and popped him into the pot to boil. The hot water made Tom kick and struggle ; and his mother, seeing the pudding jump up and down in such a furious manner, thought it was bewitched ; and a tinker coming by just at the time, she quickly gave him the pudding; he put it into his budget, and walked on.

As soon as Tom could get the batter out of his mouth, he began to cry aloud, which so frightened the poor tinker, that he flung the pudding over the hedge, and ran away from it as fast as he could. The pudding being broken to pieces by the fall, Tom was released, and walked home to his mother, who gave him a kiss and put him to bed.

Tom Thumb's mother once took him with her when she went to milk the cow; and it being a very windy day, she tied him with a needleful of thread to a thistle, that he might not be blown away. The cow, liking his oak-leaf hat, took him and the thistle up at one mouthful. While the cow chewed the thistle, Tom, terrified at her great teeth, which seemed ready to crush him to pieces, roared, "Mother, mother!" as loud as he could bawl.

"Where are you, Tommy, my dear Tommy?" said the mother.

"Here, mother, here in the red cow's mouth."

The mother began to cry and wring her hands; but the cow, surprised at such odd noises in her throat, opened her mouth and let him drop out. His mother clapped him into her apron, and ran home with him. Tom's father made him a whip of a barley straw to drive the cattle with, and being one day in the field he slipped into a deep furrow. A raven flying over picked him up with a grain of corn, and flew with him to the top of a giant's castle by the seaside, where he left him; and old Grumbo, the giant, coming soon after to walk upon his terrace, swallowed Tom like a pill, clothes and all. Tom presently made the giant very uncomfortable, and he threw him up into the sea. A great fish then swallowed him. This fish was soon after caught, and sent as a present to King Arthur. When it was cut open, everybody was delighted with little Tom Thumb. The king made him his dwarf;

he was the favourite of the whole court; and, by his merry pranks, often amused the queen and the knights of the Round Table. The king, when he rode on horseback, frequently took Tom in his hand; and if a shower of rain came on, he used to creep into the king's waistcoat-pocket, and sleep till the rain was over. The king also sometimes questioned Tom concerning his parents; and when Tom informed his majesty they were very poor people, the king led him into his treasury, and told him he should pay his friends a visit, and take with him as much money as he could carry. Tom procured a little purse, and putting a threepenny piece into it, with much labour and difficulty got it upon his back; and, after travelling two days and nights, arrived at his father's house. His mother met him at the door, almost tired to death, having in forty-eight hours travelled almost half a mile with a huge silver threepence upon his back. Both his parents were glad to see him, especially when he had brought such an amazing sum of money with him. They placed him in a walnut-shell by the fireside, and feasted him for three days upon a hazel-nut, which made him sick, for a whole nut usually served him for a month. Tom got well, but could not travel because it had rained; therefore his mother took him in her hand, and with one puff blew him into King Arthur's court; where Tom entertained the king, queen, and nobility at tilts and tournaments, at which he exerted himself so much that he brought on a fit of sickness, and his life was despaired of. At this juncture the queen of the fairies came in a chariot, drawn by flying mice, placed Tom by her side, and drove through the air without stopping till they arrived at her palace; when, after restoring him to health and permitting him to enjoy all the gay diversions of Fairyland, she commanded a fair wind, and, placing Tom before it, blew him straight to the court of King Arthur. But just as Tom should have alighted in the courtyard of the palace, the cook happened to pass along with the king's great bowl of furmenty (King Arthur loved furmenty), and poor Tom Thumb fell plump into the middle of it, and splashed the hot furmenty into the cook's eyes.   Down went the bowl.

"Oh dear ! oh dear ! " cried Tom.

"Murder ! murder ! " bellowed the cook ; and away poured the king's nice furmenty into the kennel.

The cook was a red-faced, cross fellow, and swore to the king that Tom had done it out of mere mischief ; so he was taken up, tried, and sentenced to be beheaded. Tom, hearing this dreadful sentence, and seeing a miller stand by with his mouth wide open, took a good spring, and jumped down the miller's throat, unperceived by all, even by the miller himself.

Tom being lost, the court broke up, and away went the miller to his mill.   But Tom did not leave him long at rest ; he began to roll and tumble about, so that the miller thought himself bewitched, and sent for a doctor. When the doctor came, Tom began to dance and sing ; the doctor was as much frightened as the miller, and sent in great haste for five more doctors and twenty learned men.   While all these were debating upon the affair, the miller (for they were very tedious) happened to yawn, and Tom, taking the opportunity, made another jump, and alighted on his feet in the middle of the table. The miller, provoked to be thus tormented by such a little creature, fell into a great passion, caught hold of Tom, and threw him out of the window into the river.   A large salmon swimming by snapped him up in a minute. The salmon was soon caught and sold in the market to a steward of a lord.   The lord, thinking it an uncommon fine fish, made a present of it to the king, who ordered it to be dressed immediately.   When the cook cut open the salmon, he found poor Tom, and ran with him directly to the king ; but the king, being busy with state affairs, desired that he might be brought another day. The cook resolving to keep him safely this time, as he had so lately given him the slip, clapped him into a mouse-trap, and left him to amuse himself by peeping through the wires for a whole week ; when the king sent for him, he forgave him for throwing down the furmenty, ordered him new clothes, and knighted him :

His shirt was made of butterflies' wings,
His boots were made of chicken skins ;
His coat and breeches were made with pride ;
A tailor's needle hung by his side ;
A mouse for a horse he used to ride.

Thus dressed and mounted, he rode a-hunting with the king and nobility, who all laughed heartily at Tom and his fine prancing steed. As they rode by a farmhouse one day, a cat jumped from behind the door, seized the mouse and little Tom, and began to devour the mouse ; however, Tom boldly drew his sword and attacked the cat, who then let him fall. The king and his nobles, seeing Tom falling, went to his assistance, and one of the lords caught him in his hat, but poor Tom was sadly scratched, and his clothes were torn by the claws of the cat. In this condition he was carried home, when a bed of down was made for him in a little ivory cabinet. The queen of the fairies came and took him again to Fairyland, where she kept him for some years ; and then, dressing him in bright green, sent him flying once more through the air to the earth, in the days of King Thunstone. The people flocked far and near to look at him ; and the king, before whom he was carried, asked him who he was, whence he came, and where he lived. Tom answered :

"My name is Tom Thumb,
From the Fairies I come ;
When King Arthur shone,
This court was my home.

TOM THUMB

> In me he delighted,
> By him I was knighted;
> Did you never hear of
> Sir Thomas Thumb?"

The king was so charmed with this address that he ordered a little chair to be made, in order that Tom might sit on his table, and also a palace of gold a span high, with a door an inch wide, for little Tom to live in. He also gave him a coach drawn by six small mice. This made the queen angry, because she had not a new coach too; therefore, resolving to ruin Tom, she complained to the king that he had behaved very insolently to her. The king sent for him in a rage. Tom, to escape his fury, crept into an empty snail-shell, and there lay till he was almost starved; when, peeping out of the hole, he saw a fine butterfly settle on the ground: he now ventured out, and, getting astride, the butterfly took wing, and mounted into the air with little Tom on his back. Away he flew from field to field, from tree to tree, till at last he flew to the king's court. The king, queen, and nobles all strove to catch the butterfly, but could not. At length poor Tom, having neither bridle nor saddle, slipped from his seat, and fell into a watering-pot, where he was found almost drowned. The queen vowed he should be guillotined; but while the guillotine was getting ready, he was secured once more in a mouse-trap; when the cat, seeing something stir, and supposing it to be a mouse, patted the trap about till she broke it, and set Tom at liberty. Soon afterwards a spider, taking him for a fly, made at him. Tom drew his sword and fought valiantly, but the spider's poisonous breath overcame him:

> He fell dead on the ground where late he had stood,
> And the spider suck'd up the last drop of his blood.

King Thunstone and his whole court went into mourning for little Tom Thumb. They buried him under a rosebush, and raised a nice white marble monument over his grave, with the following epitaph :

> Here lies Tom Thumb, King Arthur's knight,
> Who died by a spider's cruel bite.
> He was well known in Arthur's court,
> Where he afforded gallant sport ;
> He rode at tilt and tournament,
> And on a mouse a-hunting went ;
> Alive he fill'd the court with mirth,
> His death to sorrow soon gave birth.
> Wipe, wipe your eyes, and shake your head,
> And cry, " Alas ! Tom Thumb is dead."

RUMPELSTILZCHEN

THERE was once a miller who was very poor, but he had a beautiful daughter. Now, it happened that he came to speak to the king, and, to give himself importance, he said to him, " I have a daughter who can spin straw into gold."

The king said to the miller, "That is a talent that pleases me well ; if she be as skilful as you say, bring her to-morrow to the palace, and I will put her to the proof."

When the maiden was brought to him, he led her to a room full of straw, gave her a wheel and spindle, and said, " Now set to work, and if by the morrow this straw be not spun into gold, you shall die." He locked the door, and left the maiden alone.

The poor girl sat down disconsolate, and could not for her life think what she was to do ; for she knew not— how could she ?—the way to spin straw into gold ; and her distress increased so much that at last she began to weep. All at once the door opened, and a little man entered and said, "Good evening, my pretty miller's daughter ; why are you weeping so bitterly ?"

" Ah ! " answered the maiden, " I must spin straw into gold, and know not how to do it."

The little man said, " What will you give me if I do it for you ?"

" My neckerchief," said the maiden.

He took the kerchief, sat down before the wheel, and grind, grind, grind—three times did he grind—and the

93

spindle was full ; then he put another thread on, and grind, grind, grind, the second was full ; so he spun on till morning ; when all the straw was spun, and all the spindles were full of gold.

The king came at sunrise, and was greatly astonished and overjoyed at the sight ; but it only made his heart the more greedy of gold. He put the miller's daughter into another much larger room, full of straw, and ordered her to spin it all in one night, if life were dear to her. The poor helpless maiden began to weep, when once more the door flew open, the little man appeared, and said, " What will you give me if I spin this straw into gold ? "

" My ring from my finger," answered the maiden.

The little man took the ring, began to turn the wheel, and, by the morning, all the straw was spun into shining gold.

The king was highly delighted when he saw it, but was not yet satisfied with the quantity of gold ; so he put the damsel into a still larger room full of straw, and said, " Spin this during the night ; and if you do it you shall be my wife." " For," he thought, " if she's only a miller's daughter, I shall never find a richer wife in the whole world."

As soon as the damsel was alone the little man came the third time and said, " What will you give me if I again spin all this straw for you ? "

" I have nothing more to give you," answered the girl.

" Then promise, if you become queen, to give me your first child."

" Who knows how that may be, or how things may turn out between now and then ? " thought the girl, but in her perplexity she could not help herself ; so she promised the little man what he desired, and he spun all the straw into gold.

When the king came in the morning and saw that

his orders had been obeyed, he married the maiden, and the beautiful miller's daughter became a queen. After a year had passed she brought a lovely baby into the world, but quite forgot the little man, till he walked suddenly into her chamber, and said, "Give me what you promised me." The queen was frightened, and offered the dwarf all the riches of the kingdom if he would only leave her her child ; but he answered, "No ; something living is dearer to me than all the treasures of the world."

Then the queen began to grieve and to weep so bitterly, that the little man took pity upon her and said, "I will give you three days ; if in that time you can find out my name, you shall keep the child."

All night long the queen thought over every name she had ever heard, and sent a messenger through the kingdom, to inquire what names were usually given to people in that country. When, next day, the little man came again, she began with Caspar, Melchior, Balthazar, and repeated, each after each, all the names she knew or had heard of ; but at each one the little man said, "That is not my name."

The second day she again sent round about in all directions, to ask how the people were called, and repeated to the little man the strangest names she could hear of or imagine : to each he answered always, "That is not my name."

The third day the messenger returned and said, "I have not been able to find a single new name ; but as I came over a high mountain by a wood, where the fox and the hare bid each other good-night, I saw a little house, and before the house was burning a little fire, and round the fire danced a very funny little man, who hopped upon one leg, and cried out :

"To-day I brew, to-morrow I bake,
Next day the queen's child I shall take ;
How glad I am that nobody knows
My name is Rumpelstilzchen ! "

You may guess how joyful the queen was at hearing this; and when, soon after, the little man entered and said, "Queen, what is my name?" she asked him mischievously, "Is your name Kunz?"

"No."

"Is your name Carl?"

"No."

"Are you not sometimes called Rumpelstilzchen?"

"A witch has told you that—a witch has told you!" shrieked the poor little man, and stamped so furiously with his right foot that it sank into the earth up to the hip; then he seized his left foot with both hands with such violence that he tore himself right in two.

FORTUNATUS

IN the city of Famagosta, in the island of Cyprus, there lived a very rich gentleman. His name was Theodorus. He married a lady who was the greatest beauty in Cyprus, and she was as rich as himself; she was called Graciana. They both had every pleasure that wealth could buy, and lived in the first style. Besides all this, the Lady Graciana brought her husband a fine little son, who was named Fortunatus; so one would think nothing could have kept Theodorus from being the most happy person in the world. But this was not long the case; for when he had enjoyed all these pleasures for some time, he grew tired of them, and began to keep company with young noblemen of the court, with whom he sat up all night drinking and playing cards, so that in a few years he spent all his fortune. He was now very sorry for what he had done, but it was too late; and there was nothing he could do, but to work at some trade to support his wife and child. For all this the Lady Graciana never found fault with him, but still loved her husband the same as before; saying, "Dear Theodorus, to be sure I do not know how to work at any trade; but if I cannot help you in earning money, I will help you to save it." So Theodorus set to work; and though the Lady Graciana had always been used only to ring her bell for everything that she wanted, she now scoured the kettles and washed the clothes with her own hands.

They went on in this manner till Fortunatus was sixteen years of age. When that time came, one day, as they were all sitting at dinner, Theodorus fixed his eyes on his son, and sighed deeply.

"What is the matter with you, father?" said Fortunatus.

"Ah! my child," said Theodorus, "I have reason enough to be sorry, when I think of the noble fortune which I have spent, and that my folly will force you to labour for your living."

"Father," replied Fortunatus, "do not grieve about it. I have often thought that it was time I should do something for myself; and though I have not been brought up to any trade, yet I hope I can contrive to support myself somehow."

When Fortunatus had done his dinner, he took his hat and walked to the sea-side, thinking of what he could do, so as to be no longer a burden to his parents. Just as he reached the sea-shore, the Earl of Flanders, who had been to Jerusalem, was embarking on board his ship with all his servants, to set sail for Flanders. Fortunatus now thought he would offer himself to be the Earl's page. When the Earl saw that he was a smart-looking lad, and heard the quick replies which he made to his questions, he took him into his service; so at once they all went on board. On their way the ship stopped a short time at the port of Venice, where Fortunatus saw many strange things, which made him wish still more to travel, and taught him much that he did not know before.

Soon after this they came to Flanders; and they had not been long on shore, before the Earl, his master, was married to the daughter of the Duke of Cleves. The wedding was kept with all sorts of public feasting, and games on horseback called tilts, which lasted many days; and, among the rest, the Earl's lady gave two jewels as prizes to be played for, each of them the value of a hundred crowns. One of them was won by Fortunatus, and the other by Timothy, a servant of the Duke of Burgundy;

who afterwards ran another tilt with Fortunatus, so that the winner was to have both the jewels. So they tilted, and, at the fourth course, Fortunatus hoisted Timothy a full spear's length from his horse, and thus won both the jewels; which pleased the Earl and Countess so much that they praised Fortunatus, and thought better of him than ever. At this time, also, Fortunatus had many rich presents given him by the lords and ladies of the court. But the high favour shown him made his fellow-servants jealous; and one, named Robert, who had always pretended a great friendship for Fortunatus, made him believe that for all his seeming kindness, the Earl in secret envied him his great skill in tilting. Robert said, too, that he had heard the Earl give private orders to one of his servants to find some way of killing him next day, while they should all be out hunting.

Fortunatus thanked the wicked Robert for what he thought a great kindness; and the next day, at daybreak, he took the swiftest horse in the Earl's stables, and left the country. When the Earl heard that Fortunatus had gone away in a hurry, he was much surprised, and asked all his servants what they knew about the matter; but they all denied knowing anything of it, or why he had left them. The Earl then said, "Fortunatus was a lad for whom I had a great esteem; I am sure some of you must have given him an affront; if I discover it, I shall not fail to punish the guilty person." In the meantime Fortunatus, when he found himself out of the Earl's country, stopped at an inn to refresh himself, and began to reckon how much he had about him. He took out all his fine clothes and jewels, and could not help putting them on. He then looked at himself in the glass, and thought that, to be sure, he was quite a fine smart fellow. Next he took out his purse, and counted the money that had been given him by the lords and ladies of the Earl's court. He found that in all he had five hundred crowns, so he bought a horse, and took care to send back the one that he had taken from the Earl's stable.

He then set off for Calais, crossed the Channel, landed safely at Dover, and went on to London, where he soon made his way into genteel company, and had once the honour to dance with the daughter of a duke at the lord mayor's ball. This sort of life, as anybody may well think, soon made away with his little stock of money. When Fortunatus found that he had not a penny left, he began to think of going back again to France; and soon after went on board a ship bound to Picardy. He landed in that country; but finding no employment he set off for Brittany, when he lost his way in crossing a wood, and was forced to stay in it all night. The next morning he was little better off, for he could find no path. So he walked about from one part of the wood to another, till at last, on the evening of the second day, he saw a spring, at which he drank very heartily; but still he had nothing to eat, and was ready to die with hunger. When night came on, he heard the growling of wild beasts, so he climbed up a high tree for safety, and he had hardly seated himself in it, before a lion walked fiercely up to the spring to drink. This made him very much afraid. When the lion had gone away, a bear came to drink also, and, as the moon shone very bright, the beast looked up, and saw Fortunatus, and straightway began to climb up the tree to get at him.

Fortunatus drew his sword, and sat quiet till the bear was come within arm's length; and then he ran him through the body. This drove the bear so very savage that he made a great spring to get at him; but the bough broke, and down he fell, and lay sprawling and howling on the ground. Fortunatus now looked around on all sides; and as he saw no more wild beasts near, he thought this would be a good time to get rid of the bear at once; so down he came, and killed him at a

WARWICK GOBLE

"The butterfly took wing, and mounted into the air with little
Tom on his back." *(Page 91)*

WARWICK GOBLE

"Are you not sometimes called Rumpelstilzchen?" (*Page 96*)

single blow. Being almost starved for want of food, the poor youth stooped down, and was going to suck the blood of the bear ; but looking round once more, to see if any wild beast were coming, he on a sudden beheld a beautiful lady standing by his side, with a bandage over her eyes, leaning upon a wheel, and looking as if she were going to speak, which she soon did, in these words, " Know, young man, that my name is Fortune ; I have the power to bestow wisdom, strength, riches, health, beauty, and long life : one of these I am willing to grant you—choose for yourself which it shall be."

Fortunatus was not a moment before he answered, " Good lady, I wish to have riches in such plenty that I may never again know what it is to be so hungry as I now find myself." The lady then gave him a purse, and told him that in all the countries where he might happen to be, he need only put his hand into the purse as often as he pleased, and he would be sure to find in it ten pieces of gold ; that the purse should never fail of yielding the same sum as long as it was kept by him and his children ; but that when he and his children should be dead, then the purse would lose its power.

Fortunatus now did not know what to do with himself for joy, and began to thank the lady very much ; but she told him that he had better think of making his way out of the wood. She then directed him which path to take, and bade him farewell. He walked by the light of the moon, as fast as his weakness and fatigue would let him, till he came near an inn. But before he went into it, he thought it would be best to see whether the Lady Fortune had been as good as her word ; so he put his hand into his purse, and to his great joy he counted ten pieces of gold. Having nothing to fear, Fortunatus walked boldly up to the inn, and called for the best supper they could get ready in a minute ; " For," said he, " I must wait till to-morrow before I am very nice. I am so hungry now, that almost anything will do." Fortunatus very soon ate quite enough, and then called for every sort of wine in the house, and drank his fill. After supper, he began to think what sort of life he should lead ; " For," said he to himself, " I shall now have money enough for everything I can desire." He slept that night in the very best bed in the house ; and the next day he ordered the finest victuals of all kinds. When he rang his bell, all the waiters tried who should run fastest, to ask him what he pleased to want ; and the landlord himself, hearing what a noble guest was come to his house, took care to be standing at the door to bow to him when he should be passing out.

Fortunatus asked the landlord whether any fine horses could be got near at hand ; also, if he knew of some smart-looking, clever men-servants who wanted places. By chance the landlord was able to provide him with both. As he had now got everything he wanted, he set out on the finest horse that was ever seen, with two servants, for the nearest town. There he bought some grand suits of clothes, put his two servants into liveries laced with gold, and then went on to Paris. Here he took the best house that was to be had, and lived in great pomp. He invited the nobility, and gave grand balls to all the most beautiful ladies of the court. He went to all public places of amusement, and the first lords in the country invited him to their houses. He had lived in this manner for about a year, when he began to think of going to Famagosta to visit his parents, whom he had left very poor. " But," thought Fortunatus, " as I am young and have not seen much of the world, I should like to meet with some person of more knowledge than I have, who would make my journey both useful and pleasing to me." Soon after this he met with an old gentleman, called Loch-Fitty, who was a native of Scotland, and had left a wife and ten children a great many years ago, in hopes to better his fortune ; but now, owing to many accidents, was poorer than ever, and had not money enough to take him back to his family.

When Loch-Fitty found how much Fortunatus wished to obtain knowledge, he told him many of the strange adventures he had met with, and gave him an account of all the countries he had been in, as well as of the customs, dress, and manners of the people. Fortunatus thought to himself, " This is the very man I stand in need of " ; so at once he made him a good offer, which the old gentleman agreed to, but made the bargain that he might first go and visit his family. Fortunatus told him that he should. " And," said he, " as I am a little tired of being always in the midst of such noisy pleasures as we find at Paris, I will, with your leave, go with you to Scotland, and see your wife and children." They set out the very next day, and came safe to the house of Loch-Fitty ; and in all the journey, Fortunatus did not once wish to change his kind companion for all the pleasures and grandeur he had left behind. Loch-Fitty kissed his wife and children, five of whom were daughters, and the most beautiful creatures that were ever beheld. When they were seated, his wife said to him, " Ah ! dear Lord Loch-Fitty, how happy I am to see you once again ! Now I hope we shall enjoy each other's company for the rest of our lives. What though we are poor ! We will be content if you will but promise not to think of leaving us again to get riches, only because we have a noble title."

Fortunatus heard this with great surprise. " What ! " said he, " are you a lord ? Then you shall be a rich lord too. And that you may not think I lay you under any burden in the fortune I shall give you, I will put it in your power to make me your debtor instead. Give me your youngest daughter, Cassandra, for a wife, and accompany us as far as Famagosta, and take all your family with you, that you may have pleasant company on your way back, when you have rested in that place from your fatigue."

Lord Loch-Fitty shed some tears of joy to think he should at last see his family again raised to all the honours which it had once enjoyed. He gladly agreed to the marriage of Fortunatus with his daughter Cassandra, and then told him the reasons that had forced him to drop his title and live poor at Paris. When Lord Loch-Fitty had ended his story, they agreed that the very next morning the Lady Cassandra should be asked to accept the hand of Fortunatus ; and that, if she should consent, they would set sail in a few days for Famagosta. The next morning the offer was made to her, as had been agreed on ; and Fortunatus had the pleasure of hearing from the lips of the beautiful Cassandra that the very first time she cast her eyes on him she thought him the most handsome gentleman in the world.

Everything was soon ready for them to set out on the journey. Fortunatus, Lord Loch-Fitty, his lady, and their ten children, then set sail in a large ship ; they had a good voyage, and landed safe at the port of Famagosta. There, however, Fortunatus found, with great grief and self-reproach, that his father and mother were both dead. However, as he was an easy-tempered gentleman, and had his betrothed Cassandra and her whole family to reconcile him to his grief, it did not last very long ; the wedding took place almost immediately ; so they lived all together in Famagosta, and in very great style. By the end of the first year, the Lady Cassandra had a little son, who was christened Ampedo ; and the next year another, who was christened Andolucia. For twelve years Fortunatus lived a very happy life with his wife and children, and his wife's kindred ; and as each of her sisters had a fortune given her from the purse of Fortunatus, they soon married very well. But by this time he began to long to travel again ; and he thought, as he was now so much older and wiser than when he was at Paris, he might go by himself, for Lord Loch-Fitty was at this time too old to bear fatigue. After he had, with great trouble, got the consent of the Lady Cassandra, and made her a promise to stay away only two years, he made all things ready for his journey; and taking his lady into one of his private rooms, he showed her three chests of gold. He told her to keep one of these for herself, and take charge of the other two for their sons, in case any evil should happen to him. He then led her back to the room where the whole family were sitting, embraced them all tenderly one by one, and set sail with a fair wind for Alexandria.

When Fortunatus came to this place, he was told it was the custom to make a handsome present to the sultan; so he sent him a piece of plate that cost five thousand pounds. The sultan was so much pleased with this, that he ordered a hundred casks of spices to be given to Fortunatus in return. Fortunatus sent these straight to the Lady Cassandra, with the most tender letters, by the same ship that brought him, which was then going back to Famagosta. Having stated that he wished to travel through his country by land, he obtained from the sultan such passports and letters as he might stand in need of, to the other princes in those parts. He then bought a camel, hired proper servants, and set off on his travels. He went through Turkey, Persia, and from thence to Carthage; he next went into the country of Prester John, who rides upon a white elephant, and has kings to wait on him. Fortunatus made him some rich presents, and went on to Calcutta; and, in coming back, he took Jerusalem in the way, and so came again to Alexandria, where he had the good fortune to find the same ship that had brought him, and to learn from the captain that his wife and family were all in perfect health. The first thing he did was to pay a visit to his old friend the sultan, to whom he again made a handsome present, and was invited to dine at his palace. After dinner, the sultan said, "It must be vastly amusing, Fortunatus, to hear an account of all the places you have seen; pray favour me with a history of your travels." Fortunatus did as he was desired, and pleased the sultan very much by telling him the many odd adventures he had met with; and, above all, the manner of his first becoming known to the Lord Loch-Fitty, and the desire of that lord to maintain the honours of his family. When he had ended, the sultan said he was greatly pleased with what he had heard, but that he possessed a more curious thing than any Fortunatus had told him of. He then led him into a room almost filled with jewels, opened a large closet, and took out a cap, which he said was of greater value than all the rest. Fortunatus thought the sultan was joking, and told him he had seen many a better cap than that. "Ah!" said the sultan, "that is because you do not know its value. Whoever puts this cap on his head, and wishes to be in any part of the world, will find himself there in a moment."

"Indeed!" said Fortunatus, "and pray, is the man living who made it?"

"I know nothing about that," said the sultan.

"One would hardly believe it," said Fortunatus. "Pray, sir, is it very heavy?"

"Not at all," replied the sultan, "you may feel it."

Fortunatus took up the cap, put it on his head, and could not help wishing himself on board the ship that was going back to Famagosta. In less than a moment he was carried on board of her, just as she was ready to sail; and there being a brisk gale, they were out of sight in half an hour, before the sultan had even time to repent of his folly for letting Fortunatus try the cap on his head. The ship came safe to Famagosta, after a happy passage, and Fortunatus found his wife and children well;

but Lord Loch-Fitty and his lady had died of old age, and were buried in the same grave.

Fortunatus now began to take great pleasure in teaching his two boys all sorts of useful learning, and also such manly sports as wrestling and tilting. Now and then he thought about the curious cap which had brought him home, and then would wish he could just take a peep at what was passing in other countries, which wish was always fulfilled ; but he never stayed there more than an hour or two, so that the Lady Cassandra did not miss him, and was no longer made uneasy by his love of travelling.

At last, Fortunatus began to grow old, and the Lady Cassandra fell sick and died. The loss of her caused him so much grief, that soon after he fell sick too. As he thought he had not long to live, he called his two sons to his bedside, and told them the secrets of the purse and the cap, which he begged they would not, on any account, make known to others. "Follow my example," said he ; "I have had the purse these forty years, and no living person knew from what source I obtained my riches." He then told them to make use of the purse between them, and to live together in friendship ; and embracing them, died soon after. Fortunatus was buried with great pomp by the side of Lady Cassandra, in his own chapel, and was for a long time mourned by the people of Famagosta.

THE BREMEN TOWN MUSICIANS

THERE was a man who owned a donkey, which had carried his sacks to the mill industriously for many years, but whose strength had come to an end, so that the poor beast grew more and more unfit for work. The master determined to stop his food, but the donkey, discovering that there was no good intended to him, ran away and took the road to Bremen. "There," thought he, "I can turn Town Musician."

When he had gone a little way, he found a hound lying on the road and panting, like one who was tired with running. "Hollo! what are you panting so for, worthy Seize 'em?" asked the donkey.

"Oh!" said the dog, "just because I am old, and get weaker every day, and cannot go out hunting, my master wanted to kill me, so I have taken leave of him; but how shall I gain my living now?"

"I'll tell you what," said the donkey, "I am going to Bremen to be Town Musician, come with me and take to music too. I will play the lute, and you shall beat the drum."

The dog liked the idea, and they travelled on. It was not long before they saw a cat sitting by the road, making a face like three rainy days.

"Now then, what has gone wrong with you, old Whiskers?" said the donkey.

"Who can be merry when his neck is in danger?" answered the cat. "Because I am advanced in years, and my teeth are blunt, and I like sitting before the fire and purring better than chasing the mice about, my mistress wanted to drown me. I have managed to escape, but good advice is scarce ; tell me where I shall go to ?"

"Come with us two to Bremen ; you understand serenading ; you also can become a Town Musician."

The cat thought it a capital idea, and went with them. Soon after the three runaways came to a farmyard, and there sat a cock on the gate, crowing with might and main.

"You crow loud enough to deafen one," said the donkey, "what is the matter with you ?"

"I prophesied fair weather," said the cock, "because it is our good mistress's washing-day, and she wants to dry the clothes ; but because to-morrow is Sunday, and company is coming, the mistress has no pity on me, and has told the cook to put me into the soup to-morrow, and I must have my head cut off to-night, so now I am crowing with all my might as long as I can."

"Oh you old Redhead," said the donkey, "you had better come with us ; we are going to Bremen, where you will certainly find something better than having your head cut off ; you have a good voice, and if we all make music together, it will be something striking."

The cock liked the proposal, and they went on, all four together.

But they could not reach the city of Bremen in one day, and they came in the evening to a wood, where they agreed to spend the night. The donkey and the dog laid themselves down under a great tree, but the cat and the cock went higher—the cock flying up to the topmost branch, where he was safest. Before he went to sleep he looked round towards all the four points of the compass, and he thought he saw a spark shining in the distance. He called to his companions that there must be a house not far off, for he could see a light. The donkey said,

"Then we must rise and go to it, for the lodgings here are very bad"; and the dog said, "Yes, a few bones with a little flesh on them would do me good." So they took the road in the direction where the light was, and soon saw it shine brighter; and it got larger and larger till they came to a brilliantly-illumined robbers' house. The donkey, being the biggest, got up at the window and looked in.

"What do you see, Greybeard?" said the cock.

"What do I see?" answered the donkey, "a table covered with beautiful food and drink, and robbers are sitting round it and enjoying themselves."

"That would do nicely for us," said the cock.

"Yes, indeed, if we were only there," replied the donkey.

The animals then consulted together how they should manage to drive out the robbers, till at last they settled on a plan. The donkey was to place himself with his fore-feet on the window-sill, the dog to climb on the donkey's back, and the cat on the dog's, and, at last, the cock was to fly up and perch himself on the cat's head. When that was done, at a signal they began their music all together: the donkey brayed, the dog barked, the cat mewed, and the cock crowed; then, with one great smash, they dashed through the window into the room, so that the glass clattered down. The robbers jumped up at this dreadful noise, thinking that nothing less than a ghost was coming in, and ran away into the wood in a great fright. The four companions then sat down at the table, quite content with what was left there, and ate as if they were expecting to fast for a month to come.

When the four musicians had finished, they put out the light, and each one looked out for a suitable and comfortable sleeping-place. The donkey lay down on the dunghill, the dog behind the door, the cat on the hearth near the warm ashes, and the cock set himself on the hen-roost ; and, as they were all tired with their long journey, they soon went to sleep. Soon after midnight, as the robbers in the distance could see that no more lights were burning in the house, and as all seemed quiet, the captain said, " We ought not to have let ourselves be scared so easily," and sent one of them to examine the house. The messenger found everything quiet, went into the kitchen to light a candle, and, thinking the cat's shining fiery eyes were live coals, he held a match to them to light it. But the cat did not understand the joke, flew in his face, spat at him, and scratched. He was dreadfully frightened, ran away, and was going out of the back door, when the dog, who was lying there, jumped up and bit him in the leg. As he ran through the yard, past the dunghill, the donkey gave him a good kick with his hind-foot ; and the cock being awakened, and made quite lively by the noise, called out from the hen-roost, " Cock-a-doodle-doo ! "

The robber ran as hard as he could, back to the captain, and said, " Oh, dear ! in the house sits a horrid old witch, who flew at me, and scratched my face with her long fingers ; and by the door stands a man with a knife, who stabbed me in the leg ; and in the yard lies a black monster, who hit me with a club ; and up on the roof there sits the judge, who called out, ' Bring the rascal up here'—so I made the best of my way off."

From that time the robbers never trusted themselves again in the house ; but the four musicians liked it so well that they could not make up their minds to leave it, and spent there the remainder of their days, as the last person who told the story is ready to avouch for a fact.

RIQUET WITH THE TUFT

ONCE upon a time a queen had a little son, who was so ugly and ill-made, that for a long time the poor little baby was thought hardly human. However, a good fairy, who presided at his birth, assured his mother that, though ugly, he would have so much sense and wit that he would never be disagreeable : moreover, she bestowed on him the power of communicating these gifts to the person he should love best in the world. At this the queen was a little comforted, and became still more so, when, as soon as he could speak, the infant began to say such pretty and clever things that everybody was charmed with him. (I forgot to mention that his name was Riquet with the Tuft, because he was born with a curious tuft of hair on the top of his head.)

Seven or eight years after this, the queen of a neighbouring country had two little daughters, twins, at whose birth the same fairy presided. The elder twin was more beautiful than the day—the younger so extremely ugly that the mother's extravagant joy in the first was all turned to grief about the second. So, in order to calm her feelings, the fairy told her that the one daughter should be as stupid as she was pretty, while the other would grow up so clever and charming that nobody would miss her want of beauty.

"Heaven grant it!" sighed the queen; "but are there no means of giving a little sense to the one who is so beautiful?"

" I can do nothing for her, madam," returned the fairy —"nothing as regards her own fortunes ; but I grant her the power of making the person who best pleases her as handsome as herself."

Accordingly, as the young princesses grew up, their perfections grew with them ; and nothing was spoken of but the beauty of the elder and the wit of the younger. True, their faults increased equally : the one became uglier, and the other more stupid, day by day. Unlucky fair one ! she never had a word to say for herself, or else it was the silliest word imaginable ; and she was so awkward that she could not place four teacups in a row without breaking at least one of them, nor drink a glass of water without spilling half of it over her clothes. Beauty is a great charm ; yet, whenever the sisters went out together, those who were attracted by the elder's lovely face, in less than half an hour were sure to be seen at the side of the younger, laughing at her witty and pleasant sayings, and altogether deserting the poor beauty, who had just sense enough to find it out, and to feel that she would have given all her good looks for one-half of her sister's talents.

One day, when she had hid herself in a wood, and was crying over her hard fate, she saw coming towards her a little man, very ugly, but magnificently dressed. Who should this be but Prince Riquet with the Tuft ? He had seen her portrait, had fallen desperately in love with her, and secretly quitted his father's kingdom that he might have the pleasure of meeting her. Delighted to find her alone, he came forward with all the respect and politeness imaginable. But he could not help noticing how very melancholy she was, and that all the elegant compliments he made her did not seem to affect her in the least.

" I cannot comprehend, madam," said he, " how so charming and lovely a lady can be so very sad. Never did I see any one who could at all compare with you."

"That's all you know," said the princess, and stopped.

"Beauty," continued the prince, sighing, "is so great an advantage that, if one possessed it, one would never trouble oneself about anything else."

"I wish I were as ugly as you, and had some sense, rather than be as handsome as I am, and such a fool."

"Madam," said Riquet politely, though her speech was not exactly civil, "nothing shows intellect so much as the modesty of believing one does not possess it."

"I don't know that ; but I know I am a great fool, and it vexes me so, that I wish I was dead," cried the princess bitterly.

"If that is all, madam, I can easily put an end to your grief, for I have the power of making the person I love best as clever as I please. I will do it, provided you consent to marry me."

The princess stood dumb with astonishment. She—to marry that little frightful creature—scarcely a man at all !

"I see," said Riquet, "that my proposal offends and grieves you. Well, I will give you a year to consider it."

Now the young lady was so stupid that she thought a year's end was a long way off—so long that it seemed as if it might not come at all, or something might happen between whiles. And she had such a longing to be clever and admired that she thought at all risks she would accept the chance of becoming so. Accordingly, she promised Riquet to marry him that day twelvemonth.

No sooner had she said it than she felt herself quite another being. She found she could at once say anything she chose, and say it in the most graceful and brilliant way. She began a lively conversation with Prince Riquet, and chattered so fast and so wittily, that he began to be afraid he had given her so much cleverness as to leave himself none.

When she returned to the palace, all the court were astonished at the change. She, who had annoyed everybody by the impertinent, tasteless, or downright foolish things she uttered, now charmed everybody by her wit, her pleasantness, and her exceeding good sense. The king himself began to come to her apartment, and ask her advice in state affairs. Her mother, and indeed the whole kingdom, were delighted; the only person to be pitied was the poor younger sister, of whom nobody now took the least notice.

Meantime, princes came in throngs to ask in marriage this wonderful princess, who was as clever as she was beautiful; but she found none to suit her, probably because the more sense a lady has, the more difficult she is to please. As for her promise to Riquet with the Tuft, being given in the days when she was so dull and stupid, it now never once came into her head; until one day, being quite perplexed by her numerous suitors, she went to take a solitary walk and think the matter over, when by chance she came into the same wood where she had met the prince. There, all of a sudden, she thought she heard a queer running about and chattering underground. "Fetch me that spit," cried one; "Put some more wood on that fire," said another; and by and by the earth opened, showing a great kitchen filled with cooks, cooking a splendid banquet. They were all working merrily at their several duties, and singing together in the most lively chorus.

"What is all this about?" asked the amazed princess.

"If you please, madam," replied the head-cook, politely, "we are cooking the wedding-dinner of Prince Riquet with the Tuft, who is to be married to-morrow."

"To-morrow!" cried the princess, all at once recollecting her promise; at which she was so frightened that she thought she should have fallen to the earth. Greater still was her alarm when, at only a few steps' distance, she beheld Riquet, dressed splendidly, like a prince and a bridegroom.

"You see me, princess, exact to my word ; and I doubt not you are the same, come to make me the happiest of mankind."

"Prince," said the lady frankly, "I must confess that such was not my intention, and I fear I shall never be able to do as you desire."

"You surprise me, madam."

"I can well believe it ; and if I had to do with a brute, instead of a gentleman of sense and feeling, I should be very uneasy," returned she ; "but since I speak with the cleverest man in the world, I am sure he will hear reason, and will not bind me, now a sensible woman, to a promise I made when I was only a fool."

"If I were a fool myself, madam, I might well complain of your broken promise ; and being, as you say, a man of sense, should I not complain of what takes away all the happiness of my life? Tell me candidly, is there anything in me, except my ugliness, which displeases you? Do you object to my birth, my temper, my manners ?"

"No, truly," replied the princess ; "I like everything in you, except"—and she hesitated courteously—"except your appearance."

"Then, madam, I need not lose my happiness ; for if I have the gift of making clever whosoever I love best, you also are able to make the person you prefer as handsome as ever you please. Could you love me enough to do that?"

"I think I could," said the princess ; and her heart being greatly softened towards him, she wished that he might become the handsomest prince in all the world. No sooner had she done so than Riquet with the Tuft appeared in her eyes the most elegant young man she had ever seen.

Ill-natured people have said that this was no fairy-gift,

"The lady then gave him a purse." (*Page 101*)

"Riquet with the Tuft appeared in her eyes the most elegant
young man she had ever seen." *(Page 116)*

but that love created the change. They declare that the princess, when she thought over her lover's perseverance, patience, good-humour, and discretion, and counted his numerous fine qualities of mind and disposition, saw no longer the deformity of his body or the plainness of his features ; that his hump was merely an exaggerated stoop, and his awkward movements became only an interesting eccentricity. Nay, even his eyes, which squinted terribly, seemed always looking on all sides for her, in token of his violent love, and his great red nose gave him an air very martial and heroic.

However this may be, it is certain that the princess married him ; that either she retained her good sense, or he never felt the want or it ; and he never again became ugly—or, at least, not in his wife's eyes : so they both lived very happy until they died.

HOUSE ISLAND

There lived in Norway, not far from the city of Drontheim, a rich and prosperous gentleman. He had an only daughter, called Aslog, the fame of whose beauty spread far and wide. The greatest men of the country sought her, but all were alike unsuccessful in their suit. Her father, who thought his daughter delayed her choice only that she might choose the better, forbore to interfere, and exulted in her prudence. But when, at length, the richest and noblest had tried their fortune with as little success as the rest, he grew angry, called his daughter, and said to her :

"Hitherto I have left you to your free choice, but since I see that you reject all without any distinction, and the very best of your suitors seem not good enough for you, I will keep measures no longer with you. What ! shall my family become extinct, and my inheritance pass away into the hands of strangers? I will break your stubborn spirit. I give you now till the festival of the great Winter-night ; by that time you must make your decision, or prepare to accept the husband whom I myself shall select."

Now Aslog secretly loved a youth named Orm, handsome, noble, and brave. She loved him with her whole soul, and would sooner die than bestow her hand on another. But Orm was poor, and poverty compelled him to keep his love as secret as her own.

When Aslog saw the darkness of her father's

countenance, and heard his angry words, she turned pale as death, for she knew his temper, and doubted not but that he would put his threats into execution. Without uttering a word in reply, she retired to her chamber, and pondered vainly how to escape the storm that hung over her. The great festival approached nearer and nearer, and her anguish increased every day.

At last the lovers resolved on flight. Orm knew a secure place, where they could hide until they found an opportunity of quitting the country. So at night, when all were asleep, he led the trembling Aslog over the snow and ice-fields away to the mountains. The moon and the stars lighted them on their way. They had under their arms a few articles of dress and some skins of animals, which were all they could carry. They ascended the mountains the whole night long, till they reached a lonely spot inclosed with lofty rocks. Here Orm conducted the weary Aslog into a cave, the low and narrow entrance to which was hardly perceptible, but it soon enlarged to a great hall, reaching deep into the mountain. He kindled a fire, and they now, reposing on their skins, sat in the deepest solitude far away from all the world.

Orm was the first who had discovered this cave, which is shown to this very day. But as no one then knew anything of it, they were safe from the pursuit of Aslog's father. They passed the whole winter in this retirement, contented and even happy; for they knew they were married, and belonged to one another, and no cruel father could separate them more. Orm used to go a-hunting, and Aslog stayed at home in the cave, minded the fire, and prepared the necessary food. Frequently did she mount the points of the rocks, but her eyes, did they wander ever so far, saw only glittering snow-fields.

The spring now came on—the woods were green—the meadows put on their various colours, people began to wander out for summer pleasuring, and Aslog could but rarely and with circumspection venture to leave the cave. One evening Orm came in with the intelligence that he had recognised her father's servants in the distance, and that he could hardly have been unobserved by them. "They will surround this place," continued he, "and never rest till they have found us ; we must quit our retreat, then, without a moment's delay."

They accordingly descended on the other side of the mountain, and reached the strand, where they fortunately found a boat. Orm pushed off, and the boat drove into the open sea. They had escaped their pursuers, but they were now exposed to dangers of another kind : whither should they turn ? They could not venture to land, for Aslog's father was lord of the whole coast, and they would infallibly fall into his hands. Nothing then remained for them but to commit their bark to the wind and waves. They were driven along the entire night. At break of day the coast had disappeared, and they saw nothing but the sky, the sea, and the waves. They had not brought one morsel of food with them, and thirst and hunger began now to torment them. Three days did they toss about in this state of misery, and Aslog, faint and exhausted, saw nothing but certain death before her.

At length, on the evening of the third day, they discovered an island of tolerable magnitude, and surrounded by a number of smaller ones. Orm immediately steered for it, but, just as he came near it, there suddenly rose a violent wind, and the sea rolled every moment higher and higher. He turned about with a view of approaching it on another side, but with no better success : his vessel, as often as it neared the island, was driven back as if by an invisible power. "God help us !" he cried, and crossed himself, and looked on poor Aslog, who seemed to be dying of weakness before his eyes. But scarcely had the exclamation passed his lips when the storm ceased, the waves subsided, and the vessel came to the shore without encountering any hindrance. Orm jumped out on the beach ; some mussels that he found on the strand strengthened and revived the exhausted Aslog, so that she was soon able to leave the boat.

The island was overgrown with low dwarf shrubs, and seemed to be uninhabited ; but when they had reached the middle of it, they discovered a house, which appeared to be half under the surface of the earth. In the hope of meeting with human help, the wanderers approached it. They listened, but the most perfect silence reigned there. Orm at length opened the door, and they both walked in : but what was their surprise, to find everything regulated and arranged as if for inhabitants, yet not a single living creature visible. The fire was burning on the hearth, in the middle of the room, and a kettle with fish hung on it, apparently only waiting for some one to take it up and eat it. The beds were made, and ready to receive their wearied tenants. Orm and Aslog stood for some time dubious, and looked on with a certain degree of awe, but at last, overcome by hunger, they took up the food and ate. When they had satisfied their appetites, and still discovered no human being, they gave way to weariness, and laid themselves in the beds, which looked so peaceful and inviting to their wearied limbs.

They had expected to be awakened in the night by the owners of the house on their return home, but their expectation was not fulfilled ; they slept undisturbed till the morning sun shone in upon them. No one appeared on any of the following days, and it seemed as if some invisible power had made ready the house for their reception. They spent the whole summer in perfect happiness : they were, to be sure, solitary, yet they did not miss mankind. The wild birds' eggs, and the fish they caught, yielded them provisions in abundance.

When autumn came, Aslog brought forth a son. In the midst of their joy at this, they were surprised by a wonderful apparition. The door opened on a sudden, and an old woman stepped in. She wore a handsome blue dress : there was something proud, but, at the same time something strange, in her appearance.

"Do not be afraid," said she, "at my unexpected appearance. I am the owner of this house, and I thank you for the clean and neat state in which you have kept it, and for the good order in which I find everything with you. I would willingly have come sooner, but I had no power to do so till this little heathen (pointing to the newborn babe) was come to the light. Now I have free access. Only fetch no priest from the mainland to christen it, or I must depart again. If you will in this matter comply with my wishes, you may not only continue to live here, but all the good that ever you can wish for I will do you. Whatever you take in hand shall prosper ; good luck shall follow you wherever you go. But break this condition, and depend upon it that misfortune after misfortune will come on you, and even on this child will I avenge myself. If you want anything, or are in danger, you have only to pronounce my name three times, and I will appear and lend you assistance. I am of the race of the old giants, and my name is Guru. But beware of uttering in my presence the name of Him whom no giant may hear of, and never venture to make the sign of the cross, or to cut it on beam or board in the house. You may dwell in this house the whole year long, only be so good as to give it up to me on Yule evening, when the sun is at the lowest, as then we celebrate our great festival, and then only are we permitted to be merry. At least, if you should not be willing to go out of the house, keep yourselves up in the loft as quiet as possible the whole day long, and as you value your lives do not look down into the room below until midnight is past. After that you may take possession of everything again."

When the old woman had thus spoken she vanished, and Aslog and Orm lived without any disturbance, contented and happy. Orm never made a cast of his net without getting a plentiful draught; he never shot an arrow from his bow that it was not sure to hit; in short, whatever they took in hand, were it ever so trifling, evidently prospered.

When Christmas came, they cleaned up the house in the best manner, set everything in order, kindled a fire on the hearth, and as the twilight approached they went up to the loft, where they remained quite still and quiet. At length it grew dark; they thought they heard a sound of whizzing and snorting in the air, such as the swans use to make in the winter time. There was a hole in the roof over the fireplace, which might be opened and shut either to let in the light from above, or to afford a free passage for the smoke. Orm lifted up the lid, which was covered with a skin, and put out his head. But what a wonderful sight then presented itself to his eyes! The little islands around were all lit up with countless blue lights, which moved about without ceasing, jumped up and down, then skipped to the shore, assembled together, and came nearer and nearer to the large island where Orm and Aslog lived. At last they reached it, and arranged themselves in a circle around a large stone not far from the shore, and which Orm well knew. But what was his surprise when he saw that the stone had now completely assumed the form of a man, though a monstrous and gigantic one! He could clearly perceive that the little blue lights were borne by Dwarfs, whose pale clay-coloured faces, with their huge noses and red eyes, disfigured too by birds' bills and owls' eyes, were supported by misshapen bodies; and they tottered and wabbled about here and there, so that they seemed to be at the same time merry and in pain. Suddenly, the circle opened; the little ones retired on each side, and Guru—

who was the woman Guru, whom Orm recognised immediately, though she had risen in stature and size so as to be almost as gigantic as the stone man—advanced towards it. She threw both her arms round the image, which immediately seemed to receive life and motion. Then the Dwarfs, with wonderful capers and grimaces, began a song, or, to speak more properly, a howl, with which the whole island resounded and almost trembled at the noise. Orm, quite terrified, drew in his head, and he and Aslog remained in the dark, so still that they hardly ventured to draw their breath.

The procession moved on towards the house, as might be clearly perceived by the nearer approach of the shouting and crying. They were now all come in, light and active ; the Dwarfs were heard jumping about on the benches, and heavy and loud sounded at intervals the steps of the giants. Orm and his wife listened to the clattering of the plates, and the shouts of joy with which they celebrated their banquet. When it was over and midnight drew near, they began to dance to that ravishing fairy-tune, which some have heard in the rocky glens, and learned by listening to the underground musicians. As soon as Aslog caught the sound of this air, she felt an irresistible longing to see the dance. Nor was Orm able to keep her back. "Let me look," said she, "or my heart will burst." She took her child and placed herself at the extreme end of the loft, whence, without being observed, she could see all that passed. Long did she gaze, without taking off her eyes for an instant, on the dance—on the bold and wonderful springs of the little creatures, who seemed to float in the air, and not so much as to touch the ground, while the ravishing melody of the Elves filled her whole soul. The child, meanwhile, which lay in her arms grew sleepy and drew its breath heavily, and, without ever thinking on the promise she had given the old woman, she made, as is usual, the sign of the cross over the mouth of the child, and said, " Christ bless you, my babe ! "

The instant she had spoken the word there was raised a horrible, piercing cry. The Dwarfs tumbled head over heels out at the door with terrible crushing and crowding, their lights went out, and in a few minutes the whole house was clear of them and left desolate. Orm and Aslog, frightened to death, hid themselves in the most retired nook they could find. They did not venture to stir till daybreak, and not till the sun shone through the hole in the roof down on the fireplace did they feel courage enough to descend from the loft.

The table remained still covered as the underground people had left it ; all their vessels, which were of silver, and manufactured in the most beautiful manner, lay upon it. In the middle of the room there stood upon the ground a huge copper kettle half full of sweet mead, and by the side of it a drinking-horn of pure gold. In the corner rested, against the wall, a stringed instrument not unlike a dulcimer, which, as people believe, the Giantesses used to play on. They gazed on what was before them, full of admiration, but without venturing to lay their hands on anything ; how great and fearful was their amazement, when, on turning about, they saw sitting at the table an immense figure, which Orm instantly recognised as the Giant whom Guru had animated by her embrace. He was now a cold and hard stone. While they were standing gazing on it, Guru herself entered the room in her giant form. She wept so bitterly, that her tears trickled down on the ground. It was long ere her sobbing permitted her to utter a single word ; at last she spoke :

" Great affliction have you brought on me, and henceforth I must weep while I live ; yet as I know that you have not done this with evil intentions, I forgive you, though it were a trifle for me to crush the whole house like an egg-shell over your heads."

"What have we done?" cried Orm and Aslog, penetrated with the deepest sorrow.

"Alas!" answered she, "my husband, whom I love more than myself, there he sits, petrified for ever; never again will he open his eyes! Three hundred years lived I with my father on the island of Kunnan, happy in the innocence of youth, as the fairest among the Giant-maidens. Mighty heroes sued for my hand; the sea around that island is still filled with the rocky fragments which they hurled against each other in their combats. Andfind won the victory, and I plighted myself to him. But ere I was married came the detestable Odin into the country, who overcame my father, and drove us all from the island. My father and sisters fled to the mountains, and since that time my eyes have beheld them no more. Andfind and I saved ourselves on this island, where we for a long time lived in peace and quiet, and thought it would never be interrupted. But destiny, which no one escapes, had determined it otherwise. Oluf came from Britain. They called him the Holy, and Andfind instantly found that his voyage would be inauspicious to the Giants. When he heard how Oluf's ship rushed through the waves, he went down to the strand and blew the sea against him with all his strength. The waves swelled up like mountains. But Oluf was still more mighty than he; his ship flew unchecked through the billows like an arrow from a bow. He steered direct for our island. When the ship was so near that Andfind thought he could reach it with his hands, he grasped at the forepart with his right hand, and was about to drag it down to the bottom, as he had often done with other ships. But Oluf, the terrible Oluf, stepped forward, and crossing his hands over each other, he cried with a loud voice, 'Stand there as a stone till the last day,' and in the same instant my unhappy husband became a mass of rock. The ship sailed on unimpeded, and ran direct against the mountain, which it cut through, and separated from it the little island which lies out yonder.

"Ever have I passed my life alone and forlorn. On Yule-eve alone can petrified Giants receive back their life for the space of seven hours, if one of their race embraces them, and is at the same time willing to sacrifice a hundred years. I loved my husband too well not to bring him back to life every time that I could do it, even at this price, and I have not even counted how often I have done it, that I might not know the hour when I myself should share his fate, and at the moment when I threw my arms around him become stone like him. But, alas! even this comfort is taken from me; I can never more by any embrace awake him. He has heard the Name which I dare not utter, and never again will he see the light until the dawn of the last day shall bring it.

"I now go hence, and you will behold me no more. All that is here in the house I give you; my dulcimer alone will I keep. But let no one venture to fix his habitation on the small islands that lie around here. There dwell the little underground people whom you saw at the festival, and I will protect them as long as I live!"

With these words Guru vanished. The next spring Orm took the golden horn and the silver-ware to Drontheim, where no one knew him. The value of these precious metals was so great that he was able to purchase everything requisite for a wealthy man. He laded his ship with his purchases, and returned back to the island, where he spent many years in unalloyed happiness, and Aslog's father was soon reconciled to his wealthy son-in-law.

The huge image remained sitting in the house; no human power was able to move it. So hard was the stone, that hammer and axe flew in pieces without making the slightest impression upon it. The Giant sat there till a holy man came to the island, who with one single word removed him back to his former station, where he stands to this hour. The copper kettle, which the underground people left behind them, was preserved as a memorial upon the island, which bears the name of House Island to the present day.

SNOW-WHITE AND ROSE-RED

A poor widow lived alone in a little cottage, in front of which was a garden, where stood two little rose trees: one bore white roses, the other red. The widow had two children, who resembled the two rose trees: one was called Snow-white, and the other Rose-red. They were two of the best children that ever lived; but Snow-white was quieter and more gentle than Rose-red. Rose-red liked best to jump about in the meadows, to look for flowers and catch butterflies; but Snow-white sat at home with her mother, helped her in the house, or read to her when there was nothing else to do. The two children loved one another so much, that they always walked hand in hand; and when Snow-white said, "We will not forsake one another," Rose-red answered, "Never as long as we live"; and the mother added, "Yes, my children, whatever one has, let her divide with the other." They often ran about in solitary places, and gathered red berries; and the wild creatures of the wood never hurt them, but came confidingly up to them. The little hare ate cabbage-leaves out of their hands, the doe grazed at their side, the stag sprang merrily past them, and the birds remained sitting on the boughs, and never ceased their songs. They met with no accident if they loitered in the wood and night came on; they lay down together on the moss, and slept till morning; and the mother knew this, and was in no anxiety about them. Once, when they had spent the night in the wood, and the red morning awoke them, they saw a beautiful child in a shining white dress, sitting by the place where they had slept, who, arising, and looking at them kindly, said nothing, but went into the wood. And when they looked round, they found out that they had been sleeping close to a precipice, and would certainly have fallen down it if they had gone a few steps farther in the dark. Their mother told them it must have been the angel that takes care of good children who had sat by them all night long.

Snow-white and Rose-red kept their mother's cottage so clean, that it was a pleasure to look into it. In the summer, Rose-red managed the house, and every morning she gathered a nosegay in which was a rose off each tree, and set it by her mother's bed before she awoke. In winter Snow-white lighted the fire, and hung the kettle on the hook; and though it was only copper, it shone like gold, it was rubbed so clean. In the evening, when the snow fell, the mother said, "Go, Snow-white, and bolt the door"; and then they seated themselves on the hearth, and the mother took her spectacles, and read aloud out of a great book, and the two girls listened, and sat and span. Near them lay a lamb on the floor, and behind them, on a perch, sat a white dove, with its head under its wing.

One evening, as they were thus happy together, some one knocked to be let in. The mother said, "Quick, Rose-red, open the door; perhaps it is a traveller, who seeks shelter." Rose-red went and pushed the bolt back, and thought it was a poor man, but a bear stretched his thick black head into the door. Rose-red screamed and sprang back, the little lamb bleated, the little dove fluttered about, and Snow-white hid herself behind her mother's bed. However, the bear began to speak, and said, "Do not be frightened, I will do you no harm; I am half frozen, and only want to warm myself a little."

"You poor bear," said the mother, "lay yourself

down before the fire, only take care your fur does not
burn." Then she called out, " Snow-white and Rose-
red, come out ; the bear will not hurt you—he means
honestly by us." Then they both came out, and, by
degrees, the lamb and the dove also approached, and
ceased to be afraid. The bear said, " Children, knock
the snow a little out of my fur " ; and they fetched a
broom, and swept the bear's skin clean ; and he stretched
himself before the fire and growled softly, like a bear
that was quite happy and comfortable. In a short time,
they all became quite friendly together, and the children
played tricks with the awkward guest. They pulled his
hair, set their feet on his back, and rolled him here and
there ; or took a hazel-rod and beat him, and when he
growled they laughed. The bear was very much pleased
with this frolic, only, when they became too mischievous,
he called out, " Children, leave me alone—

> Little Snow-white and Rose-red,
> You will strike your lover dead."

When bedtime came, and the others went to sleep,
the mother said to the bear : " You can lie there on the
hearth, and then you will be sheltered from the cold and
the bad weather." At daybreak the two children let him
out, and he trotted over the snow into the wood. Hence-
forward, the bear came every evening at the same hour,
laid himself on the hearth, and allowed the children to
play with him as much as they liked ; and they became
so used to him, that the door was never bolted until
their black companion had arrived. When spring came,
and everything was green out of doors, the bear said one
morning to Snow-white : " Now I must go away, and
may not come again the whole summer."

" Where are you going, dear Bear ? " asked Snow-
white.

" I must go into the wood, and guard my treasures

131

from the bad dwarfs ; in winter, when the ground is frozen hard, they have to stay underneath, and cannot work their way through, but now that the sun has thawed and warmed the earth, they break through, come up, seek, and steal : what is once in their hands, and lies in their caverns, does not come so easily into daylight again." Snow-white was quite sorrowful at parting, and as she unbolted the door for him, and the bear ran out, the hook of the door caught him, and a piece of his skin tore off ; it seemed to Snow-white as if she had seen gold shining through, but she was not sure. But the bear ran quickly away, and soon disappeared behind the trees.

After some time, their mother sent the children into the wood to collect faggots. They found there a large tree, which had been cut down and lay on the ground, and by the trunk something was jumping up and down, but they could not tell what it was. As they came nearer, they saw that it was a dwarf, with an old withered face, and a snow-white beard a yard long. The end of the beard was stuck fast in a cleft in the tree, and the little fellow jumped about like a dog on a rope, and did not know how to help himself. He stared at the girls with his fiery red eyes, and screamed out, "Why do you stand there ? Can't you come and render me some assistance ?"

"What is the matter with you, little man ?" asked Rose-red.

"Stupid little goose !" answered the dwarf ; "I wanted to chop the tree, so as to have some small pieces of wood for the kitchen ; we only want little bits ; with thick logs, the small quantity of food that we cook for ourselves—we are not, like you, great greedy people— burns directly. I had driven the wedge well in, and it was all going on right, but the detestable wood was too smooth, and sprang out unexpectedly ; and the tree

"So at night, when all were asleep, he led the trembling Aslog
over the snow and ice-fields away to the mountains." (*Page 119*)

"The compassionate children instantly seized hold of the little
man, held him fast, and struggled so long that the eagle let his
prey go." *(Page 134)*

closed up so quickly, that I could not pull my beautiful white beard out : now it is sticking there, and I can't get away. There you foolish, soft, milk-faces! you are laughing and crying out, 'How ugly you are! how ugly you are!'"

The children took a great deal of trouble, but they could not pull the beard out ; it stuck too fast.

"I will run and fetch somebody," said Rose-red.

"You great ninny!" snarled the dwarf, "to want to call more people ; you are two too many for me now. Can't you think of anything better?"

"Only don't be impatient," said Snow-white, "I have thought of something"; and she took her little scissors out of her pocket, and cut the end of the beard off.

As soon as the dwarf felt himself free, he seized a sack filled with gold that was sticking between the roots of the tree; pulling it out, he growled to himself, "You rude people, to cut off a piece of my beautiful beard! May evil reward you!" Then he threw his sack over his shoulders and walked away, without once looking at the children.

Some time afterwards, Snow-white and Rose-red wished to catch some fish for dinner. As they came near to the stream, they saw that something like a grasshopper was jumping towards the water, as if it were going to spring in. They ran on and recognised the dwarf.

"Where are you going?" asked Rose-red. "You don't want to go into the water?"

"I am not such a fool as that," cried the dwarf. "Don't you see the detestable fish wants to pull me in?"

The little fellow had been sitting there fishing, and, unluckily, the wind had entangled his beard with the line. When directly afterwards a great fish bit at his hook, the weak creature could not pull him out, so the fish was pulling the dwarf into the water. It is true he caught hold of all the reeds and rushes, but that did not help him much; he had to follow all the movements of the fish, and was in imminent danger of being drowned. The girls, coming at the right time, held him fast and tried to get the beard loose from the line, but in vain—beard and line were entangled fast together. There was nothing to do but to pull out the scissors and to cut off the beard, in doing which a little piece of it was lost. When the dwarf saw that, he cried out: "Is that manners, you goose! to disfigure one's face so? Is it not enough that you once cut my beard shorter? But now you have cut the best part of it off. I dare not be seen by my people. I wish you had had to run, and had lost the soles of your shoes!" Then he fetched a sack of pearls that lay among the rushes, and, without saying a word more, he dragged it away and disappeared behind a stone.

Soon after, the mother sent the two girls to the town to buy cotton, needles, cord, and tape. The road led them by a heath, scattered over which lay great masses of rock. There they saw a large bird hovering in the air; it flew round and round just above them, always sinking lower and lower, and at last it settled down by a rock not far distant. Directly after, they heard a piercing, wailing cry. They ran up, and saw with horror that the eagle had seized their old acquaintance the dwarf, and was going to carry him off. The compassionate children instantly seized hold of the little man, held him fast, and struggled so long that the eagle let his prey go.

When the dwarf had recovered from his first fright, he called out, in his shrill voice: "Could not you deal rather more gently with me? You have torn my thin coat all in tatters, awkward, clumsy creatures that you are!" Then he took a sack of precious stones, and slipped behind the rock again into his den. The girls, who were used to his ingratitude, went on their way, and completed their business in the town. As they were coming home again over the heath, they surprised the dwarf, who had emptied his sack of precious stones on a little clean place, and had not thought that any one would come by there so late. The evening sun shone on the glittering stones, which looked so beautiful in all their colours, that the children could not help standing still to gaze.

"Why do you stand there gaping?" cried the dwarf, his ash-coloured face turning vermilion with anger.

With these cross words he was going away, when he heard a loud roaring, and a black bear trotted out of the wood towards them. The dwarf sprang up terrified, but he could not get to his lurking-hole again—the bear was already close upon him. Then he called out in anguish:

"Dear Mr. Bear, spare me, and you shall have all my treasures; look at the beautiful precious stones that lie there. Give me my life! for what do you want with a poor thin little fellow like me? You would scarcely feel me between your teeth. Rather seize those two wicked girls; they will be tender morsels for you, as fat as young quails; pray, eat them at once."

The bear, without troubling himself to answer, gave the malicious creature one single stroke with his paw, and he did not move again. The girls had run away, but the bear called after them, "Snow-white and Rose-red, do not be frightened; wait, I will go with you." Recognising the voice of their old friend, they stood still, and when the bear came up to them his skin suddenly fell off; and behold he was not a bear, but a handsome young man dressed all in gold.

"I am a king's son," said he; "I was changed by the wicked dwarf, who had stolen all my treasures, into a wild bear, and obliged to run about in the wood until I should be freed by his death. Now he has received his well-deserved punishment."

So they all went home together to the widow's cottage, and Snow-white was married to the prince, and Rose-red

to his brother. They divided between them the great
treasures which the dwarf had amassed. The old mother
lived many quiet and happy years with her children ; but
when she left her cottage for the palace, she took the two
rose trees with her, and they stood before her window and
bore every year the most beautiful roses—one white and
the other red.

JACK AND THE BEAN-STALK

In the days of King Alfred there lived a poor woman, whose cottage was in a remote country village, many miles from London. She had been a widow some years, and had an only child named Jack, whom she indulged so much that he never paid the least attention to anything she said, but was indolent, careless, and extravagant. His follies were not owing to a bad disposition, but to his mother's foolish partiality. By degrees, he spent all that she had—scarcely anything remained but a cow. One day, for the first time in her life, she reproached him: "Cruel, cruel boy! you have at last brought me to beggary. I have not money enough to purchase even a bit of bread; nothing now remains to sell but my poor cow! I am sorry to part with her; it grieves me sadly, but we cannot starve." For a few minutes Jack felt remorse, but it was soon over; and he began asking his mother to let him sell the cow at the next village; teasing her so much that she at last consented. As he was going along he met a butcher, who inquired why he was driving the cow from home? Jack replied, he was going to sell it. The butcher held some curious beans in his hat; they were of various colours, and attracted Jack's attention: this did not pass unnoticed by the man, who, knowing Jack's easy temper, thought now was the time to take an advantage of it; and, determined not to let slip so good an opportunity, asked what was the price of the cow, offering at the same time all the beans in his hat for her. The silly boy could not conceal the pleasure he felt at what he supposed so great an offer : the bargain was struck instantly, and the cow exchanged for a few paltry beans. Jack made the best of his way home, calling aloud to his mother before he reached the door, thinking to surprise her.

When she saw the beans, and heard Jack's account, her patience quite forsook her : she tossed the beans out of the window, where they fell on the garden-bed below. Then she threw her apron over her head, and cried bitterly. Jack attempted to console her, but in vain, and, not having anything to eat, they both went supperless to bed. Jack awoke early in the morning, and seeing something uncommon darkening the window of his bedchamber, ran downstairs into the garden, where he found some of the beans had taken root, and sprung up surprisingly : the stalks were of an immense thickness, and had twined together until they formed a ladder like a chain, and so high that the top appeared to be lost in the clouds. Jack was an adventurous lad; he determined to climb up to the top, and ran to tell his mother, not doubting but that she would be equally pleased with himself. She declared he should not go ; said it would break her heart if he did —entreated and threatened, but all in vain. Jack set out, and after climbing for some hours, reached the top of the bean-stalk, quite exhausted. Looking around, he found himself in a strange country ; it appeared to be a barren desert—not a tree, shrub, house, or living creature was to be seen ; here and there were scattered fragments of stone ;. and at unequal distances, small heaps of earth were loosely thrown together.

Jack seated himself pensively upon a block of stone, and thought of his mother ; he reflected with sorrow upon his disobedience in climbing the bean-stalk against her will, and concluded that he must die of hunger. However, he walked on, hoping to see a house, where he might beg something to eat and drink. He did not find it ;

but he saw at a distance a beautiful lady, walking all alone. She was elegantly clad, and carried a white wand, at the top of which sat a peacock of pure gold.

Jack, who was a gallant fellow, went straight up to her ; when, with a bewitching smile, she asked him how he came there. He told her all about the bean-stalk. The lady answered him by a question, " Do you remember your father, young man ? "

" No, madam ; but I am sure there is some mystery about him, for when I name him to my mother she always begins to weep, and will tell me nothing."

" She dare not," replied the lady, " but I can and will. For know, young man, that I am a fairy, and was your father's guardian. But fairies are bound by laws as well as mortals ; and by an error of mine I lost my power for a term of years, so that I was unable to succour your father when he most needed it, and he died." Here the fairy looked so sorrowful that Jack's heart warmed to her, and he begged her earnestly to tell him more.

" I will ; only you must promise to obey me in every-thing, or you will perish yourself."

Jack was brave, and, besides, his fortunes were so bad they could not well be worse—so he promised.

The fairy continued : " Your father, Jack, was a most excellent, amiable, generous man. He had a good wife, faithful servants, plenty of money ; but he had one mis-fortune—a false friend. This was a giant, whom he had succoured in misfortune, and who returned his kindness by murdering him, and seizing on all his property ; also making your mother take a solemn oath that she would never tell you anything about your father, or he would murder both her and you. Then he turned her off with you in her arms, to wander about the wide world as she might. I could not help her, as my power only returned on the day you went to sell your cow."

" It was I," added the fairy, " who impelled you to

take the beans, who made the bean-stalk grow, and inspired you with the desire to climb up it to this strange country ; for it is here the wicked giant lives who was your father's destroyer. It is you who must avenge him, and rid the world of a monster who never will do anything but evil. I will assist you. You may lawfully take possession of his house and all his riches, for everything he has belonged to your father, and is therefore yours. Now farewell ! Do not let your mother know you are acquainted with your father's history : this is my command, and if you disobey me you will suffer for it. Now go."

Jack asked where he was to go.

"Along the direct road, till you see the house where the giant lives. You must then act according to your own just judgment, and I will guide you if any difficulty arises. Farewell ! "

She bestowed on the youth a benignant smile, and vanished.

Jack pursued his journey. He walked on till after sunset, when, to his great joy, he espied a large mansion. A plain-looking woman was at the door : he accosted her, begging she would give him a morsel of bread and a night's lodging. She expressed the greatest surprise, and said it was quite uncommon to see a human being near their house ; for it was well known that her husband was a powerful giant, who would never eat anything but human flesh, if he could possibly get it ; that he would walk fifty miles to procure it, usually being out the whole day for that purpose.

This account greatly terrified Jack, but still he hoped to elude the giant, and therefore he again entreated the woman to take him in for one night only, and hide him where she thought proper. She at last suffered herself to be persuaded, for she was of a compassionate and generous disposition, and took him into. the house. First, they entered a fine large hall, magnificently furnished ; they then passed through several spacious rooms, in the same style of grandeur ; but all appeared forsaken and desolate. A long gallery came next ; it was very dark—just light enough to show that, instead of a wall on one side, there was a grating of iron which parted off a dismal dungeon, from whence issued the groans of those victims whom the cruel giant reserved in confinement for his own voracious appetite. Poor Jack was half dead with fear, and would have given the world to have been with his mother again, for he now began to doubt if he should ever see her more ; he even mistrusted the good woman, and thought she had let him into the house for no other purpose than to lock him up among the unfortunate people in the dungeon. However, she bade Jack sit down, and gave him plenty to eat and drink ; and he, not seeing anything to make him uncomfortable, soon forgot his fear, and was just beginning to enjoy himself, when he was startled by a loud knocking at the outer door, which made the whole house shake.

"Ah ! that's the giant ; and if he sees you he will kill you and me too," cried the poor woman, trembling all over. "What shall I do ?"

"Hide me in the oven," cried Jack, now as bold as a lion at the thought of being face to face with his father's cruel murderer. So he crept into the oven—for there was no fire near it—and listened to the giant's loud voice and heavy step as he went up and down the kitchen scolding his wife. At last he seated himself at table, and Jack, peeping through a crevice in the oven, was amazed to see what a quantity of food he devoured. It seemed as if he never would have done eating and drinking ; but he did at last, and, leaning back, called to his wife in a voice like thunder :

"Bring me my hen !"

She obeyed, and placed upon the table a very beautiful live hen.

"Lay!" roared the giant, and the hen laid immediately an egg of solid gold.

"Lay another!" and every time the giant said this the hen laid a larger egg than before.

He amused himself a long time with his hen, and then sent his wife to bed, while he fell asleep by the fireside, and snored like the roaring of cannon.

As soon as he was asleep, Jack crept out of the oven, seized the hen, and ran off with her. He got safely out of the house, and finding his way along the road he came, reached the top of the bean-stalk, which he descended in safety.

His mother was overjoyed to see him. She thought he had come to some ill end.

"Not a bit of it, mother. Look here!" and he showed her the hen. "Now lay"; and the hen obeyed him as readily as the giant, and laid as many golden eggs as he desired.

These eggs being sold, Jack and his mother got plenty of money, and for some months lived very happily together; till Jack got another great longing to climb the bean-stalk, and carry away some more of the giant's riches. He had told his mother of his adventure, but had been very careful not to say a word about his father. He thought of his journey again and again, but still he could not summon resolution enough to break it to his mother, being well assured that she would endeavour to prevent his going. However, one day he told her boldly, that he must take another journey up the bean-stalk; she begged and prayed him not to think of it, and tried all in her power to dissuade him. She told him that the giant's wife would certainly know him again, and that the giant would desire nothing better than to get him into his power, that he might put him to a cruel death, in order to be revenged for the loss of his hen. Jack, finding that all his arguments were useless, ceased speaking, though resolved to go at all events. He had a dress prepared which would disguise him, and something to colour his skin; he thought it impossible for any one to recollect him in this dress.

A few mornings after, he rose very early, and, unperceived by any one, climbed the bean-stalk a second time. He was greatly fatigued when he reached the top, and very hungry. Having rested some time on one of the stones, he pursued his journey to the giant's mansion, which he reached late in the evening: the woman was at the door as before. Jack addressed her, at the same time telling her a pitiful tale, and requesting that she would give him some victuals and drink, and also a night's lodging.

She told him (what he knew before very well) about her husband's being a powerful and cruel giant, and also that she had one night admitted a poor, hungry, friendless boy; that the little ungrateful fellow had stolen one of the giant's treasures; and ever since that her husband had been worse than before, using her very cruelly, and continually upbraiding her with being the cause of his misfortune. Jack felt sorry for her, but confessed nothing, and did his best to persuade her to admit him, but found it a very hard task. At last she consented, and as she led the way, Jack observed that everything was just as he had found it before: she took him into the kitchen, and after he had done eating and drinking, she hid him in an old lumber-closet. The giant returned at the usual time, and walked in so heavily, that the house was shaken to its foundation. He seated himself by the fire, and soon after exclaimed: "Wife, I smell fresh meat!"

The wife replied it was the crows, which had brought a piece of raw meat, and left it at the top of the house. While supper was preparing, the giant was very ill-tempered and impatient, frequently lifting up his hand to strike his wife for not being quick enough. He was also continually upbraiding her with the loss of his wonderful hen.

At last, having ended his supper, he cried, "Give me something to amuse me—my harp or my money-bags."

"Which will you have, my dear?" said the wife humbly.

"My money-bags, because they are the heaviest to carry," thundered he.

She brought them, staggering under the weight; two bags—one filled with new guineas, and the other with new shillings; she emptied them out on the table, and the giant began counting them in great glee. "Now you may go to bed, you old fool." So the wife crept away.

Jack from his hiding-place watched the counting of the money, which he knew was his poor father's, and wished it was his own; it would give him much less trouble than going about selling the golden eggs. The giant, little thinking he was so narrowly observed, reckoned it all up, and then replaced it in the two bags, which he tied up very carefully and put beside his chair, with his little dog to guard them. At last he fell asleep as before, and snored so loud, that Jack compared his noise to the roaring of the sea in a high wind, when the tide is coming in. At last Jack, concluding all secure, stole out, in order to carry off the two bags of money; but just as he laid his hand upon one of them, the little dog, which he had not perceived before, started from under the giant's chair and barked most furiously. Instead of endeavouring to escape, Jack stood still, though expecting his enemy to awake every instant. Contrary, however, to his expectation, the giant continued in a sound sleep, and Jack, seeing a piece of meat, threw it to the dog, who at once ceased barking, and began to devour it. So Jack carried off the bags, one on each shoulder, but they were so heavy that it took him two whole days to descend the beanstalk and get back to his mother's door.

When he came he found the cottage deserted. He ran from one room to another, without being able to find any one ; he then hastened into the village, hoping to see some of the neighbours, who could inform him where he could find his mother. An old woman at last directed him to a neighbouring house, where she was ill of a fever. He was greatly shocked at finding her apparently dying, and blamed himself bitterly as the cause of it all. However, at sight of her dear son, the poor woman revived, and slowly recovered health. Jack gave her his two money-bags : they had the cottage rebuilt and well furnished, and lived happier than they had ever done before.

For three years Jack heard no more of the bean-stalk, but he could not forget it, though he feared making his mother unhappy. It was in vain endeavouring to amuse himself ; he became thoughtful, and would arise at the first dawn of day, and sit looking at the bean-stalk for hours together. His mother saw that something preyed upon his mind, and endeavoured to discover the cause ; but Jack knew too well what the consequence would be should she succeed. He did his utmost, therefore, to conquer the great desire he had for another journey up the bean-stalk. Finding, however, that his inclination grew too powerful for him, he began to make secret preparations for his journey. He got ready a new disguise, better and more complete than the former ; and when summer came, on the longest day he woke as soon as it was light, and without telling his mother, ascended the bean-stalk. He found the road, journey, etc., much as it was on the two former times. He arrived at the giant's mansion in the evening, and found the wife standing, as usual, at the door. Jack had disguised him-self so completely, that she did not appear to have the least recollection of him ; however, when he pleaded hunger and poverty, in order to gain admittance, he found it very difficult indeed to persuade her. At last he prevailed, and was concealed in the copper. When the giant returned, he said furiously, "I smell fresh meat!" But Jack felt quite composed, as he had said so before, and had been soon satisfied. However, the giant started up suddenly, and, notwithstanding all his wife could say, he searched all round the room. Whilst this was going forward, Jack was exceedingly terrified, wishing himself at home a thousand times ; but when the giant approached the copper, and put his hand upon the lid, Jack thought his death was certain. However, nothing happened ; for the giant did not take the trouble to lift up the lid, but sat down shortly by the fireside, and began to eat his enormous supper. When he had finished, he commanded his wife to fetch down his harp. Jack peeped under the copper-lid, and saw a most beautiful harp. The giant placed it on the table, said " Play !" and it played of its own accord, without anybody touching it, the most exquisite music imaginable. Jack, who was a very good musician, was delighted, and more anxious to get this than any other of his enemy's treasures. But the giant not being particularly fond of music, the harp had only the effect of lulling him to sleep earlier than usual. As for the wife, she had gone to bed as soon as ever she could.

As soon as he thought all was safe, Jack got out of the copper, and seizing the harp, was eagerly running off with it. But the harp was enchanted by a fairy, and as soon as it found itself in strange hands, it called out loudly, just as if it had been alive, " Master ! Master !"

The giant awoke, started up, and saw Jack scampering away as fast as his legs could carry him.

"Oh, you villain ! it is you who have robbed me of my hen and my money-bags, and now you are stealing my harp also. Wait till I catch you, and I'll eat you up alive !"

"Very well ; try !" shouted Jack, who was not a bit afraid, for he saw the giant was so tipsy he could hardly stand, much less run ; and he himself had young legs and a clear conscience, which carry a man a long way. So, after leading the giant a considerable race, he contrived to be first at the top of the bean-stalk, and then scrambled down it as fast as he could, the harp playing all the while the most melancholy music, till he said, "Stop," and it stopped.

Arrived at the bottom, he found his mother sitting at her cottage-door, weeping silently.

"Here, mother, don't cry ; just give me a hatchet ; make haste." For he knew there was not a moment to spare ; he saw the giant beginning to descend the bean-stalk.

However, it was too late—the monster's ill deeds had come to an end. Jack with his hatchet cut the bean-stalk close off at the root ; the giant fell headlong into the garden, and was killed on the spot.

Instantly the fairy appeared, and explained everything to Jack's mother, begging her to forgive Jack, who was his father's own son for bravery and generosity, and who would be sure to make her happy for the rest of her days.

So all ended well, and nothing was ever more heard or seen of the wonderful Bean-stalk.

GRACIOSA AND PERCINET

ONCE upon a time there lived a king and queen, who had an only daughter. Her incomparable beauty, sweetness, and intelligence caused her to be named Graciosa. She was all her mother's joy. Every day she had given her a different dress, of gold brocade, velvet, or satin; yet she was neither conceited nor boastful. She used to pass her mornings in study, and in the afternoon she sat sewing by the queen's side. She had, however, plenty of play-time, and sweetmeats without end, so that she was altogether the happiest princess alive.

At the same court was an elderly young lady named Duchess Grognon, who was the very opposite of Graciosa. Her hair was fiery red, her face fat and spotty, and she had but one eye. Her mouth was so big that you might have thought she could eat you up, only she had no teeth to do it with; she was also humpbacked and lame. Of course she could not help her ugliness, and nobody would have disliked her for that, if she had not been of such an unpleasant temper that she hated everything sweet and beautiful, and especially Graciosa. She had also a very good opinion of herself, and when any one praised the princess, would say angrily, "That is a lie! My little finger is worth her whole body."

In course of time the queen fell sick and died, and her daughter was almost broken-hearted. So was her husband for a year, and then he began to comfort himself by hunting. One day, after a long chase, he came to a

148

"Jack . . . seized the hen, and ran off with her, . . . reached the
top of the bean-stalk, which he descended in safety." *(Page 142)*

"As soon as the rods touched her, they turned into bundles of feathers." (*Page 152*)

strange castle, which happened to be that of the Duchess Grognon. She, informed of his approach, went out to meet him, and received him most respectfully. As he was very hot with hunting, she took him into the coolest place in the palace, which was a vaulted cave, most elegantly furnished, where there were two hundred barrels arranged in long rows.

"Madam, are these all yours ?" inquired the king.

"Yes, sire, but I shall be most happy if you will condescend to taste their contents. Which wine do you prefer—canary, hermitage, champagne ?" and she ran over a long list, out of which his majesty made his choice.

Grognon took a little hammer, and struck "toc, toc," on the cask, from which there rolled out a handful of silver money. "Nay, what is this?" said she, smiling, and passed on to the next, from which, when she tapped it, out poured a stream of gold coins. "I never saw the like—what nonsense!" and she tried the third, out of which came a heap of pearls and diamonds, so that the floor of the cave was strewn with them. "Sire," she exclaimed, "some one has robbed me of my good wine, and put this rubbish in its place."

"Rubbish, madam ! Why, such rubbish would buy my whole kingdom."

"It is yours, sire," replied the duchess, "if you will make me your queen."

The king, who was a great lover of money, replied eagerly, "Certainly, madam, I'll marry you to-morrow if you will."

Grognon, highly delighted, made but one other condition—that she should have the Princess Graciosa entirely in her own rule and power, just as if she had been her real mother ; to which the foolish king consented, for he thought much more of riches than he did of his child. So he and Grognon departed hand in hand out of the cave, very well pleased.

149

When the king returned home, Graciosa ran out with joy to welcome her father, and asked him if he had had good sport in his hunting.

" Yes, my child," said he, " for I have taken a dove alive."

" Oh, give it me, and I will nourish and cherish it," cried the princess.

" That is impossible ; for it is the Duchess Grognon, whom I have promised to marry."

" She a dove !—she is rather a hawk," sighed the princess in despair ; but her father bade her hold her tongue, and promise to love her stepmother, who would have over her all the authority of a mother, and to whom he wished to present her that very day.

The obedient princess went to her apartment, where her nurse soon found out the sorrow in her face, and its cause.

" My child," said the good old woman, " princesses ought to show a good example to humbler women. Promise me to do your best to please your father, and to make yourself agreeable to the stepmother he has chosen for you. She may not be so bad after all."

And the nurse gave so much good advice, that Graciosa began to smile, and dressed herself in her best attire, a green robe embroidered with gold ; while her fair, loose-falling hair was adorned, according to the fashion of the day, with a coronet of jasmine, of which the leaves were made of large emeralds.

Grognon, on her part, made the best of herself that was possible. She put on a high-heeled shoe to appear less lame, she padded her shoulders, dyed her red hair black, and put in a false eye ; then dressed herself in a hooped petticoat of violet satin trimmed with blue, and an upper gown of yellow with green ribands. In this costume, she wished to enter the city on horseback, as she understood the queens were in the habit of doing.

Meantime, Graciosa waited in fear the moment of her arrival, and, to pass the time away, she went all alone into a little wood, where she sobbed and wept in secret, until suddenly there appeared before her a young page, whom she had never seen before.

"Who are you?" she inquired; "and when did his majesty take you into his service?"

"Princess," said the page, bowing, "I am in no one's service but your own. I am Percinet, a prince in my own country, so that there is no inequality of rank between us. I have loved you long, and seen you often, for I have the fairy gift of making myself invisible. I might longer have concealed myself from you, but for your present sorrow, in which, however, I hope to be of both comfort and assistance—a page and yet a prince, and your faithful lover."

At these words, at once tender and respectful, the princess, who had long heard of the fairy-prince Percinet, felt so happy that she feared Grognon no more. They talked a little while together, and then returned to the palace, where the page assisted her to mount her horse; on which she looked so beautiful, that all the new queen's splendours faded into nothing in comparison, and not one of the courtiers had eyes for any except Graciosa.

As soon as Grognon saw it, "What!" cried she, "has this creature the impudence to be better mounted than myself? Descend, Miss, and let me try your horse;—and your page, whom everybody thinks so much of, bid him come and hold my bridle."

Prince Percinet, who was the page, cast one look at his fair Graciosa and obeyed; but no sooner had the duchess mounted, than the horse ran away with her and dragged her over briers, stones, and mud, and finally threw her into a deep ditch. Her head was cut in several places, and her arm fractured. They picked her up in little pieces like a broken wineglass; never was there a poor bride in worse plight. But in spite of her sufferings her malice remained. She sent for the king :

"This is all Graciosa's fault ; she wished to kill me. I desire that your majesty will punish her, or leave me to do it—else I will certainly be revenged upon you both."

The king, afraid of losing his casks full of gold pieces, consented, and Graciosa was commanded to appear. She came trembling and looking round vainly for Prince Percinet. The cruel Grognon ordered four women, ugly as witches, to take her and strip off her fine clothes, and whip her with rods till her white shoulders were red with blood. But lo! as soon as the rods touched her, they turned into bundles of feathers, and the women tired themselves to death with whipping, without hurting Graciosa the least in the world !

"Ah ! kind Percinet, what do I not owe you ? What should I do without you ! " sighed the princess, when she was taken back to her own chamber and her nurse. And then she saw the prince standing before her, in his green dress and his white plume, the most charming of pages.

Percinet advised her to pretend illness on account of the cruel treatment she was supposed to have received ; which so delighted Grognon, that she got well all the sooner, and the marriage was celebrated with great splendour.

Soon after, the king, who knew that his wife's weak point was her vanity, gave a tournament, at which he ordered the six bravest knights of the court to proclaim that Queen Grognon was the fairest lady alive. No knight ventured to dispute this fact, until there appeared one who carried a little box adorned with diamonds, and proclaimed aloud that Grognon was the ugliest woman in the universe, and that the most beautiful was she whose portrait was in the box. He opened it, and behold the image of the Princess Graciosa !

The princess, who sat behind her stepmother, felt sure

that the unknown knight was Percinet ; but she dared say nothing. The contest was fixed for next day ; but in the meantime, Grognon, wild with anger, commanded Graciosa to be taken in the middle of the night to a forest a hundred leagues distant, full of wolves, lions, tigers, and bears. In vain the poor maiden implored that the attendants would kill her at once, rather than leave her in that dreadful place : the queen's orders must be obeyed ; no answer was made to her, but the servants remounted and rode away. Graciosa, in solitude and darkness, groped through the forest, sometimes falling against the trunks of trees, sometimes tearing herself with bushes and briers ; at last, overcome with fear and grief, she sank on the ground, sobbing out, " Percinet, Percinet, have you forsaken me ? "

While she spoke, a bright light dazzled her eyes, the midnight forest was changed into glittering alleys, at the end of which appeared a palace of crystal, shining like the sun. She knew it was the doing of the fairy-prince who loved her, and felt a joy mingled with fear. She turned to fly, but saw him standing before her, more handsome and charming than ever.

" Princess," said he, " why are you afraid of me ? This is the palace of the fairy-queen my mother, and the princesses my sisters, who will take care of you, and love you tenderly. Enter this chariot, and I will convey you there."

Graciosa entered, and passing through many a lovely forest glade, where it was clear daylight, and shepherds and shepherdesses were dancing to merry music, they reached the palace, where the queen and her two daughters received the forlorn princess with great kindness, and led her through many rooms of rock-crystal, glittering with jewels, where, to her amazement, Graciosa saw the history of her own life, even down to this adventure in the forest, painted on the walls.

"How is this?" she said. "Prince, you know everything about me."

"Yes; and I wish to preserve everything concerning you," said he tenderly; whereupon Graciosa cast down her eyes. She was only too happy, and afraid that she should learn to love the fairy-prince too much.

She spent eight days in his palace—days full of every enjoyment; and Percinet tried all the arguments he could think of to induce her to marry him, and remain there for ever. But the good and gentle Graciosa remembered her father, who was once so kind to her, and she preferred rather to suffer than to be wanting in duty. She entreated Percinet to use his fairy power to send her home again, and meantime to tell her what had become of her father.

"Come with me into the great tower there, and you shall see for yourself."

Thereupon he took her to the top of a tower, prodigiously high, put her little finger to his lips, and her foot upon his foot. Then he bade her look, and she saw as in a picture, or as in a play upon the stage, the King and Grognon sitting together on their throne. The latter was telling how Graciosa had hanged herself in a cave.

"She will not be much loss, sire; and as, when dead, she was far too frightful for you to look at, I have given orders to bury her at once."

She might well say that, for she had had a large faggot put into a coffin, and sealed up; the king and all the nation mourned over it; and, now that she was no more, they declared there never was such a sweet creature as the lost princess.

The sight of her father's grief quite overcame Graciosa: "Oh, Percinet!" she cried, "my father believes me dead. If you love me, take me home."

The prince consented, though very sorrowfully, saying that she was as cruel to him as Grognon was to her, and mounted with her in his chariot, drawn by four white stags. As they quitted the courtyard, they heard a great noise, and Graciosa saw the palace all falling to pieces with a great crash.

" What is this ? " she cried, terrified.

" Princess, my palace, which you forsake, is among the things which are dead and gone. You will enter it no more till after your burial."

" Prince, you are angry with me," said Graciosa sorrowfully ; only she knew well that she suffered quite as much as he did in thus departing and quitting him.

Arrived in her father's presence, she had great difficulty in persuading him that she was not a ghost, until the coffin with the faggot inside it was taken up, and Grognon's malice discovered. But even then, the king was so weak a man, that the queen soon made him believe he had been cheated, that the princess was really dead, and that this was a false Graciosa. Without more ado, he abandoned his daughter to her stepmother's will.

Grognon, transported with joy, dragged her to a dark prison, took away her clothes, made her dress in rags, feed on bread and water, and sleep upon straw. Forlorn and hopeless, Graciosa dared not now call upon Percinet ; she doubted if he still loved her enough to come to her aid.

Meantime, Grognon had sent for a fairy, who was scarcely less malicious than herself. " I have here," said she, " a little wretch of a girl for whom I wish to find all sorts of difficult tasks ; pray assist me in giving her a new one every day."

The fairy promised to think of it, and soon brought a skein as thick as four persons, yet composed of thread so fine, that it broke if you only blew upon it, and so tangled that it had neither beginning nor end. Grognon, delighted, sent for her poor prisoner.

" There, miss, teach your clumsy fingers to unwind

this skein, and if you break a single thread, I will flay you alive. Begin when you like, but you must finish at sunset, or it will be the worse for you." Then she sent her to her miserable cell, and treble-locked the door.

Graciosa stood dismayed, turning the skein over and over, and breaking hundreds of threads each time. " Ah! Percinet," she cried in despair, "come and help me, or at least receive my last farewell."

Immediately Percinet stood beside her, having entered the cell as easily as if he carried the key in his pocket. "Behold me, princess, ready to serve you, even though you forsook me." He touched the skein with his wand, and it untangled itself, and wound itself up in perfect order. "Do you wish anything more, madam?" asked he coldly.

"Percinet, Percinet, do not reproach me; I am only too unhappy!"

"It is your own fault. Come with me, and make us both happy." But she said nothing, and the fairy-prince disappeared.

At sunset, Grognon eagerly came to the prison-door with her three keys, and found Graciosa smiling and fair, her task all done. There was no complaint to make, yet Grognon exclaimed that the skein was dirty, and boxed the princess's ears till her rosy cheeks turned yellow and blue. Then she left her, and overwhelmed the fairy with reproaches.

"Find me, by to-morrow, something absolutely impossible for her to do."

The fairy brought a great basket full of feathers, plucked from every kind of bird—nightingales, canaries, linnets, larks, doves, thrushes, peacocks, ostriches, pheasants, partridges, magpies, eagles—in fact, if I told them all over, I should never come to an end; and all these feathers were so mixed up together, that they could not be distinguished.

"See," said the fairy, "even one of ourselves would find it difficult to separate these, and arrange them as belonging to each sort of bird. Command your prisoner to do it; she is sure to fail."

Grognon jumped for joy, sent for the princess, and ordered her to take her task, and finish it, as before, by set of sun.

Graciosa tried patiently, but she could see no difference in the feathers; she threw them all back again into the basket and began to weep bitterly. "Let me die," said she, "for death only will end my sorrows. Percinet loves me no longer; if he did, he would already have been here."

"Here I am, my princess," cried a voice from under the basket; and the fairy-prince appeared. He gave three taps with his wand—the feathers flew by millions out of the basket, and arranged themselves in little heaps, each belonging to a different bird.

"What do I not owe you?" cried Graciosa.

"Love me!" answered the prince tenderly, and said no more.

When Grognon arrived, she found the task done. She was furious at the fairy, who was as much astonished as herself at the result of their malicious contrivances. But she promised to try once more; and for several days employed all her industry in inventing a box, which, she said, the prisoner must be forbidden on any account to open. "Then," added the cunning fairy, "of course, being such a disobedient and wicked girl, as you say, she will open it, and the result will satisfy you to your heart's content."

Grognon took the box, and commanded Graciosa to carry it to her castle, and set it on a certain table, in an apartment she named, but not, upon any account, to open it or examine the contents.

Graciosa departed. She was dressed like any poor

peasant, in a cotton gown, a woollen hood, and wooden shoes ; yet, as she walked along, people took her for a queen in disguise, so lovely were her looks and ways. But being weak with imprisonment, she soon grew weary, and, sitting down upon the edge of a little wood, took the box upon her lap. Suddenly a wonderful desire seized her to open it.

" I will take nothing out, I will touch nothing," said she to herself, " but I must see what is inside."

Without reflecting on the consequences, she lifted up the lid, and instantly there jumped out a number of little men and little women, carrying little tables and chairs, little dishes, and little musical instruments. The whole company were so small, that the biggest giant among them was scarcely the height of a finger. They leaped into the green meadow, separated into various bands, and began dancing and singing, eating and drinking, to Graciosa's wonder and delight. But when she recollected herself, and wished to get them into the box again, they all scampered away, played at hide-and-seek in the wood, and by no means could she catch a single one.

Again, in her distress, she called upon Percinet, and again he appeared ; and, with a single touch of his wand, sent all the little people back into the box. Then, in his chariot drawn by stags, he took her to the castle, where she did all that she had been commanded, and returned in safety to her stepmother, who was more furious than ever. If a fairy could be strangled, Grognon certainly would have done it in her rage. At last, she resolved to ask help no more, but to work her own wicked will upon Graciosa.

She caused to be dug a large hole in the garden, and taking the princess there, showed her the stone which covered it.

" Underneath this stone lies a great treasure ; lift it up, and you will see."

Graciosa obeyed; and while she was standing at the edge of the pit, Grognon pushed her in, and let the stone fall down again upon her, burying her alive. After this, there seemed no more hope for the poor princess.

"Oh, Percinet," cried she, "you are avenged. Why did I not return your love, and marry you? Still, death will be less bitter, if only you regret me a little."

While she spoke, she saw through the blank darkness a glimmer of light; it came through a little door. She remembered what Percinet had said: that she would never return to the fairy palace, until after she was buried. Perhaps this final cruelty of Grognon would be the end of her sorrows. So she took courage, crept through the little door, and lo! she came out into a beautiful garden, with long alleys, fruit trees, and flower-beds. Well she knew it, and well she knew the glitter of the rock-crystal walls. And there, at the palace-gate, stood Percinet, and the queen his mother, and the princesses his sisters. "Welcome, Graciosa!" cried they all; and Graciosa, after all her sufferings, wept for joy.

The marriage was celebrated with great splendour; and all the fairies, for a thousand leagues round, attended it. Some came in chariots drawn by dragons, or swans, or peacocks; some were mounted upon floating clouds, or globes of fire. Among the rest, appeared the very fairy who had assisted Grognon to torment Graciosa. When she discovered that Grognon's poor prisoner was now Prince Percinet's bride, she was overwhelmed with confusion, and entreated her to forget all that had passed, because she really was ignorant who she had been so cruelly afflicting.

"But I will make amends for all the evil that I have done," said the fairy; and, refusing to stay for the wedding-dinner, she remounted her chariot, drawn by two terrible serpents, and flew to the palace of Graciosa's father. There, before either king or courtiers, or ladies-in-waiting could stop her—even had they wished to do it, which remains doubtful—she came behind the wicked Grognon, and twisted her neck, just as a cook does a barn-door fowl. So Grognon died, and was buried, and nobody was particularly sorry for the same.

THE IRON STOVE

In the days when magic was still of some avail, a king's son was enchanted by an old witch, and compelled to spend his life sitting inside a great Iron Stove in a wood. There he passed many years, and nobody could release him.

Once a king's daughter came into the wood. She had gone astray, and could not find her father's kingdom again ; and having wandered about for nine days, at last she stood before the Iron Stove. Then a voice came out of it, and said, " Whence do you come, and where do you want to go ? "

She answered, " I have wandered from my father's kingdom, and lost myself, and cannot get home again."

Then the voice spoke out of the Iron Stove : " I will help you home again, and that, too, in a short time, if you will promise to do what I desire. I am a greater prince than you are a princess, and I wish to marry you."

She was very much frightened, and thought, " Oh, what shall I do ? How can I marry an Iron Stove ? "

However, as she wanted very much to go home to her father, she promised what was demanded of her. " Very well," said the voice ; " you must come again, and bring a knife with you, and scrape a hole in the iron."

And the Iron Stove gave her for a companion something, or somebody—she was not quite sure what—who walked by her side and did not speak, but took her safe home within two hours. Then there was great joy in her father's palace, and the old king fell on her neck, and kissed her many times. But she was very sorrowful, and said, "Dear father, you little know what has happened to me ; I should never have come home again out of the great wild wood, if I had not passed by an Iron Stove. But I had to promise faithfully that I would return back to it, and marry it."

The old king was so terrified that he nearly fell into a swoon ; for he had only this one child. They therefore consulted together, and decided to send, not the princess, but a miller's daughter, who was very beautiful ; and leading her out, they gave her a knife, and told her how she was to scrape the Iron Stove. When she reached the wood, she scraped away for four-and-twenty hours, but could not make the slightest impression. But when day began to break, a voice in the Iron Stove called out, "It seems to me that it is day out there."

She answered, "It seems so to me too ; I think I hear my father's mill turning."

"Oh, then, you are a miller's daughter ; go straight back and send the king's daughter here!"

Then she returned and told the old king that the Iron Stove would not have her ; he wanted the princess only. The old king was greatly frightened, and the princess wept. But they had still a swineherd's daughter, who was still more beautiful than the miller's girl ; so they gave her a piece of gold, in order that she might be persuaded to go, instead of the king's daughter, to the Iron Stove. She was taken to the wood as before, and had also to scrape for four-and-twenty hours ; but she could make no impression.

Now when dawn broke, a voice called out of the Stove, "It seems to me it is day out there."

Then she answered, "It seems so to me too ; I think I hear my father's little horn sounding."

"So you are the swineherd's daughter : go away

directly, and bid the king's daughter come, and tell her it shall happen to her as I forewarned her ; if she does not come, everything in the kingdom shall fall to pieces and tumble down, and no stone remain upon another."

When the king's daughter heard this, she began to cry ; but there was nothing else to be done—she must keep her promise. She took leave of her father, put a knife in her pocket, and went out to the Iron Stove in the wood. When she arrived there, she began to scrape and scrape ; the iron yielded, and in two hours she had already scraped a little hole. She looked in and saw a most beautiful youth : oh ! he shone so with gold and precious stones, that he pleased her to the very bottom of her heart. She scraped away faster than ever, till she made the hole so large that he was able to get out.

Then he said, " You are mine, and I am yours ; you have freed me, and you are my bride."

He wished to take her home to his kingdom, but she begged that she might go once more to see her father ; and the prince gave her leave, on condition that she should speak no more than three words with him, and come back again. So she went home ; but, alas ! being a little chatterbox, she spoke more than three words. The Iron Stove disappeared instantly, and was removed far away, over glass mountains and sharp swords ; but the king's son, being now freed, was not shut up in it.

The princess took leave of her father, and took some money with her, but not much, and went again into the great wood. There she looked everywhere for the Iron Stove, but it was not to be found.

She sought it for nine days, until her hunger was so great that she did not know what to do ; for she had eaten all the food she could find, and had nothing left to keep her alive. At evening-tide she climbed up into a little tree, and purposed spending the night there, for fear of the wild beasts. But when midnight came she saw afar off a little glimmering light, and thinking, " Oh ! there I should be safe," climbed down and went towards it.

Then she came to a little old house, overgrown with grass, with a little heap of wood before the door. Wondering how it came there, she looked in through the window, and saw nothing inside but a number of fat little frogs, and a table beautifully spread. There were on it roast meats and wines, and the plates and cups were all of silver. So she took heart, and knocked. Immediately the fattest frog called out :

> " Maiden sweet and small,
> Hutzelbein I call;
>   Hutzelbein's little dog,
> Creep about and see
> Who this can be."

Then a little frog came and opened the door for her ; and as soon as she came in, the frogs all bade her welcome, and persuaded her to sit down. They asked—" Whence do you come ? where do you want to go ? "

Then she told them all that had happened to her, and how, because she had disobeyed the command not to speak to her father more than three words, the Stove had disappeared, as well as the king's son ; now she was determined to seek him, and to wander over mountain and valley till she found him.

The old fat frog said :

> " Maiden sweet and small,
> Hutzelbein I call ;
>   Hutzelbein's little dog,
> Creep about and see ;
> Bring the great box to me."

Then the little frog went and brought the box. Afterwards they gave the princess food and drink, and took her to a beautifully-made bed, all of silk and velvet ; she laid herself in it, and slept peacefully.

When day came she arose, and the old frog gave her

"At evening-tide she climbed up into a little tree, and purposed
spending the night there, for fear of the wild beasts." *(Page 163)*

WARWICK GOBLE.

"Madam,' said he, 'since I have had the honour to serve you, I know not any other happiness that I can wish for.'" (*Page 172*) three needles out of the great box, and told her to take them with her. They would be very necessary to her, for she would have to go over a high glass mountain, and three sharp swords, and a great sea ; if she passed all those, she would recover her dearest prince. The frog also gave her, besides the three needles, other gifts, which she was to take great care of—namely, a plough-wheel, and three nuts.

With these she set off, and when she came to the slippery glass mountain, she stuck the three needles into it as she walked—some before her feet, and some behind —and so managed to get across. When she was on the other side, she hid the needles, in a place which she had noticed particularly, and went on her way. Afterwards she came to the sharp-cutting swords, but she set herself on her plough-wheel and rolled safely over them. At last she came before a great lake, which she had to sail across, and when she had done so she saw a great castle. She went in and said she was a poor maiden, who wished very much to hire herself out, if she might be taken in there as a servant. For the frogs had told her that the king's son, whom she had released out of the Iron Stove in the great wood, dwelt there ; so she was content to be taken as kitchen-maid, for very small pay.

Now the king's son had thought the princess was dead ; and there was now with him another maiden, whom he had been persuaded he ought to marry, which grieved the poor kitchen-maid very much.

In the evening, when she had washed up the dishes, and had done all her work, she felt in her pocket, and found the three nuts which the old frog had given her. She bit one open, and was going to eat the kernel, when, behold, inside it was the most beautiful dress imaginable —so beautiful that the bride soon heard of it, came and asked to see it, and wanted to buy it, saying it was no dress for a kitchen-maid. But the kitchen-maid thought differently, and refused to sell it, but offered to give it as a present, if the bride would grant her one favour— namely, to sleep one night on the mat outside the bride- groom's door. The bride gave her leave, because the dress was so beautiful, and she had none like it.

Now when it was evening, she said to her bridegroom : " The foolish kitchen-maid wants to sleep on the mat outside your door."

" If you are content, I am," said he.

But the bride gave him a glass of wine, in which she had put a sleeping-draught ; so that he slept so soundly, nothing could wake him. While, outside the door, the princess wept the whole night, saying : " I have released you out of the wild wood — out of an Iron Stove ; in seeking you, I have gone over a glass mountain, over three sharp swords, and over a great lake ; yet, now that I find you, you will not hear me."

Next evening, when she had washed up everything, she bit the second nut open ; and inside it was a far more beautiful dress than the first, which, when the bride saw, she wished to buy also. But the girl again refused to take money, and again begged that she might spend the night outside the bridegroom's door. Once more the bride gave him a sleeping-draught, and he slept so soundly, that he could hear nothing. But the kitchen-maid wept the whole night long, crying, " I have released you out of a wild wood, and out of an Iron Stove ; and have gone over a glass mountain, over three sharp swords, and over a great lake, before I found you ; and yet, when I find you, you will not hear me."

The third evening, she bit open the third nut ; and there was in it a still more beautiful dress, which shone stiff with pure gold. When the bride saw it, she wished more earnestly than ever to have it; but the kitchen-maid would only give it to her on condition that she might sleep, for the third time, on the mat at the bridegroom's door. But this time the prince was cautious, and left the sleeping-draught untouched. Now, when she began to weep, and to call out, "Dearest treasure, I have released you out of the horrible wild wood, and out of an Iron Stove," the king's son sprang up, crying out, "This is my right true love—she is mine, and I am hers." Then he declared he would not marry the other bride, whom he did not love ; and so, still in the middle of the night, he got into a carriage with the kitchen-maid, and drove away.

When they came to the great lake, they sailed over ; and at the three sharp swords, they seated themselves on the plough-wheel ; and at the glass mountain, they found the three needles, and stuck them in step by step. So they came at last to the little old house ; but, as they went in, lo ! it changed to a great castle ; the frogs turned to princes and princesses, all kings' children, and received them both with great joy. There the wedding was celebrated, and they remained in the castle, which was much larger than that which belonged to the princess's father. But as the old man lamented very much his daughter's loss, and his own loneliness, they soon went and fetched him home to themselves. So they had two kingdoms, instead of one, and live happily together all their days.

THE INVISIBLE PRINCE

THERE was a king and queen who were dotingly fond of their only son, notwithstanding that he was equally deformed in mind and person. The king was quite sensible of the evil disposition of his son, but the queen, in her excessive fondness, saw no fault whatever in her dear Furibon, as he was named. The surest way to win her favour was to praise Furibon for charms he did not possess. When he came of age to have a governor, the king made choice of a prince who had an ancient right to the crown, but was not able to support it. This prince had a son, named Leander, handsome, accomplished, amiable—in every respect the opposite of Prince Furibon. The two were frequently together, which only made the deformed prince more repulsive.

One day, certain ambassadors having arrived from a far country, the princes stood in a gallery to see them ; when, taking Leander for the king's son, they made their obeisance to him, treating Furibon as a mere dwarf, at which the latter was so offended that he drew his sword, and would have done them a mischief had not the king just then appeared. As it was, the affair produced a quarrel, which ended in Leander's being sent to a far-away castle belonging to his father.

There, however, he was quite happy, for he was a great lover of hunting, fishing, and walking : he understood painting, read much, and played upon several instruments ; so that he was glad to be freed from the fantastic humours of Furibon. One day as he was walking in the garden, finding the heat increase, he retired into a shady grove, and began to play upon the flute to amuse himself. As he played, he felt something wind about his leg, and looking down saw a great adder : he took his handkerchief, and, catching it by the head, was going to kill it. But the adder, looking stedfastly in his face, seemed to beg his pardon. At this instant one of the gardeners happened to come to the place where Leander was, and spying the snake, cried out to his master, " Hold him fast, sir ; it is but an hour since we ran after him to kill him : it is the most mischievous creature in the world."

Leander, casting his eyes a second time upon the snake, which was speckled with a thousand extraordinary colours, perceived the poor creature still looked upon him with an aspect that seemed to implore compassion, and never tried in the least to defend itself.

" Though thou hast such a mind to kill it," said he to the gardener, " yet, as it came to me for refuge, I forbid thee to do it any harm ; for I will keep it, and when it has cast its beautiful skin I will let it go." He then returned home, and carrying the snake with him, put it into a large chamber, the key of which he kept himself, and ordered bran, milk, and flowers to be given to it, for its delight and sustenance ; so that never was snake so happy. Leander went sometimes to see it, and when it perceived him it made haste to meet him, showing him all the little marks of love and gratitude of which a poor snake was capable, which did not a little surprise him, though, however, he took no further notice of it.

In the meantime all the court ladies were extremely troubled at his absence, and he was the subject of all their discourse. " Alas ! " cried they, " there is no pleasure at court since Leander is gone, of whose absence the wicked Furibon is the cause ! " Furibon also had his parasites, for his power over the queen made him feared ;

they told him what the ladies said, which enraged him to such a degree that in his passion he flew to the queen's chamber, and vowed he would kill himself before her face if she did not find means to destroy Leander. The queen, who also hated Leander, because he was handsomer than her son, replied that she had long looked upon him as a traitor, and therefore would willingly consent to his death. To which purpose she advised Furibon to go a-hunting with some of his confidants, and contrive it so that Leander should make one of the party.

"Then," said she, "you may find some way to punish him for pleasing everybody."

Furibon understood her, and accordingly went a-hunting ; and Leander, when he heard the horns and the hounds, mounted his horse, and rode to see who it was. But he was surprised to meet the prince so unexpectedly : he alighted immediately, and saluted him with respect ; and Furibon received him more graciously than usual, and bade him follow him. All of a sudden he turned his horse, and rode another way, making a sign to the ruffians to take the first opportunity to kill him ; but before he had got quite out of sight, a lion of prodigious size, coming out of his den, leaped upon Furibon : all his followers fled, and only Leander remained ; who, attacking the animal sword in hand, by his valour and agility saved the life of his most cruel enemy, who had fallen in a swoon from fear. When he recovered, Leander presented him his horse to remount. Now, any other than such a wretch would have been grateful : but Furibon did not even look upon him : nay, mounting the horse, he rode in quest of the ruffians, to whom he repeated his orders to kill him. They accordingly surrounded Leander, who, setting his back to a tree, behaved with so much bravery, that he laid them all dead at his feet. Furibon, believing him by this time slain, rode eagerly up to the spot. When Leander saw him, he advanced to meet him.

"Sir," said he, "if it was by your order that these assassins came to kill me, I am sorry I made any defence."

"You are an insolent villain!" replied Furibon, "and if ever you come into my presence again, you shall surely die."

Leander made no answer, but retired sad and pensive to his own home, where he spent the night in pondering what was best for him to do; for there was no likelihood he should be able to defend himself against the power of the king's son; therefore he at length concluded he would travel abroad and see the world. Being ready to depart, he recollected his snake, and, calling for some milk and fruits, carried them to the poor creature, for the last time; but on opening the door he perceived an extraordinary lustre in one corner of the room, and casting his eye on the place he was surprised to see a lady, whose noble and majestic air made him immediately conclude she was a princess of royal birth. Her habit was of purple satin, embroidered with pearls and diamonds; and advancing towards him with a gracious smile—

"Young prince," said she, "you find no longer your pet snake, but me, the Fairy Gentilla, ready to requite your generosity. For know, that we fairies live a hundred years in flourishing youth, without diseases, without trouble or pain; and this term being expired, we become snakes for eight days. During that time it is not in our power to prevent any misfortune that may befall us; and if we happen to be killed, we never revive again. But these eight days being expired, we resume our usual form, and recover our beauty, our power, and our riches. Now you know how much I am obliged to your goodness, and it is but just that I should repay my debt of gratitude: think how I can serve you, and depend on me."

The young prince, who had never conversed with a fairy till now, was so surprised that it was a long time before he could speak. But at length, making a profound reverence, "Madam," said he, "since I have had the honour to serve you, I know not any other happiness that I can wish for."

"I should be sorry," replied she, "not to be of service to you in something; consider, it is in my power to bestow on you long life, kingdoms, riches: to give you mines of diamonds, and houses full of gold; I can make you an excellent orator, poet, musician, and painter; or, if you desire it, a spirit of the air, the water, or the earth."

Here Leander interrupted her: "Permit me, madam," said he, "to ask you what benefit it would be to me to be a spirit?"

"Much," replied the fairy; "you would be invisible when you pleased, and might in an instant traverse the whole earth; you would be able to fly without wings, to descend into the abyss of the earth without dying, and walk at the bottom of the sea without being drowned; nor doors, nor windows, though fast shut and locked, could hinder you from entering anywhere: and whenever you had a mind, you might resume your natural form."

"Oh, madam!" cried Leander, "then let me be a spirit; I am going to travel, and should prefer it above all those other advantages you have so generously offered me."

Gentilla thereupon stroking his face three times, "Be a spirit," said she; and then, embracing him, she gave him a little red cap with a plume of feathers. "When you put on this cap, you shall be invisible; but when you take it off, you shall again become visible."

Leander, overjoyed, put his little red cap upon his head, and wished himself in the forest, that he might gather some wild roses which he had observed there: his body immediately became as light as thought; he flew through the window like a bird; though, in flying over the river, he was not without fear, lest he should fall into it, and the power of the fairy not be able to save him.

But he arrived in safety at the rose-bushes, plucked three roses, and returned immediately to his chamber ; presented his roses to the fairy, overjoyed that his first experiment had succeeded so well. She bade him keep the roses, for that one of them would supply him with money whenever he wanted it ; that if he put the other into his mistress's bosom, he would know whether she was faithful or not ; and that the third would keep him always in good health. Then, without staying to receive his thanks, she wished him success in his travels and disappeared.

Leander, infinitely pleased, settled his affairs, mounted the finest horse in the stable, called Gris-de-line, and attended by some of his servants in livery, made his return to court. Now you must know Furibon had given out that had it not been for his courage Leander would have murdered him when they were a-hunting ; so the king, being importuned by the queen, gave orders that Leander should be apprehended. But when he came, he showed so much courage and resolution that Furibon ran to the queen's chamber, and prayed her to order him to be seized. The queen, who was extremely diligent in everything that her son desired, went immediately to the king. Furibon, being impatient to know what would be resolved, followed her ; but stopped at the door, and laid his ear to the keyhole, putting his hair aside that he might the better hear what was said. At the same time, Leander entered the court-hall of the palace with his red cap upon his head, and perceiving Furibon listening at the door of the king's chamber, he took a nail and a hammer, and nailed his ear to the door. Furibon began to roar, so that the queen, hearing her son's voice, ran and opened the door, and, pulling it hastily, tore her son's ear from his head. Half out of her wits, she set him in her lap, took up his ear, kissed it, and clapped it again upon its place ; but the invisible Leander, seizing upon a handful of twigs, with which they corrected the king's little dogs, gave the queen several lashes upon her hands, and her son as many on the nose : upon which the queen cried out, " Murder ! murder ! " and the king looked about, and the people came running in ; but nothing was to be seen. Some cried that the queen was mad, and that her madness proceeded from her grief to see that her son had lost one ear ; and the king was as ready as any to believe it, so that when she came near him he avoided her, which made a very ridiculous scene. Leander, then leaving the chamber, went into the garden, and there, assuming his own shape, he boldly began to pluck the queen's cherries, apricots, strawberries, and flowers, though he knew she set such a high value on them, that it was as much as a man's life was worth to touch one. The gardeners, all amazed, came and told their majesties that Prince Leander was making havoc of all the fruits and flowers in the queen's garden.

" What insolence ! " said the queen : then turning to Furibon, " My pretty child, forget the pain of thy ear but for a moment, and fetch that vile wretch hither ; take our guards, both horse and foot, seize him, and punish him as he deserves."

Furibon, encouraged by his mother, and attended by a great number of armed soldiers, entered the garden, and saw Leander ; who, taking refuge under a tree, pelted them all with oranges. But when they came running towards him, thinking to have seized him, he was not to be seen : he had slipped behind Furibon, who was in a bad condition already. But Leander played him one trick more ; for he pushed him down upon the gravel-walk, and frightened him so that the soldiers had to take him up, carry him away, and put him to bed.

Satisfied with this revenge, he returned to his servants, who waited for him, and, giving them money, sent them back to his castle, that none might know the secret of his red cap and roses. As yet he had not determined whither to go ; however, he mounted his fine horse Gris-de-line, and, laying the reins upon his neck, let him take his own road : at length he arrived in a forest, where he stopped to shelter himself from the heat. He had not been above a minute there before he heard a lamentable noise of sighing and sobbing ; and looking about him, beheld a man, who ran, stopped, then ran again, sometimes crying, sometimes silent, then tearing his hair, then thumping his breast like some unfortunate madman. Yet he seemed to be both handsome and young : his garments had been magnificent, but he had torn them all to tatters. The prince, moved with compassion, made towards him, and mildly accosted him : "Sir," said he, "your condition appears so deplorable, that I must ask the cause of your sorrow, assuring you of every assistance in my power."

"Oh, sir," answered the young man, "nothing can cure my grief ; this day my dear mistress is to be sacrificed to a rich old ruffian of a husband who will make her miserable."

"Does she love you, then ? " asked Leander.

" I flatter myself so," answered the young man.

" Where is she ? " continued Leander.

" In a castle at the end of this forest," replied the lover.

"Very well," said Leander ; "stay you here till I come again, and in a little while I will bring you good news."

He then put on his little red cap, and wished himself in the castle. He had hardly got thither before he heard all sorts of music ; he entered into a great room, where the friends and kindred of the old man and the young lady were assembled. No one could look more amiable than she ; but the paleness of her complexion, the melancholy that appeared in her countenance, and the tears that now and then dropped, as it were by stealth, from her eyes, betrayed the trouble of her mind.

Leander now became invisible, and placed himself in a corner of the room. He soon perceived the father and mother of the bride ; and coming behind the mother's chair, whispered in her ear, " If you marry your daughter to that old dotard, before eight days are over you shall certainly die." The woman, frightened to hear such a terrible sentence pronounced upon her, and yet not know from whence it came, gave a loud shriek, and dropped upon the floor. Her husband asked what ailed her : she cried that she was a dead woman if the marriage of her daughter went forward, and therefore she would not consent to it for all the world. Her husband laughed at her, and called her a fool. But the invisible Leander, accosting the man, threatened him in the same way, which frightened him so terribly, that he also insisted on the marriage being broken off. When the lover complained, Leander trod hard upon his gouty toes, and rang such an alarum in his ears, that, not being able any longer to hear himself speak, away he limped, glad enough to go. The real lover soon appeared, and he and his fair mistress fell joyfully into one another's arms, the parents consenting to their union. Leander, assuming his own shape, appeared at the hall-door, as if he were a stranger drawn thither by the report of this extraordinary wedding.

From hence he travelled on, and came to a great city, where, upon his arrival, he understood there was a great and solemn procession, in order to shut up a young woman, against her will, among the vestal nuns. The prince was touched with compassion ; and thinking the best use he could make of his cap was to redress public wrongs and relieve the oppressed, he flew to the temple, where he saw the young woman, crowned with flowers, clad in white, and with her dishevelled hair flowing about her shoulders. Two of her brothers led her by each hand, and her mother followed her with a great crowd of men and women. Leander, being invisible, cried out, " Stop, stop, wicked brethren : stop, rash and inconsiderate mother ; if you proceed any farther, you shall be squeezed to death like so many frogs." They looked about, but could not conceive from whence these terrible menaces came. The brothers said it was only their sister's lover, who had hid himself in some hole; at which Leander, in wrath, took a long cudgel, and they had no reason to say the blows were not well laid on. The multitude fled, the vestals ran away, and Leander was left alone with the victim; immediately he pulled off his red cap, and asked her wherein he might serve her. She answered him, that there was a certain gentleman whom she would be glad to marry, but that he wanted an estate. Leander then shook his rose so long, that he supplied them with ten millions; after which they married, and lived happily together.

But his last adventure was the most agreeable. Entering into a wide forest, he heard lamentable cries. Looking about him every way, at length he spied four men well armed, who were carrying away by force a young lady, thirteen or fourteen years of age; upon which, making up to them as fast as he could, "What harm has that girl done?" said he.

"Ha, ha! my little master," cried he who seemed to be the ringleader of the rest, "who bade you inquire?"

"Let her alone," said Leander, "and go about your business."

"Oh yes, to be sure," cried they, laughing; whereupon the prince alighting, put on his red cap, not thinking it otherwise prudent to attack four who seemed strong enough to fight a dozen. One of them stayed to take care of the young lady, while the three others went after Gris-de-line, who gave them a great deal of unwelcome exercise.

Meantime the young lady continued her cries and complaints: "Oh, my dear princess," said she, "how happy was I in your palace! Did you but know my sad misfortune, you would send your Amazons to rescue poor Abricotina."

Leander, having listened to what she said, without delay seized the ruffian that held her, and bound him fast to a tree, before he had time or strength to defend himself. He then went to the second, and taking him by both arms, bound him in the same manner to another tree. In the meantime Abricotina made the best of her good fortune, and betook herself to her heels, not knowing which way she went. But Leander, missing her, called out to his horse Gris-de-line ; who, by two kicks with his hoof, rid himself of the two ruffians who had pursued him : one of them had his head broken ; and the other, three of his ribs. And now Leander only wanted to overtake Abricotina ; for he had thought her so handsome that he wished to see her again. He found her leaning against a tree. When she saw Gris-de-line coming towards her, " How lucky am I ! " cried she ; " this pretty little horse will carry me to the Palace of Pleasure." Leander heard her, though she saw him not : he rode up to her ; Gris-de-line stopped, and when Abricotina mounted him, Leander clasped her in his arms, and placed her gently before him. Oh, how great was Abricotina's fear to feel herself fast embraced, and yet see nobody ! She durst not stir, and shut her eyes for fear of seeing a spirit. But Leander took off his little cap : " How comes it, fair Abricotina," said he, " that you are afraid of me, who delivered you out of the hands of the ruffians ? "

With that she opened her eyes, and knowing him again, " Oh, sir," said she, " I am infinitely obliged to you ; but I was afraid, for I felt myself held fast, and could see no one."

" Surely," replied Leander ; " the danger you have been in has disturbed you, and cast a mist before your eyes."

Abricotina would not seem to doubt him, though she was otherwise extremely sensible. And after they had talked for some time of indifferent things, Leander

178

requested her to tell him her age, her country, and by
what accident she fell into the hands of the ruffians.

"Know then, sir," said she, "there was a certain very
great fairy married to a prince who wearied of her ; she
therefore banished him from her presence, and established
herself and daughter in the Island of Calm Delights.   The
princess, who is my mistress, being very fair, has many
lovers—among others, one named Furibon, whom she
detests : he it was whose ruffians seized me to-day when I
was wandering in search of a stray parrot.   Accept, noble
prince, my best thanks for your valour, which I shall
never forget."

Leander said how happy he was to have served her,
and asked if he could not obtain admission into the island.
Abricotina assured him this was impossible, and therefore
he had better forget all about it.   While they were thus
conversing, they came to the bank of a large river :
Abricotina alighting with a nimble jump from the horse—

"Farewell, sir," said she to the prince, making a
profound reverence, "I wish you every happiness."

"And I," said Leander, "wish that I may now and
then have a small share in your remembrance."

So saying, he galloped away, and soon entered into
the thickest part of a wood, near a river, where he un-
bridled and unsaddled Gris-de-line ; then, putting on his
little cap, wished himself in the Island of Calm Delights,
and his wish was immediately accomplished.

The palace was of pure gold, and stood upon pillars
of crystal and precious stones, which represented the
zodiac, and all the wonders of nature ; all the arts and
sciences ; the sea, with all the variety of fish therein
contained ; the earth, with all the various creatures which
it produces ; the chases of Diana and her nymphs ; the
noble exercises of the Amazons ; the amusements of a
country life ; flocks of sheep with their shepherds and
dogs ; the toils of agriculture, harvesting, gardening.

And among all this variety of representations there was neither man nor boy to be seen—not so much as a little winged Cupid : so highly had the princess been incensed against her inconstant husband, as not to show the least favour to his fickle sex.

"Abricotina did not deceive me," said Leander to himself ; "they have banished from hence the very idea of men ; now let us see what they have lost by it." With that he entered into the palace, and at every step he took, he met with objects so wonderful, that when he had once fixed his eyes upon them, he had much ado to take them off again. He viewed a vast number of these apartments, some full of china, no less fine than curious ; others lined with porcelain, so delicate that the walls were quite transparent. Coral, jasper, agates, and cornelians adorned the rooms of state, and the presence-chamber was one entire mirror. The throne was one single pearl, hollowed like a shell ; the princess sat, surrounded by her maidens, none of whom could compare with herself. In her was all the innocent sweetness of youth, joined to the dignity of maturity ; in truth, she was perfection ; and so thought the invisible Leander.

Not seeing Abricotina, she asked where she was. Upon that, Leander, being very desirous to speak, assumed the tone of a parrot, for there were many in the room ; and addressing himself invisibly to the princess :

"Most charming princess," said he, "Abricotina will return immediately. She was in great danger of being carried away from this palace, but for a young prince who rescued her."

The princess was surprised at the parrot, his answer was so extremely pertinent.

"You are very rude, little parrot," said the princess ; "and Abricotina, when she comes, shall chastise you for it."

"I shall not be chastised," answered Leander, still

180

"These beasts of prey were instantly turned into three little lambs." (*Page 200*)

WARWICK GOBLE

"The king took the beautiful maiden on his own horse and conducted her to his castle." (*Page 222*)

WARWICK GOBLE.

counterfeiting the parrot's voice; " moreover, she will let you know the great desire that stranger had to be admitted into this palace, that he might convince you of the falsehood of those ideas which you have conceived against his sex."

" In truth, pretty parrot," cried the princess, " it is a pity you are not every day so diverting; I should love you dearly."

" Ah! if prattling will please you, madam," replied Leander, " I will prate from morning till night."

" But," continued the princess, " how shall I be sure my parrot is not a sorcerer ? "

" He is more in love than any sorcerer can be," replied the prince.

At this moment Abricotina entered the room, and falling at her lovely mistress's feet, gave her a full account of what had befallen her, and described the prince in the most glowing colours.

" I should have hated all men," added she, " had I not seen him ! Oh, madam, how charming he is ! His air and all his behaviour have something in them so noble ; and though whatever he spoke was infinitely pleasing, yet I think I did well in not bringing him hither."

To this the princess said nothing, but she asked Abricotina a hundred other questions concerning the prince ; whether she knew his name, his country, his birth, from whence he came, and whither he was going ; and after this she fell into a profound thoughtfulness.

Leander observed everything, and continued to chatter as he had begun—

" Abricotina is ungrateful, madam," said he ; " that poor stranger will die for grief if he sees you not."

" Well, parrot, let him die," answered the princess, with a sigh ; " and since thou undertakest to reason like a person of wit, and not like a little bird, I forbid thee to talk to me any more of this unknown person."

Leander was overjoyed to find that Abricotina's and the parrot's discourse had made such an impression on the princess. He looked upon her with pleasure and delight. "Can it be," said he to himself, "that the masterpiece of nature, that the wonder of our age, should be confined eternally in an island, and no mortal dare to approach her? But," continued he, "wherefore am I concerned that others are banished hence, since I have the happiness to be with her, to see her, to hear and to admire her; nay more, to love her above all the women in the universe?"

It was late, and the princess retired into a large room of marble and porphyry, where several bubbling fountains refreshed the air with an agreeable coolness. As soon as she entered, the music began, a sumptuous supper was served up, and the birds from several aviaries on each side of the room, of which Abricotina had the chief care, opened their little throats in the most agreeable manner.

Leander had travelled a journey long enough to give him a good appetite, which made him draw near the table, where the very smell of such viands was agreeable and refreshing. The princess had a curious tabby-cat, for which she had a great kindness. This cat one of the maids of honour held in her arms, saying, "Madam, Bluet is hungry!" With that a chair was presently brought for the cat; for he was a cat of quality, and had a necklace of pearl about his neck. He was served on a gold plate, with a laced napkin before him; and the plate being supplied with meat, Bluet sat with the solemn importance of an alderman.

"Ho, ho!" cried Leander to himself; "an idle tabby malkin, that perhaps never caught a mouse in his life, and I daresay is not descended from a better family than myself, has the honour to sit at table with my mistress: I would fain know whether he loves her so well as I do."

Saying this, he placed himself in the chair with the cat

upon his knee, for nobody saw him, because he had his little red cap on; finding Bluet's plate well supplied with partridge, quails, and pheasants, he made so free with them, that whatever was set before master puss disappeared in a trice. The whole court said no cat ever ate with a better appetite. There were excellent ragouts, and the prince made use of the cat's paw to taste them; but he sometimes pulled his paw too roughly, and Bluet, not understanding raillery, began to mew and be quite out of patience. The princess observing it, "Bring that fricassee and that tart to poor Bluet," said she; "see how he cries to have them."

Leander laughed to himself at the pleasantness of this adventure; but he was very thirsty, not being accustomed to make such large meals without drinking. By the help of the cat's paw he got a melon, with which he somewhat quenched his thirst; and when supper was quite over, he went to the beaufet, and took two bottles of delicious wine.

The princess now retired into her boudoir, ordering Abricotina to follow her and make fast the door; but they could not keep out Leander, who was there as soon as they. However, the princess, believing herself alone with her confidante—

"Abricotina," said she, "tell me truly, did you exaggerate in your description of the unknown prince, for methinks it is impossible he should be as amiable as you say?"

"Madam," replied the damsel, "if I have failed in anything, it was in coming short of what was due to him."

The princess sighed, and was silent for a time; then resuming her speech: "I am glad," said she, "thou didst not bring him with thee."

"But, madam," answered Abricotina, who was a cunning girl, and already penetrated her mistress's thoughts, "suppose he had come to admire the wonders of these beautiful mansions, what harm could he have done us? Will you live eternally unknown in a corner of the world, concealed from the rest of human kind? Of what use is all your grandeur, pomp, magnificence, if nobody sees it?"

"Hold thy peace, prattler," replied the princess, "and do not disturb that happy repose which I have enjoyed so long."

Abricotina durst make no reply; and the princess, having waited her answer for some time, asked her whether she had anything to say. Abricotina then said she thought it was to very little purpose her mistress having sent her picture to the courts of several princes, where it only served to make those who saw it miserable; that every one would be desirous to marry her, and as she could not marry them all, indeed none of them, it would make them desperate.

"Yet for all that," said the princess, "I could wish my picture were in the hands of this same stranger."

"Oh, madam," answered Abricotina, "is not his desire to see you violent enough already; would you augment it?"

"Yes," cried the princess; "a certain impulse of vanity, which I was never sensible of till now, has bred this foolish fancy in me."

Leander heard all this discourse, and lost not a tittle of what she said; some of her expressions gave him hope, others absolutely destroyed it. The princess presently asked Abricotina whether she had seen anything extraordinary during her short travels?

"Madam," said she, "I passed through one forest where I saw certain creatures that resembled little children: they skip and dance upon the trees like squirrels; they are very ugly, but have wonderful agility and address."

"I wish I had one of them," said the princess: "but if they are so nimble as you say they are, it is impossible to catch one."

Leander, who passed through the same forest, knew what Abricotina meant, and presently wished himself in the place. He caught a dozen of little monkeys, some bigger, some less, and all of different colours, and with much ado put them into a large sack; then, wishing himself at Paris, where, he had heard, a man might have everything for money, he went and bought a little gold chariot. He taught six green monkeys to draw it; they were harnessed with fine traces of flame-coloured morocco leather. He went to another place, where he met with two monkeys of merit; the most pleasant of which was called Briscambril, the other Pierceforest—both very spruce and well educated. He dressed Briscambril like a king, and placed him in the coach; Pierceforest he made the coachman: the others were dressed like pages; all which he put into his sack, coach and all.

The princess not being gone to bed, heard a rumbling of a little coach in the long gallery; at the same time, her ladies came to tell her that the king of the dwarfs was arrived, and the chariot immediately entered her chamber with all the monkey train. The country monkeys began to show a thousand tricks, which far surpassed those of Briscambril and Pierceforest. To say the truth, Leander conducted the whole machine. He drew the chariot where Briscambril sat arrayed as a king, and making him hold a box of diamonds in his hand, he presented it with a becoming grace to the princess. The princess's surprise may be easily imagined. Moreover, Briscambril made a sign for Pierceforest to come and dance with him. The most celebrated dancers were not to be compared with them in activity. But the princess, troubled that she could not guess from whence this curious present came, dismissed the dancers sooner than she would otherwise have done, though she was extremely pleased with them.

Leander, satisfied with having seen the delight the princess had taken in beholding the monkeys, thought of nothing now but to get a little repose, which he greatly wanted. He stayed some time in the great gallery; afterwards, going down a pair of stairs, and finding a door open, he entered into an apartment the most delightful that ever was seen. There was in it a bed of cloth of gold, enriched with pearls, intermixed with rubies and emeralds; for by this time there appeared daylight sufficient for him to view and admire the magnificence of this sumptuous furniture. Having made fast the door, he composed himself to sleep. Next day he rose very early, and looking about on every side, he spied a painter's pallet, with colours ready prepared and pencils. Remembering what the princess had said to Abricotina touching her own portrait, he immediately (for he could paint as well as the most excellent masters) seated himself before a mirror, and drew his own picture first; then, in an oval, that of the princess. He had all her features so strong in his imagination, that he had no occasion for her sitting; and as his desire to please her had set him to work, never did portrait bear a stronger resemblance. He had painted himself upon one knee, holding the princess's picture in one hand, and in the other a label with this inscription: "She is better in my heart." When the princess went into her cabinet, she was amazed to see the portrait of a man; and she fixed her eyes upon it with so much the more surprise, because she also saw her own with it, and because the words which were written upon the label afforded her ample room for curiosity. She persuaded herself that it was Abricotina's doing; and all she desired to know was, whether the portrait were real or imaginary. Rising in haste, she called Abricotina, while the invisible Leander, with his

little red cap, slipped into the cabinet, impatient to know
what passed. The princess bid Abricotina look upon the
picture, and tell her what she thought of it.

After she had viewed it, "I protest," said she, " 'tis
the picture of that generous stranger to whom I am
indebted for my life. Yes, yes, I am sure it is he; his
very features, shape, and hair."

"Thou pretendest surprise," said the princess, "but I
know it was thou thyself who put it there."

"Who! I, madam?" replied Abricotina; "I protest,
I never saw the picture before in my life. Should I be
so bold as to conceal from your knowledge a thing that
so nearly concerns you? And by what miracle could
I come by it? I never could paint, nor did any man
ever enter this place; yet here he is painted with you."

"Some spirit, then, must have brought it hither,"
cried the princess.

"How I tremble for fear, madam!" said Abricotina.
"Was it not rather some lover? And therefore, if you
will take my advice, let us burn it immediately."

"'Twere a pity to burn it," cried the princess,
sighing; "a finer piece, methinks, cannot adorn my
cabinet." And saying these words, she cast her eyes
upon it. But Abricotina continued obstinate in her
opinion that it ought to be burnt, as a thing that could
not come there but by the power of magic.

"And these words—'She is better in my heart,'" said
the princess; "must we burn them too?"

"No favour must be shown to anything," said
Abricotina, "not even to your own portrait."

Abricotina ran away immediately for some fire, while
the princess went to look out at the window. Leander,
unwilling to let his performance be burnt, took this
opportunity to convey it away without being perceived.
He had hardly quitted the cabinet, when the princess
turned about to look once more upon that enchanting

picture, which had so delighted her. But how was she surprised to find it gone! She sought for it all the room over; and Abricotina returning, was no less surprised than her mistress; so that this last adventure put them both in the most terrible fright.

Leander took great delight in hearing and seeing his incomparable mistress; even though he had to eat every day at her table with the tabby-cat, who fared never the worse for that; but his satisfaction was far from being complete, seeing he durst neither speak nor show himself; and he knew it was not a common thing for ladies to fall in love with persons invisible.

The princess had a universal taste for amusement. One day, she was saying to her attendants that it would give her great pleasure to know how the ladies were dressed in all the courts of the universe. There needed no more words to send Leander all over the world. He wished himself in China, where he bought the richest stuffs he could lay his hands on, and got patterns of all the court fashions. From thence he flew to Siam, where he did the same; in three days he travelled over all the four parts of the world, and, from time to time, brought what he bought to the Palace of Calm Delights, and hid it all in a chamber, which he kept always locked. When he had thus collected together all the rarities he could meet with—for he never wanted money, his rose always supplying him—he went and bought five or six dozen of dolls, which he caused to be dressed at Paris, the place in the world where most regard is paid to fashions. They were all dressed differently, and as magnificent as could be, and Leander placed them all in the princess's closet. When she entered it, she was agreeably surprised to see such a company of little mutes, every one decked with watches, bracelets, diamond buckles or necklaces; and the most remarkable of them held a picture-box in its hand, which the princess opening, found it contained Leander's portrait. She gave a loud shriek, and looking upon Abricotina, "There have appeared of late," said she, "so many wonders in this place, that I know not what to think of them :—my birds are all grown witty ; I cannot so much as wish, but presently I have my desires ; twice have I now seen the portrait of him who rescued thee from the ruffians ; and here are silks of all sorts, diamonds, embroideries, laces, and an infinite number of other rarities. What fairy is it that takes such care to pay me these agreeable civilities ?"

Leander was overjoyed to hear and see her so much interested about his picture, and calling to mind that there was in a grotto which she often frequented a certain pedestal, on which a Diana, not yet finished, was to be erected, on this pedestal he resolved to place himself, crowned with laurel, and holding a lyre in his hand, on which he played like another Apollo. He most anxiously waited the princess's retiring to the grotto, which she did every day since her thoughts had been taken up with this unknown person ; for what Abricotina had said, joined to the sight of the picture, had almost destroyed her repose : her lively humour changed into a pensive melancholy, and she grew a great lover of solitude. When she entered the grotto, she made a sign that nobody should follow her, so that her young damsels dispersed themselves into the neighbouring walks. The princess threw herself upon a bank of green turf, sighed, wept, and even talked, but so softly that Leander could not hear what she said. He had put his red cap on, that she might not see him at first ; but having taken it off, she beheld him standing on the pedestal. At first she took him for a real statue, for he observed exactly the attitude in which he had placed himself, without moving so much as a finger. She beheld with a kind of pleasure intermixed with fear, but pleasure soon dispelled her fear, and she continued to view the pleasing figure, which so exactly resembled life. The prince having tuned his lyre, began to play ; at which the princess, greatly surprised, could not resist the fear that seized her ; she grew pale, and fell into a swoon. Leander leaped from the pedestal, and putting on his little red cap, that he might not be perceived, took the princess in his arms, and gave her all the assistance that his zeal and tenderness could inspire. At length she opened her charming eyes, and looked about in search of him, but she could perceive nobody ; yet she felt somebody who held her hands, kissed them, and be-dewed them with his tears. It was a long time before she durst speak, and her spirits were in a confused agitation between fear and hope. She was afraid of the spirit, but loved the figure of the unknown. At length she said : "Courtly invisible, why are you not the person I desire you should be ?" At these words, Leander was going to declare himself, but durst not do it yet ; "For," thought he, "if I again affright the object I adore, and make her fear me, she will not love me." This con-sideration caused him to keep silence.

The princess then, believing herself alone, called Abricotina and told her all the wonders of the animated statue ; that it had played divinely, and that the invisible person had greatly assisted her when she lay in a swoon.

"What pity 'tis," said she, "that this person should be so frightful, for nothing can be more amiable or accept-able than his behaviour !"

"Who told you, madam," answered Abricotina, "that he is frightful? If he is the youth who saved me, he is beautiful as Cupid himself."

"If Cupid and the unknown are the same," replied the princess, blushing, "I could be content to love Cupid ; but alas ! how far am I from such a happiness ! I love a mere shadow ; and this fatal picture, joined to what thou hast told me, have inspired me with inclinations so contrary to the precepts which I received from my mother, that I am daily afraid of being punished for them."

"Oh! madam," said Abricotina, interrupting her, "have you not troubles enough already? Why should you anticipate afflictions which may never come to pass?"

It is easy to imagine what pleasure Leander took in this conversation.

In the meantime, the little Furibon, still enamoured of the princess whom he had never seen, expected with impatience the return of the four servants whom he had sent to the Island of Calm Delights. One of them at last came back, and after he had given the prince a particular account of what had passed, told him that the island was defended by Amazons, and that unless he sent a very powerful army, it would be impossible to get into it. The king his father was dead, and Furibon was now lord of all: disdaining, therefore, any repulse, he raised an army of four hundred thousand men, and put himself at the head of them, appearing like another Tom Thumb upon a war-horse. Now, when the Amazons perceived his mighty host, they gave the princess notice of it, who immediately despatched away her trusty Abricotina to the kingdom of the fairies, to beg her mother's instructions as to what she should do to drive the little Furibon from her territories. But Abricotina found the fairy in an angry humour.

"Nothing that my daughter does," said she, "escapes my knowledge. The Prince Leander is now in her palace; he loves her, and she has a tenderness for him. All my cares and precepts have not been able to guard her from the tyranny of love, and she is now under its fatal dominion. But it is the decree of destiny, and I must submit: therefore, Abricotina, begone! nor let me hear a word more of a daughter whose behaviour has so much displeased me."

Abricotina returned with these ill tidings, whereat the princess was almost distracted; and this was soon perceived by Leander, who was near her, though she did not see him.

He beheld her grief with the greatest pain.   However, he durst not then open his lips ; but recollecting that Furibon was exceedingly covetous, he thought that, by giving him a sum of money, he might perhaps prevail with him to retire.   Thereupon, he dressed himself like an Amazon, and wished himself in the forest, to catch his horse.   He had no sooner called him than Gris-de-line came leaping, prancing, and neighing for joy, for he was grown quite weary of being so long absent from his dear master ; but when he beheld him dressed as a woman, he hardly knew him.   However, at the sound of his voice, he suffered the prince to mount, and they soon arrived in the camp of Furibon, where they gave notice that a lady was come to speak with him from the Princess of Calm Delights. Immediately the little fellow put on his royal robes, and having placed himself upon his throne, he looked like a great toad counterfeiting a king.

Leander harangued him, and told him that the princess, preferring a quiet and peaceable life to the fatigues of war, had sent to offer his majesty as much money as he pleased to demand, provided he would suffer her to continue in peace ; but if he refused her proposal, she would omit no means that might serve for her defence.   Furibon replied that he took pity on her, and would grant her the honour of his protection ; but that he demanded a hundred thousand thousand millions of pounds, and without which he would not return to his kingdom.   Leander answered that such a vast sum would be too long a-counting, and therefore, if he would say how many rooms full he desired to have, the princess was generous and rich enough to satisfy him.   Furibon was astonished to hear that, instead of entreating, she would rather offer more ; and it came into his wicked mind to take all the money he could get, and then seize the Amazon and kill her, that she might never return to her mistress.   He told Leander, therefore, that he would have thirty chambers of gold, all full to the ceiling. Leander, being conducted into the chambers, took his rose and shook it, till every room was filled with all sorts of coin. Furibon was in an ecstasy, and the more gold he saw the greater was his desire to get hold of the Amazon; so that when all the rooms were full, he commanded his guards to seize her, alleging she had brought him counterfeit money. Immediately Leander put on his little red cap and disappeared. The guards, believing that the lady had escaped, ran out and left Furibon alone; when Leander, availing himself of the opportunity, took the tyrant by the hair, and twisted his head off with the same ease he would a pullet's; nor did the little wretch of a king see the hand that killed him.

Leander having got his enemy's head, wished himself in the Palace of Calm Delights, where he found the princess walking, and with grief considering the message which her mother had sent her, and on the means to repel Furibon. Suddenly she beheld a head hanging in the air, with nobody to hold it. This prodigy astonished her so, that she could not tell what to think of it; but her amazement was increased when she saw the head laid at her feet, and heard a voice utter these words:

> "Charming princess, cease your fear
> Of Furibon: whose head see here."

Abricotina, knowing Leander's voice, cried, "I protest, madam, the invisible person who speaks is the very stranger that rescued me."

The princess seemed astonished, but yet pleased.

"Oh," said she, "if it be true that the invisible and the stranger are the same person, I confess I shall be glad to make him my acknowledgments."

Leander, still invisible, replied, "I will yet do more to deserve them"; and so saying he returned to Furibon's army, where the report of the king's death was already spread throughout the camp. As soon as Leander

O

appeared there in his usual habit, everybody knew him; all the officers and soldiers surrounded him, uttering the loudest acclamations of joy. In short, they acknowledged him for their king, and that the crown of right belonged to him; for which he thanked them, and, as the first mark of his royal bounty, divided the thirty rooms of gold among the soldiers. This done, he returned to his princess, ordering the army to march back into his kingdom.

The princess was gone to bed. Leander, therefore, retired into his own apartment, for he was very sleepy— so sleepy that he forgot to bolt his door; and so it happened that the princess, rising early to taste the morning air, chanced to enter into this very chamber, and was greatly astonished to find a young prince asleep upon the bed. She took a full view of him, and was convinced that he was the person whose picture she had in her diamond box. "It is impossible," said she, "that this should be a spirit; for can spirits sleep? Is this a body composed of air and fire, without substance, as Abricotina told me?" She softly touched his hair, and heard him breathe, and looked at him as if she could have looked for ever. While she was thus occupied, her mother, the fairy, entered with such a dreadful noise that Leander started out of his sleep. But how deeply was he afflicted, to behold his beloved princess in the most deplorable condition! Her mother dragged her by the hair, and loaded her with a thousand bitter reproaches. In what grief and consternation were the two young lovers, who saw themselves now upon the point of being separated for ever! The princess durst not open her lips, but cast her eyes upon Leander, as if to beg his assistance. He judged rightly, that he ought not to deal rudely with a power superior to his own, and therefore he sought, by his eloquence and submission, to move the incensed fairy. He ran to her, threw himself at her feet, and besought her to have pity upon a young prince, who would never change in his affection for her daughter. The princess, encouraged, also embraced her mother's knees, and declared that without Leander she should never be happy.

"Happy!" cried the fairy, "you know not the miseries of love, nor the treacheries of which lovers are capable. They bewitch us only to poison our lives; I have known it by experience; and why will you suffer the same?"

"Is there no exception, madam?" replied Leander, and his countenance showed him to be one.

But neither tears nor entreaties could move the implacable fairy; and it is very probable that she would never have pardoned them, had not the lovely Gentilla appeared at that instant in the chamber, more brilliant than the sun. Embracing the old fairy—

"Dear sister," said she, "I am persuaded you cannot have forgotten the good office I did you when, after your unhappy marriage, you besought a readmittance into Fairyland: since then I never desired any favour at your hands, but now the time is come. Pardon, then, this lovely princess; consent to her nuptials with this young prince. I will engage he shall be ever constant to her; the thread of their days shall be spun of gold and silk; they shall live to complete your happiness; and I will never forget the obligation you lay upon me."

"Charming Gentilla," cried the fairy, "I consent to whatever you desire. Come, my dear children, and receive my love." So saying, she embraced them both.

Abricotina, just then entering, cast her eyes upon Leander: she knew him again, and saw he was perfectly happy, at which she, too, was quite satisfied.

"Prince," condescendingly said the fairy-mother, "I will remove the Island of Calm Delights into your own kingdom, live with you myself, and do you great services."

Whether or not Prince Leander appreciated this offer, he bowed low and assured his mother-in-law that no favour could be equal to the one he had that day received from her hands. This short compliment pleased the fairy exceedingly, for she belonged to those ancient days when people used to stand a whole day upon one leg complimenting one another. The nuptials were performed in a most splendid manner, and the young prince and princess lived together happily for many years, beloved by all around them.

THE WOODCUTTER'S DAUGHTER

THERE was once a poor woodcutter, very miserable, though prudent and industrious; he had a wife and three grown-up sons, yet their united labours scarcely sufficed for bread. No hope appeared of improving his lot, when he was one day fortunate enough to save the life of his master when attacked by robbers in the forest.

This master was not ungrateful; he desired the woodcutter to repair to him on the following day in order to receive a reward. The poor man did not fail, hoping to gain two or three crowns; for it appeared so natural to defend an unarmed man that he attached little value to his services, considering his own danger not worth a thought. He put on his best array, shaved, and made many reverences to the porter and the numerous lackeys previous to an introduction to the master, who was much more polite than the valets.

"Well, Thomas," said he, "how can I recompense what you have done for me? Without your assistance I should have perished; and as my life is a very happy one, I value it accordingly."

Poor Thomas was at a loss how to reply; he stammered out, "My Lord—your Grace," but could get no further.

The master, in order to relieve the poor man, interrupted him thus: "I understand better than yourself, perhaps, what would suit you; I would not wish to draw you from your native condition, for I believe that none is more truly happy ; but I present to you and your children's children, in perpetuity, the cottage which you inhabit in the forest. You and they shall have the power of cutting as much wood every year as you can use ; you shall work for yourself ; and if your sons like to hunt, all the game which they kill shall be for their own use. I only exact that you sell nothing, and that while possessing every comfort, you seek not to quit your peaceful obscurity."

Thomas was so astonished that he could find no words to express his gratitude. He came home to his wife, who heartily shared his joy. The sons immediately set off for a large supply of faggots, and made a great fire ; but when they had been thoroughly warmed, Mother Thomas began to say what a pity it was they could make no use of all the wood which was not burned.

"An idea has just struck me," replied the husband ; "our master gives us all we can *use* ; these are his own words,—very well ; I shall be able to use enough to bring us in a pretty little income !"

"How ? " said his wife.

"When I was a boy," rejoined the woodcutter, "my father taught me to make wooden shoes ; and I made them so light and so neat, that they were everywhere sought for. What need now prevent me from exercising this trade ? James shall cut wood in the forest, Peter shall kill game for dinner, and Paul, who has not the least brains of the three, shall go to sell my merchandise at the neighbouring town. This will be a public benefit, by enabling the poor about us to dress with more decency and comfort, and it will also serve to furnish our own cottage, of which we shall make a little palace."

The boys, who were present, highly relished this idea. Mother Thomas, who was rather inclined to gluttony, made the most of the game which Peter provided. A little labour, good cheer, a blazing fire, and perfect family concord, rendered this family the happiest in the world. The master came to the cottage, and seeing them so united and industrious, encouraged the trade of the wooden shoes, which increased their comforts without exposing them to the vices attendant on avarice and luxury.

But happiness such as this seldom remains permanent. A flock of furious wolves appeared in the forest ; every day they devoured either helpless children or travellers ; they tore up the roots of the trees, attacking even each other, while their wild howlings were heard night and day in the cottage of the woodcutter.

Mother Thomas would no longer suffer her boys to leave home ; and when they did go in spite of her, she remained watching at the door, refusing either to eat or drink until they returned.

Such a situation was deplorable ; when at length the young men, who were very brave, resolved to deliver themselves and their master. Taking arms, in case they should be attacked, they went into the forest and digged deep pits, covering them with a little earth, laid over some branches of trees ; and during this heavy labour, which lasted several days, they lighted great fires around them, in order to hinder the wolves from approaching.

Success crowned their enterprise, for in returning to the spot at sunrise, they perceived that one of the pits had been broken into during the night, and that it was now quite uncovered. They charged their muskets, and each were disputing the honour of first firing, when they heard issue from the depths below, a mild and supplicating voice imploring assistance.

" What shall we do? " said Peter ; " assuredly that is not the roaring of a wolf ; it is, perhaps, some unfortunate little wandering child. How lucky that we did not draw the trigger ! "

They approached, and distinguished a beautiful lady richly dressed, wearing on her head a cluster of diamonds, which shone like a star. She appeared very young, and was trembling with cold. Much rain had fallen during the night, and her robe, of silver gauze, was dabbled in mud and water ; her fair and tender hands were all dirty, which seemed to vex her even more than the dangers she had experienced. She continued, however, to struggle and to make signs for relief, when three enormous wolves appeared at a distance. The brothers looked at each other expressively, like people who feel that all is lost, but who resolve to do their duty. They had a cord about them, which Peter fastened round his body, and let himself down into the pit. He took the beautiful lady on his shoulders, while his brothers assisted in drawing them up. They then stretched her on the grass, for she had fainted ; and now the wolves had just reached them,—when, lo ! these beasts of prey were instantly turned into three little lambs, and licked the feet of the lady, who slowly returned to life.

" My good lads," said she to the woodcutters, " fear nothing. From henceforth no more dangerous animals than these shall trouble you. But I owe you a still greater recompense : lead me to your father, I wish to felicitate him on the generosity and bravery of his sons."

The poor youths were so astonished by this adventure, that they felt unable to reply ; but they respectfully lifted her long train from the ground, it having now recovered all its splendour.

The three lambs followed, skipping and frolicking before them—they seemed to know the way ; and Mother Thomas, who sat at the door looking out for her children, was not a little surprised to behold their companion.

She had, however, presence of mind to invite her noble guest to enter and rest ; much ashamed of having nothing better to offer than a straw chair, and some spring-water, which was in a very clean pitcher on the dresser.

" I shall willingly rest an hour with you," said the lady.

"Although you now see me for the first time, I am one of your best friends, of which I shall give you a proof. I accept a glass of water, on condition that your husband and children will also pledge me."

A glance of Mother Thomas's eye directed her family ; they each sought their ordinary drinking-cup, which was of wood, and then bent the neck of the pitcher ; but what was their astonishment to perceive the vessel turn into wrought-silver in their hands, and to taste, instead of water, a liquor so delicious, that when the woodcutter and his wife had drunk, they felt themselves ten years younger than before !

They threw themselves at the feet of the beautiful lady, in terror ; for a natural instinct made them feel that great power is always more or less to be dreaded, even when employed in acts of beneficence. The lady meanwhile kindly raised them, and having spoken of the courage and generosity of their sons, who exposed themselves to the fury of wolves rather than take flight and abandon her, she said that her name was the Fairy Coquette, and that she would willingly relate her history.

"Previously, madam," said the woodcutter, "will you have the goodness to tell me, what is a fairy ? During thirty years that I have inhabited this forest, I have heard of the devil, of the Were wolf, of the monster of Gévaudan, but never have I heard of fairies."

"We exist, notwithstanding," replied Coquette, "but not in all ages, nor in all countries. We are supernatural beings, to whom has been imparted a portion of supernatural power, which we make use of for good or evil, according to our natural disposition ; in that alone consists our resemblance to men."

The woodcutter, who was very simple, understood little of this explanation ; but, like many others, had a profound respect for what he could not comprehend. He bowed down to the ground, and only requested the fairy to inform him, why a supernatural being, so highly gifted, could have fallen into a pit prepared for wolves.

"It is," replied Coquette, "because I have an enemy still more powerful than myself, the Enchanter Barabapatapouf, the most wicked ogre in the world ; he has but three teeth, three hairs, one eye, and is fifteen feet high. With all these charms he happened to fall in love with me, and merely for mischief I affected to accept him. He then invited his friends to the nuptials ; when, to his great mortification, I took them to witness that I would never be the wife of such a monster. Barabapatapouf was deeply incensed, swore to be revenged, and has never lost an opportunity of keeping his word. I should have remained three days in that horrible pit but for the generosity of your children."

"They have done nothing more than their duty," replied the woodcutter.

"I must also do mine," said Coquette, "but my power is limited. I can satisfy but two wishes, and it is necessary that each of you should choose freely, unbiassed by the other. You must separate accordingly, and to-morrow, at early dawn, come to inform me what you have all resolved on during the night."

Mother Thomas was very uneasy in thinking how she could accommodate the fairy, for neither her children's beds nor her own were worthy of offering to such a grand lady ; but Coquette desired her to feel at ease, as she would provide everything needful. She then drew forth some grains of sand, which she scattered on the floor. Instantly there arose on the spot a bed of rose-leaves three feet high ; the bolster was of violets, heartsease, and orange flowers, all breathing delicious perfumes ; and the counterpane, entirely composed of butterflies' wings, exhibited colours so brilliant and varied that one could never be weary of examining it. The three lambs which had followed the fairy lay down at her feet, and as the room was rather damp, they gently warmed it with their breath, with a care and intelligence almost human. The woodcutter and his sons felt so surprised at all these wonders, that they imagined themselves dreaming. Coquette warned Mother Thomas that if she should speak once to her husband before she again saw her, the wishes could not be realised. The strictest injunctions were indeed necessary, to prevent their communicating on a subject which interested both so deeply. When day appeared, Coquette summoned them to her presence.

The woodcutter first came, and said, with his usual simplicity, that he never could have believed it so difficult to form a wish. Till that moment he had considered himself happy, but now, finding it possible to obtain one thing, he desired a thousand. Wearied with the fatigue of thought, he had fallen asleep without coming to a determination ; but seeing in his dreams five purses filled with gold, it seemed as if one were for him, one for his wife, and one for each of his children.

" Well," said Coquette, " these purses are apparently your desire ; go then to the bin where you deposit your bread, and you will find them. Only say how many pounds you wish them to contain."

" Oh, if there were but a hundred pounds in each," replied Thomas, " that would be sufficient to extend our little commerce, and send our wooden shoes to China itself."

" Your wish is accomplished," said the fairy ; " go away, and permit your wife to come in her turn."

The good dame had also passed a sleepless night, and had never before been so much agitated or so unhappy ; sometimes she wished for riches, and then thought, riches would not prevent her from dying—so she had better wish that she might live a hundred years. Now one idea filled her mind, now another : it seemed as if the fairy should have given her at least a month to deliberate. At last she suddenly said, "Madam Fairy, I am very old, and what I desire most is a daughter, to assist me in household management and to keep me company : my husband almost lives in the woods and leaves me at break of day ; my sons also go about their business ; we are without neighbours, and I have nobody to speak to."

"Be it so," said the fairy ; "you shall have the prettiest daughter imaginable, and she shall speak from her birth, in order that no time may be lost. Call your husband and sons ; I hope to find all parties content."

The little family assembled, but harmony was not the result of their communications. The young men thought their father's wish quite pitiful, and the woodcutter by no means relished the idea of another child. The fairy, however, provided an excellent breakfast, and the wine reanimated his spirits.

"Now I promise," said Coquette, "that you shall have a daughter, who at the moment of her birth will be endowed with the figure and the intelligence of twelve years old. Call her Rose, for her complexion shall shame the flower which bears that name."

"And *I* pronounce that she shall also be as black as ebony, and become, before the age of fifteen, the wife of a great king," said a very strong voice in clear and distinct accents, accompanied by shouts of laughter, which evidently proceeded from a great pitcher placed at the corner of the chimney.

The Fairy Coquette turned pale, and consternation was general ; but the woodcutter, now merry with wine, joined in the laugh. "Ah ! how droll," said he, "red and black roses ! A likely story, indeed, that a great king would come a-wooing to a woodcutter's daughter ! Only a pitcher could invent such nonsense, and I shall teach it to utter no more."

Thus saying, he gave the pitcher a great kick and broke it in pieces ; when there issued from it a smoke thick and black, and so stifling that Coquette was obliged to use two bottles of essence to dissipate its noxious effects.

"Ah, cruel Barabapatapouf!" cried she, "must your malignity then extend even to those whom I wish to benefit? I indeed recognise my enemy," said she to the woodcutter; "beware of him, and believe that it is with no good intention he destines your daughter for the bride of a king. Some mystery is here concealed, foreboding evil."

Every one was rendered quite melancholy by this adventure, and Coquette, beginning to weary of these poor foresters, opened the window and disappeared.

A great quarrel then arose between the woodcutter and his sons, who, forgetting that respect in which they had never before failed, reproached him for losing an opportunity of rendering them all happy. "We might," said they, "have purchased estates, finery of all kinds, and been as rich and noble as many who now despise us. One or two millions would have been as easy said as five hundred pounds; that sum would obtain a marquisate for my father, and baronies for each of us. What extraordinary stupidity our parents have shown!"

"My children," said the woodcutter, "are these things, then, necessary for happiness? It appeared to me that you were well satisfied when our master only made our poverty a little less oppressive; and now, while you have more gold than you ever saw in your lives, one would suppose that you had been deeply injured, and could never know contentment more."

As for Mother Thomas, she was wiser, and so well pleased with the idea of her daughter, that her imagination roamed no farther. In course of time she gave birth to an infant; but scarcely had it seen the light than it glided from her arms, and started up to the stature of a well-formed girl of twelve or thirteen years old, who made a low courtesy to the woodcutter, kissed the hand of her mother, and offered her brothers a cordial embrace. But these lads ill-naturedly repulsed the young stranger; they felt jealous, fearing that she would now be preferred to them.

Rose, one might say, was born dressed, for flowing ringlets fell around her shoulders, forming a complete covering; and with her increase of size, appeared a little smart petticoat and brown bodice in peasant fashion. Her delicate feet were clad in wooden shoes, but both the foot and the shoe were so shapely, that any lady in the land might have been proud to exhibit them. Her little plump hand was so white that it hardly appeared formed for rustic labours, yet she immediately prepared to assist in household matters, and the poor old dame was never weary of caressing such a charming child.

A bed was prepared for Rose beside her mother. This good girl arose at dawn to prepare the young men's breakfast; for she had an excellent natural disposition, and so much intelligence that she seemed to know by instinct that her birth was displeasing to them, and sought to gain their regard by good-natured attentions.

Mother Thomas soon rose likewise, and returned to the kitchen. But what was her horror on beholding her daughter's face black as ebony, her hair woolly and crisped like a negro's! As there was no mirror in the cottage, Rose could not understand what had so alarmed her mother; she asked if she had involuntarily had the misfortune to give offence?

"No, no," said the old dame, weeping; "shouldst thou remain all thy life as black as ink, I shall not love thee less: but I cannot without pain recall thy beauties of yesterday. Thou wilt be laughed at; and us too. Still, we will keep thee—thou must never leave us."

Rose readily promised she never would. But when her brothers returned, they considered the change in her quite as a matter of course. They recollected the prediction of the pitcher, and seemed quite delighted to think that, since it was fulfilled in the first instance, they might yet become the brothers of a queen.

Meanwhile they lived on better terms with Rose, hoping that one day she might be of service to them. Far from listening to the counsels of their father, they endeavoured to awaken in her mind the seeds of ambition; and in order to further views interested and selfish, flattered her beauty, her talents, and her sense, rendering the future queen the most respectful homage, which diverted her exceedingly.

But, strange to say, Rose was not always black; every second day she recovered her natural beauty, from whence it might be concluded, that the influence of the fairy and the Enchanter Barabapatapouf operated alternately. The woodcutter's family grew gradually accustomed to these successions; and as habit reconciles people to all things, each colour became indifferent to them.

Thomas was too old to change his mode of life; he would not hear of going to live in town, although they had money sufficient for that purpose; he also still continued the making of wooden shoes. Those which Rose wore in winter were trimmed with lamb's-wool, which she wrought very dexterously: she was clever and ingenious but, it must be confessed, a little imperious; and was sometimes surprised sighing like a person indulging in visionary wishes, and languishing under some secret chagrin.

A year passed: Rose grew tall, and her brothers, weary of waiting for an event so uncertain as her marriage with a king, executed a crime which they had long meditated. Seeing that their father had touched but one of the purses, they easily obtained possession of the rest, and rising with the dawn, all three departed, saying, to satisfy their consciences, that these purses must be finally theirs, and that they would, meanwhile, turn them to advantage. When they should become very rich, they would come back to their parents and take care of their latter days. Each of them made a belt, in which he concealed his gold; and with perfect concord, more frequently found amongst knaves than honest men, they travelled a hundred leagues in eight days.

The woodcutter and his wife did not at first comprehend the extent of their misfortune. They thought their children must have gone astray in the forest, and the old man wandered everywhere in search of them. But when he observed the loss of the purses, the truth was revealed, and he felt ready to die with grief. "Cursed gold!" cried he, "thou hast corrupted my brave and honest boys; they were poor, but virtuous; they are now become villains, and will meet punishment from either man or God!"

Thus saying, he took the remaining purse, and flung it into the bottom of a well. Mother Thomas was vexed, but dared not speak, for the unfortunate man was so much irritated and troubled that he would have beaten her.

When his reason cleared a little, however, he felt that he had committed an error in parting with his money, they being both old and unable to work as formerly. The dame sold some articles which had been purchased during their prosperity. But poverty was nothing; it was the conduct of their sons which inflicted the bitter sting. How was this then augmented, when some officers of justice arrived, and announced that James, Peter, and Paul had been arrested. It seemed that while drinking together in a public-house, they had spread on a table all their gold. The host surprised them, and not believing that young peasants, so coarsely clothed and wearing wooden shoes, could lawfully be in possession of such a sum, he had given them in charge. The poor boys, quite terrified, related the story of the Fairy Coquette; but as the magistrate had never seen a fairy, he did not believe one word of the matter.

Having then no hope but in the kindness of their father, they sent to summon the woodcutter and his wife, who confirmed all their assertions. But as no money was found in the cottage, whose inhabitants appeared to subsist on their labour, the officers knew not what to think.

Meantime they arrested the woodcutter for the purpose of identifying his children. Pale, and trembling like criminals, the old couple followed the guards. Mother Thomas was ready to faint, and doubly grieved for leaving poor Rose all alone, especially as this was her day for being white and beautiful. She begged her not to leave the house, but to live on the milk of her sheep, and to bake cakes of some meal which was in the bin. Their adieus were heartrending; although the soldiers declared that in three days the forester should be at liberty to return, provided the innocence of his family was established. Rose believed them, and endeavoured to take courage. But more than a month passed, and no tidings of her parents. She could not then prevent herself from wandering a little on the highway; and having walked till sunset, wept so bitterly, that her beauty indeed must have been a fairy-gift to remain uninjured.

One evening, being more worn out than usual, she seated herself at the foot of a tree and fell asleep. A slight noise awoke her, and, on looking up, she perceived a young gentleman richly dressed, who was contemplating her with evident astonishment. "Art thou a goddess, or a simple mortal?" cried he.

"Sir," replied Rose, "I am the daughter of a poor woodcutter, who lives in the forest;—it is late, and I beg you will not detain me."

"You are a wayward beauty, indeed!" replied the prince, for so he was; "but as my way lies in that direction I hope you will permit me to see you home."

"It is not in my power to prevent you," said Rose, without raising her eyes.

The prince at this moment remarked that she had been weeping, and, delighted to have an opportunity of offering sympathy and consolation, entreated her to impart her grief to him. "I am not actuated by mere curiosity," added he; "I never can behold a woman in tears without feeling moved to the bottom of my soul! Tell me your distress, and I will neither sleep nor eat till I have aided you."

Rose timidly raised her lovely blue eyes, to see whether the countenance of the prince harmonised with his discourse; but although he was not actually ugly, his features wore an expression too stern and hypocritical to invite her confidence. She therefore walked silently forward, and when near the cottage felt so uneasy, that, for the first time, she invented a lie in order to get rid of him. "You seem to compassionate my sorrows," said she; "meanwhile you only increase them. When my mother sees me accompanied by a great gentleman like you, she will beat me, and not believe that you have followed me against my will."

This reasoning appeared so just to the prince, who felt himself affected by a passion such as he had never before experienced, that he consented to retire, entreating Rose to meet him the next evening at the same hour. She refused to give a decisive answer, and returned home much dejected; recalling all the words of the stranger, and almost reproaching herself for having behaved so harshly to him.

The following day Rose took mechanically the same route, going always in the path by which her parents might be expected. Her provisions being nearly exhausted, she feared to die of hunger, and began to think that this gentleman, who had been repulsed so rudely, could, perhaps, obtain news of her family. Suddenly beholding him leaning against a tree, looking very melancholy and dejected, she threw herself at his feet, bathed in tears, and said :

" Sir, a wretch who has lost everything dear, supplicates your compassion. You, who are so kind — so tender-hearted——"

" What does the vile creature want ? " exclaimed the prince, with a savage expression. "How dare you have the impertinence to address me ? I wonder what prevents me from shooting you ? I lost my sport all yesterday in following a pretty girl ; here is game of a new description."

Rose started up, overwhelmed with terror, while the prince laughed most brutally. It was not till that moment she recollected that this was her black day, which accounted for his not recognising her. " Ah ! " thought she, " this is the humane man who could not behold a woman weep ; because my colour displeases him, he is ready to take my life. No hope now remains for me—my misfortunes are at their height ! "

Rose wept all night ; yet she could not prevent herself from returning to the same spot on the following day ; she felt irresistibly led thither, dreading, and yet wishing, to meet the prince.

He had been already waiting above an hour, and accosted her with a degree of respect quite unusual for him ; but he was in love, and love makes the worst of people better for the time.

" Cruel beauty ! " said he, in a courtier-like style, to which Rose was little accustomed, " what have I not suffered during your absence ? I even remained all night in the wood, in expectation of you, and the queen my mother despatched messengers everywhere, fearing some accident had befallen me."

" The queen, your mother ! " exclaimed Rose. " Are you, then, the son of a queen ? "

" I have betrayed myself ! " said the prince, striking

his forehead in a theatrical manner. "Yes, it is true, I have that misfortune. You will now fear me ; and what we fear, we never love."

"The wicked alone are to be feared," answered Rose. "I am very glad to hear that you are a king, for I know that you will be my husband."

The prince, who little guessed the enchanter's communication, was confounded by the unembarrassed freedom of her manner ; but it was far from displeasing to him. "You are ambitious," said he, smiling ; "but there is nothing to which beauty may not pretend. Tell me only how I can have the happiness of serving you, and you shall see that everything is possible to love."

Rose sat down on the grass, and related in very simple terms the story of the purse ; confessed that she had deceived him, and that, so far from being severely treated at home, she was now weeping her mother's loss ; that the king must take measures for the discovery and liberation of her family, before he could hope to win her affections, or pretend to her hand.

The enamoured monarch vowed he would not lose a moment ; and although she behaved with much dignity, her every word and look was adorable in his eyes. Rose thought all night of the fine fortune of being a queen ; she would then no longer wear wooden shoes ; and, above all, might have an opportunity of being useful to her dear parents.

These meetings continued every alternate day during a week ; and the queen dowager was informed that her son neglected all business, and thought of nothing but making love. She was in despair. This prince was surnamed the Terrible, by reason of his ferocity to women : till that moment he had never loved, but he had frequently made pretence of it, and when successful, it was not unusual with him to cut out the poor ladies' tongues, put out their eyes, or even throw them into the sea. The least pretext sufficed for this ; and the queen, who was of a kind disposition, lamented that yet another victim was preparing. The courtiers begged her to be tranquil ; said it was nothing more than the daughter of a poor woodcutter whom his majesty now admired, and that if he did kill her, it would be of little consequence.

But the courtiers, and the queen dowager herself, were altogether bewildered when the king, having liberated the woodcutter and his family, brought Rose to the palace as his wife. She was not at all abashed or out of countenance ; she behaved with the utmost respect to the queen, and with affability to all. It was universally remarked : "The king has committed a folly, but that charming girl is his excuse, and no man would have been wiser under similar circumstances."

A grand ball was given in the evening. Rose danced well enough for a queen ; and she yielded herself up entirely to the enchantment of such a happy day. The prince, ever eager to be near her, was figuring away in a quadrille, when twelve o'clock struck : great, then, was his astonishment, while gazing passionately on his partner, he beheld—a negress !

"What metamorphosis is this ?" cried he, rudely seizing her arm ; "where is the princess I married to-day ?"

Rose bent her head in confusion ; it still bore her diamonds, and her crown,—no doubt could exist of her identity.

"Wretched, hideous black, thou shalt surely die !" cried the king ; "none shall deceive me with impunity." He then drew a poniard, and was preparing to take instant vengeance, when, recollecting himself—"I do thee too much honour," said he ; "rather let my cooks cut thee in pieces to make a hash for my hounds."

The old queen, as humane as her son was cruel, knew there was but one means of saving the unfortunate victim ; this was to appear still more enraged than the king.

"I truly feel this injury," said she; "sometimes you have reproached my weakness, but now behold a proof that I also can avenge. Your orders must be strictly fulfilled—I myself shall witness the execution." She then signed to the guards to lay hold of the unfortunate Rose, who was dragged away by an iron chain fastened round her neck. She gave herself up for lost, and uttering the most heartrending cries, was led away to a pigeon-house at the end of the palace, furnished with some clean straw; where, however, the queen promised to come on the following day.

Her majesty kept her word. Much affected by the sweetness of the hapless bride, she promised to mitigate, as far as possible, her melancholy situation.

Rose, very grateful, supplicated her benefactress to inform the woodcutter's family that she was still alive, knowing what they would suffer should the story reach them of the black Rose having breakfasted the king's hounds. The queen promised to employ a confidential domestic; and Rose, who had still preserved her wooden shoes, sent one, that her father might recognise his handiwork.

A few days afterwards a young peasant arrived from the cottage; he brought some cakes and cheese, made by Mother Thomas, which Rose preferred to all the delicacies of the palace.

This young peasant, who was named Mirto, related to Rose everything concerning her dear parents, and took back very loving messages from her to them.

Mirto found so much pleasure in conversing with the fair prisoner, and had so often cakes to carry, that they were seldom asunder. He said he was an orphan, and having some work to do in the prison where Thomas had been confined, there formed a friendship with the family. In return for some little services then rendered them, he desired to learn the trade of the wooden shoes; being very ingenious, he became a valuable acquisition. He never had felt so happy before. In truth, he was not aware that this happiness received its date from the hour in which he first saw Rose.

Alas! the poor Rose was only too sensible of his affection, and feeling the duty of struggling against it, found herself still more miserable than before.

"Whatever may be the conduct of Prince Terrible," said she to herself, "I have married him. It is certainly very hard to love a husband who wished to kill me, but still I should not permit myself to love another."

For a whole month following she had sufficient resolution to see Mirto no more, and was becoming sick with chagrin and weariness. The queen visited her frequently, bringing all sorts of sweetmeats, and a singing-bird, to divert her captivity. She brought no finery; indeed, that would have been quite thrown away on the pigeons.

At length, one day Rose heard a great noise in the palace. People kept running to and fro—all the bells were rung, and all the cannons fired. The poor prisoner mounted up to one of the pigeon-holes, and peeping through, perceived the palace hung with black. She knew not what to think. But soon one of the queen's officers appeared, and conducted her in due form to the court. Rose, all trembling, inquired what had happened.

"Your majesty is a widow," replied the officer; "the king has been killed in hunting; here are your weeds, of which the queen begs your acceptance."

Rose was much agitated, but she followed the officer in silence, with a sad and serious aspect, as a dignified personage should do when informed of the death of a husband.

The queen was a tender mother, and although fully conscious of the ferocious disposition of her son, she deeply lamented him, and wept bitterly on embracing her daughter-in-law. "Your husband is no more," said she; "forget his errors, my dear child; the remainder of my life shall be devoted to making atonement for them."

The princess threw herself at her benefactress' feet, and declared all was forgotten. "If your majesty deigns to permit me to speak candidly," added she, "and will bestow a moment's attention, I shall confess the dearest wishes of my heart!"

"Speak," said the queen; "nothing now can assuage my grief, save an opportunity of proving to you my friendship."

"I was not born for a queen," continued Rose. "My mother is a poor forester, but she has been a tender parent, and weeps incessantly for my absence."

"Let her be conducted hither," replied the queen.

"This is not all, madam," continued Rose; "I confess that I love a young peasant, who has assisted my father to make wooden shoes. If I were the wife of Mirto, and your majesty would have the goodness to give some assistance to my family, my old father might be freed from labour, and I the happiest woman in the world."

The queen embraced Rose, and promised all she wished. She then conducted her to the forest; and just as they had reached its boundary, they perceived in the air a mahogany car, mounted on wheels of mother-o'-pearl; two pretty white lambs were yoked to it, which Rose immediately recognised as those of the Fairy Coquette.

The car descended, and the fairy alighting, thus addressed the queen: "Madam, I come to seek my child, and am delighted to find you willing to part with her, for she has a lover whom I approve;—who loves her faithfully, though hopelessly, which is a thing more rare than all the treasures of your majesty's crown."

The fairy then addressing herself to Rose, related

that her enemy, the Enchanter Barabapatapouf, had just been killed in combat with another giant. "Now," added Coquette, "I have full power to render you happy"; and passing her fair hand over Rose's face, the negro colour and features vanished—to reappear no more.

The queen, convinced that her daughter-in-law required nothing further, offered only her portrait, as a token of esteem and friendship. Rose received it with grateful respect, then ascended the fairy's car, and was in a few minutes surrounded by the foresters, who never wearied of caressing her. Poor Mirto drew back, trembling, not knowing whether to hope or fear; but Coquette, perceiving their mutual embarrassment, declared that she had ordained this marriage from the very beginning. She blessed them, gave them a flock of beautiful white sheep, a cottage covered with honeysuckles and roses, a lovely garden abounding with fruits and flowers, and a moderate sum of money; endowing them also with life for a hundred years, uninterrupted health, and constant love.

BROTHER AND SISTER

A BROTHER took his sister by the hand and said, "Since our mother is dead we have no more happy hours : our stepmother beats us every day, and whenever we come near her she kicks us away. She gives us hard crusts and nasty scraps to eat, and the dog under the table fares better than we do, for he does sometimes get a nice bit thrown to him. It would break our mother's heart if she knew it ! Come, we will go out into the wide world together."

They went along the whole day through meadows, over rocks and stones, and when it rained the little sister said, "Heaven and our hearts are crying together." In the evening they came to a great wood, and were so worn out with grief, hunger, and weariness, that they sat down in a hollow tree and went to sleep.

The next morning, when they awoke, the sun was already high in the heavens, and shone down very hot on the tree. Upon which said the brother : "Sister, I am thirsty ; I would go and have a drink if I knew where there was a spring : I think I can hear one trickling." He got up, took his sister by the hand, and they went to look for the spring.

The wicked stepmother, however, who was a witch and well knew how the children had run away, had crept after them secretly, in the way witches do, and had bewitched all the springs in the wood. When they had found a spring that was dancing brightly over the stones, the brother stooped down to drink ; but his sister heard a voice in its murmur, which said, " Whoever drinks of me will become a tiger." Eagerly the little sister cried, " I pray thee, brother, do not drink, lest thou become a wild beast and tear me to pieces."

The brother did not drink, although he was so thirsty, but said, " I will wait for the next spring." When they came to the next, the little sister heard it say, " Who drinks of me will become a wolf ; who drinks of me will become a wolf!" and cried out, " O brother, I pray thee do not drink, lest thou become a wolf and eat me up."

The brother did not drink, but said : " I will wait till I come to the next spring, but then I must drink, say what you will, for my thirst is getting unbearable."

And when they came to the third spring, the little sister heard a voice in its murmur, saying, " Whoever drinks of me will become a roe," and she cried, " O brother, do not drink, I pray thee, lest thou become a roe and run away from me." But the brother had already knelt down by the stream, stooped down, and drank of the water ; and as soon as the first drop touched his lips, there he lay—a white roe.

The little sister cried over her poor bewitched brother, and the roe cried also as he rested mournfully beside her. At last the maiden said, " Never mind, dear Roe, I will never forsake you." So she took off her golden garter and put it round the roe's neck, then pulled some rushes and wove them into a cord. To this she tied the little animal and led him on, and they both went still deeper into the wood. When they had gone a long, long way, they came at last to a little house, into which the maiden peeped ; and as it was empty, she thought, " Here we may stay and live." So she made a pretty bed of leaves and moss for the roe ; and every morning she went out and gathered roots, berries, and nuts for herself ; and for the roe she brought tender grass, which he ate out of her hand, and played about and was very happy. In the evening, when the little sister was tired and had said her prayers, she laid her head upon the roe, who was her pillow, and went sweetly to sleep; and if her brother had only kept his proper shape, they would have led a very happy life.

They had lived alone in this way during a long time, when it happened that the king of the country held a great hunt in the forest. Through the trees might be heard the blowing of horns, the barking of dogs, and the joyous cries of the hunters, which when the little roe heard he was almost beside himself with delight. "Oh," said he to his sister, "let me go and see the hunt—I can no longer refrain"; and he begged hard till she consented.

"But," said she, "when you return at evening I shall have shut my door against the wild huntsmen, and in order that I may know you, knock and say—'My little sister, let me in'; but if you do not say so, I shall not open the door."

Now off sprang the roe, and was so happy to find himself in the open air. The king and his huntsmen saw the beautiful beast and set off after him, but they could not catch him; for when they thought they had certainly got him, he sprang over a bush and disappeared. When it was dark he galloped up to the little house, knocked, and cried, "My little sister, let me in." And when the door was opened he sprang in, and rested all night on his pretty little bed. Next morning the hunt began again, and when the roe heard the blast of the horns, and the "Ho! ho!" of the hunters, he could not rest, and cried, "Sister, open the door—I must go."

His sister opened the door and said, "But mind you must be back in the evening and make your little speech, that I may let you in."

When the king and his huntsmen saw the white roe

with the gold band once more, they all rode after him, but
he was too quick and agile for them.   This chase lasted
the whole day;   at last, towards evening, the hunters
surrounded him, and wounded him with an arrow in the
foot, so that he was forced to limp and go slowly.   One
of the hunters creeping softly after him to the little house,
heard him say, "My sister, let me in," and saw that the
door was opened and immediately shut to again; so he
went back to the king, and told him all he had seen and
heard.

"We will have another hunt to-morrow," said the
king.

The little sister was greatly alarmed when she saw her
white roe was wounded; she washed off the blood, laid
herbs upon the place, and said, "Go now to thy bed, dear
Roe, and get well."

The wound, however, was so slight that the next
morning he felt nothing of it, and when he heard the
noise of the hunt, he said, "I cannot keep away,—I must
go, and nothing shall keep me."

His sister cried and said, "Now you will go and be
killed, and leave me here alone in the forest, forsaken by
all the world; I will not let you go out."

"Then I shall die here of grief," answered the roe:
"for when I hear the sound of the horn, I do feel as if I
could jump out of my shoes."   So his sister could not do
less than open the door with a heavy heart, and the roe
sprang out joyfully into the forest.

As soon as the king saw him, he said to his huntsmen,
"Now hunt him all day till evening, but don't do
anything to hurt him."

When the sun was set the king said to his huntsman,
"Now come and show me the little house you saw in the
wood."   And when he was before the door he knocked
and cried, "Dear little sister, let me in."   Immediately
the door opened, the king entered, and there stood a

maiden more beautiful than any one he had ever seen. The damsel was frightened when she found there had come in, not her roe, but a man who wore a golden crown on his head. But the king looked kindly at her, took her hand and said, " Wilt thou go with me to my castle, and be my dear wife ? "

"Oh yes," answered the maiden, "but the roe must come with me, for I cannot forsake him."

The king replied, " He shall remain with you as long as you live, and shall want for nothing."

At this moment he came springing in, his sister tied the cord of rushes round his neck, led him with her own hand, and they all left the little house together.

The king took the beautiful maiden on his own horse and conducted her to his castle, where the marriage was celebrated with great pomp. She was now queen, and they lived a long time very happily together ; while the roe was petted and taken care of, and played all day about the palace-garden.

But the wicked stepmother, on whose account these children had been driven into the wide world, thought nothing less than that the little sister had been torn to pieces by wild beasts in the forest, and that the brother, in the shape of a roe, had been killed by the hunters. When she now heard they were so happy, and that everything went well with them, envy and spite raged in her heart and gave her no rest, and her only thought was how she could do some mischief to them both. Her own daughter, who was as ugly as the night and had only one eye, was continually reproaching her, and saying, " It is I who ought to have been made queen."

"Never mind," said the old witch to console her ; " when the time comes I will manage it."

By and by the queen gave birth to a beautiful little boy ; and the king being away at the hunt, the old witch took upon herself the form of the lady-in-waiting, entered the room where the queen lay, and said to her, "Come, the bath is ready, which will do you good and give you new strength ; make haste before it gets cold." Her daughter was also at hand, and they carried the poor weak queen between them into the bath-room, and laid her in the bath : then they shut the door and ran away. But under the bath they had first lighted a great furnace-fire, so that the beautiful young queen could not save herself from being scorched alive.

When that was done the old witch took her own daughter, put a cap on her, and laid her on the bed in the queen's room. She changed her also into the shape of the young queen, all except her one eye, and she could not give her another. But in order that the king might not observe it, she was obliged to lie on that side where there was no eye. In the evening, when he was come home, and heard that he had a little son, he was very much delighted, and wished to visit his dear wife and see how she was getting on ; on which the old woman cried out in a great hurry, " As you value your life, don't touch the curtain ; the queen must not see the light, and must be left quite quiet." So the king went away, and never found out that it was a false queen in the bed.

But when it was midnight, and all the world was asleep, the nurse who was sitting beside the cradle, and who was the only person awake, saw the door open and the true queen come in. She took the baby out of the cradle, laid it in her arms, and nursed it tenderly. She then shook up the pillows, laid it down again, and covered it with the counterpane. She did not forget the roe either, but went into the corner where it lay, and stroked it gently. After this she passed out, quite silently, through the door ; and the nurse inquired next morning of the sentinels whether any one had gained entrance into the palace during the night, but they answered, " No—we have seen nobody." She continued to come in the same way for several nights, though she spoke never a word : the nurse always saw her, but never dared to mention it.

When some time had passed, the queen at last began to speak, and said :

"How is my baby ?   How is my roe ?
I can come again twice, then for ever must go."

The nurse could not answer her ; but when she had disappeared she went to the king, and told him all about it, upon which he cried, "What does it mean?   I will myself watch by the child to-night."

In the evening he came to the nursery, and there at midnight the dead queen appeared, and said :

"How is my baby ?   How is my roe ?
I can come but once more, then for ever must go ; "

and nursed and fondled the baby as before, then vanished. The king did not dare to address her, but watched again the following night.   This time she said :

"How is my baby ?   How is my roe ?
I can come but this once, then for ever must go."

Upon which the king could no longer contain himselr, but sprang forward and cried, "Thou canst surely be no one but my own dear wife ! "

She replied, "Yes, I am thy dear wife " ; and as soon as she had spoken these words she was restored to life, and became once more fresh and blooming.

Then she related to the king the crime committed on her by the old witch and her ugly daughter, whom he at once commanded to be brought to judgment, and had sentence passed upon them.   The daughter was taken forth into the woods, where the wild beasts tore her in pieces, and the witch was burnt.   And behold ! as soon as there was nothing left of her but ashes, the white roe became changed again and resumed his human form ; so they all lived happily together till the end of their lives.

LITTLE RED-RIDING-HOOD

ONCE there was a little village maiden, the prettiest ever seen. Her mother was foolishly fond of her and her grandmother likewise. The old woman made for her a little hood, which became the damsel so well, that ever after she went by the name of Little Red-Riding-Hood. One day, when her mother was making cakes, she said, "My child, you shall go and see your grandmother, for I hear she is not well; and you shall take her some of these cakes, and a pot of butter."

Little Red-Riding-Hood was delighted to go, though it was a long walk; but she was a good child, and fond of her kind grandmother. Passing through a wood, she met a great wolf, who was most eager to eat her up, but dared not, because of a woodcutter who was busy hard by. So he only came and asked her politely where she was going. The poor child, who did not know how dangerous it is to stop and speak to wolves, replied, "I am going to see my grandmother, and to take her a cake and a pot of butter, which my mother has sent her."

"Is it very far from hence?" asked the wolf.

"Oh yes, it is just above the mill which you may see up there—the first house you come to in the village."

"Well," said the wolf, "I will go there also, to inquire after your excellent grandmother; I will go one way, and you the other, and we will see who can be there first."

So he ran as fast as ever he could, taking the shortest road, but the little maiden took the longest; for she stopped to pluck roses in the wood, to chase butterflies, and gather nosegays of the prettiest flowers she could find—she was such a happy and innocent little soul.

The wolf was not long in reaching the grandmother's door. He knocked, Toc—toc, and the grandmother said, "Who is there?"

"It is your child, Little Red-Riding-Hood," replied the wicked beast, imitating the girl's voice; "I bring you a cake and a pot of butter, which my mother has sent you."

The grandmother, who was ill in her bed, said, "Very well, my dear, pull the string and the latch will open." The wolf pulled the string—the door flew open; he leaped in, fell upon the poor old woman, and ate her up in less than no time, tough as she was, for he had not tasted anything for more than three days. Then he carefully shut the door, and laying himself down snugly in the bed, waited for Little Red-Riding-Hood, who was not long before she came and knocked, Toc—toc, at the door.

"Who is there?" said the wolf; and the little maiden, hearing his gruff voice, felt sure that her poor grandmother must have caught a bad cold and be very ill indeed.

So she answered cheerfully, "It is your child, Little Red-Riding-Hood, who brings you a cake and a pot of butter that my mother has sent you."

Then the wolf, softening his voice as much as he could, said, "Pull the string, and the latch will open."

So Little Red-Riding-Hood pulled the string and the door opened. The wolf, seeing her enter, hid himself as much as he could under the coverlid of the bed, and said in a whisper, "Put the cake and the pot of butter on the shelf, and then make haste and come to bed, for it is very late."

Little Red-Riding-Hood did not think so; but to please her grandmother, she undressed herself and began to get ready for bed, when she was very much astonished to find how different the old woman looked from ordinary.

"Grandmother, what great arms you have!"

"That is to hug you the better, my dear."

"Grandmother, what great ears you have!"

"That is to hear you the better, my dear."

"Grandmother, what great eyes you have!"

"That is to see you the better, my dear."

"Grandmother, what a great mouth you have!"

"That is to eat you up," cried the wicked wolf; and immediately he fell upon poor Little Red-Riding-Hood, and ate her up in a moment.

PUSS IN BOOTS

A MILLER, dying, divided all his property between his three children. This was a very simple matter, as he had nothing to leave but his mill, his ass, and his cat; so he made no will, and called in no lawyer, who would, probably, have taken a large slice out of these poor possessions. The eldest son took the mill, the second the ass, while the third was obliged to content himself with the cat, at which he grumbled very much. "My brothers," said he, "by putting their property together, may gain an honest livelihood, but there is nothing left for me, except to die of hunger; unless, indeed, I were to kill my cat and eat him, and make a coat out of his skin, which would be very scanty clothing."

The cat, who heard the young man talking to himself, sat up on his four paws, and looking at him with a grave and wise air, said, "Master, I think you had better not kill me; I shall be much more useful to you alive."

"How so?" asked his master.

"You have but to give me a sack, and a pair of boots such as gentlemen wear when they go shooting, and you will find you are not so ill off as you suppose."

Now, though the young miller did not much depend upon the cat's words, still he thought it rather surprising that a cat should speak at all. And he had before now seen him show so much adroitness and cleverness in catching rats and mice, that it seemed advisable to trust

"You have but to give me a sack, and a pair of boots such as
gentlemen wear when they go shooting." *(Page 228)*

"Avenant delivered up his phial; the owl flew with it into the grotto, and in less than half-an-hour reappeared, bringing it quite full and well corked." (*Page 247*)

WARWICK GOBLE

him a little further ; especially as, poor young fellow ! he
had nobody else to trust.

When the cat got his boots, he drew them on with a
grand air, and slinging his sack over his shoulder, and
drawing the cords of it round his neck, he marched
bravely to a rabbit-warren hard by, with which he was
well acquainted. Then, putting some bran and lettuces
into his bag, and stretching himself out beside it as if he
were dead, he waited till some fine fat young rabbit,
ignorant of the wickedness and deceit of the world, should
peer into the sack to eat the food that was inside. This
happened very shortly, for there are plenty of foolish
young rabbits in every warren ; and when one of them,
who really was a splendid fat fellow, put his head inside,
Master Puss drew the cords immediately, and took him
and killed him without mercy. Then, very proud of his
prey, he marched direct up to the palace, and begged to
speak with the king. He was desired to ascend to the
apartment of his majesty, where, making a low bow,
he said :

"Sire, here is a magnificent rabbit, killed in the warren
which belongs to my lord the Marquis of Carabas, and
which he has desired me to offer humbly to your majesty."

"Tell your master," replied the king politely, "that I
accept his present, and am very much obliged to him."

Another time, Puss went and hid himself and his sack
in a wheat-field, and there caught two splendid fat partridges in the same manner as he had done the rabbit.
When he presented them to the king, with a similar
message as before, his majesty was so pleased that he
ordered the cat to be taken down into the kitchen and
given something to eat and drink ; where, while enjoying
himself, the faithful animal did not cease to talk in the
most cunning way of the large preserves and abundant
game which belonged to my lord the Marquis of Carabas.

One day, hearing that the king was intending to take

229

a drive along the river-side with his daughter, the most beautiful princess in the world, Puss said to his master, "Sir, if you would only follow my advice, your fortune is made."

"Be it so," said the miller's son, who was growing very disconsolate, and cared little what he did: "Say your say, cat."

"It is but little," replied Puss, looking wise, as cats can. "You have only to go and bathe in the river, at a place which I shall show you, and leave all the rest to me. Only remember that you are no longer yourself, but my lord the Marquis of Carabas."

"Just so," said the miller's son, "it's all the same to me"; but he did as the cat told him.

While he was bathing, the king and all the court passed by, and were startled to hear loud cries of "Help, help! my lord the Marquis of Carabas is drowning." The king put his head out of the carriage, and saw nobody but the cat, who had, at different times, brought him so many presents of game: however, he ordered his guards to fly quickly to the succour of my lord the Marquis of Carabas. While they were pulling the unfortunate marquis out of the water, the cat came up, bowing, to the side of the king's carriage, and told a long and pitiful story about some thieves, who, while his master was bathing, had come and carried away all his clothes, so that it would be impossible for him to appear before his majesty and the illustrious princess.

"Oh, we will soon remedy that," answered the king kindly; and immediately ordered one of the first officers of the household to ride back to the palace with all speed, and bring back the most elegant supply of clothes for the young gentleman, who kept in the background until they arrived. Then, being handsome and well-made, his new clothes became him so well, that he looked as if he had been a marquis all his days, and advanced with an air of respectful ease to offer his thanks to his majesty.

The king received him courteously, and the princess admired him very much. Indeed, so charming did he appear to her, that she hinted to her father to invite him into the carriage with them, which, you may be sure, the young man did not refuse. The cat, delighted at the success of his scheme, went away as fast as he could, and ran so swiftly that he kept a long way ahead of the royal carriage. He went on and on, till he came to some peasants who were mowing in a meadow. " Good people," said he in a very firm voice, " the king is coming past here shortly, and if you do not say that the field you are mowing belongs to my lord the Marquis of Carabas, you shall all be chopped as small as mince-meat."

So when the king drove by, and asked whose meadow it was where there was such a splendid crop of hay, the mowers all answered, trembling, that it belonged to my lord the Marquis of Carabas.

" You have very fine land, Marquis," said his majesty to the miller's son ; who bowed, and answered " that it was not a bad meadow, take it altogether."

Then the cat came to a wheat-field, where the reapers were reaping with all their might. He bounced in upon them : " The king is coming past to-day, and if you do not tell him that this wheat belongs to my lord the Marquis of Carabas, I will have you every one chopped as small as mince-meat." The reapers, very much alarmed, did as they were bid, and the king congratulated the Marquis upon possessing such beautiful fields, laden with such an abundant harvest.

They drove on—the cat always running before and saying the same thing to everybody he met, that they were to declare the whole country belonged to his master ; so that even the king was astonished at the vast estate of my lord the Marquis of Carabas.

But now the cat arrived at a great castle where dwelt an Ogre, to whom belonged all the land through which the royal equipage had been driving. He was a cruel tyrant, and his tenants and servants were terribly afraid of him, which accounted for their being so ready to say whatever they were told to say by the cat, who had taken pains to inform himself of all about the Ogre. So, putting on the boldest face he could assume, Puss marched up to the castle with his boots on, and asked to see the owner of it, saying that he was on his travels, but did not wish to pass so near the castle of such a noble gentleman, without paying his respects to him. When the Ogre heard this message, he went to the door, received the cat as civilly as an Ogre can, and begged him to walk in and repose himself.

"Thank you, sir," said the cat; "but first I hope you will satisfy a traveller's curiosity. I have heard in far countries of your many remarkable qualities, and especially how you have the power to change yourself into any sort of beast you choose—a lion for instance, or an elephant."

"That is quite true," replied the Ogre; "and lest you should doubt it, I will immediately become a lion."

He did so; and the cat was so frightened that he sprang up to the roof of the castle and hid himself in the gutter—a proceeding rather inconvenient on account of his boots, which were not exactly fitted to walk with upon tiles. At length, perceiving that the Ogre had resumed his original form, he came down again stealthily, and confessed that he had been very much frightened.

"But, sir," said he, "it may be easy enough for such a big gentleman as you to change himself into a large animal: I do not suppose you can become a small one—a rat or mouse for instance. I have heard that you can; still, for my part, I consider it quite impossible."

"Impossible?" cried the other indignantly. "You shall see!" and immediately the cat saw the Ogre no longer, but a little mouse running along on the floor.

This was exactly what he wanted; and he did the very best a cat could do, and the most natural under the circumstances—he sprang upon the mouse and gobbled it up in a trice. So there was an end of the Ogre.

By this time the king had arrived opposite the castle, and was seized with a strong desire to enter it. The cat, hearing the noise of the carriage-wheels, ran forward in a great hurry, and standing at the gate, said in a loud voice, " Welcome, sire, to the castle of my lord the Marquis of Carabas."

" What ! " cried his majesty, very much surprised, " does the castle also belong to you ? Truly, Marquis, you have kept your secret well up to the last minute. I have never seen anything finer than this courtyard and these battlements. Indeed, I have nothing like them in the whole of my dominions."

The Marquis, without speaking, offered his hand to the princess to assist her to descend, and, standing aside that the king might enter first—for he had already acquired all the manners of a court—followed his majesty to the great hall, where a magnificent collation was laid out, and where, without more delay, they all sat down to feast.

Before the banquet was over, the king, charmed with the good qualities of the Marquis of Carabas — and likewise with his wine, of which he had drunk six or seven cups—said, bowing across the table at which the princess and the miller's son were talking very confidentially together, " It rests with you, Marquis, whether you will not become my son-in-law."

" I shall be only too happy," said the complaisant Marquis, and the princess's cast-down eyes declared the same.

So they were married the very next day, and took possession of the Ogre's castle, and of everything that had belonged to him.

As for the cat, he became at once a grand personage, and had never more any need to run after mice, except for his own diversion.

THE WOLF AND THE SEVEN YOUNG GOSLINGS

THERE was once an old goose who had seven young goslings, and loved them as only a mother can love her children. One day she was going into the wood to seek for provender, and before setting off she called all seven to her and said, " Dear children, I am obliged to go into the wood, so be on your guard against the wolf ; for if he gets in here he will eat you up, feathers, skin, and all. The villain often disguises himself, but you can easily recognise him by his rough voice and black paws."

The children answered, " Dear mother, we will take great care ; you may go without any anxiety." So the old lady was comforted, and set off cheerfully for the wood.

Before long, some one knocked at the door, and cried, " Open, open, my dear children ; your mother is here, and has brought something for each of you."

But the goslings soon perceived, by the rough voice, that it was the wolf. " We will not open," said they ; " you are not our mother, for she has a sweet and lovely voice ; but your voice is rough—you are the wolf."

Thereupon the wolf set off to a merchant and bought a large lump of chalk ; he ate it, and it made his voice sweet. Back he came, knocked at the door, and cried, " Open, open, my dear children ; your mother is here, and has brought something for each of you."

But the wolf had laid his black paw on the window-sill,

and when the children saw it, they cried, "We will not open ; our mother has not black feet like you—you are the wolf."

So the wolf ran off to the baker, and said, "I have hurt my foot, put some dough on it." And when the baker had plastered it with dough, the wolf went to the miller and cried, "Strew some meal on my paws." But the miller thought to himself, "The wolf wants to deceive some one," and he hesitated to do it ; till the wolf said, "If you don't do it at once, I will eat you up." So the miller was afraid and made his paws white. Such is the way of the world !

Now came the rogue back for the third time, knocked and said, "Open the door, dear children ; your mother has come home, and has brought something for each of you out of the wood."

The little goslings cried, "Show us your paws first, that we may see whether you are indeed our mother." So he laid his paws on the window-sill, and when the goslings saw that they were white, they believed it was all right, and opened the door ; and who should come in but the wolf !

They screamed out and tried to hide themselves ; one jumped under the table, another into the bed, the third into the oven ; the fourth ran into the kitchen, the fifth hopped into a chest, the sixth under the wash-tub, and the seventh got into the clock-case. But the wolf seized them, and stood on no ceremony with them ; one after another he gobbled them all up, except the youngest, who being in the clock-case he couldn't find. When the wolf had eaten his fill, he strolled forth, laid himself down in the green meadow under a tree, and went fast asleep.

Not long after, back came the old goose home from the wood ; but what, alas ! did she see ? The house-door stood wide open ; table, chairs, benches, were all overthrown ; the wash-tub lay in the ashes ; blankets and pillows were torn off the bed. She looked for her children, but nowhere could she find them; she called them each by name, but nobody answered. At last, when she came to the youngest, a little squeaking voice answered, "Dear mother, I am in the clock-case." She pulled him out, and he told her how the wolf had come and had eaten up all the others. You may think how she wept for her dear children.

At last, in her grief, she went out, and the youngest gosling ran beside her. And when she came to the meadow there lay the wolf under the tree, snoring till the boughs shook. She walked round and examined him on all sides, till she perceived that something was moving and kicking about inside him.

"Can it be," thought she, "that my poor children whom he has swallowed for his supper are yet alive?" So she sent the little gosling back to the house for scissors, needle, and thread, and began to slit up the monster's stomach. Scarcely had she given one snip, when out came the head of a gosling, and when she had cut a little further, the six jumped out one after another, not having taken the least hurt, because the greedy monster had swallowed them down whole. That was a joy! They embraced their mother tenderly, and skipped about as lively as a tailor at his wedding.

But the old goose said, "Now go and find me six large stones, which we will put inside the greedy beast while he is still asleep." So the goslings got the stones in all haste, and they put them inside the wolf; and the old goose sewed him up again in a great hurry, while he never once moved nor took any notice.

Now when the wolf at last woke up and got upon his legs, he found he was very thirsty, and wished to go to the spring to drink. But as soon as he began to move the stones began to shake and rattle inside him, till he cried :

THE WOLF AND YOUNG GOSLINGS

"What's this rumbling and tumbling,
What's this rattling like bones ?
I thought I had eaten six little geese.
But they've turn'd out only stones."

And when he came to the spring and bent down his head
to drink, the heavy stones overbalanced him, and in he
went head over heels.   Now when the seven goslings saw
this, they came running up, crying loudly, "The wolf is
dead, the wolf is dead!" and danced for joy all round
the spring, and their mother with them.

THE FAIR ONE WITH GOLDEN LOCKS

THERE was once a king's daughter so beautiful that they named her the Fair One with Golden Locks. These golden locks were the most remarkable in the world, soft and fine, and falling in long waves down to her very feet. She wore them always thus, loose and flowing, surmounted with a wreath of flowers; and though such long hair was sometimes rather inconvenient, it was so exceedingly beautiful, shining in the sun like ripples of molten gold, that everybody agreed she fully deserved her name.

Now there was a young king of a neighbouring country, very handsome, very rich, and wanting nothing but a wife to make him happy. He heard so much of the various perfections of the Fair One with Golden Locks, that at last, without even seeing her, he fell in love with her so desperately that he could neither eat nor drink, and resolved to send an ambassador at once to demand her in marriage. So he ordered a magnificent equipage— more than a hundred horses and a hundred footmen—in order to bring back to him the Fair One with Golden Locks, who, he never doubted, would be only too happy to become his queen. Indeed, he felt so sure of her that he refurnished the whole palace, and had made, by all the dressmakers of the city, dresses enough to last a lady for a lifetime. But, alas! when the ambassador arrived and delivered his message, either the princess was in a bad humour, or the offer did not appear to be to her taste; for she returned her best thanks to his majesty, but said she had not the slightest wish or intention to be married. She also, being a prudent damsel, declined receiving any of the presents which the king had sent her; except that, not quite to offend his majesty, she retained a box of English pins, which were in that country of considerable value.

When the ambassador returned, alone and unsuccessful, all the court was very much affected, and the king himself began to weep with all his might. Now, there was in the palace household a young gentleman named Avenant, beautiful as the sun, besides being at once so amiable and so wise that the king confided to him all his affairs; and every one loved him, except those people—to be found in all courts—who were envious of his good fortune. These malicious folk hearing him say gaily, "If the king had sent me to fetch the Fair One with Golden Locks, I know she would have come back with me," repeated the saying in such a manner, that it appeared as if Avenant thought so much of himself and his beauty, and felt sure the princess would have followed him all over the world; which when it came to the ears of the king, as it was meant to do, irritated him so much that he commanded Avenant to be imprisoned in a high tower, and left to die there of hunger. The guards accordingly carried off the young man, who had quite forgotten his idle speech, and had not the least idea what fault he had committed. They ill-treated him very much, and then left him, with nothing to eat and only water to drink. This, however, kept him alive for a few days, during which he did not cease to complain aloud, and to call upon the king, saying, "O king, what harm have I done? You have no subject more faithful than I. Never have I had a thought which could offend you."

And it so befell that the king, coming by chance, or else with a sort of remorse, past the tower, was touched by the voice of the young Avenant, whom he had once so much regarded. In spite of all the courtiers could do to prevent him, he stopped to listen, and overheard these words. The tears rushed into his eyes; he opened the door of the tower, and called, "Avenant!" Avenant came, creeping feebly along, fell at the king's knees, and kissed his feet:

"Oh, sire, what have I done that you should treat me so cruelly?"

"You have mocked me and my ambassador; for you said, if I had sent you to fetch the Fair One with Golden Locks, you would have been successful and brought her back."

"I did say it, and it was true," replied Avenant fearlessly; "for I should have told her so much about your majesty and your various high qualities, which no one knows so well as myself, that I am persuaded she would have returned with me."

"I believe it," said the king, with an angry look at those who had spoken ill of his favourite; he then gave Avenant a free pardon, and took him back with him to the court.

After having supplied the famished youth with as much supper as he could eat, the king admitted him to a private audience, and said, "I am as much in love as ever with the Fair One with Golden Locks, so I will take thee at thy word, and send thee to try and win her for me."

"Very well, please your majesty," replied Avenant cheerfully; "I will depart to-morrow."

The king, overjoyed with his willingness and hopefulness, would have furnished him with a still more magnificent equipage and suite than the first ambassador; but Avenant refused to take anything except a good horse to ride, and letters of introduction to the princess's father. The king embraced him, and eagerly saw him depart.

It was on a Monday morning when, without any pomp or show, Avenant thus started on his mission. He rode slowly and meditatively, pondering over every possible means of persuading the Fair One with Golden Locks to marry the king ; but, even after several days' journey towards her country, no clear project had entered into his mind. One morning, when he had started at break of day, he came to a great meadow with a stream running through it, along which were planted willows and poplars. It was such a pleasant, rippling stream that he dismounted and sat down on its banks. There he perceived, gasping on the grass, a large golden carp, which, in leaping too far after gnats, had thrown itself quite out of the water, and now lay dying on the greensward. Avenant took pity on it, and though he was very hungry, and the fish was very fat, and he would well enough have liked it for his breakfast, still he lifted it gently and put it back into the stream. No sooner had the carp touched the fresh cool water than it revived and swam away ; but shortly returning, it spoke to him from the water in this wise :

" Avenant, I thank you for your good deed. I was dying, and you have saved me : I will recompense you for this one day."

After this pretty little speech, the fish popped down to the bottom of the stream, according to the habit of carp, leaving Avenant very much astonished, as was natural.

Another day he met with a raven that was in great distress, being pursued by an eagle, which would have swallowed him up in no time. "See," thought Avenant, " how the stronger oppress the weaker ! What right has an eagle to eat up a raven?" So taking his bow and rrow, which he always carried, he shot the eagle dead, and the raven, delighted, perched in safety on an opposite tree.

" Avenant," screeched he, though not in the sweetest voice in the world ; " you have generously succoured me, a poor miserable raven. I am not ungrateful, and I will recompense you one day."

" Thank you," said Avenant, and continued his road.

Entering in a thick wood, so dark with the shadows of
early morning that he could scarcely find his way, he heard
an owl hooting, like an owl in great tribulation. She had
been caught by the nets spread by bird-catchers to entrap
finches, larks, and other small birds. "What a pity,"
thought Avenant, "that men must always torment poor
birds and beasts who have done them no harm!" So he
took out his knife, cut the net, and let the owl go free.
She went sailing up into the air, but immediately returned,
hovering over his head on her brown wings.

"Avenant," said she, "at daylight the bird-catchers
would have been here, and I should have been caught and
killed. I have a grateful heart; I will recompense you
one day."

These were the three principal adventures that befell
Avenant on his way to the kingdom of the Fair One with
Golden Locks. Arrived there, he dressed himself with
the greatest care, in a habit of silver brocade, and a hat
adorned with plumes of scarlet and white. He threw
over all a rich mantle, and carried a little basket, in which
was a lovely little dog, an offering of respect to the
princess. With this he presented himself at the palace-
gates, where, even though he came alone, his mien was so
dignified and graceful, so altogether charming, that every
one did him reverence, and was eager to run and tell the
Fair One with Golden Locks that Avenant, another
ambassador from the king her suitor, awaited an audience.

"Avenant!" repeated the princess, "that is a pretty
name; perhaps the youth is pretty too."

"So beautiful," said the ladies of honour, "that while
he stood under the palace window we could do nothing
but look at him."

"How silly of you!" sharply said the princess. But
she desired them to bring her robe of blue satin, to comb
out her long hair, and adorn it with the freshest garland
of flowers; to give her her high-heeled shoes, and her

fan. "Also," added she, "take care that my audience-chamber is well swept and my throne well dusted. I wish in everything to appear as becomes the Fair One with Golden Locks."

This done, she seated herself on her throne of ivory and ebony, and gave orders for her musicians to play, but softly, so as not to disturb conversation. Thus, shining in all her beauty, she admitted Avenant to her presence.

He was so dazzled that at first he could not speak : then he began and delivered his harangue to perfection.

"Gentle Avenant," returned the princess, after listening to all his reasons for her returning with him, "your arguments are very strong, and I am inclined to listen to them ; but you must first find for me a ring, which I dropped into the river about a month ago. Until I recover it, I can listen to no propositions of marriage."

Avenant, surprised and disturbed, made her a profound reverence and retired, taking with him the basket and the little dog Cabriole, which she refused to accept. All night long he sat sighing to himself, "How can I ever find a ring which she dropped into the river a month ago ? She has set me an impossibility."

"My dear master," said Cabriole, "nothing is an impossibility to one so young and charming as you are : let us go at daybreak to the river-side."

Avenant patted him, but replied nothing : until, worn out with grief, he slept. Before dawn Cabriole wakened him, saying, "Master, dress yourself and let us go to the river."

There Avenant walked up and down, with his arms folded and his head bent, but saw nothing. At last he heard a voice, calling from a distance, "Avenant, Avenant!"

The little dog ran to the water-side—"Never believe me again, master, if it is not a golden carp, with a ring in its mouth !"

"Yes, Avenant," said the carp, "this is the ring which

the princess has lost. You saved my life in the willow meadow, and I have recompensed you. Farewell!"

Avenant took the ring gratefully and returned to the palace with Cabriole, who scampered about in great glee. Craving an audience, he presented the princess with her ring, and begged her to accompany him to his master's kingdom. She took the ring, looked at it, and thought she was surely dreaming.

"Some fairy must have assisted you, fortunate Avenant," said she.

"Madam, I am only fortunate in my desire to obey your wishes."

"Obey me still," she said graciously. "There is a prince named Galifron, whose suit I have refused. He is a giant as tall as a tower, who eats a man as a monkey eats a nut; he puts cannons into his pockets instead of pistols; and when he speaks, his voice is so loud that every one near him becomes deaf. Go and fight him, and bring me his head."

Avenant was thunderstruck; but after a time he recovered himself—"Very well, madam. I shall certainly perish, but I will perish like a brave man. I will depart at once to fight the Giant Galifron."

The princess, now in her turn, surprised and alarmed, tried every persuasion to induce him not to go, but in vain. Avenant armed himself and started, carrying his little dog in its basket. Cabriole was the only creature that gave him consolation : "Courage, master! While you attack the giant, I will bite his legs : he will stoop down to strike me, and then you can knock him on the head." Avenant smiled at the little dog's spirit, but he knew it was useless.

Arrived at the castle of Galifron, he found the road all strewn with bones and carcases of men. Soon he saw the giant walking. His head was level with the highest trees, and he sang in a terrific voice :

"The fairy there welcomed her majesty." *(Page 251)*

WARWICK GOBLE

"The king's daughter was overjoyed when she beheld her pretty plaything again, picked it up, and ran away with it." (*Page 267*)

"Bring me babies to devour;
More—more—more—more—
Men and women, tender and tough;
All the world holds not enough."

To which Avenant replied, imitating the tune :

"Avenant you here may see,
He is come to punish thee :
Be he tender, be he tough,
To kill thee, giant, he is enough."

Hearing these words, the giant took up his massive club, looked around for the singer, and, perceiving him, would have slain him on the spot, had not a raven, sitting on a tree close by, suddenly flown out upon him and picked out both his eyes. Then Avenant easily killed him and cut off his head, while the raven, watching him, said :

"You shot the eagle who was pursuing me : I promised to recompense you, and to-day I have done it. We are quits."

"No, it is I who am your debtor, Sir Raven," replied Avenant, as, hanging the frightful head to his saddle-bow, he mounted his horse and rode back to the city of the Fair One with Golden Locks.

There everybody followed him, shouting, "Here is brave Avenant, who has killed the giant," until the princess, hearing the noise, and fearing it was Avenant himself who was killed, appeared, all trembling ; and even when he appeared with Galifron's head, she trembled still, although she had nothing to fear.

"Madam," said Avenant, "your enemy is dead : so I trust you will accept the hand of the king my master."

"I cannot," replied she thoughtfully, "unless you first bring me a phial of the water in the Grotto of Darkness. It is six leagues in length, and guarded at the entrance by two fiery dragons. Within it is a pit, full of scorpions, lizards, and serpents, and at the bottom of this place flows the Fountain of Beauty and Health. All who wash in it become, if ugly, beautiful, and if beautiful, beautiful for ever ; if old, young ; and if young, young for ever. Judge then, Avenant, if I can quit my kingdom without carrying with me some of this miraculous water."

"Madam," replied Avenant, "you are already so beautiful that you require it not ; but I am an unfortunate ambassador whose death you desire : I will obey you, though I know I shall never return."

So he departed with his only friends—his horse and his faithful dog Cabriole ; while all who met him looked at him compassionately, pitying so pretty a youth bound on such a hopeless errand. But, however kindly they addressed him, Avenant rode on and answered nothing, for he was too sad at heart.

He reached a mountain-side, where he sat down to rest, leaving his horse to graze, and Cabriole to run after the flies. He knew that the Grotto of Darkness was not far off, yet he looked about him like one who sees nothing. At last he perceived a rock, as black as ink, whence came a thick smoke ; and in a moment appeared one of the two dragons, breathing out flames. It had a yellow and green body, claws, and a long tail. When Cabriole saw the monster, the poor little dog hid himself in terrible fright. But Avenant resolved to die bravely ; so, taking a phial which the princess had given him, he prepared to descend into the cave.

"Cabriole," said he, "I shall soon be dead : then fill this phial with my blood, and carry it to the Fair One with Golden Locks, and afterwards to the king my master, to show him I have been faithful to the last."

While he was thus speaking, a voice called, "Avenant, Avenant!"—and he saw an owl sitting on a hollow tree. Said the owl, "You cut the net in which I was caught, and I vowed to recompense you. Now is the time. Give me the phial : I know every corner of the Grotto of Darkness—I will fetch you the water of beauty."

Delighted beyond words, Avenant delivered up his phial; the owl flew with it into the grotto, and in less than half-an-hour reappeared, bringing it quite full and well corked. Avenant thanked her with all his heart, and joyfully took once more the road to the city.

The Fair One with Golden Locks had no more to say. She consented to accompany him back, with all her suite, to his master's court. On the way thither she saw so much of him, and found him so charming, that Avenant might have married her himself had he chosen; but he would not have been false to his master for all the beauties under the sun. At length they arrived at the king's city, and the Fair One with Golden Locks became his spouse and queen. But she still loved Avenant in her heart, and often said to the king her lord—"But for Avenant I should not be here; he has done all sorts of impossible deeds for my sake; he has fetched me the water of beauty, and I shall never grow old—in short, I owe him everything."

And she praised him in this sort so much, that at length the king became jealous; and though Avenant gave him not the slightest cause of offence, he shut him up in the same high tower once more—but with irons on his hands and feet, and a cruel jailer besides, who fed him with bread and water only. His sole companion was his little dog Cabriole.

When the Fair One with Golden Locks heard of this, she reproached her husband for his ingratitude, and then, throwing herself at his knees, implored that Avenant might be set free. But the king only said, "She loves him!" and refused her prayer. The queen entreated no more, but fell into a deep melancholy.

When the king saw it, he thought she did not care for him because he was not handsome enough; and that if he could wash his face with her water of beauty, it would make her love him more. He knew that she kept it in a cabinet in her chamber, where she could find it always.

Now it happened that a waiting-maid, in cleaning out this cabinet, had, the very day before, knocked down the phial, which was broken in a thousand pieces, and all the contents were lost. Very much alarmed, she then remembered seeing, in a cabinet belonging to the king, a similar phial. This she fetched, and put in the place of the other one, in which was the water of beauty. But the king's phial contained the water of death. It was a poison, used to destroy great criminals—that is, noble-men, gentlemen, and such like. Instead of hanging them or cutting their heads off, like common people, they were compelled to wash their faces with this water ; upon which they fell asleep, and woke no more. So it happened that the king, taking up this phial, believing it to be the water of beauty, washed his face with it, fell asleep, and—died.

Cabriole heard the news, and, gliding in and out among the crowd which clustered round the young and lovely widow, whispered softly to her—" Madam, do not forget poor Avenant." If she had been disposed to do so, the sight of his little dog would have been enough to remind her of him—his many sufferings, and his great fidelity. She rose up, without speaking to anybody, and went straight to the tower where Avenant was confined. There, with her own hands, she struck off his chains, and putting a crown of gold on his head, and a purple mantle on his shoulders, said to him, " Be king—and my husband."

Avenant could not refuse ; for in his heart he had loved her all the time. He threw himself at her feet, and then took the crown and sceptre, and ruled her kingdom like a king. All the people were delighted to have him as their sovereign. The marriage was celebrated in all imaginable pomp, and Avenant and the Fair One with Golden Locks lived and reigned happily together all their days.

THE BUTTERFLY

In the time of the illustrious Merinous, it was indeed a pleasure to be a king : the laws were just, the people obedient, and peace was over the land. This monarch would have been the happiest of men, but for the continual complaints of his consort, which tore his very heart in twain. She wept continually for her daughters, nineteen of whom had perished in the flower of youth. The Fairy of the Fountain had promised a twentieth ; but years passed away in fruitless expectation. "You have neglected to do the fairy sufficient homage," said the king one day ; "I shall give orders to conduct you to the foot of the mountain with pomp and splendour. But when arrived there the mountain itself must be climbed on foot, with many fatigues : most women would rather die childless than encounter them."

"Courage shall not be wanting on my part," said the queen, "and I wish to set out immediately."

The king kissed her forehead, bade her good-night, and fell asleep.

At early dawn appeared in the grand court of the palace an equipage, dazzling as the sun itself ; the wheels were of massy gold, with emerald nails, which sparkled in the light. It was drawn by forty-two horses, white as snow, whose reins were of rose-coloured satin, the fashion of that period. They snorted impatiently, striking fire from the pavement beneath their feet ; their eyes were inflamed ; their bits covered with foam ; and their proud and triumphant air seemed already to announce the success of the queen's enterprise. Three thousand chevaliers, armed at all points and mounted on fiery coursers, wheeled about the chariot, the air resounding with their joyful acclamations of—" *Long live King Merinous and his august spouse !* "

The queen saluted the people with the utmost grace and condescension, which caused such immoderate joy, that she was almost stifled by the pressure of the crowd : but the guards gently kept them at a distance, and the procession passed on.

When her majesty had reached the foot of the mountain, she alighted from her chariot, and, accompanied by only four maids-of-honour, proceeded on foot.

This mountain was formed of slippery earth, slightly covered over with green turf, but giving way at every step. The queen's pretty little white satin shoes were soon left behind ; and her feet next stuck so fast that she could not withdraw them ; her fair hands were in the same plight ; she cried aloud for succour, fearing she should be completely buried alive.

Turning then round to look for her maids-of-honour, she perceived that they had fallen flat on their faces (the impression remains till this day), and were struggling, making the most desperate efforts, less in consideration of their own danger than that of the queen. In fine, after four hours and a half's patient perseverance, they succeeded in regaining their feet ; and, strange to say, no mud or clay attached itself to their clothes ; nothing worse than a slight shade of the green turf, which assumed the appearance of a gauze veil. The fairy then, seeing the queen willing to overcome difficulties, would not try her further, but with one stroke of a wand reduced the mountain two or three hundred feet ; the remaining height was very dry and easy of ascent.

The queen was thus conducted to a delicious grove :

a coral fountain rose in the midst ; its waters, of the purest rose-colour, wound along the meadow, murmuring plaintive airs, whose words were perfectly distinguishable. The fairy there welcomed her majesty, who prepared to explain the occasion of her journey ; but that was quite unnecessary. The fairy, exacting profound secrecy, presented her with a phial of water drawn from the fountain, strictly ordering that it should be broken when she had drank it all. The queen, charmed by this reception, made presents of inestimable value, and rejoined her maids-of-honour, who had been thrown into an enchanted sleep. They then returned to the palace in such high spirits, that all the court danced and sung for a month afterwards.

In due course, her majesty became, for the twentieth time, a joyful mother.

The magnificence and liberality displayed on this occasion exceed belief. The royal palace was surrounded by three hundred large spouts, which poured forth alternately, night and day, the choicest sweetmeats, confectionery, and money ; the streets, in fact, were filled—the passengers had only to stoop down and be satisfied.

But in the midst of these festivities the Fairy of the Fountain, uncovering the little princess's cradle, which was of mother-o'-pearl studded with diamonds, perceived a beautiful butterfly, placed immediately under the infant's left eye.

The chief cradle-rocker, who dreaded being taxed with negligence, took a humming-bird's wing, and endeavoured to chase it away, but all in vain : it remained quite unconcerned in the same spot, extending its large wings of rose-colour and azure-blue on the face of the princess, appearing rather to caress than to wish to do her any injury. " Ah ! " said the fairy, " this butterfly is not what you imagine. It is a powerful fairy, who presides at the birth of the most distinguished princesses, and endows them with a degree of levity which generally leads to misfortune. I can lessen the evil, without doubt, but I cannot entirely avert it." The queen wept bitterly at this sad news, and the king saw no person during eight days. He then ceased to think on the subject.

Misfortunes rarely enter into the speculations of kings. Masters of the destinies of others, mankind flatter them into a belief that their power can almost control fate itself. Accordingly, the visit of the butterfly did not produce much permanent inquietude. The poets-laureate and literati of the court turned it into numerous sentimental conceits ; amongst others, that the insect had fastened on the princess's cheek mistaking it for a rose. This idea branched out into a hundred elegies, a thousand madrigals, and fifteen hundred songs, which were sung in all the principal families, and adapted to airs, some already known, and others composed for the occasion.

The fairy frequently visited her little charge, but was unable to conquer her fickle disposition. Ten different nurses had already been obliged to give her up ; she scratched them, bit them, and obstinately refused to be fed. When she grew older, and began her education, she was so easily wearied and vexed, that no one dared to contradict her. The fairy was consulted ; who made her smell at a very rare flower. This produced a degree of intelligence so extraordinary, that in three days she could read, write, speak all languages, and play on every instrument after just twenty-three minutes' application.

The queen was now delighted, for the princess's talents were noised abroad equally with her beauty. She had scarcely attained the age of fourteen when many kings sought the honour of her hand. The good King Merinous was well stricken in years, and fondly desired to see Papillette established. All who seemed worthy of her received a favourable reception, and amongst this number was the accomplished Prince Favourite. After he had been presented in due form, the old monarch asked his daughter what she thought of their new guest.

" Sire," replied the maiden, " I have been brought up with too much modesty and reserve to bestow attention on strangers of the other sex."

" That is true," returned the monarch ; " but merely regarding him as a picture, how has he appeared to you ? "

" Tall and handsome," answered Papillette, " his chestnut hair clinging in close and crisping curls to his ivory brow ; his eyes of violet-blue, filled with soft vivacity ; his teeth, of the most brilliant white, divide lips of coral ; his nose is perfect Grecian, and his limbs like the rarest statuary. I might say more, had I ventured to look at the prince."

" It is enough," said the king, " your first glance has shown you enough. I am delighted that you are so sensible to the merits of Prince Favourite, as I design him for your husband. Love him accordingly."

" Your majesty's commands are laws to your dutiful daughter," replied Papillette.

One may easily imagine with what magnificence preparations were made for the nuptials ; the king hastened them, lest his daughter's fickleness and levity might cause disappointment to their dearest hopes.

Papillette one day, while steadily regarding her lover, who was kneeling before her, appeared struck by something which made an impression as sudden as disagreeable. She repulsed Prince Favourite, saying she was seized with a headache, and could not be troubled with company.

The lover submissively arose and went to seek the queen, beseeching her to find out what he had done, and to intercede in his favour. Her majesty accordingly questioned the princess, who, bathed in tears, threw herself into the arms of her mother, confessing that she had made a discovery which totally altered her sentiments regarding the prince. "Is it possible," added she, "that you have not perceived his ears, of so unusual a size, and a deep red colour?"

"Is that all?" cried the queen. "In truth, I have not observed it ; but to take notice of an imperfection so very trifling, would make us appear ridiculous indeed."

"People cannot help their feelings," replied Papillette ; "I have quite a horror of red ears ; it is little worth while to be daughter of a great king, if one must be crossed and thwarted in the most important arrangement of life."

The queen reasoned long ; but this only increased Papillette's resistance : therefore, being quite defenceless against the tears of a child so dear, her majesty promised to speak to the king.

Merinous was firm in all his resolutions ; he therefore declared that his daughter should become the wife of Prince Favourite, whether she liked it or not.

The queen had not courage to impart this dreadful intelligence ; but she threw herself on the generosity of the prince, beseeching that he would himself break the engagement—thus shielding Papillette from the resentment of the king.

The distracted lover was ready to die with grief : but promised to do all she requested. He asked but three days' grace.

The queen consented ; and Prince Favourite then summoned Queséca, chief barber to the king. "Barber," said he, "each country has its particular prejudices—its own ideas of beauty ; here I find large ears are deemed a deformity ; therefore, I command thee to cut off mine."

"I cannot do it," replied the barber ; "your royal highness has been grossly deceived. I have the honour of shaving the first lords of the court, and I know many of them whose ears are equally red and ten times as long as those of your royal highness. These very lords are amongst the most distinguished favourites of the king."

"I have summoned thee," replied the prince, "to operate and not to prate ; obey my orders, and inflame not my ears still further by thy discourse."

"Alas!" said the barber, "since your royal highness means to sacrifice them to an unreasonable caprice, what signifies it whether they are inflamed or not?"

At these words the prince made a threatening gesture ; and Queséca, no longer daring to resist, took his razor, and with a trembling hand separated two of the handsomest ears from one of the finest heads in the world : for be it known, that the princess only made a pretext of this assertion, because she had taken a fancy for somebody else.

The wound bled profusely : the prince applied healing balm ; and when in a condition to appear before her, enclosed his two ears in a little box, rare and precious, and presented it to Papillette, his heart once more filled with hope and love.

The princess eagerly opened the beautiful little casket, then dashed it with horror to the ground. "Prince!" she cried, "what can have induced you to mutilate yourself so cruelly? Could you imagine that I would ever wed a man who submitted to lose his ears?"

"Madam," said the prince, in consternation, "it was by my own order that——"

"What a fool you were then!" cried Papillette. "If you are not willing to become the ridicule of the court, I advise you to quit it with the greatest expedition imaginable."

The prince dared not call her cruel and ungrateful : he retired to the thickest retreats of a forest, and soon after entirely lost his reason.

The princess, once more free, confessed that amongst her numerous suitors there was one whom she preferred ; this was Prince Malabar, whose martial mien announced the soul of a hero. The queen did not deny that Malabar had sought her daughter's hand, even before Favourite aspired to that honour, and King Merinous could now no longer insist on a marriage with this unfortunate prince, since he was quite insane, ran naked through the woods, sometimes believing himself a hind, sometimes a wolf, and never stopping until exhausted by grief and despair. But in consenting to the marriage of his daughter with Prince Malabar, the king declared that, should she again change her mind, he would never forgive her.

The happy day was once more fixed, and Papillette, three days preceding, invited her lover to meet her in a delightful grove at the extremity of the gardens. This grove was planted with myrtles, so thick and high that they afforded a pleasant shade. Beautiful flowers sprang up on all sides ; and, added to the warblings of the birds in the trees, were the voices of hidden musicians, singing a chorus, composed by the princess herself. This, however, Malabar, who was a soldier, and not a musician, and who naturally wished to have his lady-love's society all to himself, did not sufficiently appreciate.

"Princess," said he, "I had much rather hear you talk than these people sing."

"Are then those cares despised," replied Papillette, "which I have so assiduously employed to amuse and gratify you by the display of my talents?"

"Your dearest talent," cried he, "is that of pleasing : it comprises every other. Send away these people, I pray." He added, in a tone of the utmost irritation, "I hate—I detest music!"

"Have I rightly heard?" exclaimed the princess angrily ; "and do you pretend to love, if your soul is insensible to such transporting sounds?"

"I wish they would transport themselves far enough away," returned the lover, who, like most other lovers, could be in an ill humour sometimes. "My princess, do order this scraping and squalling to cease."

"On the contrary, I order my musicians to remain,"

answered Papillette, quite indignant; "and never, never will I unite myself to him whom divine melody hath no power to move. Go, prince, barbarous alike in taste and science, seek some rustic maid, best suited to your insensibility."

The musicians, too far distant to hear these words, struck up a lively tune. Malabar imagined this done in derision, and it required all his respect for the princess to prevent him from falling upon them sword in hand. He repented much his words, but considered it beneath his dignity to retract them; the princess also refused to retract hers: so they parted.

Malabar resolved on instant death. Mounting the noblest courser in his stable, he rode down to the sea-coast, and plunged him right over a perpendicular cliff into the waters below.

The tide happened to be coming in, so that the body was soon washed on shore, and brought before the eyes of the cruel princess, laid on a litter formed of willow, hung with draperies of black crape.

She was standing at the window when the melancholy procession passed, and inquired what it was. None dared answer; they only removed the covering from the face of the corpse. She uttered a loud shriek, and fainted away.

The king and queen lavished on her the most tender cares, but all in vain: she declared that she regarded herself as an inconsolable widow, and insisted upon putting on the deepest weeds.

King Merinous respected this caprice, and ordered twenty thousand yards of crape for her use. She was just giving orders to have her apartments festooned with it, and holding a cambric handkerchief to her eyes, when a little green ape (a drawing-room favourite) dressed itself in weepers, and disposed one of the widow's caps most tastefully under its chin.

At this sight the princess burst out laughing so loudly and heartily, that all the court ladies, who had been trying which could pull the longest and most sympathetic countenance, were greatly relieved, and began immediately to smile a little.

Gradually, they removed from her eyes the trappings of woe, and substituted ribbons of rose-colour and blue of every shade and variety : trying on these, so diverted Papillette's melancholy, that the poor drowned prince was soon forgotten. Her tears indeed were vain ; he had already enough of water.

The king was in despair. "Alas !" said he to the queen, "we shall never have the consolation of marrying Papillette, or beholding our grandchildren. Of two monarchs so worthy of her, one has lost his reason, the other has cast himself into the sea ; and while we continue to weep, she, already consoled, thinks only of diverting herself ! "

"Sire," replied the queen, "calm your apprehensions. Our daughter is yet too young to feel true love in all its fervour ; let us have patience, and seek alliance with none but those truly worthy of her affections."

"Such is my wish," replied the king, "and I begin to turn my views upon Prince Patipata ; he has seen the portrait of Papillette, and is satisfied ; but, though a wise and noble monarch, his personal qualifications are little in his favour."

"How so?" rejoined the queen.

"Because he is stiff, tall, and spare ; his eyes bleared and filmy ; his hair red, and so scanty withal, that it seems like a few stripes of blasted flax hung around a distaff."

A few days after this conversation, Prince Patipata arrived at court ; and the queen did not conceal from Papillette, that, notwithstanding his personal disadvantages, he was intended for her spouse.

The princess laughed immoderately, yet, just for amusement, she displayed towards him all the arts and graces of coquetry to perfection.

Prince Patipata having been informed of the deplorable end of his predecessors, concealed his love as carefully as the others had proclaimed theirs. He was so reserved and cold, that the princess longed exceedingly to discover the state of his feelings. Accordingly, one day, while Patipata was walking with Salmoé, his intimate confidant, she hid herself in the trunk of an old tree, which had been hollowed out by lightning, and afforded apparently a secure retreat. The prince seated himself at the foot of it, but he had observed the princess; and, making a sign of intelligence to his companion, feigned to continue a conversation of which she was the subject. "Assuredly," said he, "the princess is very handsome; but flatterers, poets, and painters always overstep the truth. Her portrait has deceived me: its large blue eyes bear assuredly some resemblance to those of Papillette, but they bespeak an ardent and feeling heart, while hers is frivolous, volatile, and incapable of love. Her smile would be charming, but for its satirical irony. And what is the value of the loveliest lips in the world, if they open but to deceive and betray!"

"I am much surprised," replied Salmoé; "I believed that your royal highness was equally loving and beloved."

"Far from it," returned Patipata; "it would ill become me, plain as I am, to be confident of pleasing; and I am not dupe enough to yield my heart without return. Do not you approve of this?"

"No," answered Salmoé, "your royal highness is too modest; I cannot sufficiently appreciate your humility."

The prince affected to be dissatisfied with this praise, and then moved onwards in order to liberate Papillette, who was very inconveniently cramped, and almost suffocated with anger. Disagreeable truths seldom reach the ear of princesses; her resentment, therefore, was to be expected. Meanwhile, her heart being equally capricious as her understanding, she felt ready to pardon, and even, on reflection, to justify Patipata. But pride soon combated this weakness ; and she determined to send him away. She complained to her father ; assured him, that by mere chance she had heard the most odious calumnies uttered by a prince who sported with their dignity, by falsely pretending to the hand of her whom he slighted and despised. The king was surprised ; but, not having entered into any positive engagements with Patipata, he readily entered into her feelings, and intimated to the prince that his adieus would be well received. This Patipata expected ; but, although not naturally presumptuous, he had read sufficiently into the heart of Papillette to feel some degree of consolation.

As no decisive explanation of any kind occurred, he was permitted to take leave of the princess. This he did with much firmness ; while she appeared so much agitated, that it was remarked by all the court. The men attributed this to hatred ; but the ladies, who knew better, pronounced it love. They were convinced of the fact, when day by day she began to pine and refused to eat ; and had not the chief cook every day invented some new ragout, she would inevitably have died of hunger.

The queen was in despair, and despatched a billet to the Fairy of the Fountain, fastening it to the tail of a little white mouse, which served as a messenger on this occasion ; it was perfectly acquainted with the way, and in a few minutes the fairy arrived at the palace. The late events were mentioned to her, and the melancholy situation of the princess.

" I understand this case," said the fairy ; " but it is necessary that Papillette should give me her confidence."

The fairy was so amiable and so much beloved by the princess, that she easily yielded ; and casting down her eyes, confessed that she loved one who regarded her with contemptuous indifference ; and what rendered her choice still more degrading was, its object being equally ugly as insensible.

"I am then to understand," replied the fairy, "that you wish to be cured of this unfortunate passion?"

"Alas, no!" rejoined Papillette, "for my only pleasure is in thinking of him, speaking to him as if he could hear, and persuading myself that, notwithstanding appearances, he could have loved me, had he believed my heart capable of steady affections. I shall therefore die, leaving him alike ignorant of my regrets and my repentance."

"I would not advise you to die," said the fairy; "that is the only evil in the world without a remedy. But, my dear Papillette, what can I do to console you?"

"Let me see the prince once more, under some metamorphose in which it is impossible for him to recognise me."

"Very well," replied the fairy. "But since you wish to risk it, and that a simple butterfly can scarcely compromise her dignity in following a king, under this form I shall transport you to his court."

So saying, the Fairy of the Fountain placed on her finger a little emerald ring, and the princess distinctly felt her arms change their shape—expand—become flexible, and form two light wings, clothed in the most brilliant colours. Her little feet quitted the earth, and as the window was open, she flew out, traversing the air, with a degree of rapidity which at first caused some sensations of fear. But soon the eager desire of seeing Patipata urged her forward, although natural instinct so far prevailed, as to cause frequent descents to earth, where she rested on every tempting flower.

At length, entering the prince's gardens, she beheld him walking on a terrace watering a beautiful orange tree. Her heart beat so violently, that her first emotion was to hide, but, soon recovering self-possession, she flew forwards and rested on a branch which he had just gathered.

"What a charming butterfly!" observed the king to his chief gardener. "Its colours are truly exquisite; I never recollect having seen any such before."

"Some new species, come to do mischief, I suppose," said the gardener, preparing to brush it rudely away. But it took refuge on the bosom of the king, with such caressing and tender familiarity, that only a hard heart could have done it injury.

"Ah, little traitor!" cried Patipata, "thou wishest to win me by thy fleeting charms, and then escape for ever. I already know too well the pain of loving fickle beings such as thou. Yet still I must defend thee, and permit thy return to my orange tree as often as thou desirest."

Papillette easily penetrated the thoughts of the prince, and although they uttered a reproach for her inconstancy, she fancied they also breathed the language of love; and returned in better spirits than usual to her father's palace, where her absence had been unobserved. From thenceforward she never omitted making use of the emerald ring, which transported her in a few moments to her royal lover: she followed him to his palace, saw him give audiences, preside in council, and everywhere prove himself just, great, generous, and worthy of all her affection. It is true that his eyes were still filmy, his body spare, and his hair as red as ever; but what signifies an outside casket when containing a priceless jewel within?

Patipata was determined against marriage; he therefore adopted as heir to the crown the son of a cousin, a young orphan, whom he purposed bringing up beneath his own eye. This prince little resembled his uncle: he had been much spoiled in infancy, and it was impossible to improve him. One day, while conversing with Patipata, "Sire," said he, "I have a favour to ask your majesty, and I pray you not to refuse me."

"I shall willingly grant you anything reasonable," replied the king.

"It is but your beautiful rose-coloured butterfly, which follows you everywhere."

"And if I were to give it to you, what then?"

"I would run this golden pin through its body, and stick it to a branch of the orange tree, to see how long it would live. Oh, nothing could be more amusing!"

"Nothing could be more barbarous!" answered Patipata indignantly. "Go, you inspire me with horror; I banish you from my presence during three entire days, and remember, that if my butterfly should receive any injury, you shall be punished with unexampled severity!"

The poor butterfly, who had heard this discourse, knew not how to express its gratitude and joy; it flapped its wings, and sported around its benefactor. The king held out his finger, and it rested there. "Thou shalt quit me no more," said he. "It is so sweet to be loved, even by a butterfly, that I would not willingly prove myself ungrateful: thou shalt feed at my table; I will serve thee with the finest fruits, the fairest flowers. Ah! if I can only make thee happy!"

On the following day, Patipata went out hunting. In vain Papillette sought him in the park, in the garden, and near the favourite orange tree. But his nephew, taking advantage of his absence, began chasing the pretty butterfly. The courtiers knew that he would one day be in power, and, eager to gratify his whims, assisted in the wanton sport: ministers the most pompous, members of council the most profound, climbed on trees, and capered through the meadows,—one would have supposed them mad. But the royal insect, so familiar with the king, was for all others the most capricious of butterflies. It amused itself in leading the court a long chase, and at length rested in the private cabinet of the king, where they never once thought of seeking it.

Papillette, now all alone, could not resist the opportunity afforded of looking over a great quantity of writing which lay on the bureau. What was her surprise and joy, on there finding verses, the most passionate and tender, which Patipata had written in her praise! They indeed revealed that he was proud, and would not risk a second refusal; but they vowed to remain faithful to her, and never to wed another.

The princess was so affected, that two little tiny tears stood in her butterfly-eyes. Well indeed she might shed them, for at this moment, the wicked little prince, her enemy, came behind, and seizing her by her two lovely wings, popped her into his hat.

"Now I have you!" cried he; and it is impossible to say what would have happened, had not the king opportunely returned; when, in taking off his hat to his uncle, he let the butterfly go.

She, recovering from her fright, testified affection by many little endearments; and Patipata, now accustomed to speak to her, exclaimed: "Beautiful insect, how happy art thou!—thou wanderest from flower to flower, without giving the preference to any—thou knowest not love—thou hast not found ingratitude! I, a king, cannot boast of such happiness. I adore the lovely Princess Papillette, and am dismissed from her court. I am ugly, it is true; but were I ever so handsome, I should not be more fortunate, for I too well know her fickle——"

The butterfly here sighed so deeply, that the king started.

"Is it possible thou canst feel?" said he. "Oh, if my princess had but as much sensibility, I would know no other care! With her I would live in a hut, far, far from the deceitful splendour of a throne!"

"The Princess Papillette would willingly accompany you," said a little voice, in tones of the finest and purest melody, and the butterfly's rosy wings blushed deep as crimson.

"What a prodigy!" cried Patipata. "Ah! butterfly, what dost thou know of my Papillette?"

"Suppose it were herself!" said a voice, which seemed to proceed from a little fountain of rock-crystal which stood between the windows.

The prince turned round ; but instead of the butterfly, he beheld the Fairy of the Fountain, holding the fair Papillette by the hand. They were both encircled by a light rose-coloured cloud, which shed a softly brilliant light around the apartment.

Patipata bent one knee to the earth, and kissed the hem of the princess's garment.

"Come, prince," said the fairy, "King Merinous is apprised of what passes here. Papillette has overcome her evil destiny. Her affections are fixed and sure ; and their object is yourself. And however ready you may both be to live in a hut together, I advise you not to do it. Love is sweeter than royalty, no doubt, but it is not impossible to unite both."

The lovers, transported with joy, placed their feet on the rose-coloured cloud, which instantly carried them to the palace of the king. The Fairy of the Fountain, to complete her benefactions, rendered Patipata as handsome as he was amiable, and the nuptials were celebrated with suitable pomp and festivity. We are informed that Papillette had, at first, some slight returns of her natural disposition ; but in one year she became a mother, and from thenceforward never knew frivolity more.

THE FROG-PRINCE

In times of yore, when wishes were both heard and granted, lived a king whose daughters were all beautiful, but the youngest was so lovely that the sun himself, who has seen so much, wondered at her beauty every time he looked in her face. Now, near the king's castle was a large dark forest; and in the forest, under an old linden-tree, was a deep well. When the day was very hot, the king's daughter used to go to the wood and seat herself at the edge of the cool well; and when she became wearied, she would take a golden ball, throw it up in the air, and catch it again. This was her favourite amusement. Once it happened that her golden ball, instead of falling back into the little hand that she stretched out for it, dropped on the ground, and immediately rolled away into the water. The king's daughter followed it with her eyes, but the ball had vanished, and the well was so deep that no one could see down to the bottom. Then she began to weep, wept louder and louder every minute, and could not console herself at all.

While she was thus lamenting some one called to her : "What is the matter with you, king's daughter? You weep so, that you would touch the heart of a stone."

She looked around to see whence the voice came, and saw a frog stretching his thick ugly head out of the water.

"Ah! it is you, old water-paddler!" said she. "I am crying for my golden ball, which has fallen into the well."

"Be content," answered the frog, "I daresay I can give you some good advice; but what will you give me if I bring back your plaything to you?"

"Whatever you like, dear frog," said she; "my clothes, my pearls and jewels, even the golden crown I wear."

The frog answered, "Your clothes, your pearls and jewels, even your golden crown, I do not care for; but if you will love me, and let me be your companion and play-fellow; sit near you at your little table, eat from your little golden plate, drink from your little cup, and sleep in your little bed;—if you will promise me this, then I will bring you back your golden ball from the bottom of the well."

"Oh yes!" said she; "I promise you everything, if you will only bring me back my golden ball."

She thought to herself, meanwhile: "What nonsense the silly frog talks! He sits on the water with the other frogs, and croaks, and cannot be anybody's play-fellow!"

But the frog, as soon as he had received the promise, dipped his head under the water and sank down. In a little while up he came again with the ball in his mouth, and threw it on the grass. The king's daughter was overjoyed when she beheld her pretty plaything again, picked it up, and ran away with it.

"Wait! wait!" cried the frog; "take me with you. I cannot run as fast as you."

Alas! of what use was it that he croaked after her as loud as he could. She would not listen to him, but hastened home, and soon forgot the poor frog, who was obliged to plunge again to the bottom of his well.

The next day, when she was sitting at dinner with the king and all the courtiers, eating from her little gold plate, there came a sound of something creeping up the marble staircase—splish, splash; and when it had reached the top, it knocked at the door and cried, "Youngest king's daughter, open to me."

She ran, wishing to see who was outside ; but when she opened the door, and there sat the frog, she flung it hastily to again, and sat down at table, feeling very, very uncomfortable. The king saw that her heart was beating violently, and said, " How, my child, why are you afraid ? Is a giant standing outside the door to carry you off ? "

"Oh no ! " answered she, " it is no giant, but a nasty frog, who yesterday, when I was playing in the wood near the well, fetched my golden ball out of the water. For this I promised him he should be my companion, but I never thought he could come out of his well. Now he is at the door, and wants to come in."

Again, the second time, there was a knock, and a voice cried :

> "Youngest king's daughter,
>   Open to me ;
>   Know you what yesterday
>   You promised me,
>   By the cool water ?
>   Youngest king's daughter,
>   Open to me."

Then said the king, " What you promised you must perform. Go and open the door."

She went and opened the door ; the frog hopped in, always following and following her till he came up to her chair. There he sat, and cried out, " Lift me up to you on the table."

She refused, till the king, her father, commanded her to do it. When the frog was on the table, he said, " Now push your little golden plate nearer to me, that we may eat together." She did as he desired, but one could easily see that she did it unwillingly. The frog seemed to enjoy his dinner very much, but every morsel she ate stuck in the throat of the poor little princess.

Then said the frog, "I have eaten enough, and am tired ; carry me to your little room, and make your little silken bed smooth, and we will lay ourselves down to sleep together."

At this the daughter of the king began to weep ; for she was afraid of the cold frog, who wanted to sleep in her pretty clean bed.

But the king looked angrily at her, and said again : "What you have promised you must perform. The frog is your companion."

It was no use to complain whether she liked it or not ; she was obliged to take the frog with her up to her little bed. So she picked him up with two fingers, hating him bitterly the while, and carried him upstairs ; but when she got into bed, instead of lifting him up to her, she threw him with all her strength against the wall, saying, "Now, you nasty frog, there will be an end of you."

But what fell down from the wall was not a dead frog, but a living young prince, with beautiful and loving eyes, who at once became, by her own promise and her father's will, her dear companion and husband. He told her how he had been cursed by a wicked sorceress, and that no one but the king's youngest daughter could release him from his enchantment and take him out of the well.

The next day a carriage drove up to the palace-gates with eight white horses, having white feathers on their heads and golden reins. Behind it stood the servant of the young prince, called the Faithful Henry. This faithful Henry had been so grieved when his master was changed into a frog, that he had been compelled to have three iron bands fastened round his heart, lest it should break. Now the carriage came to convey the prince to his kingdom, so the faithful Henry lifted in the bride and bridegroom, and mounted behind, full of joy at his lord's release. But when they had gone a short distance, the prince heard behind him a noise as if something was breaking. He turned round, and cried out, "Henry, the carriage is breaking!"

But Henry replied, "No, sir, it is not the carriage, but one of the bands from my heart, with which I was forced to bind it up, or it would have broken with grief, while you sat as a frog at the bottom of the well."

Twice again this happened, and the prince always thought the carriage was breaking; but it was only the bands breaking off from the heart of the faithful Henry, out of joy that his lord the Frog-Prince was a frog no more.

THE WHITE CAT

THERE was once a king who had three sons, all handsome, brave and noble of heart. Nevertheless, some wicked courtiers made their father believe they were eager to wear his crown, which, though he was old, he had no mind to resign. He therefore invented a plan to get them out of the kingdom, and prevent their carrying out any undutiful projects. Sending for them to a private audience, he conversed with them kindly, and said : "You must be sensible, my dear children, that my great age prevents me from attending so closely as I have hitherto done to state affairs. I fear this may be injurious to my subjects ; I therefore desire to place my crown on the head of one of you ; but it is no more than just that, in return for such a present, you should procure me some amusement in my retirement, before I leave the capital for ever. I cannot help thinking that a little dog, handsome, faithful, and engaging, would be the very thing to make me happy ; so that, without bestowing a preference on either of you, I declare that he who brings me the most perfect little dog shall be my successor."

The princes were much surprised at the fancy of their father to have a little dog, yet they accepted the proposition with pleasure ; and accordingly, after taking leave of the king, who presented them with abundance of money and jewels, and appointed that day twelvemonth for their return, they set off on their travels.

Before separating, however, they took some refreshment together, in an old palace about three miles out of town, where they mutually agreed to meet in the same place on that day twelvemonth, and go all together with their presents to court. They also agreed to change their names, and travel incognito.

Each took a different road ; but it is intended to relate the adventures of only the youngest, who was the most beautiful, amiable, and accomplished prince in the world. As he travelled from town to town, he bought all the handsome dogs that fell in his way ; and as soon as he saw one that was handsomer than those he had, he made a present of the rest ; for twenty servants would scarcely have been sufficient to take care of all the dogs he was continually purchasing. At length, wandering he knew not whither, he found himself in a forest ; night suddenly came on, and with it a violent storm of thunder, lightning, and rain : to add to his perplexity, he lost his way. After he had groped about for a long time, he perceived a light, which made him suppose that he was not far from some house : he accordingly pursued his way towards it, and in a short time found himself at the gates of the most magnificent palace he had ever beheld. The entrance-door was of gold, covered with sapphires, which shone so that scarcely could the strongest eyesight bear to look at it : this was the light the prince had seen from the forest. The walls were of transparent porcelain, variously coloured, and represented the history of all the fairies that had existed from the beginning of the world. The prince, coming back to the golden door, observed a deer's foot fastened to a chain of diamonds ; he could not help wondering at the magnificence he beheld, and the security in which the inhabitants seemed to live ; "For," said he to himself, "nothing could be easier than for thieves to steal this chain, and as many of the sapphire stones as would make their fortunes." He pulled the chain, and heard a bell, the sound of which was exquisite. In a few moments the door was opened ; yet he perceived nothing but twelve hands in the air, each holding a torch. The prince was so astonished that he durst not move a step— when he felt himself gently pushed on by some other hands from behind him. He walked on, in great perplexity, till he entered a vestibule inlaid with porphyry and lapis-stone, where the most melodious voice he had ever heard chanted the following words :

> "Welcome, prince, no danger fear,
> Mirth and love attend you here ;
> You shall break the magic spell,
> That on a beauteous lady fell.
>
> Welcome, prince, no danger fear,
> Mirth and love attend you here."

The prince now advanced with confidence, wondering what these words could mean ; the hands moved him forward towards a large door of coral, which opened of itself to give him admittance into a splendid apartment built of mother-o'-pearl, through which he passed into others, so richly adorned with paintings and jewels, and so resplendently lighted with thousands of lamps, girandoles, and lustres, that he imagined he must be in an enchanted palace. When he had passed through sixty apartments, all equally splendid, he was stopped by the hands, and a large easy-chair advanced of itself towards the fireplace ; then the hands, which he observed were extremely white and delicate, took off his wet clothes, and supplied their place with the finest linen imaginable, adding a comfortable wrapping-gown, embroidered with gold and pearls.

The hands next brought him an elegant dressing-table, and combed his hair so very gently that he scarcely felt their touch. They held before him a beautiful basin, filled with perfumes, for him to wash his face and hands, and afterwards took off the wrapping-gown, and dressed him in a suit of clothes of still greater splendour. When his toilet was complete, they conducted him to an apartment he had not yet seen, and which also was magnificently furnished. There was a table spread for supper, and everything upon it was of the purest gold, adorned with jewels. The prince observed there were two covers set, and was wondering who was to be his companion, when his attention was suddenly caught by a small figure not a foot high, which just then entered the room, and advanced towards him. It had on a long black veil, and was supported by two cats dressed in mourning, and with swords by their sides: they were followed by a numerous retinue of cats, some carrying cages full of rats, and others mouse-traps full of mice.

The prince was at a loss what to think. The little figure now approached, and throwing aside her veil, he beheld a most beautiful white cat: she seemed young and melancholy; and, addressing herself to him, she said, "My prince, you are welcome; your presence affords me the greatest pleasure."

"Madam," replied he, "I would fain thank you for your generosity, nor can I help observing that you must be an extraordinary creature to possess, with your present form, the gift of speech, and the most magnificent palace I have ever seen."

"All this is very true," answered the beautiful cat; "but, prince, I am not fond of talking, and least of all do I like compliments; let us therefore sit down to supper."

The trunkless hands then placed the dishes on the table, and the prince and white cat seated themselves at it. The first dish was a pie made of young pigeons, and the next was a fricassee of the fattest mice. The view of the one made the prince almost afraid to taste the other, till the white cat, who guessed his thoughts, assured him that there were certain dishes at table which had been dressed on purpose for him, in which there was not a morsel of either rat or mouse: accordingly, he ate heartily of such as she recommended. When supper was over, he perceived that the white cat had a portrait set in gold hanging to one of her feet. He begged her permission to look at it; when, to his astonishment, he saw the portrait of a handsome young man, who exactly resembled himself! He thought there was something most extraordinary in all this : yet, as the white cat sighed and looked very sorrowful, he did not venture to ask any questions. He conversed with her on different subjects, and found her extremely well versed in everything that was passing in the world. When night was far advanced, his hostess wished him a good night, and he was conducted by the hands to his bedchamber, which was different still from anything he had seen in the palace, being hung with the wings of butterflies mixed with the most curious feathers. His bed was of gauze, festooned with bunches of the gayest ribands, and the looking-glasses reached from the floor to the ceiling. The prince was undressed and put into bed by the hands, without speaking a word. He, however, slept little, and in the morning was awakened by a confused noise. The hands took him out of bed, and put on him a handsome hunting-jacket. He looked into the courtyard, and perceived more than five hundred cats, busily employed in preparing for the field—for this was a day of festival. Presently the white cat came to his apartment ; and having politely inquired after his health, she invited him to partake of their amusement. The prince willingly acceded, and mounted a wooden horse, richly caparisoned, which had been prepared for him, and which he was assured would gallop to admiration. The beautiful white cat mounted a monkey; she wore a dragoon's cap, which made her look so fierce that all the rats and mice ran away in the utmost terror.

Everything being ready, the horns sounded, and away they went : no hunting was ever more agreeable. The cats ran faster than the hares and rabbits ; and when they caught any, they turned them out to be hunted in the presence of the white cat, and a thousand cunning tricks were played. Nor were the birds in safety; for the monkey made nothing of climbing up the trees, with the white cat on his back, to the nests of the young eagles. When the chase was over, the whole retinue returned to the palace; the white cat immediately exchanged her dragoon's cap for the veil, and sat down to supper with the prince, who, being very hungry, ate heartily, and afterwards partook with her of the most delicious wines. He then was conducted to his chamber as before, and wakened in the morning to renew the same sort of life, which day after day became so pleasant to him that he no longer thought of anything but of pleasing the sweet little creature who received him so courteously: accordingly, every day was spent in new amusements. The prince had almost forgotten his country and relations, and sometimes even regretted that he was not a cat, so great was his affection for his mewing companions.

"Alas!" said he to the white cat, "how will it afflict me to leave you, whom I love so much! Either make yourself a lady, or make me a cat." She smiled at the prince's wish, but offered no reply.

At length, the twelvemonth was nearly expired: the white cat, who knew the very day when the prince was to reach his father's palace, reminded him that he had but three days longer to look for a perfect little dog. The prince, astonished at his own forgetfulness, began to afflict himself; when the cat told him not to be so sorrowful, since she would not only provide him with a little dog, but also with a wooden horse, which should convey him safely home in less than twelve hours.

"Look here," said she, showing him an acorn; "this contains what you desire."

The prince put the acorn to his ear, and heard the barking of a little dog. Transported with joy, he thanked the cat a thousand times ; and the next day, bidding her tenderly adieu, he set out on his return.

The prince arrived first at the place of rendezvous, and was soon joined by his brothers : they mutually embraced, and began to give an account of their success ; when the youngest showed them only a little mongrel cur, telling them that he thought it could not fail to please the king, from its extraordinary beauty. The brothers trod on each other's toes under the table, as much as to say, "We have little to fear from this sorry-looking animal." The next day they went together to the palace. The dogs of the two elder brothers were lying on cushions, and so curiously wrapped around with embroidered quilts, that one would scarcely venture to touch them. The youngest produced his cur, and all wondered how the prince could hope to receive a crown for such a shabby present. The king examined the two little dogs of the elder princes, and declared he thought them so equally beautiful that he knew not to which, with justice, he could give the preference. They accordingly began to dispute ; when the youngest prince, taking his acorn from his pocket, soon ended their contention ; for a little dog appeared, which could with ease go through the smallest ring, and was besides a miracle of beauty. The king could not possibly hesitate in declaring his satis- faction ; yet, as he was not more inclined than the year before to part with his crown, he told his sons that he was extremely obliged to them for the pains they had taken : and since they had succeeded so well, he wished they would make a second attempt ; he therefore begged they would take another year in order to procure a piece of cambric, fine enough to be drawn through the eye of a small needle.

The three princes thought this very hard ; yet they set out, in obedience to the king's command. The two eldest took different roads, and the youngest remounted his wooden horse, and in a short time arrived at the palace of his beloved white cat, who received him with the greatest joy, while the trunkless hands helped him to dismount, and provided him with immediate refreshment. Afterwards the prince gave the white cat an account of the admiration which had been bestowed on the beautiful little dog, and informed her of the further injunction of his father.

" Make yourself perfectly easy, dear prince," said she ; " I have in my palace some cats who are perfect adepts in making such cambric as the king requires ; so you have nothing to do but to give me the pleasure of your company while it is making, and I will procure you all the amusement possible."

She accordingly ordered the most curious fireworks to be played off in sight of the window of the apartment in which they were sitting ; and nothing but festivity and rejoicing was heard throughout the palace for the prince's return. As the white cat frequently gave proofs of an excellent understanding, the prince was by no means tired of her company ; she talked with him of state affairs, of theatres, of fashions : in short, she was at a loss on no subject whatever ; so that when the prince was alone, he had plenty of amusement in thinking how it could possibly be, that a small white cat could be endowed with all the attractions of the very best and most charming of women.

The twelvemonth in this manner again passed insensibly away ; but the cat took care to remind the prince of his duty in proper time. " For once, my prince," said she, " I will have the pleasure of equipping you as suits your high rank." And, looking into the courtyard, he saw a superb car, ornamented all over with gold, silver, pearls, and diamonds, drawn by twelve horses as white as snow, and harnessed in the most sumptuous trappings ; and behind the car a thousand guards, richly apparelled, were waiting to attend on the prince's person. She then presented him with a nut : " You will find in it," said she, " the piece of cambric I promised you : do not break the shell till you are in the presence of the king your father." Then, to prevent the acknowledgments which the prince was about to offer, she hastily bade him adieu.

Nothing could exceed the speed with which the snow-white horses conveyed this fortunate prince to his father's palace, where his brothers had just arrived before him. They embraced each other, and demanded an immediate audience of the king, who received them with the greatest of kindness. The princes hastened to place at the feet of his majesty the curious present he had required them to procure. The eldest produced a piece of cambric so extremely fine, that his friends had no doubt of its passing through the eye of the needle, which was now delivered to the king, having been kept locked up in the custody of his majesty's treasurer all the time. But when the king tried to draw the cambric through the eye of the needle, it would not pass, though it failed but very little. Then came the second prince, who made as sure of obtaining the crown as his brother had done, but, alas ! with no better success ; for though his piece of cambric was exquisitely fine, yet it could not be drawn through the eye of the needle. It was now the turn of the youngest prince, who accordingly advanced, and opening an elegant little box inlaid with jewels, took out a walnut and cracked the shell, imagining he should immediately perceive his piece of cambric ; but what was his astonishment to see nothing but a filbert ! He did not, however, lose his hopes ; he cracked the filbert, and it presented him with a cherry-stone. The lords of the court, who had assembled to witness this extraordinary trial, could not, any more than the princes his brothers, refrain from laughing, to think he should be so silly as to claim the crown on no better pretensions. The prince, however, cracked the cherry-stone, which was filled with a kernel ; he divided it, and found in the middle a grain of wheat, and in that a grain of millet-seed. He was now absolutely confounded, and could not help muttering between his teeth, "O white cat, white cat, thou hast deceived me!" At this instant he felt his hand scratched by the claw of a cat; upon which he again took courage, and opening the grain of millet-seed, to the astonishment of all present, he drew forth a piece of cambric four hundred yards long, and fine enough to be threaded with perfect ease through the eye of the needle.

When the king found he had no pretext left for refusing the crown to his youngest son, he sighed deeply, and it was easy to be seen that he was sorry for the prince's success.

"My sons," said he, "it is so gratifying to the heart of a father to receive proofs of his children's love and obedience, that I cannot refuse myself the satisfaction of requiring of you one thing more. You must undertake another expedition. That one of you, who, by the end of a year, brings me the most beautiful lady, shall marry her and obtain my crown."

So they again took leave of the king and of each other, and set out without delay; and in less than twelve hours, our young prince arrived, in his splendid car, at the palace of his dear white cat. Everything went on as before till the end of another year. At length only one day remained of the year, when the white cat thus addressed him: "To-morrow, my prince, you must present yourself at the palace of your father, and give him a proof of your obedience. It depends only on yourself to conduct thither the most beautiful princess ever yet beheld, for the time is come when the enchantment by which I am bound may be ended. You must cut off my head and tail," continued she, "and throw them into the fire."

"I!" said the prince, hastily—"I cut off your head and tail! You surely mean to try my affection, which, believe me, beautiful cat, is truly yours."

" You mistake me, generous prince," said she ; " I do not doubt your regard ; but if you wish to see me in any other form than that of a cat, you must consent to do as I desire, when you will have done me a service I shall never be able sufficiently to repay."

The prince's eyes filled with tears as she spoke, yet he considered himself obliged to undertake the dreadful task ; and the cat continuing to press him with the greatest eagerness, with a trembling hand he drew his sword, cut off her head and tail, and threw them into the fire. No sooner was this done, than the most beautiful lady his eyes had ever seen stood before him : and ere he had sufficiently recovered from his surprise to speak to her, a long train of attendants, who, at the same moment as their mistress, were changed to their natural shapes, came to offer their congratulations to the queen, and inquire her commands. She received them with the greatest kindness, and ordering them to withdraw, thus addressed the astonished prince :

" Do not imagine, dear prince, that I have always been a cat, or that I am of obscure birth. My father was the monarch of six kingdoms ; he tenderly loved my mother, and left her always at liberty to follow her own inclinations. Her prevailing passion was to travel ; and a short time before my birth, having heard of some fairies who were in possession of the largest gardens filled with the most delicious fruits, she had so strong a desire to eat some of them, that she set out for the country where they lived. She arrived at their abode, which she found to be a magnificent palace, on all sides glittering with gold and precious stones. She knocked a long time at the gates ; but no one came, nor could she perceive the least sign that it had any inhabitant. The difficulty, however, did but increase the violence of my mother's longing ; for she saw the tops of the trees above the garden-walls, loaded with the most luscious fruits. The queen, in despair, ordered her attendants to place tents close to the door of the palace ; but, having waited six weeks without seeing any one pass the gates, she fell sick of vexation, and her life was despaired of.

"One night, as she lay half asleep, she turned herself about, and, opening her eyes, perceived a little old woman, very ugly and deformed, seated in the easy-chair by her bed-side. 'I and my sister fairies,' said she, 'take it very ill that your majesty should so obstinately persist in getting some of our fruit ; but since so precious a life is at stake, we consent to give you as much as you can carry away, provided you will give us in return what we shall ask.' 'Ah ! kind fairy,' cried the queen, 'I will give you anything that I possess, even my very kingdoms, on condition that I eat of your fruit.' The old fairy then informed the queen that what they required was, that she should give them the child she was going to have, as soon as it should be born ; adding, that every possible care should be taken of it, and that it should become the most accomplished princess. The queen replied that, however cruel the conditions, she must accept them, since nothing but the fruit could save her life. In short, dear prince," continued the lady, "my mother instantly got out of bed, was dressed by her attendants, entered the palace, and satisfied her longing. Having eaten her fill, she ordered four thousand mules to be procured and loaded with the fruit, which had the virtue of continuing all the year round in a state of perfection. Thus provided, she returned to the king my father, who, with the whole court, received her with rejoicings, as it was before imagined she would die of disappointment. All this time the queen said nothing to my father of the promise she had made to give her daughter to the fairies ; so that when the time was come that she expected my birth, she grew very melancholy ; till at length, being pressed by the king, she declared to him the truth. Nothing could exceed his affliction when he heard that his only child, when

born, was to be given to the fairies. He bore it, however, as well as he could, for fear of adding to my
mother's grief ; and also believing he should find some
means of keeping me in a place of safety, which the fairies
would not be able to approach. As soon, therefore, as I
was born, he had me conveyed to a tower in the palace, to
which there were twenty flights of stairs, and a door to
each, of which my father kept the key, so that none came
near me without his consent. When the fairies heard of
what had been done, they sent first to demand me ; and
on my father's refusal, they let loose a monstrous dragon,
which devoured men, women, and children, and which, by
the breath of its nostrils, destroyed everything it came
near, so that even the trees and plants began to die. The
grief of the king was excessive ; and, finding that his
whole kingdom would in a short time be reduced to
famine, he consented to give me into their hands. I was
accordingly laid in a cradle of mother-o'-pearl, ornamented
with gold and jewels, and carried to their palace, when the
dragon immediately disappeared. The fairies placed me
in a tower, elegantly furnished, but to which there was no
door, so that whoever approached was obliged to come by
the windows, which were a great height from the ground :
from these I had the liberty of getting out into a delightful garden, in which were baths, and every sort of cooling
fruit. In this place was I educated by the fairies, who
behaved to me with the greatest kindness ; my clothes
were splendid, and I was instructed in every kind of
accomplishment ; in short, prince, if I had never seen
any one but themselves, I should have remained very
happy. One day, however, as I was talking at the
window with my parrot, I perceived a young gentleman
who was listening to our conversation. As I had never
seen a man but in pictures, I was not sorry for the
opportunity of gratifying my curiosity. I thought him a
very pleasing object, and he at length bowed in the most

respectful manner, without daring to speak, for he knew that I was in the palace of the fairies. When it began to grow dark, he went away, and I vainly endeavoured to see which road he took. The next morning, as soon as it was light, I again placed myself at the window, and had the pleasure of seeing that the gentleman had returned to the same place. He now spoke to me through a speaking-trumpet, and informed me he thought me a most charming lady, and that he should be very unhappy if he did not pass his life in my company.

"I resolved to find some means of escaping from my tower, and was not long in devising the means for the execution of my project : I begged the fairies to bring me a netting-needle, a mesh, and some cord, saying I wished to make some nets to amuse myself with catching birds at my window. This they readily complied with, and in a short time I completed a ladder long enough to reach to the ground. I now sent my parrot to the prince, to beg he would come to the usual place, as I wished to speak with him. He did not fail ; and finding the ladder, mounted it, and quickly entered my tower. This at first alarmed me, but the charms of his conversation had restored me to tranquillity, when all at once the window opened, and the Fairy Violent, mounted on the dragon's back, rushed into the tower. My beloved prince thought of nothing but how to defend me from their fury ; for I had had time to relate to him my story, previous to this cruel interruption ; but their numbers overpowered him, and the Fairy Violent had the barbarity to command the dragon to devour my lover before my eyes. In my despair, I would have thrown myself also into the mouth of the horrible monster ; but this they took care to prevent, saying, my life should be preserved for greater punishment. The fairy then touched me with her wand, and I instantly became a white cat. She next conducted me to this palace, which belonged to my father, and gave me a train of cats for my attendants, together with the twelve hands that waited on your highness. She then informed me of my birth and the death of my parents, and pronounced upon me what she imagined the greatest of maledictions : that I should not be restored to my natural figure until a young prince, the perfect resemblance of him I had lost, should cut off my head and tail. You are that perfect resemblance ; and accordingly you ended the enchantment. I need not add, that I already love you more than my life ; let us therefore hasten to the palace of the king your father, and obtain his approbation to our marriage."

The prince and princess accordingly set out side by side, in a car of still greater splendour than before, and reached the palace just as the two brothers had arrived with two beautiful princesses. The king, hearing that each of his sons had succeeded in finding what he had required, again began to think of some new expedient to delay the time of his resigning the crown ; but when the whole court were with the king assembled to pass judgment, the princess who accompanied the youngest, perceiving his thoughts by his countenance, stepped majestically forward and thus addressed him :

"It is a pity that your majesty, who is so capable of governing, should think of resigning the crown ! I am fortunate enough to have six kingdoms in my possession ; permit me to bestow one on each of the eldest princes, and to enjoy the remaining four in the society of the youngest. And may it please your majesty to keep your own kingdom, and make no decision concerning the beauty of three princesses, who, without such a proof of your majesty's preference, will no doubt live happily together ! "

The air resounded with the applauses of the assembly : the young prince and princess embraced the king and next their brothers and sisters : the three weddings immediately took place, and the kingdoms were divided as the princess had proposed.

PRINCE CHERRY

LONG ago there lived a monarch, who was such a very honest man that his subjects entitled him the Good King. One day, when he was out hunting, a little white rabbit which had been half killed by his hounds, leaped right into his majesty's arms. Said he, caressing it: "This poor creature has put itself under my protection, and I will allow no one to injure it." So he carried it to his palace, had prepared for it a neat little rabbit-hutch, with abundance of the daintiest food, such as rabbits love, and there he left it.

The same night, when he was alone in his chamber, there appeared to him a beautiful lady. She was dressed neither in gold, nor silver, nor brocade; but her flowing robes were white as snow, and she wore a garland of white roses on her head. The Good King was greatly astonished at the sight; for his door was locked, and he wondered how so dazzling a lady could possibly enter: but she soon removed his doubts.

"I am the Fairy Candide," said she, with a smiling and gracious air. "Passing through the wood, where you were hunting, I took a desire to know if you were as good as men say you are. I therefore changed myself into a white rabbit, and took refuge in your arms. You saved me; and now I know that those who are merciful to dumb beasts will be ten times more so to human beings. You merit the name your subjects give you: you are the Good King. I thank you for your protection, and shall be always one of your best friends. You have but to say what you most desire, and I promise you your wish shall be granted."

"Madam," replied the king, "if you are a fairy, you must know, without my telling you, the wish of my heart. I have one well-beloved son, Prince Cherry : whatever kindly feeling you have towards me, extend it to him."

"Willingly," said Candide. "I will make him the handsomest, richest, or most powerful prince in the world : choose whichever you desire for him."

"None of the three," returned the father. "I only wish him to be good—the best prince in the whole world. Of what use would riches, power, or beauty be to him if he were a bad man ? "

"You are right," said the fairy ; "but I cannot make him good : he must do that himself. I can only change his external fortunes ; for his personal character, the utmost I can promise is to give him good counsel, reprove him for his faults, and even punish him, if he will not punish himself. You mortals can but do the same with your children."

"Ah, yes ! " said the king, sighing. Still, he felt that the kindness of a fairy was something gained for his son, and died not long after, content and at peace.

Prince Cherry mourned deeply, for he dearly loved his father, and would have gladly given all his kingdoms and treasures to keep him in life a little longer. Two days after the Good King was no more, Prince Cherry was sleeping in his chamber, when he saw the same dazzling vision of the Fairy Candide.

"I promised your father," said she, " to be your best friend, and in pledge of this take what I now give you " ; and she placed a small gold ring upon his finger. " Poor as it looks, it is more precious than diamonds ; for whenever you do ill it will prick your finger. If, after that warning, you still continue in evil, you will lose my friendship, and I shall become your direst enemy."

So saying, she disappeared, leaving Cherry in such amazement, that he would have believed it all a dream, save for the ring on his finger.

He was for a long time so good that the ring never pricked him at all; and this made him so cheerful and pleasant in his humour that everybody called him, "Happy Prince Cherry." But, one unlucky day, he was out hunting and found no sport, which vexed him so much that he showed his ill temper by his looks and ways. He fancied his ring felt very tight and uncomfortable, but as it did not prick him, he took no heed of this: until, re-entering his palace, his little pet dog, Bibi, jumped up upon him, and was sharply told to get away. The creature, accustomed to nothing but caresses, tried to attract his attention by pulling at his garments, when Prince Cherry turned and gave it a severe kick. At this moment he felt in his finger a prick like a pin.

"What nonsense!" said he to himself. "The fairy must be making game of me. Why, what great evil have I done? I, the master of a great empire, cannot I kick my own dog?"

A voice replied, or else Prince Cherry imagined it, "No, sire; the master of a great empire has a right to do good, but not evil. I—a fairy—am as much above you as you are above your dog. I might punish you, kill you, if I chose; but I prefer leaving you to amend your ways. You have been guilty of three faults to-day —bad temper, passion, cruelty: do better to-morrow."

The prince promised, and kept his word awhile; but he had been brought up by a foolish nurse, who indulged him in every way, and was always telling him that he would be a king one day, when he might do as he liked in all things. He found out now that even a king cannot always do that; it vexed him, and made him angry. His ring began to prick him so often that his little finger was continually bleeding. He disliked this, as was natural; and soon began to consider whether it would not be easier to throw the ring away altogether than to be constantly annoyed by it. It was such a queer thing for a king to have always a spot of blood on his finger! At last, unable to put up with it any more, he took his ring off, and hid it where he would never see it; and believed himself the happiest of men, for he could now do exactly what he liked. He did it, and became every day more and more miserable.

One day he saw a young girl, so beautiful that, being always accustomed to have his own way, he immediately determined to espouse her. He never doubted that she would be only too glad to be made a queen, for she was very poor. But Zelia—that was her name—answered, to his great astonishment, that she would rather not marry him.

"Do I displease you?" asked the prince, into whose mind it had never entered that he could displease anybody.

"Not at all, my prince," said the honest peasant-maiden. "You are very handsome, very charming; but you are not like your father the Good King. I will not be your queen, for you would make me miserable."

At these words the prince's love seemed all to turn to hatred: he gave orders to his guards to convey Zelia to a prison near the palace; and then took counsel with his foster-brother, the one of all his ill companions who most incited him to do wrong.

"Sir," said this man, "if I were in your majesty's place, I would never vex myself about a poor silly girl. Feed her on bread and water till she comes to her senses; and if she still refuses you, let her die in torment, as a warning to your other subjects should they venture to dispute your will. You will be disgraced should you suffer yourself to be conquered by a simple girl."

"But," said Prince Cherry, "shall I not be disgraced if I harm a creature so perfectly innocent?"

"No one is innocent who disputes your majesty's authority," said the courtier, bowing ; "and it is better to commit an injustice than allow it to be supposed you can ever be contradicted with impunity."

This touched Cherry on his weak point—his good impulses faded : he resolved once more to ask Zelia if she would marry him, and, if she again refused, to sell her as a slave. Arrived at the cell in which she was confined, what was his astonishment to find her gone ! He knew not who to accuse, for he had kept the key in his pocket the whole time. At last, the foster-brother suggested that the escape of Zelia might have been contrived by an old man, Suliman by name, the prince's former tutor, who was the only one who now ventured to blame him for anything that he did. Cherry sent immediately, and ordered his old friend to be brought to him, loaded heavily with irons. Then, full of fury, he went and shut himself up in his own chamber, where he went raging to and fro, till startled by a noise like a clap of thunder. The Fairy Candide stood before him.

"Prince," said she, in a severe voice, "I promised your father to give you good counsels, and to punish you if you refused to follow them. My counsels were forgotten, my punishments despised. Under the figure of a man, you have been no better than the beasts you chase : like a lion in fury, a wolf in gluttony, a serpent in revenge, and a bull in brutality. Take, therefore, in your new form the likeness of all these animals."

Scarcely had Prince Cherry heard these words, than to his horror he found himself transformed into what the fairy had named. He was a creature with the head of a lion, the horns of a bull, the feet of a wolf, and the tail of a serpent. At the same time he felt himself transported to a distant forest, where, standing on the bank of a stream, he saw reflected in the water his own frightful shape, and heard a voice saying :

"Look at thyself, and know thy soul has become a thousand times uglier even than thy body."

Cherry recognised the voice of Candide, and in his rage would have sprung upon her and devoured her; but he saw nothing, and the same voice said behind him:

"Cease thy feeble fury, and learn to conquer thy pride by being in submission to thine own subjects."

Hearing no more, he soon quitted the stream, hoping at least to get rid of the sight of himself; but he had scarcely gone twenty paces when he tumbled into a pitfall that was laid to catch bears; the bear-hunters, descending from some trees hard by, caught him, chained him, and, only too delighted to get hold of such a curious-looking animal, led him along with them to the capital of his own kingdom.

There great rejoicings were taking place, and the bear-hunters, asking what it was all about, were told that it was because Prince Cherry, the torment of his subjects, had just been struck dead by a thunderbolt—just punishment of all his crimes. Four courtiers, his wicked companions, had wished to divide his throne between them; but the people had risen up against them, and offered the crown to Suliman, the old tutor whom Cherry had ordered to be arrested.

All this the poor monster heard. He even saw Suliman sitting upon his own throne, and trying to calm the populace by representing to them that it was not certain Prince Cherry was dead; that he might return one day to re-assume with honour the crown which Suliman only consented to wear as a sort of viceroy.

"I know his heart," said the honest and faithful old man; "it is tainted, but not corrupt. If alive, he may reform yet, and be all his father over again to you, his people, whom he has caused to suffer so much."

These words touched the poor beast so deeply that he ceased to beat himself against the iron bars of the cage in which the hunters carried him about, became gentle as a lamb, and suffered himself to be taken quietly to a menagerie, where were kept all sorts of strange and ferocious animals — a place which he had himself often visited as a boy, but never thought he should be shut up there himself.

However, he owned he had deserved it all, and began to make amends by showing himself very obedient to his keeper. This man was almost as great a brute as the animals he had charge of, and when he was in ill humour he used to beat them without rhyme or reason. One day, while he was sleeping, a tiger broke loose, and leaped upon him, eager to devour him. Cherry at first felt a thrill of pleasure at the thought of being revenged ; then, seeing how helpless the man was, he wished himself free, that he might defend him. Immediately the doors of his cage opened. The keeper, waking up, saw the strange beast leap out, and imagined, of course, that he was going to be slain at once. Instead, he saw the tiger lying dead, and the strange beast creeping up, and laying itself at his feet to be caressed. But as he lifted up his hand to stroke it, a voice was heard saying, " Good actions never go unrewarded " ; and, instead of the frightful monster, there crouched on the ground nothing but a pretty little dog.

Cherry, delighted to find himself thus metamorphosed, caressed the keeper in every possible way, till at last the man took him up into his arms and carried him to the king, to whom he related this wonderful story, from beginning to end. The queen wished to have the charming little dog : and Cherry would have been exceedingly happy, could he have forgotten that he was originally a man and a king. He was lodged most elegantly, had the richest of collars to adorn his neck, and heard himself praised continually. But his beauty rather brought him into trouble, for the queen, afraid lest he might grow too large for a pet, took advice of dog-doctors, who ordered

WARWICK GOBLE

"'I was accordingly laid in a cradle of mother-of-pearl,
ornamented with gold and jewels.'" *(Page 283)*

"He flew in, perched on her shoulder, and expressed his delight and affection by a thousand caresses." (*Page 294*)

that he should be fed entirely upon bread, and that very sparingly ; so poor Cherry was sometimes nearly starved.

One day, when they gave him his crust for breakfast, a fancy seized him to go and eat it in the palace garden ; so he took the bread in his mouth, and trotted away towards a stream which he knew, and where he sometimes stopped to drink. But instead of the stream he saw a splendid palace, glittering with gold and precious stones. Entering the doors was a crowd of men and women, magnificently dressed ; and within there was singing and dancing, and good cheer of all sorts. Yet, however grandly and gaily the people went in, Cherry noticed that those who came out were pale, thin, ragged, half-naked, covered with wounds and sores. Some of them dropped dead at once ; others dragged themselves on a little way and then lay down, dying of hunger, and vainly begged a morsel of bread from others who were entering in— who never took the least notice of them.

Cherry perceived one woman, who was trying feebly to gather and eat some green herbs. " Poor thing ! " said he to himself ; " I know what it is to be hungry, and I want my breakfast badly enough ; but still it will not kill me to wait till dinner-time, and my crust may save the life of this poor woman."

So the little dog ran up to her, and dropped his bread at her feet ; she picked it up, and ate it with avidity. Soon she looked quite recovered, and Cherry, delighted, was trotting back again to his kennel, when he heard loud cries, and saw a young girl dragged by four men to the door of the palace, which they were trying to compel her to enter. Oh, how he wished himself a monster again, as when he slew the tiger !—for the young girl was no other than his beloved Zelia. Alas ! what could a poor little dog do to defend her ? But he ran forward and barked at the men, and bit their heels, until at last they chased him away with heavy blows. And then he lay down outside the palace-door, determined to watch and see what had become of Zelia.

Conscience pricked him now. "What!" thought he, "I am furious against these wicked men, who are carrying her away ; and did I not do the same myself? Did I not cast her into prison, and intend to sell her as a slave? Who knows how much more wickedness I might not have done to her and others, if heaven's justice had not stopped me in time?"

While he lay thinking and repenting, he heard a window open, and saw Zelia throw out of it a bit of dainty meat. Cherry, who felt hungry enough by this time, was just about to eat it, when the woman to whom he had given his crust snatched him up in her arms.

"Poor little beast!" cried she, patting him, "every bit of food in that palace is poisoned : you shall not touch a morsel."

And at the same time the voice in the air repeated again, "Good actions never go unrewarded"; and Cherry found himself changed into a beautiful little white pigeon. He remembered with joy that white was the colour of the Fairy Candide, and began to hope that she was taking him into favour again.

So he stretched his wings, delighted that he might now have a chance of approaching his fair Zelia. He flew up to the palace-windows, and, finding one of them open, entered and sought everywhere, but he could not find Zelia. Then, in despair, he flew out again, resolved to go over the world until he beheld her once more.

He took flight at once, and traversed many countries, swiftly as a bird can, but found no trace of his beloved. At length in a desert, sitting beside an old hermit in his cave, and partaking with him his frugal repast, Cherry saw a poor peasant-girl, and recognised Zelia. Transported with joy, he flew in, perched on her shoulder, and expressed his delight and affection by a thousand caresses.

She, charmed with the pretty little pigeon, caressed it in her turn, and promised it that, if it would stay with her, she would love it always.

"What have you done, Zelia?" said the hermit, smiling; and while he spoke the white pigeon vanished, and there stood Prince Cherry in his own natural form. "Your enchantment ended, prince, when Zelia promised to love you. Indeed, she has loved you always, but your many faults constrained her to hide her love. These are now amended, and you may both live happy if you will, because your union is founded upon mutual esteem."

Cherry and Zelia threw themselves at the feet of the hermit, whose form also began to change. His soiled garments became of dazzling whiteness, and his long beard and withered face grew into the flowing hair and lovely countenance of the Fairy Candide.

"Rise up, my children," said she; "I must now transport you to your palace, and restore to Prince Cherry his father's crown, of which he is now worthy."

She had scarcely ceased speaking when they found themselves in the chamber of Suliman, who, delighted to find again his beloved pupil and master, willingly resigned the throne, and became the most faithful of his subjects.

King Cherry and Queen Zelia reigned together for many years, and it is said that the former was so blameless and strict in all his duties, that though he constantly wore the ring which Candide had restored to him it never once pricked his finger enough to make it bleed.

LITTLE SNOWDROP

ONCE upon a time, in the middle of winter, when the flakes of snow fell like feathers from the sky, a queen sat at a window set in an ebony frame, and sewed. While she was sewing and watching the snow fall, she pricked her finger with her needle, and three drops of blood dropped on the snow. And because the crimson looked so beautiful on the white snow, she thought, "Oh that I had a child as white as snow, as red as blood, and as black as the wood of this ebony frame!"

Soon afterwards she had a little daughter, who was as white as snow, as red as blood, and had hair as black as ebony. And when the child was born, the queen died.

After a year had gone by, the king took another wife. She was a handsome lady, but proud and haughty, and could not endure that any one should surpass her in beauty. She had a wonderful mirror, and whenever she walked up to it, and looked at herself in it, she said :

> "Little glass upon the wall,
> Who is fairest among us all?"

Then the mirror replied :

> "Lady queen, so grand and tall,
> Thou art the fairest of them all."

And she was satisfied, for she knew the mirror always told the truth. But Snowdrop grew ever taller and fairer, and at seven years old was beautiful as the day, and more beautiful than the queen herself.   So once, when the queen asked of her mirror :

> "Little glass upon the wall,
> Who is fairest among us all ? "

it answered :

> "Lady queen, you are grand and tall,
> But Snowdrop is fairest of you all."

Then the queen was startled, and turned yellow and green with envy.   From that hour she so hated Snowdrop, that she burned with secret wrath whenever she saw the maiden.   Pride and envy grew apace like weeds in her heart, till she had no rest day or night.   So she called a huntsman and said, " Take the child out in the forest, for I will endure her no longer in my sight.   Kill her, and bring me her lungs and liver as tokens that you have done it."

The huntsman obeyed, and led the child away ; but when he had drawn his hunting-knife, and was about to pierce Snowdrop's innocent heart, she began to weep, and said, " Ah ! dear huntsman, spare my life, and I will run deep into the wild forest, and never more come home."

The huntsman took pity on her, because she looked so lovely, and said, "Run away then, poor child ! "— "The wild beasts will soon make an end of thee," he thought ; but it seemed as if a stone had been rolled from his heart, because he had avoided taking her life ; and as a little bear came by just then, he killed it, took out its liver and lungs, and carried them as tokens to the queen.   She made the cook dress them with salt, and then the wicked woman ate them, and thought she had eaten Snowdrop's lungs and liver.   The poor child was now all alone in the great forest, and she felt frightened as she looked at all the leafy trees, and knew not what to do.   So she began to run, and ran over the sharp stones, and through the thorns ; and the wild beasts passed close to her, but did her no harm. She ran as long as her feet could carry her, and when evening closed in, she saw a little house, and went into it to rest herself. Everything in the house was very small, but I cannot tell you how pretty and clean it was.

There stood a little table, covered with a white table-cloth, on which were seven little plates (each little plate with its own little spoon)—also seven little knives and forks, and seven little cups. Round the walls stood seven little beds close together, with sheets as white as snow. Snowdrop being so hungry and thirsty, ate a little of the vegetables and bread on each plate, and drank a drop of wine from every cup, for she did not like to empty one entirely.

Then, being very tired, she laid herself down in one of the beds, but could not make herself comfortable, for one was too long, and another too short. The seventh, luckily, was just right; so there she stayed, said her prayers, and fell asleep.

When it was grown quite dark, home came the masters of the house, seven dwarfs, who delved and mined for iron among the mountains. They lighted their seven candles, and as soon as there was a light in the kitchen, they saw that some one had been there, for it was not quite so orderly as they had left it.

The first said, "Who has been sitting on my stool?"

The second, "Who has eaten off my plate?"

The third, "Who has taken part of my loaf?"

The fourth, "Who has touched my vegetables?"

The fifth, "Who has used my fork?"

The sixth, "Who has cut with my knife?"

The seventh, "Who has drunk out of my little cup?"

Then the first dwarf looked about, and saw that there was a slight hollow in his bed, so he asked, "Who has been lying in my little bed?"

The others came running, and each called out, "Some one has also been lying in my bed."

But the seventh, when he looked in his bed, saw Snowdrop there, fast asleep. He called the others, who flocked round with cries of surprise, fetched their seven candles, and cast the light on Snowdrop.

"Oh, heaven!" they cried, "what a lovely child!" and were so pleased that they would not wake her, but let her sleep on in the little bed. The seventh dwarf slept with all his companions in turn, an hour with each, and so they spent the night. When it was morning, Snowdrop woke up, and was frightened when she saw the seven dwarfs. They were very friendly, however, and inquired her name.

"Snowdrop," answered she.

"How have you found your way to our house?" further asked the dwarfs.

So she told them how her stepmother had tried to kill her, how the huntsman had spared her life, and how she had run the whole day through, till at last she had found their little house.

Then the dwarfs said, "If thou wilt keep our house, cook, make the beds, wash, sew and knit, and make all neat and clean, thou canst stay with us, and shalt want for nothing."

"I will, right willingly," said Snowdrop. So she dwelt with them, and kept their house in order. Every morning they went out among the mountains, to seek iron and gold, and came home ready for supper in the evening.

The maiden being left alone all day long, the good dwarfs warned her, saying, "Beware of thy wicked stepmother, who will soon find out that thou art here; take care that thou lettest nobody in."

The queen, however, after having, as she thought, eaten Snowdrop's lungs and liver, had no doubt that she was again the first and fairest woman in the world; so she walked up to her mirror, and said :

"Little glass upon the wall,
  Who is fairest among us all?"

The mirror replied:

"Lady queen, so grand and tall,
  Here, you are fairest of them all;
  But over the hills, with the seven dwarfs old,
  Lives Snowdrop, fairer a hundredfold."

She trembled, knowing the mirror never told a falsehood; she felt sure that the huntsman had deceived her, and that Snowdrop was still alive. She pondered once more, late and early, early and late, how best to kill Snowdrop; for envy gave her no rest, day or night, while she herself was not the fairest lady in the land. When she had planned what to do, she painted her face, dressed herself like an old pedlar-woman, and altered her appearance so much, that no one could have known her. In this disguise she went over the seven hills, to where the seven dwarfs dwelt, knocked at the door, and cried, "Good wares, cheap! very cheap!"

Snowdrop looked out of the window and cried, "Good-morning, good woman: what have you to sell?"

"Good wares, smart wares," answered the queen—"bodice laces of all colours"; and drew out one which was woven of coloured silk.

"I may surely let this honest dame in!" thought Snowdrop; so she unfastened the door, and bought for herself the pretty lace.

"Child," said the old woman, "what a figure thou art! Let me lace thee for once properly." Snowdrop feared no harm, so stepped in front of her, and allowed her bodice to be fastened up with the new lace.

But the old woman laced so quick and laced so tight, that Snowdrop's breath was stopped, and she fell down as if dead. "Now I am fairest at last," said the old woman to herself, and sped away.

The seven dwarfs came home soon after, at eventide, but how alarmed were they to find their poor Snowdrop lifeless on the ground! They lifted her up, and, seeing that she was laced too tightly, cut the lace of her bodice; she began to breathe faintly, and slowly returned to life. When the dwarfs heard what had happened, they said, "The old pedlar-woman was none other than the wicked queen. Be careful of thyself, and open the door to no one if we are not at home."

The cruel stepmother walked up to her mirror when she reached home, and said:

"Little glass upon the wall,
    Who is fairest among us all?"

To which it answered, as usual:

"Lady queen, so grand and tall,
    Here, you are fairest of them all;
    But over the hills, with the seven dwarfs old,
    Lives Snowdrop, fairer a hundredfold."

When she heard this, she was so alarmed that all the blood rushed to her heart, for she saw plainly that Snowdrop was still alive.

"This time," said she, "I will think of some means that shall destroy her utterly"; and with the help of witchcraft, in which she was skilful, she made a poisoned comb. Then she changed her dress and took the shape of another old woman.

Again she crossed the seven hills to the home of the seven dwarfs, knocked at the door, and cried, "Good wares, very cheap!"

Snowdrop looked out and said, "Go away—I dare let no one in."

"You may surely be allowed to look!" answered the old woman, and she drew out the poisoned comb and held it up. The girl was so pleased with it that she let herself be cajoled, and opened the door.

When the bargain was struck, the dame said, "Now let me dress your hair properly for once." Poor Snowdrop took no heed, and let the old woman begin; but the comb had scarcely touched her hair before the poison worked, and she fell down senseless.

"Paragon of beauty!" said the wicked woman, "all is over with thee now," and went away.

Luckily, it was near evening, and the seven dwarfs soon came home. When they found Snowdrop lifeless on the ground, they at once distrusted her stepmother. They searched, and found the poisoned comb; and as soon as they had drawn it out, Snowdrop came to herself, and told them what had happened. Again they warned her to be careful, and open the door to no one.

The queen placed herself before the mirror at home and said:

> "Little glass upon the wall,
>   Who is fairest among us all?"

But it again answered:

> "Lady queen, so grand and tall,
>   Here, you are fairest of them all;
>   But over the hills, with the seven dwarfs old,
>   Lives Snowdrop, fairer a thousandfold."

When she heard the mirror speak thus, she quivered with rage. "Snowdrop shall die," she cried, "if it costs my own life!"

Then she went to a secret and lonely chamber, where no one ever disturbed her, and compounded an apple of deadly poison. Ripe and rosy-cheeked, it was so beautiful to look upon, that all who saw it longed for it; but it brought death to any who should eat it. When the apple was ready, she painted her face, disguised herself as a peasant-woman, and journeyed over the seven hills to where the seven dwarfs dwelt. At the sound of the knock, Snowdrop put her head out of the window, and said, " I cannot open the door to anybody, for the seven dwarfs have forbidden me to do so."

" Very well," replied the peasant-woman ; " I only want to be rid of my apples. Here, I will give you one of them ! "

" No ! " said Snowdrop, " I dare not take it."

" Art thou afraid of being poisoned? " asked the old woman. " Look here ; I will cut the apple in two, and you shall eat the rosy side, and I the white."

Now the fruit was so cunningly made, that only the rosy side was poisoned. Snowdrop longed for the pretty apple ; and when she saw the peasant-woman eating it, she could resist no longer, but stretched out her hand and took the poisoned half. She had scarcely tasted it, when she fell lifeless to the ground.

The queen, laughing loudly, watched her with a barbarous look, and cried, "O thou who art white as snow, red as blood, and black as ebony, the seven dwarfs cannot awaken thee this time ! "

And when she asked the mirror at home :

> " Little glass upon the wall,
> Who is fairest among us all ? "

the mirror at last replied :

> " Lady queen, so grand and tall,
> You are the fairest of them all."

So her envious heart had as much repose as an envious heart can ever know.

When the dwarfs came home in the evening, they found Snowdrop lying breathless and motionless on the ground. They lifted her up, searched whether she had anything poisonous about her, unlaced her, combed her hair, washed her with water and with wine ; but all was useless, for they could not bring the darling back to life. They laid her on a bier, and all the seven placed themselves round it, and mourned for her three long days.

Then they would have buried her, but that she still looked so fresh and life-like, and had such lovely rosy cheeks. "We cannot lower her into the dark earth," said they; and caused a transparent coffin of glass to be made, so that she could be seen on all sides, and laid her in it, writing her name outside in letters of gold, which told that she was the daughter of a king. Then they placed the coffin on the mountain above, and one of them always stayed by it and guarded it. But there was little need to guard it, for even the wild animals came and mourned for Snowdrop: the birds likewise—first an owl, and then a raven, and afterwards a dove.

Long long years did Snowdrop lie in her coffin unchanged, looking as though asleep, for she was still white as snow, red as blood, and her hair was black as ebony. At last the son of a king chanced to wander into the forest, and came to the dwarfs' house for a night's shelter. He saw the coffin on the mountain with the beautiful Snowdrop in it, and read what was written there in letters of gold. Then he said to the dwarfs, "Let me have the coffin! I will give you whatever you like to ask for it."

But the dwarfs answered, "We would not part with it for all the gold in the world."

He said again, "Yet give it me; for I cannot live without seeing Snowdrop, and though she is dead, I will prize and honour her as my beloved."

Then the good dwarfs took pity on him, and gave him the coffin. The prince had it borne away by his servants. They happened to stumble over a bush, and the shock forced the bit of poisoned apple which Snowdrop had tasted out of her throat. Immediately she opened her eyes, raised the coffin-lid, and sat up alive once more. "Oh, heaven!" cried she, "where am I?"

The prince answered joyfully, "Thou art with me," and told her what had happened, saying, "I love thee more dearly than anything else in the world. Come with me to my father's castle, and be my wife."

Snowdrop, well pleased, went with him, and they were married with much state and grandeur.

The wicked stepmother was invited to the feast. Richly dressed, she stood before the mirror, and asked of it :

> " Little glass upon the wall,
>   Who is fairest among us all ? "

The mirror answered :

> " Lady queen, so grand and tall,
>   Here, you are fairest among them all ;
>   But the young queen over the mountains old,
>   Is fairer than you a thousandfold."

The evil-hearted woman uttered a curse, and could scarcely endure her anguish. She first resolved not to attend the wedding, but curiosity would not allow her to rest. She determined to travel, and see who that young queen could be, who was the most beautiful in all the world. When she came, and found that it was Snowdrop alive again, she stood petrified with terror and despair. Then two iron shoes, heated burning hot, were drawn out of the fire with a pair of tongs, and laid before her feet. She was forced to put them on, and to go and dance at Snowdrop's wedding—dancing, dancing on these red-hot shoes till she fell down dead.

THE BLUE BIRD

A POWERFUL and wealthy king, having lost his wife, was so inconsolable, that he shut himself up for eight entire days, in a little cabinet, where he spent his time in knocking his head against the wall, until the courtiers were afraid he would kill himself! They accordingly placed stuffed mattresses over every wall, and allowed all his subjects, who desired, to pay him a visit, trusting that something would be said to alleviate his grief. But neither grave nor lively discourse made any impression upon him; he scarcely heard what was spoken. At last there presented herself before him a lady, covered from head to foot in a long crape veil, who wept and sobbed so much that the king noticed her. She told him that she did not come, like the rest, to console him, but rather to encourage his grief. She herself had lost the best of husbands, and here she began to weep so profusely, that it was a wonder her eyes were not melted out of her head. The king began to weep in company, and to talk to her of his dear wife— she did the same of her dear husband : in fact they talked so much, that they talked their sorrow quite away. Then, lifting up her veil, she showed lovely blue eyes and dark eyelashes. The king noticed her more and more— he spoke less and less of the departed queen ; by and by he ceased to speak of her at all. The end was, that he courted the inconsolable lady in the black veil, and married her.

By his first marriage he had one daughter, called

306

Florina, or the little Flora, because she was so fresh and lovely ; at the time of his second marriage she was quite fifteen years old. The new queen also had a daughter, who was being brought up by her godmother, the fairy Soussio—her name was Troutina, because her complexion was all spotted like a trout's back. Indeed, she was altogether ugly and disagreeable ; and when contrasted with Florina, the difference between the two made the mother so envious, that she and Troutina spared no pains to make the princess's life unhappy, and to speak ill of her to her father.

One day the king observed that both girls were now old enough to be married, and that he intended to choose for one of them the first prince who visited his court.

"Be it so," said the queen ; "and as my daughter is older, handsomer, and more amiable than yours, she shall have the first choice." The king disputed nothing ; indeed, he never did—the queen ruled him in all things.

Some time after, news came that King Charming would shortly arrive, and that he was as charming as his name. When the queen heard this news, she sent for milliners, dressmakers, jewellers, and decked Troutina from head to foot ; but to Florina she allowed not a single new frock. The poor princess had to put on her old one, which was very old and shabby indeed ; she was so much ashamed of it that she hid herself in a corner of the saloon, lest King Charming should see her. But he did not, being overwhelmed with the ceremonious reception given him by the queen, who presented to him Troutina, all blazing with jewels, yet so ugly that King Charming involuntarily turned away his eyes.

"But, madam, is there not another princess, called Florina?"

They pointed to the corner where Florina was hidden, and she came out, blushing so much, that the young king was dazzled with her beauty, in spite of her shabby gown.

307

He rose, and made her a profound reverence, paying her besides so many elegant compliments, that the queen became very much displeased. King Charming took no heed, but conversed with Florina for three hours without stopping. Indeed, his admiration of her was so plain, that the queen and Troutina begged of the king that she might be shut up in a tower during the whole time of his visit ; so, as soon as she had returned to her apartment, four men in masks entered, and carried her off, leaving her in a dark cell, and in the utmost desolation.

Meantime King Charming eagerly awaited her reappearance, but he saw her no more ; and by the queen's orders, every one about him spoke all the evil they could of poor Florina, but he refused to believe one word. "No," said he, "nature could not have united a base nature to such a sweet innocent face. I will rather suppose that she is maligned by her stepmother and by Troutina, who is so ugly herself that no wonder she bears envy towards the fairest woman in the world."

Meanwhile Florina, shut up in her tower, lamented bitterly. "Ah, would I had been sent here before I saw this amiable prince, who was so kind to me! It is to prevent my meeting him again that the queen treats me so cruelly. Alas! the little beauty I have has cost me sore ! "

The queen, to win King Charming for her daughter, made him many presents ; among the rest an order of knighthood, a golden heart, enamelled in flame-colour, surrounded with many arrows, but pierced by one only, the motto being "*She alone.*" The heart was made of a single ruby, as big as an ostrich's egg. Each arrow was a diamond, a finger's length, and the chain was of pearls, each weighing a pound. When the young king received this very handsome present, he was much perplexed, until they told him it came from the princess whom he had lately seen, and who requested him to be her knight.

"They were very friendly, however, and inquired her name.
'Snow-drop,' answered she." (*Page 299*)

WARWICK GOBLE

"Stopping beside a fountain, she let her hair fall loose, and
dipped her weary feet in the cool water." *(Page 318)*

" Florina ! " cried he, enchanted.

" No, Troutina."

" Then I am sorry I cannot accept the honour," replied King Charming. "A monarch is surely at liberty to form his own engagements. I know what is a knight's duty to his lady, and should wish to fulfil it ; as I cannot fulfil it to Troutina, I would rather decline the favour she offers me than become unworthy of it."

Civil as this answer was, it irritated the queen and her daughter exceedingly ; and when, since in all his audiences with their majesties he never saw Florina, he at last inquired where the younger princess was, the queen answered fiercely, that she was shut up in prison, and would remain there till Troutina was married.

" And for what reason ? " asked King Charming.

" I do not know ; and if I did, I would not tell you," replied the queen, more angrily than ever ; so that King Charming quitted her presence as soon as ever he could.

When he was alone, he sent for one of his attendants, whom he trusted very much, and begged him to gain information from some court lady about the Princess Florina. This scheme succeeded so well, that Florina was persuaded to promise she would speak to him for a few moments next night, from a small window at the bottom of the tower. But the faithless lady-in-waiting betrayed her to the queen, who locked her up in her chamber, and determined to send her own daughter to the window instead. The night was so dark that King Charming never found out the difference, but made to Troutina all the tender speeches that he meant for Florina, offering her his crown and his heart, and ending by placing his own ring on her finger, as a pledge of eternal fidelity. He also made her agree to fly with him next night, in a chariot drawn by winged frogs, of which a great magician, one of his friends, had made him a present. He thought she talked very little, and that little not in quite so pleasant a voice as formerly; still, he was too much in love to notice much, and departed very joyful in having obtained her promise.

Next night Troutina, thickly veiled, quitted the palace by a secret door. King Charming met her, received her in his arms, and vowed to love her for ever. Then he lifted her into the fairy chariot, and they sailed about in the air for some hours. But as he was not likely to wish to sail about for ever, he at last proposed that they should descend to earth, and be married. Troutina agreed with all her heart, but wished that the ceremony should be performed at her godmother's, the fairy Soussio. So they entered together into the fairy-palace, and she told her godmother privately how all had happened, and how she had won King Charming, begging the fairy to pacify him when he found out his mistake.

"My child," replied the godmother, "that is more easily said than done; he is too deeply in love with Florina."

Meantime the king was left waiting in a chamber with diamond walls, so thin and transparent, that through them he saw Troutina and Soussio conversing together. He stood like a man in a dream: "What! am I betrayed? Has this enemy to my peace carried away my dear Florina?"

How great was his despair, when Soussio said to him in a commanding voice, "King Charming, behold the princess Troutina, to whom you have promised your faith: marry her immediately!"

"Do you think me a fool?" cried the king; "I have promised her nothing. She is——"

"Stop—if you show me any disrespect——"

"I will respect you as much as a fairy deserves to be respected, if you will only give me back my princess."

"Am not I she?" said Troutina. "It was to me you gave this ring; to me you spoke at the window."

"I have been wickedly deceived!" cried the king; "come, my winged frogs, we will depart immediately."

"You cannot," said Soussio; and, touching him, he found himself fixed as if his feet were glued to the pavement.

"You may turn me into stone!" exclaimed he; "but I will love no one, except Florina."

Soussio employed persuasions, threats, promises, entreaties. Troutina wept, groaned, shrieked, and then tried quiet sulkiness; but the king uttered not a word. For twenty days and twenty nights he stood there, without sleeping, or eating, or once sitting down—they talking all the while.

At length, Soussio, quite worn out, said, "Choose, seven years of penitence and punishment, or marry my god-daughter."

"I choose," answered the king; "and I will not marry your god-daughter."

"Then fly out of this window, in the shape of a Blue Bird."

Immediately the king's figure changed. His arms formed themselves into wings; his legs and feet turned black and thin, and claws grew upon them; his body wasted into the slender shape of a bird, and was covered with bright blue feathers; his eyes became round and beady; his nose an ivory beak; and his crown was a white plume on the top of his head. He began to speak in a singing voice, and then uttering a doleful cry, fled away as far as possible from the fatal palace of Soussio.

But, though he looked only a blue bird, the king was his own natural self still, and remembered all his misfortunes, and did not cease to lament for his beautiful Florina. Flying from tree to tree, he sang melancholy songs about her and himself, and wished he were dead many a time.

The fairy Soussio sent back Troutina to her mother, who was furious. "Florina shall repent having pleased

King Charming!" cried she; and dressing her own daughter in rich garments, with a gold crown on her head, and King Charming's ring on her finger, she took her to the tower. "Florina, your sister is come to see and bring you marriage presents, for she is now the wife of King Charming."

Florina, doubting no more her lover's loss, fell down in a swoon, and the queen immediately went to tell her father that she was mad for love, and must be watched closely lest she should in some way disgrace herself. The king said, her stepmother might do with her exactly what she pleased.

When the princess recovered from her swoon, she began to weep, and wept all night long, sitting at the open window of her tower. The Blue Bird, who kept continually flying about the palace, but only at night time, lest any one should see him, happened to come and perch upon a tall cypress opposite the window, and heard her; but it was too dark to see who she was, and at daylight she shut the window. Next night, it was broad moonlight, and then he saw clearly the figure of a young girl, weeping sore, and knew that it was his beloved Florina.

When she paused in her lamentations, "Adorable princess," said he, "why do you mourn? Your troubles are not without remedy."

"Who speaks to me so gently?" asked she.

"A king, who loves you, and will never love any other."

So saying he flew up to the window, and at first frightened the princess very much, for she could not understand such an extraordinary thing as a bird who talked in words like a man, yet kept still the piping voice of a nightingale. But soon she began stroking his beautiful plumage, and caressing him.

"Who are you, charming bird?"

"You have spoken my name. I am King Charming,

condemned to be a bird for seven years, because I will not renounce you."

"Ah! do not deceive me. I know you have married Troutina. She came to visit me with your diamonds on her neck, and your ring on her finger, wearing the golden crown and royal mantle which you had given her, while I was laden with iron chains."

"It is all false," sang the Blue Bird, and told her his whole story, which comforted her so much that she thought no more of her misfortunes. They conversed till daybreak, and promised faithfully every night to meet again thus.

Meantime the princess could not sleep for thinking of her Blue Bird. "Suppose sportsmen should shoot him, or eagles and kites attack him, and vultures devour him just as if he were a mere bird and not a great king? What should I do if I saw his poor feathers scattered on the ground, and knew that he was no more?" So she grieved all day long.

The beautiful Blue Bird, hid in a hollow tree, spent the hours in thinking of his princess. "How happy I am to have found her again, and found her so engaging and so sweet." And as he wished to pay her all the attentions that a lover delights in, he flew to his own kingdom, entered his palace by an open window, and sought for some diamond ear-rings, which he brought back in his beak, and, when night came, offered them to Florina. So night after night he brought her something beautiful, and they talked together till day, when he flew back to the hollow tree, where he sang her praises in a voice so sweet that the passers-by thought it was not a bird but a spirit. Rumours went about that the place was haunted, and no one would go near the spot. Thus, for two years, Florina spent her time, and never once regretted her captivity. Her Blue Bird visited her every night, and they loved one another dearly. And though she saw nobody, and he lived in the hollow of a tree, they always found plenty to say to one another.

The malicious queen tried with all her might to get Troutina married, but in vain. Nobody would have her. "If it were Florina, now," said the kings, or the kings' ambassadors, "we should be most happy to sign the contract."

"That girl thwarts us still," said the queen. "She must have some secret correspondence with foreign suitors. But we will find her out and punish her."

The mother and daughter finished talking so late that it was midnight before they reached Florina's apartment. She had dressed herself as usual, with the utmost care, to please her Blue Bird, who liked to see her lovely ; and she had adorned herself with all the pretty things he had given her. He perched on the window-sill, and she sat at the window, and they were singing together a duet, which the queen heard outside. She burst the door open, and rushed into the chamber.

The first thing Florina did was to open her little window that the Blue Bird might fly away. But he would not. He had seen the queen and Troutina, and though he could not defend his princess, he refused to leave her. The two rushed upon her like furies. Her wonderful beauty and her splendid jewels startled them. "Whence came all these ornaments ? " cried they.

"I found them," replied Florina, and refused to answer more.

"Some one has given them to you that you might join in treason against your father and the kingdom."

"Am I likely to do this ? I, a poor princess, kept in captivity for two years, with you as my gaoler ?"

"In captivity," repeated the queen. "Why, then, do you dress yourself so fine, and adorn your chamber with flowers ? "

"I have leisure enough : I may just as well spend

some of it in adorning myself, instead of bemoaning my misfortune—innocent as I am."

"Innocent, indeed!" cried the queen, and began to search the room. In it she found all King Charming's presents—diamonds, rubies, emeralds, amethysts—in short, jewels without end. Meantime, from the window, the Blue Bird, who had the eye of a lynx, sang aloud, "Beware, Florina!"

"You see, madam," said Florina, "even the spirits of the air take pity upon me."

"I see that you are in league with demons; but your father shall judge you"; and, very much frightened, the queen left her, and went to hold counsel with Troutina as to what was to be done. They agreed to put in Florina's chamber a waiting-maid, who should watch her from morning till night. When the princess learnt this she was in great grief.

"Alas!" cried she, "I can no longer talk with my bird who loved me so; and our love was consolation for all our misfortunes. What will he do? What shall I do?" And she melted into floods of tears.

She dared not open the window, though she heard continually his wings fluttering round it. For more than a month she waited; but the serving-maid watched her night and day. At last, overcome with weariness, the girl fell asleep, and then Florina opened her little window, and sang in a low voice:

> "Blue Bird, Blue Bird,
> Come to my side."

The Blue Bird flew to the window-sill, and they lavished on one another a hundred caresses, and talked together till dawn. Next night it happened the same, till they began to hope that the waiting-maid, who seemed to enjoy her sleep so much, would sleep every night to come. But on the third night, hearing a noise, she wakened, and saw by the light of the moon the Princess Florina sitting at the window with a beautiful Blue Bird, who warbled in her ear and touched her gently with his beak. The spy listened and heard all their conversation, very much astonished that a princess could be so fond of a mere bird. When day came, she related all to the queen and Troutina, who concluded that the bird could be no other than King Charming. They sent the girl back, told her to express no curiosity, but to feign sleep, and to go to bed earlier than usual. Then the poor deceived princess opened her little window, and sang her usual song :

> "Blue Bird, Blue Bird,
> Come to my side."

But no Blue Bird appeared. The queen had caused sharp knives to be hung outside the hollow of the tree : he flew against them and cut his feet and wings, till he dropped down, covered with blood.

"Oh, Florina, come to my help!" sighed he. "But she is dead, I know, and I will die also."

At that moment, his friend, the magician, who, since he had seen the chariot with flying frogs return without King Charming, had gone eight times round the world in search of him, made his ninth journey, and came to the tree where the poor Blue Bird lay, calling out, "King Charming, King Charming!"

The king recognised the voice of his best friend : whereupon the magician took him out of the hollow tree, healed his wounds, and heard all his history. He persuaded King Charming that, overcome with fear and cruel treatment, Florina must have betrayed him.

"Then do as you will with me!" cried the king. "Put me into a cage and take me back with you. I shall at least be safe there for the five years that are to be endured."

316

"But," said the enchanter, "can you remain five years in so undignified a position? And you have enemies who will assuredly seize on your kingdom."

"Why can I not return and govern it as before?"

"I fear," replied his friend, "that the thing is difficult. Who would obey a Blue Bird?"

"Ah, that is too true!" cried the king sadly. "People only judge by the outside."

Meantime Florina, overcome with grief, fell dangerously sick, and in her sickness she kept singing, day and night, her little song:

> "Blue Bird, Blue Bird,
> Come to my side."

But no one regarded her.

At last a sudden change took place in her fortunes. The king her father died, and the people, who knew she was his heir, began to inquire, with one accord, where was the Princess Florina? They assailed the palace in crowds, demanding her for their sovereign. The riot became so dangerous that Troutina and her mother fled away to the fairy Soussio. Then the populace stormed the tower, rescued the sick and almost dying princess, and crowned her as their queen.

The exceeding care that was taken of her, and her longing to live in order to see again her Blue Bird, restored Florina's health, and gave her strength to call a council and arrange all the affairs of her kingdom. Then she departed by night, and alone, to go over the world in search of her Blue Bird.

The magician, who was King Charming's friend, went to the fairy Soussio, whom he knew, for they had quarrelled and made it up again, as fairies and magicians do, many times within the last five or six hundred years. She received him civilly, and asked him what he wanted. He tried to make a bargain with her, but could effect nothing, unless King Charming would consent to marry Troutina. The enchanter found this bride so ugly that he could not advise. Still, the Blue Bird had run so many risks in his cage : the nail it was hung upon had broken, and the king suffered much in the fall ; Minetta, the cat, had glowered at him with her green eyes ; the attendants had forgotten his hemp-seed and his water-glass, so that he was half dying of hunger and thirst ; and a monkey had plucked at his feathers through the wires as disrespectfully as if, instead of a king, he had been a linnet or a jay. Worse than all, his next heir spread reports of his death, and threatened to seize on his throne.

Under these circumstances the magician thought it best to agree with Soussio that King Charming should be restored to his kingdom and his natural shape for six months, on condition that Troutina should remain in his palace, and that he should try to like her and marry her. If not, he was to become again a Blue Bird. So he found himself once more King Charming, and as charming as ever ; but he would rather have been a bird and near his beloved, than a king in the society of Troutina. The enchanter gave him the best reasons for what had been done, and advised him to occupy himself with the affairs of his kingdom and people ; but he thought less of these things than how to escape from the horror of marrying Troutina.

Meanwhile the Queen Florina, in a peasant's dress, with a straw hat on her head, and a canvas sack on her shoulder, began her journey : sometimes on horseback, sometimes on foot, sometimes by sea, sometimes by land, wandering evermore after her beloved King Charming. One day, stopping beside a fountain, she let her hair fall loose, and dipped her weary feet in the cool water, when an old woman, bent, and leaning on a stick, came by.

"My pretty maiden, what are you doing here all alone ?"

"Good mother," replied the queen, "I have too many troubles to be pleasant company for anybody."

"Tell me your troubles, and I may be able to soften them."

Florina obeyed, and told her whole history, and how she was travelling over the world in search of the Blue Bird. The little woman listened attentively, and then, in the twinkling of an eye, became, instead of an old woman, a beautiful fairy.

"Incomparable Florina, the king you seek is no longer a bird; my sister Soussio has restored him to his proper shape, and he reigns in his own kingdom. Do not afflict yourself; happiness will yet be yours. Take these four eggs, and whenever you are in trouble, break them, and see what ensues." So saying, the fairy vanished.

Florina, greatly comforted, put the eggs in her sack, and turned her steps towards the country of King Charming. She walked eight days and nights without stopping, and then came to a mountain made entirely of ivory, and nearly perpendicular. Despairing of ever climbing it, she sank down at the foot, prepared to die there, when she bethought herself of the eggs. "Let me see," said she, "if the fairy has deceived me or not." So she broke one, and inside it were little hooks of gold, which she fitted on her feet and hands, and by means of which she climbed the mountain with ease. Arrived at the summit she found new difficulties; for the valley below was one large smooth mirror, in which sixty thousand women stood admiring themselves. They had need, for the charm of the mirror was that each saw herself therein, not as she was, but as she wished to be; and the grimaces they made were enough to cause a person to die of laughter. Not one of them had ever gained the top of the mountain; and when they saw Florina there, they all burst into angry outcries, "How has this woman got up the hill? If she descends upon our mirror her first footstep will crack it into a thousand pieces."

The queen, uncertain what to do, broke the second egg, and there flew out two pigeons harnessed to a fine chariot, in which Florina mounted, and descended lightly over the mirror to the valley's foot. "Now, my pretty pigeons," said she, "will you convey me to the palace of King Charming?" The obedient pigeons did so, flying day and night till they reached the city gates; when the queen dismissed them with a sweet kiss, which was worth more than her crown.

How her heart beat as she entered, and begged to see the king! "You!" cried the servants, mocking. "Little peasant-girl, your eyes are not half good enough to see the king. Besides, he is going to-morrow to the temple with the Princess Troutina, whom he has at last agreed to marry."

Florina sat down on a doorstep, and hid her face under her straw hat and her drooping hair. "Alas!" she cried, "my Blue Bird has forsaken me."

She neither ate nor slept, but rose with the dawn, and pushed her way through the guards to the temple, where she saw two thrones, one for King Charming, and the other for Troutina. They arrived shortly; he more charming and she more repulsive than ever. Knitting her brows, Troutina exclaimed, "What creature is that who dares approach so near my golden throne?"

"I am a poor peasant-girl," said Florina. "I come from afar to sell you curiosities." And she took out of her sack the emerald bracelets which the Blue Bird had given her.

"These are pretty trinkets," said Troutina; and going up to the king she asked him what he thought of them. At sight of the ornaments he turned pale, remembering those he had given to Florina.

"These bracelets are worth half my kingdom; I did

not think there had been more than one pair in the world."

"Then I will buy these," said Troutina; but Florina refused to sell them for money: the price she asked was permission to sleep a night in the Chamber of Echoes.

"As you will; your bargains are cheap enough," replied Troutina, laughing: and when she laughed she showed teeth like the tusks of a wild boar.

Now the king, when he was a Blue Bird, had informed Florina about this Chamber of Echoes, where every word spoken could be heard in his own chamber; she could not have chosen a better way of reproaching him for his infidelity. But vain were her sobs and complainings; the king had taken opium to lull his grief; he slept soundly all night long. Next day, Florina was in great disquietude. Could he have really heard her, and been indifferent to her sorrow; or had he not heard her at all? She determined to buy another night in the Chamber of Echoes; but she had no more jewels to tempt Troutina; so she broke the third egg. Out of it came a chariot of polished steel, inlaid with gold, drawn by six green mice, the coachman being a rose-coloured rat, and the postilion a grey one. Inside the carriage sat little puppets, who behaved themselves just like live ladies and gentlemen.

When Troutina went to walk in the palace garden, Florina awaited her in a green alley, and made the mice gallop, and the ladies and gentlemen bow, till the princess was delighted, and ready to buy the curiosity at any price. Again Florina exacted permission to pass the night in the Chamber of Echoes; and again the king, undisturbed by her lamentation, slept without waking till dawn.

The third day, one of the palace valets, passing her by, said, "You stupid peasant-girl, it is well the king takes opium every night, or you would disturb him by that terrible sobbing of yours."

"Does he so?" said the queen, now comprehending

all. "Then if you will promise to-night to keep the opium cup out of his way, these pearls and diamonds," and she took a handful of them out of her sack, "shall assuredly be yours."

The valet promised; and then Florina broke her fourth egg, out of which came a pie composed of birds, which, though they had been plucked, baked, and made ready for the table, sang as beautifully as birds that are alive. Troutina, charmed with this marvellous novelty, bought it at the same price as the rest, adding generously a small piece of gold.

When all the palace were asleep, Florina for the last time, hoping King Charming would hear her, called upon him with all sorts of tender expressions, reminding him of their former vows, and their two years of happiness. "What have I done to thee, that thou shouldst forget me and marry Troutina?" sobbed she; and the king, who this time was wide awake, heard her. He could not make out whose voice it was, or whence it came, but it somehow reminded him of his dearest Florina, whom he had never ceased to love. He called his valet, inquired who was sleeping in the Chamber of Echoes, and heard that it was the little peasant-girl who had sold to Troutina the emerald bracelet. Then he rose up, dressed himself hastily, and went in search of her. She was sitting mournfully on the floor, with her hair hiding her face, and her eyes swollen with tears; but he knew at once his faithful Florina. He fell on his knees before her, covered her hands with kisses, and they embraced and wept together. For what was the good of all their love when they were still in the power of the fairy Soussio?

But at this moment appeared the friendly enchanter, with a fairy still greater than Soussio, the one who had given Florina the four eggs. They declared that their united power was stronger than Soussio's, and that the lovers should be married without further delay.

THE BLUE BIRD

When this news reached Troutina, she ran to the Chamber of Echoes, and there beheld her beautiful rival, whom she had so cruelly afflicted. But the moment she opened her mouth to speak, her wicked tongue was silenced for ever ; for the magician turned her into a trout, which he flung out of the window into the stream that flowed through the castle garden.

As for King Charming and Queen Florina, delivered out of all their sorrows, and given to one another, their joy was quite inexpressible, and it lasted to the end of their lives.

Note.—It will be seen that this tale, which is from the French, bears a curious resemblance to Grimm's story of "The Iron Stove," except that the latter retains a brevity and German simplicity, not found here. This family likeness may be traced in the fairy tales of all countries. I merely refer to it to show that the repetition of incidents was not unobserved or unintentional. —EDITOR.

THE YELLOW DWARF

THERE was once a queen, who had been the mother of several children, but all were dead, except one daughter, of whom she was excessively fond, humouring and indulging her in all her ways and wishes. This princess was so extremely beautiful, that she was called All-Fair, and twenty kings were, at one time, paying their addresses to her. She had so many lovers, indeed, that she did not know which to choose, and refused them all. Her mother, being advanced in years, was anxious to see her married and settled before she died; but as no entreaties could prevail, she determined to go to the Desert Fairy to ask advice concerning her stubborn daughter.

Now, this fairy being guarded by two fierce lions, the queen made a cake of millet, sugar-candy, and crocodiles' eggs, in order to appease their fury, and pass by them; and having thus provided herself, she set out. After travelling some time she found herself weary, and lying down under a tree fell asleep. When she awoke, she heard the roaring of the lions which guarded the fairy, and on looking for her cake she found it was gone. This threw her into the utmost agony, as she felt sure she should be devoured; when, hearing somebody approach, she raised her eyes, and saw in a tree a little yellow man half a yard high, picking and eating oranges.

"Ah! queen," said the Yellow Dwarf, for so he was called on account of his complexion, and the orange tree in which he lived, "how will you escape the lions? There

"There, one day, he heard a voice, and presently after was
surprised by the appearance of a mermaid." *(Page 328)*

"The queen threw one of the shirts over each of them, and when
the shirts touched their bodies, they were changed into swans,
and flew away over the wood." *(Page 332)*

WARWICK GOBLE

is but one way ; I know what business brought you here ; promise me your daughter in marriage and I will save you."

The queen, though she could not look without horror upon so frightful a figure, was forced to consent ; and having agreed to the terms proposed, she instantly found herself in her own palace, and all that had passed seemed much like a dream : nevertheless, she was so thoroughly persuaded of the reality of it, that she became melancholy.

The young princess being unable to learn the cause of her mother's dejection, resolved in her turn to go and inquire of the Desert Fairy ; and, accordingly, having prepared a cake for the lions, she also set off on the same journey. It happened that All-Fair took exactly the route her mother had done before her ; and coming to the fatal tree which was loaded with oranges, she felt inclined to pick some ; therefore, laying down her basket, in which she carried the cake, she plentifully indulged herself with the delicious fruit.

The lions now began to roar ; All-Fair, looking for her cake, was thrown into the utmost despair to find it gone ; and as she was lamenting her deplorable situation, the Yellow Dwarf presented himself to her with these words : "Lovely princess, dry your tears, and hear what I am going to say. You need not proceed to the Desert Fairy, to know the reason of your mother's indisposition—it is this : she is ungenerous enough to repent having promised you, her only daughter, to me in marriage——"

"How !" interrupted the princess ; "my mother promised me to you in marriage ;—you ! such a fright as you !"

"None of your scoffs," returned the Yellow Dwarf ; "I warn you not to rouse my anger. If you will promise to marry me, I will be the tenderest and most loving husband in the world ; if not, save yourself from the lions, if you can."

The princess, overcome with terror, gave the promise; but such was the agony of her mind, that she fell into a swoon, and, when she recovered, she found herself in her own bed, finely adorned with ribands, with a ring of a single red hair so fastened round her finger that it could not be got off.

This adventure had the same effect upon All-Fair as the former one had had upon her mother. She grew melancholy, which was remarked and wondered at by the whole court. The best way to divert her, they thought, would be to urge her to marry; which the princess, who was now become less obstinate on that point than formerly, consented to. Trusting that such a pigmy as the Yellow Dwarf would not dare to contend with so gallant a person as the King of the Golden Mines, she fixed upon that prince for her husband. He was exceedingly rich and powerful, and loved her to distraction. The most superb preparations were made for the nuptials, and the happy day was fixed when, as they were proceeding to the ceremony, they saw moving towards them a box, upon which sat an old woman remarkable for her ugliness.

"Hold, queen and princess!" cried she, knitting her brows; "remember the promises you have both made to my friend the Yellow Dwarf. I am the Desert Fairy; and unless All-Fair consent to marry him, I solemnly swear to burn my crutch."

The queen and princess were struck almost motionless by this unexpected address of the fairy; but the Prince of the Golden Mines was exceeding angry, and holding his sword to her throat, he said, "Fly, wretch! or thy malice shall cost thee thy life."

No sooner had he uttered these words, than the top of the box flying off, out came the Yellow Dwarf, mounted upon a large Spanish cat. Placing himself between the king and the fairy, he exclaimed, "Rash youth! thy rage shall be levelled at me, not at the Desert Fairy. I am

thy rival, and claim thy princess, who is fast bound to
me by her own promise, her mother's, and the single red
hair that you see round her finger."

This so enraged the king, that he cried out, "Con-
temptible creature! wert thou worthy of notice, I would
sacrifice thee for thy presumption."

The Yellow Dwarf, clapping spurs to his cat, and
drawing a cutlass, now defied the king to combat; and
down they went into the courtyard. The sun was
immediately turned as red as blood, the air became dark,
it thundered heavily, and the flashes of lightning discovered
two giants vomiting fire on each side of the Yellow Dwarf.
The king behaved with such undaunted courage, as to
give the dwarf great trouble; but he was dismayed when
he saw the Desert Fairy, mounted on a winged griffin,
and with her head covered with snakes, strike the princess
so hard with a lance, that she fell into the queen's arms,
covered with blood. He immediately left the combat, to
go to the relief of his beloved, but the dwarf was too quick
for him; and flying on his Spanish cat to the balcony
where she was, he took her from her mother's arms, leaped
with her upon the top of the palace, and immediately
disappeared.

As the king stood confused and astonished at this
strange adventure, he suddenly found a mist before his
eyes, and felt himself lifted up in the air by some extraordinary power; for the Desert Fairy had fallen in love
with him. To secure him for herself, therefore, she
carried him to a frightful cavern, hoping he would there
forget All-Fair. But finding this scheme ineffectual, she
resolved to carry him to a place altogether as pleasant as the
other was terrible; and accordingly placed him in a chariot
drawn by swans. In passing through the air, he was
unspeakably surprised to see his beloved princess in a
castle of polished steel, leaning her head on one hand, and
wiping away her tears with the other. She happened to

look up, and had the mortification to see the king sitting by the fairy, who then, by her art, made herself appear extremely beautiful. Had not the king been sensible of the fairy's power, he would certainly have tried to free himself from her by some means or other ; but he knew it would be in vain, and therefore made believe to have a liking for her. At last they came to a stately palace, fenced on one side by walls of emeralds, and on the other by a boisterous sea. The king, by pretending an attachment to the fairy, obtained the liberty to walk by himself on the shore. There, one day, he heard a voice, and presently after was surprised by the appearance of a mermaid, who, swimming up to him with a pleasing smile, spoke to this effect : "O King of the Golden Mines, I well know all that has befallen you and the Princess All-Fair. Do not suspect this to be a contrivance of the fairy to try you, for I am an inveterate enemy both to her and the Yellow Dwarf ; therefore, if you will place confidence in me, I will lend you my assistance to procure the release, not only of yourself, but of All-Fair also."

The overjoyed king promised to do whatever the mermaid should direct, and seating himself by her desire upon her fish's tail, they sailed away together over the rolling sea.

When they had sailed some time, " Now," said the mermaid to the king, "we are approaching the place where your princess is kept prisoner by the Yellow Dwarf. You will have many enemies to fight before you can come to her ; take, therefore, this sword, with which you may overcome everything, provided you never let it go out of your hand."

The king returned her all the thanks that the most grateful heart could suggest ; and the mermaid landed and took leave of him, promising him further assistance when necessary. The king boldly advanced, and, meeting with two terrible sphinxes, laid them dead at his feet with the sword. Next he attacked six dragons that opposed him, and despatched them also. Then he met four-and-twenty nymphs, crowned with garlands of flowers, at the sight of whom he stopped, being unwilling to destroy so much beauty; when he heard a voice say, "Strike! strike! or you will lose your princess for ever!" So he threw himself into the midst of the nymphs, smiting right and left, and soon dispersed them.

Presently he came to the castle, where was imprisoned the princess All-Fair. "Oh, my princess," exclaimed he, "behold your faithful lover!"

"Faithful lover!" she replied, drawing herself back. "Did I not see you passing through the air with a beautiful nymph? were you faithful then?"

"Yes," replied the king, "I was. That was the detested Desert Fairy, who was carrying me to a place where I must have languished out all my days, had it not been for a kind mermaid, by whose assistance it is that I am now come to release you." Having uttered these words, he threw himself at her feet; but, catching hold of her gown he unfortunately let go the magic sword, which the Yellow Dwarf no sooner discovered, than, leaping from behind a shrub, where he had been concealed, he ran and seized it. By two cabalistical words he then conjured up a couple of giants, who laid the king in irons.

"Now," said the Dwarf, "my rival's fate is in my own hands; however, if he will consent to my marriage with the princess All-Fair, he shall have his life and liberty."

"No," said the king, "I scorn thy favour on such terms."

The dwarf was so exasperated by this reply, that he instantly stabbed the king to the heart. The disconsolate princess stood a moment petrified, and then exclaimed, "Thou hideous creature! since entreaties could not avail thee, perhaps thou now reliest upon force; but thou shalt be disappointed. I will die for the love I have for the King of the Golden Mines!" and so saying she sank down upon his body, and expired without a sigh.

Thus ended the fate of these two faithful lovers, whom the mermaid very much regretted ; but as all her power lay in the sword, she could only change them into two palm trees, which, preserving a constant and mutual affection, still fondly unite their branches together.

THE SIX SWANS

ONCE upon a time, a king, hunting in a great forest, chased a wild boar so eagerly, that none of his people could follow him. When evening came, he stopped to look about him, and saw that he had lost himself. He sought everywhere for a way out of the wood, but could find none. Then he perceived coming towards him an old woman, whose head kept constantly shaking. She was a witch.

"My good woman," said he to her, "cannot you show me the way through the wood?"

"Oh yes, your majesty," answered she, "that I can, but only on one condition, and if you do not agree to it, you will never get out, and must die here of hunger."

"What is the condition?" asked the king.

"I have an only daughter," said the old woman, "she is as beautiful as any one you could find in the wide world, and well deserves to be your wife; if you will make her your queen, I will show you the way out of the wood."

The king, in the fear of his heart, consented, and the old woman led him to her house, where her daughter sat by the fire. She received the king as if she had expected him, and he saw that she was very beautiful; but still she did not please him, and he could not look at her without a secret shudder. After he had lifted up the maiden beside him on his horse, the old woman showed him the way, and the king arrived again at his royal castle, where the wedding was celebrated.

He had been married once before, and had by his first wife seven children, six boys and a girl, whom he loved more than anything in the world. But, because he was afraid that the stepmother might not treat them well, or might even do them some harm, he took them to a lonely castle which stood in the middle of a wood. It was so hidden, and the road was so difficult to find, that he himself would not have found it, if a wise woman had not given him a wonderful skein of thread; which, when he threw it down before him, unrolled of itself and showed him the way. The king went out so often to his dear children, that the queen noticed his absence, and was full of curiosity to know what business took him thus alone to the wood. So she gave his servants a sum of money, and they told her the secret, and also told her of the skein, which was the only thing that could show the way. After that she never rested till she had found out where the king kept the skein. Then she made some little white silk shirts, and as she had learned witchcraft from her mother, she sewed a spell into every one of them. And one day when the king was gone out to hunt, she took the little shirts and went into the wood, and the skein showed her the way.

The six brothers, who saw some one in the distance, thought their dear father was coming, and ran to meet him, full of joy. As they approached, the queen threw one of the shirts over each of them, and when the shirts touched their bodies, they were changed into swans, and flew away over the wood. The witch's daughter went home quite happy, and thought she had got rid of all her stepchildren; but the one little girl had not run out with her brothers, and the queen knew nothing about her.

Next day, the king came joyfully to visit his children, but he found nobody except the little sister.

"Where are your brothers?" asked he.

" Oh, dear father," she answered, " they are gone and have left me alone," and then she told him all that she had seen out of her window ; how her brothers were turned into swans, and had flown away over the wood ; she also showed him the feathers which they had dropped into the courtyard, and which she had picked up.

The king was grieved, but he never thought that the queen had done this wicked deed ; however, because he dreaded lest the little girl would be stolen from him likewise, he wished to take her away with him. But she was afraid of the stepmother, and begged the king to let her stay one night more in the castle in the wood.

The poor little girl thought, " I cannot rest here any longer, I will go and look for my brothers."

And when the night came, she ran away, and went straight into the wood. She went on all through the night, and the next day too, till she was so tired that she could go no further. Then she saw a little house, and went in, and found a room with six little beds ; she did not dare to lie down in any, but crept under one of them, laid herself on the hard floor, and meant to pass the night there. But when the sun was just going to set, she heard a rustling, and saw six swans come flying in at the window. They sat down on the floor, and blew at one another, and blew all their feathers off, and took off their swan's-skins like shirts. Then the little girl saw them and recognised her brothers, and was very glad, and crept out from under the bed.

The brothers were not less rejoiced when they saw their little sister, but their joy did not last long.

" You cannot stop here," said they to her, " this is a house belonging to robbers ; if they come home, and find you, they will kill you."

" Cannot you protect me ? " asked the little sister.

" No," answered they, " we can only take off our swan's-skins for a quarter of an hour every evening, and have our natural shape for that time, but afterwards we are turned into swans again."

The little sister cried and said, " Cannot you be released ? "

" Oh no ! " answered they, " the conditions are too hard. You must not speak or laugh for six years, and must make for us six shirts out of stitchweed during that time. If while you are making them a single word comes from your mouth, all your work will be of no use." When her brothers had said this, the quarter of an hour was over, and they turned into swans again, and flew out of the window.

But the little girl made a firm resolution to release her brothers, even if it cost her her life. She left the house, and went into the middle of the wood, and climbed up in a tree and spent the night there. Next morning she got down, collected a quantity of stitchweed, and began to sew. She could not speak to any one, and she did not want to laugh, so she sat, and only looked at her work.

When she had been there a long time, it happened that the king of the country was hunting in the wood, and his hunters came to the tree on which the little girl sat. They called to her, and said, " Who are you ? "

But she gave them no answer.

" Come down to us," said they, " we will not do you any harm."

But she only shook her head. As they kept teasing her with their questions, she threw them down her gold necklace, and thought they would be satisfied with that. But they did not leave off, so she threw her sash down to them, and as that was no good, she threw down her garters, and at last everything that she had on, and could spare ; so that she had nothing left but her shift. But the hunters would not be sent away, and climbed up the tree and brought down the little girl and took her to the king.

The king asked, "Who are you? what were you doing up in the tree?"

But she did not answer. He asked it in all the languages that he knew, but she remained as dumb as a fish. But, because she was so beautiful, the king's heart was moved, and he fell deeply in love with her. He wrapped his cloak round her, took her before him on his horse, and brought her to his castle. Then he had her dressed in rich clothes, and she shone in her beauty like bright sunshine; but they could not get a word out of her. He set her by him at the table, and her modest look and proper behaviour pleased him so much, that he said, "I will marry her, and no one else in the world," and after a few days he was married to her.

But the king had a wicked mother, who was not pleased with this marriage, and spoke ill of the young queen. "Who knows where the girl comes from," said she, "she cannot speak; she is not good enough for a king."

A year after, when the queen brought her first child into the world, the old mother took it away, and smeared her mouth with blood while she was asleep. Then she went to the king, and accused her of eating her child. The king would not believe it, and would not let any one do her any harm. And she always sat and sewed the shirts, and took no notice of anything else. Next time, when she had another beautiful baby, the wicked step-mother did the same as before; but the king could not resolve to believe what she said.

He said, "My wife is too pious and good to do such a thing; if she were not dumb, and if she could defend herself, her innocence would be made clear."

But when for the third time the old woman took away the new-born child, and accused the queen, who could not say a word in her own defence, the king could not help himself; he was forced to give her up to the court of justice, and she was condemned to suffer death by fire.

When the day came upon which the sentence was to be executed, it was exactly the last day of the six years, in which she might not speak or laugh ; and she had freed her dear brothers from the power of the spell. The six little shirts were finished, except that on the last one a sleeve was wanting. When she came to the place of execution, she laid the shirts on her arm, and when she stood at the stake, and the fire was just going to be lit, she looked round, and there came six swans flying through the air. Then her heart leaped with joy, for she saw that her deliverance was near.

The swans flew to her, and crouched down, so that she could throw the shirts over them ; as soon as the shirts were touched by them, their swan's-skins fell off, and her brothers stood before her. They were all grown up, strong and handsome ; only the youngest had no left arm, but instead of it a swan's wing.

They hugged and kissed their sister many times, and then the queen went to the king, and began to speak, and said, " Dearest husband, now I may speak, and declare to you that I am innocent and falsely accused " ; and she told him about the deceit of the old mother, who had taken away her three children, and hidden them.

However they were soon fetched safely back, to the great joy of the king ; and the wicked mother-in-law was tied to the stake, and burnt to ashes. But the king and queen, with their six brothers, lived many years in peace and happiness.

THE PRINCE WITH THE NOSE

THERE was once a king who was passionately in love with a beautiful princess, but she could not be married because a magician had enchanted her. The king went to a good fairy to inquire what he should do. Said the fairy, after receiving him graciously : "Sir, I will tell you a secret. The princess has a great cat whom she loves so well that she cares for nothing and nobody else ; but she will be obliged to marry any person who is adroit enough to walk upon the cat's tail."

"That will not be very difficult," thought the king to himself, and departed, resolving to trample the cat's tail to pieces rather than not succeed in walking upon it. He went immediately to the palace of his fair mistress and the cat ; the animal came in front of him, arching its back in anger as it was wont to do. The king lifted up his foot, thinking nothing would be so easy as to tread on the tail, but he found himself mistaken. Minon—that was the creature's name—twisted itself round so sharply that the king only hurt his own foot by stamping on the floor. For eight days did he pursue the cat everywhere : up and down the palace he was after it from morning till night, but with no better success ; the tail seemed made of quick-silver, so very lively was it. At last the king had the good fortune to catch Minon sleeping, when tramp, tramp ! he trod on the tail with all his force.

Minon woke up, mewed horribly, and immediately changed from a cat into a large, fierce-looking man, who regarded the king with flashing eyes.

"You must marry the princess," cried he, "because you have broken the enchantment in which I held her; but I will be revenged on you. You shall have a son with a nose as long as—that"; he made in the air a curve of half a foot; "yet he shall believe it is just like all other noses, and shall be always unfortunate till he has found out it is not. And if you ever tell anybody of this threat of mine, you shall die on the spot." So saying, the magician disappeared.

The king, who was at first much terrified, soon began to laugh at this adventure. "My son might have a worse misfortune than too long a nose," thought he. "At least it will hinder him neither in seeing nor hearing. I will go and find the princess, and marry her at once."

He did so, but he only lived a few months after, and died before his little son was born, so that nobody knew anything about the secret of the nose.

The little prince was so much wished for, that when he came into the world they agreed to call him Prince Wish. He had beautiful blue eyes, and a sweet little mouth, but his nose was so big that it covered half his face. The queen, his mother, was inconsolable; but her ladies tried to satisfy her by telling her that the nose was not nearly so large as it seemed, that it would grow smaller as the prince grew bigger, and that if it did not a large nose was indispensable to a hero. All great soldiers, they said, had great noses, as everybody knew. The queen was so very fond of her son that she listened eagerly to all this comfort. Shortly she grew so used to the prince's nose that it did not seem to her any larger than ordinary noses of the court; where, in process of time, everybody with a long nose was very much admired, and the unfortunate people who had only snubs were taken very little notice of.

Great care was observed in the education of the prince; and as soon as he could speak they told him all sorts of amusing tales, in which all the bad people had short noses, and all the good people long ones. No person was suffered to come near him who had not a nose of more than ordinary length; nay, to such an extent did the courtiers carry their fancy, that the noses of all the little babies were ordered to be pulled out as far as possible several times a day, in order to make them grow. But grow as they would, they never could grow as long as that of Prince Wish. When he was old enough his tutor taught him history; and whenever any great king or lovely princess was referred to, the tutor always took care to mention that he or she had a long nose. All the royal apartments were filled with pictures and portraits having this peculiarity, so that at last Prince Wish began to regard the length of his nose as his greatest perfection, and would not have had it an inch less even to save his crown.

When he was twenty years old his mother and his people wished him to marry. They procured for him the likenesses of many princesses, but the one he preferred was Princess Darling, daughter of a powerful monarch and heiress to several kingdoms. Alas! with all her beauty, this princess had one great misfortune, a little turned-up nose, which, every one else said, made her only the more bewitching. But here, in the kingdom of Prince Wish, the courtiers were thrown by it into the utmost perplexity. They were in the habit of laughing at all small noses; but how dared they make fun of the nose of Princess Darling? Two unfortunate gentlemen, whom Prince Wish had overheard doing so, were ignominiously banished from the court and capital.

After this, the courtiers became alarmed, and tried to correct their habit of speech; but they would have found themselves in constant difficulties, had not one clever person struck out a bright idea. He said that though it was indispensably necessary for a man to have a great nose, women were different; and that a learned man had discovered in a very old manuscript that the celebrated Cleopatra, Queen of Egypt, the beauty of the ancient world, had a turned-up nose. At this information Prince Wish was so delighted that he made the courtier a very handsome present, and immediately sent off ambassadors to demand Princess Darling in marriage.

She accepted his offer at once, and returned with the ambassadors. He made all haste to meet and welcome her; but when she was only three leagues distant from his capital, before he had time even to kiss her hand, the magician who had once assumed the shape of his mother's cat, Minon, appeared in the air and carried her off before the lover's very eyes.

Prince Wish, almost beside himself with grief, declared that nothing should induce him to return to his throne and kingdom till he had found Darling. He would suffer none of his courtiers or attendants to follow him; but, bidding them all adieu, mounted a good horse, laid the reins on the animal's neck, and let him take him wherever he would.

The horse entered a wide-extended plain, and trotted on steadily the whole day without finding a single house. Master and beast began almost to faint with hunger; and Prince Wish might have wished himself safe at home again, had he not discovered, just at dusk, a cavern, where there sat, beside a bright lantern, a little woman who might have been more than a hundred years old.

She put on her spectacles the better to look at the stranger, and he noticed that her nose was so small that the spectacles would hardly stay on; then the prince and the fairy,—for it was a fairy,—burst into a mutual fit of laughter.

"What a funny nose!" cried the one.

"Not so funny as yours, madam," returned the other. "But pray let us leave our noses alone, and be good

WARWICK GOBLE

"By the care of the Fairy Tulip, she was not wounded."
(Page 358)

"Out of the fire flew a beautiful bird, who, singing deliciously,
rose up high in the air." *(Page 368)*

enough to give me something to eat, for I am dying with hunger, and so is my poor horse."

" With all my heart," answered the fairy. " Although your nose is ridiculously long, you are no less the son of one of my best friends. I loved your father like a brother ; *he* had a very handsome nose."

" What is wanting to my nose ? " asked Wish, rather savagely.

" Oh ! nothing at all. On the contrary, there is a great deal too much of it ; but never mind, one may be a very honest man, and yet have too big a nose. As I said, I was a great friend of your father's ; he came often to see me. I was very pretty then, and oftentimes he used to say to me, ' My sister——' "

" I will hear the rest, madam, with pleasure, when I have supped ; but will you condescend to remember that I have tasted nothing all day ? "

" Poor boy ! " said the fairy, " I will give you some supper directly ; and while you eat it I will tell you my history in six words, for I hate much talking. A long tongue is as insupportable as a long nose ; and I remember when I was young how much I used to be admired because I was not a talker ; indeed, some one said to the queen, my mother,—for poor as you see me now, I am the daughter of a great king, who always——"

" Ate when he was hungry, I hope," interrupted the prince, whose patience was fast departing.

" You are right," said the imperturbable old fairy; " and I will bring you your supper directly, only I wish first just to say that the king my father——"

" Hang the king your father ! " Prince Wish was about to exclaim, but he stopped himself, and only observed that however the pleasure of her conversation might make him forget his hunger, it could not have the same effect upon his horse, who was really starving.

The fairy, pleased at his civility, called her servants

and bade them supply him at once with all he needed
"And," added she, "I must say you are very polite and
very good-tempered, in spite of your nose."

"What has the old woman to do with my nose?"
thought the prince. "If I were not so very hungry I would
soon show her what she is—a regular old gossip and
chatter-box. She to fancy she talks little, indeed! One
must be very foolish not to know one's own defects.
This comes of being born a princess. Flatterers have
spoiled her, and persuaded her that she talks little. Little,
indeed! I never knew anybody chatter so much."

While the prince thus meditated, the servants were
laying the table, the fairy asking them a hundred unnecessary questions, simply for the pleasure of hearing
herself talk. "Well," thought Wish, "I am delighted
that I came hither, if only to learn how wise I have been
in never listening to flatterers, who hide from us our faults,
or make us believe they are perfections. But they could
never deceive me. I know all my own weak points, I
trust." As truly he believed he did.

So he went on eating contentedly, nor stopped till the
old fairy began to address him.

"Prince," said she, "will you be kind enough to turn
a little? Your nose casts such a shadow that I cannot see
what is in my plate. And, as I was saying, your father
admired me and always made me welcome at court.
What is the court etiquette there now? Do the ladies
still go to assemblies, promenades, balls?—I beg your
pardon for laughing, but how *very* long your nose is."

"I wish you would cease to speak of my nose," said
the prince, becoming annoyed. "It is what it is, and I do
not desire it any shorter."

"Oh! I see that I have vexed you," returned the
fairy. "Nevertheless, I am one of your best friends, and so
I shall take the liberty of always——" She would doubtless
have gone on talking till midnight; but the prince, unable

342

to bear it any longer, here interrupted her, thanked her for her hospitality, bade her a hasty adieu, and rode away.

He travelled for a long time, half over the world, but he heard no news of Princess Darling. However, in each place he went to, he heard one remarkable fact—the great length of his own nose. The little boys in the streets jeered at him, the peasants stared at him, and the more polite ladies and gentlemen whom he met in society used to try in vain to keep from laughing, and to get out of his way as soon as they could. So the poor prince became gradually quite forlorn and solitary ; he thought all the world was mad, but still he never thought of there being anything queer about his own nose.

At last the old fairy, who, though she was a chatter-box, was very good-natured, saw that he was almost breaking his heart. She felt sorry for him, and wished to help him in spite of himself, for she knew the enchantment, which hid from him the Princess Darling, could never be broken till he had discovered his own defect. So she went in search of the princess, and being more powerful than the magician, since she was a good fairy, and he was an evil magician, she got her away from him, and shut her up in a palace of crystal, which she placed on the road which Prince Wish had to pass.

He was riding along, very melancholy, when he saw the palace ; and at its entrance was a room, made of the purest glass, in which sat his beloved princess, smiling and beautiful as ever. He leaped from his horse, and ran towards her. She held out her hand for him to kiss, but he could not get at it for the glass. Transported with eagerness and delight, he dashed his sword through the crystal, and succeeded in breaking a small opening, to which she put up her beautiful rosy mouth. But it was in vain, Prince Wish could not approach it. He twisted his neck about, and turned his head on all sides, till at length, putting up his hand to his face, he discovered the impediment.

"It must be confessed," exclaimed he, "that my nose *is* too long."

That moment the glass walls all split asunder, and the old fairy appeared, leading Princess Darling.

"Avow, prince," said she, "that you are very much obliged to me, for now the enchantment is ended. You may marry the object of your choice. But," added she, smiling, "I fear I might have talked to you for ever on the subject of your nose, and you would not have believed me in its length, till it became an obstacle to your own inclinations. Now behold it!" and she held up a crystal mirror. "Are you satisfied to be no different from other people?"

"Perfectly," said Prince Wish, who found his nose had shrunk to an ordinary length. And, taking the Princess Darling by the hand, he kissed her, courteously, affectionately, and satisfactorily. Then they departed to their own country, and lived very happy all their days.

THE HIND OF THE FOREST

A BEAUTIFUL queen, whose subjects adored her, and whose husband thought her the best woman in the world, had but one sorrow, which was equally a sorrow both to the king and the country—she brought him no heir to the throne. She, at last, grew so melancholy, that she was ordered for her health to drink the medicinal waters that were found in a celebrated wood ; and one day, sitting beside one of these fountains, which fell into a marble and porphyry basin, she sent all her ladies away, that she might the better weep and lament unobserved.

"How unhappy am I," said she ; "five years I have been married, and am still childless, while the poorest women in the land have children by the dozen. Am I to die without ever giving the king an heir ?"

While she spoke, she noticed that the water of the fountain was slightly disturbed, and there issued thence a large cray-fish, who thus addressed her, " Great queen, you shall have what you desire ; but first you must go to the fairy-palace which is near here, though so surrounded by mists and clouds as to be invisible to mortal eyes, unless you will be conducted there by a poor cray-fish."

Though very much surprised, the queen answered courteously that she had no objection, except that the animal's method of walking would not well suit her own.

The shell-fish smiled—if a shell-fish can smile—and immediately took the shape of a pretty little old woman. " Madam," said she, " we now need not walk crab-fashion.

345

Consider me as your friend, for, indeed, I am desirous of being so."

So saying, she jumped out of the fountain, her clothes not being the least wet, though they were made of white and crimson velvet, nor her grey hair damp : it was tied with green ribbons, and appeared all in order and smooth as silk. She saluted the queen, and then conducted her by a road which, strange to say, well as she knew every portion of the wood, her majesty had never before seen, to a palace of which the walls, roofs, and balconies were built entirely of diamonds.

" Is all this a dream ? " cried the delighted queen.

But no, it was a reality, for the gates straightway opened, and six beautiful fairies appeared, who, making her a profound reverence, presented her with six flowers composed of jewels : a rose, a tulip, an anemone, a jasmine, a carnation, and a heartsease.

" Madam," said they, " we could not give you a greater mark of our favour than in permitting you to come here. We are delighted to tell you that by and by you will have a little daughter, whom you must name Désirée—the Desired. As soon as she is born, call us, and we will endow her with all sorts of good qualities. You have only to take this bouquet, and name each separate flower, thinking of us, when immediately we shall be present in your chamber."

The queen, transported with joy, embraced all the fairies, spent the day with them, and returned, laden with presents, to the fountain side ; where the little old woman jumped into the water, became a cray-fish again, and disappeared.

In due time the Princess Désirée was born, and the queen did as she was told in naming the flowers. Soon, all the six fairies appeared, in different chariots ; of ebony, drawn by white pigeons—of ivory, drawn by black crows, and so on, in great variety. They entered the royal chamber with an air at once cheerful and majestic, embraced the queen and the little princess, and spread out all their presents. These were, linen, so fine that none but fairy hands could have spun it ; lace and embroidery without end ; and a cradle, the wonder of the world. It was made of wood more precious than gold, and at each corner stood four animated images, little cupids, who, as soon as the baby cried, began to rock it of their own accord. Then the six fairies kissed and dandled the princess, bestowing on her for her portion beauty, good temper, good health, talents, long life, and the faculty of doing thoroughly well everything she tried to do. The queen, overcome with gratitude, was thanking them with all her heart for their kindness to her little daughter, when she saw enter her chamber a cray-fish, so large that it could hardly pass through the door.

"Ungrateful queen," said the crab, "have you forgotten the fairy of the fountain ? You sent for these my sisters, and not for me, who am the one to whom you owed most of all."

The queen made a hundred apologies, and the six fairies tried vainly to pacify the other one ; but she was determined, as she said, to punish ingratitude. "However," added she, "I will give no worse gift to the princess than to warn you, that if you let her see daylight before she is fifteen years old, you will repent it." So saying, she retired backwards, crab-fashion, resisting all entreaties to resume her proper form and join in the festivities.

The afflicted mother took council with the six fairies how she was to save her baby from this impending evil, and after many conflicting opinions they advised her to build a tower without doors or windows, and with a subterranean entrance, which the princess might inhabit till she had passed the fatal age. Everything is easy to fairies ; so three strokes of their wands, making eighteen strokes in all, began and finished the edifice. It was built of green and white marble, ornamented inside with diamonds and emeralds, and hung with tapestry—all fairy work—on which was pictured the lives of heroes. Though there was only lamp-light allowed, yet the lamps were so numerous, that they made the tower seem as bright as day. Whether the princess was ever permitted any fresh air, or taken out for a walk by starlight or moonlight, the history does not say ; but it does say one thing, that she grew up very happy, very lovely, and very well educated.

The six fairies came frequently to see her, and were most kind and affectionate to her ; but the one she loved best among them all was Tulip. By this fairy's advice, the nearer she approached the age of fifteen, the more carefully was Désirée shut up from daylight. But her mother, who was very proud of her beauty, caused her portrait to be painted, and sent among all the neighbouring courts, in order that some prince might seek her in marriage. There was one prince who was so captivated by this likeness, that he shut himself up with it, and talked to it, as if it had been alive, making love to it in the most passionate manner, and then falling into a hopeless melancholy.

When his father tried to discover the cause of this —"Sir," said Prince Warrior (he went by that name, because, young as he was, he had already gained three battles), "my grief is that you wish me to marry the Black Princess, while I will only marry the Princess Désirée. I have seen her portrait, and without her I shall surely die. Behold her ! "

The king looked at the portrait. "Well, my son, I cannot wish for a more charming daughter-in-law ; we will retract our offers for the Black Princess, and send an ambassador to propose for the Princess Désirée."

The prince, kissing his father's hand, overwhelmed

him with his gratitude and joy. A courtier, Becafico by name, young and gallant, was despatched with eighty equipages, a hundred mounted squires, and the portrait of the Prince Warrior, to ask the Princess Désirée in marriage. The report of his splendours travelled before him, till it reached the ears of the king and queen, and of the six fairies, who were all equally delighted.

"But," said the Fairy Tulip, who was the sagest of them, "beware, queen, of allowing Becafico to see our child," as they tenderly called Désirée, "and do not upon any account suffer her to leave her tower for the kingdom of Prince Warrior until her fifteenth birthday is past."

The ambassador arrived ; his magnificent train took twenty-three days in going through the gates of the city. He made his harangue to the king and queen, and much state ceremonial passed between them; then he begged for the honour of an audience with the princess, and was very much astonished to find it denied him—still more so, when the king candidly told him the whole story.

The queen had strictly enjoined the ladies of honour not to tell her daughter one word of the ambassador's visit, or her intended marriage ; yet somehow the princess already knew it quite well. But she was wise enough to say nothing about it ; and when her mother showed her the prince's portrait, and asked her if she should like such a gallant young man for her husband, she replied humbly that she should be quite satisfied with any choice her parents made for her. So her hand was promised, but as she still wanted three months of fifteen, the prince was requested to wait thus long.

He took this delay so much to heart, that he could neither eat nor sleep ; meantime Désirée was little better —she did nothing but look at the prince's portrait, and was exceedingly irritable with Longthorn and Gilliflower, her two maids of honour. The other lady—the Black Princess—was in equally sore plight, for she, too, had fallen in love with the prince's portrait, and his rejection of her hand offended her much.

"What," said she to the ambassador, "your master does not find me handsome enough, or rich enough?"

"Madam," said the ambassador, "as much as a subject dare blame a sovereign, I blame my prince; had I the first throne in the world, I should know to whom to offer it."

He said this, because he feared the bastinado, for Ethiopians are warm haters as well as warm lovers. The Black Princess was softened, and dismissed him, on which he gladly took himself out of the country.

But the Ethiopian lady was too deeply offended with Prince Warrior to pardon him so readily. She mounted her ivory car, drawn by six ostriches which ran at the rate of six leagues an hour, and went to the palace of her godmother, the Fairy of the Fountain, who had been so offended by being forgotten at the birth of Désirée. Arrived there, she unfolded all her annoyances. The fairy consoled her, and promised to aid her in her revenge.

Meantime Becafico had travelled with all diligence to the capital of Désirée's father, where with earnest entreaties he begged that the princess might be sent back with him to her betrothed spouse, who otherwise would certainly die; at which tidings the princess herself was so much moved that she fainted away. Thus her parents discovered how deeply in love she was with Prince Warrior.

"Do not disquiet yourself, my dear child," said the queen; "if the prince suffers, it is you who can console him. My only fear is on account of the menaces of the Fairy of the Fountain."

But Désirée was so eager to start, that she suggested being sent away in a closed carriage, where the light of day should never penetrate, and which should only be opened at night-time to give her food. She was willing to suffer any inconvenience for the sake of saving the life of Prince Warrior.

The parents assented. So there was built a magnificent equipage of green velvet outside, and lined with rose-colour and silver brocade. It was very large, but it shut up as tight as a box, and it had a huge lock, the key of which was entrusted to one of the highest noblemen of the court. In this carriage Désirée was placed, after most affecting adieus, by her father and mother ; and with her were sent her maids of honour, Longthorn and Gilliflower, and a lady-in-waiting, who was the mother of both. Now, Longthorn cared little for the princess, but she cared very much for Prince Warrior, whose portrait she had seen ; and when the bridal train departed, she said to her mother that she should certainly die if this marriage were accomplished ; so the mother, notwith-standing the confidence placed in her by the queen, that she should watch over the princess, and carefully seclude her from daylight until she had reached the age of fifteen, yielded to her own child's persuasions, and determined to betray her trust.

Longthorn, who learned each evening from the officers of the household, when they came to bring the princess her supper, how far they were on their journey, at last persuaded her mother, who put off the cruel act as long as she could, that it would never do to wait any longer. They were nearly at the capital, and the young prince might, in his impatience, come to meet them, and the opportunity be lost. So next day, at noon, when the sun was at the hottest, the lady-in-waiting took out a knife, which she had brought with her for the purpose, cut a large hole in the side of the carriage where they were all shut up together, and the princess, for the first time in her life, beheld daylight. She uttered a deep sigh, and immediately leaped out of the carriage in the form of a white hind, which fled away like lightning, and hid itself in the thickest recesses of a neighbouring wood.

None of the train perceived her, or if they had, they would not have known it was she ; besides, the Fairy of the Fountain immediately sent such a storm of thunder and lightning that the whole cavalcade took shelter in the nearest place they could find. The only persons who knew what had happened were Longthorn, her mother, and Gilliflower ; but Gilliflower, overwhelmed with grief, had sprung out of the carriage after her beloved mistress ; so the two others were left alone. Longthorn immediately put on the garments of Désirée, and adorned herself with her royal mantle, her crown of diamonds, her sceptre of a single ruby, and the globe which she carried in her left hand, composed of one enormous pearl. Thus attired, with her mother bearing her train, the false Désirée marched into the city—they two alone ; for, by the fairy's contrivance, the rest of the attendants had been scattered in all directions. Longthorn doubted not the prince would be already advancing to meet his bride, which was indeed the case ; though he was so weak that he had to be conveyed in a litter, surrounded by courtiers and knights, who all wore splendid armour and green plumes, green being the favourite colour of the princess. Seeing the two ladies, so richly dressed, coming forward on foot and unattended, they dismounted, and respectfully greeted them.

" May I inquire," said Longthorn, " who is in that litter ? "

"Madam," replied a knight, "it is the Prince Warrior, who comes to meet his betrothed, the Princess Désirée."

" Tell him," said Longthorn, " that I am she. A fairy, jealous of my happiness, has driven away all my attendants, but that I am Désirée is proved by these my royal ornaments, and the letters of my father, borne by my lady-of-honour here."

Immediately the courtiers kissed the hem of her robe, and made all diligence to announce to the prince, and the king his father, who accompanied him, that the Princess Désirée had arrived.

"What!" cried the king; "arrived here in full daylight?" But the prince, burning with impatience, asked no questions, except about the lady herself: "Is she not a miracle of beauty—according to her portrait?" There was no reply. "You are afraid to speak, gentlemen, lest you should praise her too much."

But the courtiers were still silent. "Sir," at last said one of the boldest of them, "you had better go and see the princess yourself."

The prince, much surprised, would have thrown himself out of his litter; but he was too feeble, and his father went instead. When the king beheld the false princess, he involuntarily drew back; but the lady-of-honour advancing boldly, said:

"Sire, this is the Princess Désirée;—I bear letters from the king and queen her parents, and also a casket of priceless jewels, which they charged me to place in your hands."

The king kept a mournful silence, and regarded his son, who now approached, leaning on one of the courtiers. When he looked at the girl, he recoiled with disgust; for she was so gaunt and tall that the clothes of Désirée scarcely covered her knees, and her extreme thinness, her red hooked nose, her black and ill-shaped teeth, made her as ugly as Désirée was beautiful. Prince Warrior, who for months had thought of nothing but his lovely bride, stood petrified. "King," said he to his father, "I am betrayed! this is not the lady whose portrait was sent me, and to whom I have plighted my faith; I have been deceived, and the deception will cost me my life."

"What do I hear?" replied Longthorn haughtily.

" Prince, who has deceived you ? you will be no victim in marrying me."

" Ah ! my beautiful princess," exclaimed the lady-of-honour, " it is we who are victims. What a reception for one of your rank ! what inconstancy—what falsehood ! But the king your father shall make them hear reason."

" We will make him hear reason ! " cried the other king indignantly. " He promised us a beautiful princess, and he has sent us a skeleton, a fright. I do not wonder he has kept it shut up for fifteen years, and now he wishes to foist it upon us."

And without taking any more notice of Longthorn, he and his son remounted each into his litter, and departed.

Prince Warrior was so overcome by this unexpected affliction, that for a long time he did not speak a word. Then he resolved, as soon as his health allowed, to depart secretly from the capital, and seek some solitary place where he might pass the remainder of his sad life. He communicated this design to no one but the faithful Becafico, who insisted upon following his fortunes wherever he went. So, one day, the prince left a letter for his father, assuring him, that as soon as his mind was tranquillized he would return to the court, but imploring that in the meantime no search might be made after him ; then he and Becafico departed together.

Meanwhile, the poor white hind fled into the wood. She wandered about till she came to a fountain, where, as in a mirror, she saw her own changed shape, and wept, convulsed with grief. Then hunger began to attack her— she bent her head, and browsed upon the green grass, which she was surprised to find tasted very good. She laid herself down on a bank of moss, but passed the night in extreme terror, hearing the wild beasts roaring around her, and often forgetting that she was a hind, trying to save herself by climbing a tree like a human being.

Daybreak reassured her a little ; she admired for the first time the wonderful beauty of dawn ; and when the sun rose, it appeared to her such a marvellous sight that she could not take her eyes from it. She was strangely comforted, spite of all her misfortune, by the charm that she found out, every minute more and more, in the new world which now for the first time she beheld in daylight.

The Fairy Tulip, who loved Désirée, was very sorry for her, although somewhat offended that the queen had not taken her advice, and detained the princess safe in her tower till she was fifteen ; however, she would not leave her a prey to the malice of the Fairy of the Fountain, so contrived invisibly to conduct the faithful Gilliflower to the place where the poor forlorn hind reposed. As soon as Désirée saw her, she leaped the stream, and came towards her former companion, lavishing on her a thousand caresses.

At first Gilliflower was very much astonished to be so taken notice of by a deer of the forest ; but looking at it attentively, she saw two great tears rolling down from the soft human-like eyes, and some instinct told her that it was her dear princess. She took the fore-feet of the hind, and kissed them as respectfully as if they had been her mistress's hands. She spoke to her, and though the hind could not reply, yet it was clear she understood, for the tears flowed faster than ever, and she showed, by as much intelligence as a dumb beast could possibly evince, that she responded to the love of the faithful girl. When Gilliflower promised that she would never quit her, by a hundred little signs the poor hind tried to express how happy she was.

They passed the day together, Désirée leading her companion to a place where she had seen plenty of wild fruits ; so that Gilliflower, who was dying of hunger, became strengthened and refreshed. But when night came, the girl's terrors returned.

"Dear hind," said she, "where shall we sleep ? If

we stay here the wild beasts will devour us; is there no little hut where we can hide?"

The poor hind shook her pretty head, and the tears again began to flow, almost as if she were a human being. Her tears melted the heart of the Fairy Tulip, who had watched her invisibly all the time, and now made herself known—appearing suddenly in a shady alley of the wood. Gilliflower and the white hind threw themselves at her feet —the latter licking her hands, and caressing her as prettily as a deer could—the former imploring her to take pity on the princess, and restore her to her natural shape.

"I cannot do that," said the fairy; "her enemy has too much power; but I can shorten her term of punishment, and soften it a little, by granting that during every night she becomes a woman, though as soon as day breaks she must again wander about as a hind of the forest."

It was a great comfort to be a woman every night; and the hind showed her joy by innumerable leaps and bounds, which delighted the good Tulip.

"Follow this by-path," said she, "and you will find a hut that will serve you as a quiet home. Farewell."

She disappeared, and Gilliflower, with the hind trotting after her, went on and on, till she came to a little hut, before which sat an old woman, making a basket of osiers.

"My good woman," said she, "have you a room to let, for me and my pet here?"

"Yes, truly," replied the old woman; and took them into a room where were two little beds, hung with white dimity, with fine white sheets, and everything as neat and comfortable as possible. As soon as it grew dark, the princess recovered her own shape, and kissed and embraced a thousand times her dear Gilliflower, who, on her part, was full of delight and thankfulness. Then they had their supper, and went to sleep in their two little beds.

When morning broke, Gilliflower was awakened by a

scratching, and there she saw the hind, just as much a hind as before, waiting to be let out. The faithful attendant opened the door, and the deer sprang out quickly, and disappeared in the forest.

Now, by an extraordinary chance, it happened that Prince Warrior, wandering about, indifferent to where he went, lost himself in this very forest, where he had come with his companion Becafico. The latter, seeking for fruits to satisfy their hunger, reached the same cottage-door where the old woman lived, and being received kindly, asked her for some food for his master. She put some bread into a basket, and was going to give it to him, when her charity made her offer the wanderers shelter for the night.

" It is a poor cottage," said she ; " but I have still one empty room, which will at least save you from being eaten up by wolves and lions."

So the prince was persuaded ; and the old woman, who appeared ignorant of his rank, admitted him and Becafico cautiously, so as not to disturb the lady and the hind, who occupied the next room. Thus the two lovers were so near, that they might almost have heard one another speak, yet did not know it.

The prince rarely slept much ; his sorrow was still too great ; and when the first rays of the sun shone through his window, he arose, and went out into the forest. There he wandered a long time without finding any sure track : at last he came upon a sort of bower, overhung with trees, and carpeted with moss, out of which started a beautiful white hind, who immediately fled away.

Now the prince had formerly been a great hunter, until his passion for the chase was swallowed up by his love for Désirée ; but the old fancy returned when he saw the white hind. He could not help following her, and sending after her arrows, not a few, from the bow which he always carried, causing her almost to die of fear ;

although, by the care of the Fairy Tulip, she was not wounded. All through the day he pursued her ; until, towards twilight, she escaped from him towards the cottage, where Gilliflower was watching in the utmost anxiety. The faithful girl received tenderly into her arms the poor hind, breathless, exhausted ; and eagerly awaited the moment when her mistress should become a woman again, and tell her what had happened. When darkness came on, the deer vanished, and it was the Princess Désirée who lay on Gilliflower's bosom.

"Alas !" cried she, weeping. "I have more to fear than the Fairy of the Fountain, and the wild beasts of the forest. I have been pursued all day by a young hunter, whom I had scarcely seen, before he obliged me to fly ; and sent so many arrows after me that I marvel I was not killed, or at least wounded."

"My princess, you must never quit this room again," said Gilliflower.

"I must ; for the same enchantment which makes me a hind forces me to do as hinds do. I feel myself every morning irresistibly compelled to run into the wood, to leap and bound, and eat grass, and behave myself exactly like a wild creature of the forest. Oh, how weary I am !"

Her soft eyes closed, and she fell asleep until the dawn of day, when again she was driven out in the shape of a poor four-footed creature, to fulfil her sad destiny.

The prince on his part came home also very much wearied and vexed. "Becafico," he said, "I have spent the day in chasing the most beautiful hind I ever saw. She has slipped from me time after time with the most wondrous adroitness ; yet my arrows were so true that I marvel how she escaped. At dawn to-morrow I must be after her once more."

So he did not fail to go, at earliest dawn, to her hiding-place ; but the hind took care not to revisit her favourite haunt. He sought her everywhere, and could see nothing ; then being very tired and hot, he gathered some luscious apples which he saw hanging upon a tree over his head. As soon as he ate them he fell fast asleep.

Meantime the hind, roaming stealthily about, came to the place where he lay—came quite suddenly, or else she would have taken to flight ; but now seeing her enemy sound asleep, she paused a minute to look at him ; and in his features, wasted with grief, but still so lovable and beautiful, she recognised the face which had long been engraven on her heart. The poor hind ! she crouched down at a little distance, and watched him, her eyes beaming with joy. Then she sighed : at length, become bolder, she approached nearer, and softly touched him with her fore-foot.

Awaking, what was the prince's surprise to see beside him, tame and familiar, the pretty creature whom he had hunted all yesterday ; but when he put out his hand to seize her, she fled away like lightning. He followed with all the speed he could, and thus, she flying and he pursuing, they passed the whole day. Towards evening her strength failed ; and when the hunter came up to her it was a poor half-dying deer that he found lying on the grass. She thought her death was certain—still, from his hands, it did not seem so terrible as from any one else ; but instead of killing her he caressed her.

" Beautiful hind," said he, " do not be afraid. I only wish to take you home with me, and have you with me always." He cut branches of trees, wove them ingeniously into a sort of couch, which he strewed with roses and moss ; then took the creature in his arms, laid her gently down upon them, and sat beside her, feeding her from time to time with the softest grass he could find. She ate contentedly from his hand, and he almost fancied she understood all the sweet things he said to her, and so time passed till it grew dusk.

"My pretty hind," said he, "I will go in search of a stream where you can drink, and then we will take our way home together." But while he was absent she stole away, and had only time to reach the cottage when the transformation happened, and it was not a hind but a weeping princess who threw herself on the bed beside the faithful Gilliflower.

"I have seen him!" she cried. "My Prince Warrior is himself in this forest: he was the hunter who has pursued me these two days, and has taken me at last. But he did not slay me: he saved and caressed me. Ah, he is gentler and sweeter even than the image in my heart."

Here she began again to weep; but Gilliflower consoled her, and they went to sleep, wondering much how this adventure would end.

The prince, returning from the stream, missed his beautiful white hind, and came back to Becafico full of grief, mingled with a certain anger at the ingratitude of the creature to whom he had been so kind. But at break of day he rose, determined again to pursue her. She, however, in order to avoid him, took a quite different route. Still, the forest was not so large but that at last he saw her, leaping and bounding among the bushes. Seized by an irresistible impulse, he shot an arrow after her; it struck her, she felt a violent pain dart through one of her slender limbs, and fell helpless on the grass. When the prince came up to her, he was overcome with remorse for his cruelty. He took a handful of herbs and bound up her wound, made her a bed of branches and moss, laid her head upon his knees, and wept over her.

"My lovely hind," said he, "why did I wound you so cruelly? You will hate me, when I wish you to love me." So he tended and cherished her all day, and, towards nightfall, he knotted a ribbon round her neck, with the intention of gently leading her home. But she struggled with him; and the struggle was so sore that

Gilliflower, coming out in search of her dear mistress, heard the rustling, and saw her hind in the hunter's power. She rushed to rescue her, to the prince's great astonishment.

"Whatever consideration I owe you, madam," said he, "you must know that you are committing a robbery; this hind is mine."

"No, sir, she is mine," returned Gilliflower respectfully. "She knows she is, and will prove it if you will only give her a little liberty. My pretty pet, come and embrace me." The hind crept into her arms. "Now kiss me on my right cheek." She obeyed. "Now touch my heart." She laid her foot against Gilliflower's bosom.

"I allow she is yours," said the prince discontentedly. "Take her, and go your ways."

But he followed them at a distance, and was very much surprised to see them enter the cottage. He asked the old woman who the damsel was, but she said she did not know, except that the lady and the hind lived there together in solitude, and paid her well. But when Becafico, who had eyes as sharp as needles, coming to meet his master, by chance caught sight of Gilliflower, he recognised her at once.

"Here is some great mystery," said he, "for that is the lady who was the favourite of the Princess Désirée."

"Do not utter that name, which only recalls my grief," said the prince sadly; but Becafico, determined to gratify his curiosity, made all sorts of inquiries, and discovered that Gilliflower was lodged in the next room.

"I should like to see her again," thought he; "and since only a thin partition divides us, I will bore a hole through."

He did so, and beheld a wonderful sight. There sat the fairest princess in all the world, attired in a robe of silver brocade, her hair falling in long curls, and her eyes sparkling through tears. Gilliflower knelt before her, binding up her beautiful arm, from which the blood was flowing.

"Do not heed it," sighed the princess; "better let me die, for death itself would be sweeter than the life I lead. Alas! how hard it is to be a hind all day; to see my betrothed, to feel his tenderness and goodness, yet be unable to speak to him, or to tell him the fatal destiny which divides me from him."

When Becafico heard this, words cannot describe his astonishment and delight. He ran towards the prince, who sat moodily at the window. "Sir," cried he, "only look through this hole, and you will see the original of the portrait which so fascinated you."

The prince looked, and recognised at once his beloved princess. He would have died with joy, had he not believed himself deceived by some enchantment. He knocked at the door, Gilliflower opened it; he entered, and threw himself at the feet of Désirée. What followed —of explanations, vows, tears, and embraces—was never very clearly related, not even by Gilliflower and Becafico, who were present, but who considerately drew aside, and spent the time in conversing with one another. So passed the night; and anxiously they awaited for the dawn, to see whether the beautiful princess would again become a hind of the forest. But the day broke, grew clearer, brightened into sunrise, and the princess, with the prince sitting beside her, remained a beautiful maiden still. Then came a knock at the door, and there entered the little old woman, who had been such a kind hostess for all this while.

"The period of enchantment is ended, my children," said she. "Go home, and be happy." And then they knew her as no longer the little old woman, but the Fairy Tulip, who had thus faithfully watched her charge.

So the bride and bridegroom returned to their capital, where the marriage was solemnized with all splendour, and, at Désirée's request, Longthorn and her mother, who had been imprisoned by the old king's order, were set free, with no further punishment than banishment to their own country, where they were to remain for life. As for the faithful Gilliflower, she stayed at court, with her beloved mistress, and became the wife of the equally faithful Becafico, who had served Prince Warrior as devotedly as she the Princess Désirée. The two were laden with wealth and honours, and shared the happiness of the other two lovers, which was as great as any mortal could desire. After their death the story of the White Hind of the Forest was commanded to be written down in the archives of the State, and thence it has been told in tradition, or sung in poetry, half over the world.

THE JUNIPER-TREE

ONE or two thousand years ago, there was a rich man who had a beautiful and pious wife; they loved one another dearly, but they had no children. They wished and prayed for some night and day, but still they had none. In front of their house was a yard, where stood a Juniper-tree, and under it the wife stood once in winter, and peeled an apple, and as she peeled the apple she cut her finger, and the blood fell on the snow.

"Oh," said she, sighing deeply and looking sorrowfully at the blood, "if I only had a child as red as blood, and as white as snow!"

While she spoke, she became quite happy; it seemed to her as if her wish would surely come to pass. Then she went into the house; and a month passed, and the snow melted; and two months, and the ground was green; and three months, and the flowers came up out of the earth; and four months, and all the trees in the wood burst forth, and the green twigs all grew thickly together; the little birds sang so that the whole wood rang, and the blossoms fell from the trees. The fifth month passed, and she stood under the Juniper-tree, and it smelt so beautiful, and her heart leaped for joy. She fell upon her knees, but could not speak. When the sixth month was gone, the fruit was large and ripe, and she was very quiet; the seventh month, she took the juniper berries, ate them eagerly, and was sick and sorrowful; and the eighth month went by, and she called to her husband,

364

and cried and said, "If I die, bury me under the Juniper-tree."

After this she was quite comforted and happy, till the next month was past, and then she had a child as white as snow and as red as blood. When she beheld it, she was so glad, that she died.

Her husband buried her under the Juniper-tree, and began to mourn very much; but after a little time, he became calmer, and when he had wept a little more, he left off weeping entirely, and soon afterwards he took another wife.

The second wife brought him a daughter, but the child of the first wife was a little son, and was as red as blood, and as white as snow. When the wife looked at her daughter, she loved her; but when she looked at the little boy, she hated him, and it seemed as if he were always in her way, and she was always thinking how she could get all the property for her daughter. The Evil One possessed her so, that she was quite angry with the little boy, and pushed him about from one corner to another, and cuffed him here and pinched him there, until the poor child was always in fear. When he came home from school, he could not find a quiet place to creep into.

Once, when the woman went up to her room, her little daughter came up too, and said, "Mother, give me an apple."

"Yes, my child," said the woman, and gave her a beautiful apple out of the chest; and the chest had a great heavy lid, with a great sharp iron lock.

"Mother," said the little daughter, "shall not brother have one too?"

That vexed the woman, but she said, "Yes, when he comes from school."

And when she saw from the window that he was coming, it was just as if the Evil One came into her, and she snatched away the apple from her daughter, and said, "You shall not have one before your brother."

Then she threw the apple into the chest, and shut the

lid close down. When the little boy came in at the door, the Evil One made her say kindly, "My son, will you have an apple?"

Yet she looked so angry all the time, that the little boy said, "Mother, how dreadful you look! Yes, give me an apple."

Then she felt that she must speak to him. "Come with me," said she, and opened the lid; "pick out an apple for yourself."

And as the little boy stooped over, the Evil One prompted her, and smash! she banged the lid down, so that his head flew off and fell among the red apples. Then she was seized with terror, and thought, "Can I get rid of the blame of this?" So she went up to her room to her chest of drawers, and took out of the top drawer a white cloth, and placed the head on the neck again, and tied the handkerchief round it, so that one could see nothing, and set him before the door on a chair, and gave him the apple in his hand.

Soon after, little Margery came to her mother, who stood by the kitchen fire, and had a pot of hot water before her, which she kept stirring round.

"Mother," said little Margery, "brother sits before the door, and looks quite white, and has an apple in his hand; I asked him to give me the apple, but he did not answer me, and I was frightened."

"Go to him again," said her mother, "and if he will not answer you, give him a box on the ear."

Then Margery went, and said, "Brother, give me the apple."

But he was silent, so she gave him a box on the ear, and the head fell down.

She was frightened, and began to cry and sob, and ran to her mother, and said, "Oh, mother, I have knocked my brother's head off!" and cried and cried, and would not be comforted.

"Margery," said her mother, "what have you done!
—but now be quiet, and no one will notice; it cannot be
helped now—we will cook him in vinegar."

Then the mother took the little boy, and chopped him
in pieces, put him into the pot, and cooked him in vinegar.
But Margery stood by, and cried and cried, and all her
tears fell into the pot, so that the cookery did not want
any salt.

When the father came home, and sat down to dinner,
he said, "Where is my son?"

The mother brought a great big dish of black soup,
and Margery cried and cried without ceasing. Then the
father said again, "Where is my son?"

"Oh," said the mother, "he is gone into the country,
to see his uncle, where he is going to stay awhile."

"What does he want there? And he has not even
said good-bye to me!"

"Oh, he wished very much to go, and asked if he
might remain away six weeks; he is well taken care of
there, you know."

"Well," said the father, "I am sorry; for he ought
to have bade me good-bye."

After that he began to eat, and said, "Margery, what
are you crying for? Brother will be sure to come back.
Oh, wife," continued he, "how delicious this food tastes;
give me some more." And the more he ate, the more he
wanted; and he said, "Give me more, you shall not have
any of it; I feel as if it were all mine." And he ate and
ate, throwing the bones under the table, till he had
finished it all.

But Margery went to her drawers, and took out of
the bottom drawer her best silk handkerchief, and fetched
out all the bones from under the table; she tied them up
in the silk handkerchief, and took them out of doors, and
shed bitter tears over them. Then she laid them under
the Juniper-tree in the green grass; and when she had

put them there, she felt all at once quite happy, and did not cry any more.

Soon the Juniper began to move, and the twigs kept dividing and then closing, just as if the tree were clapping its hands for joy. After that there went up from it a sort of mist, and right in the centre of the mist burnt a fire, and out of the fire flew a beautiful bird, who, singing deliciously, rose up high in the air. When he was out of sight, the Juniper-tree was just as it had been before, only the handkerchief with the bones was gone. But Margery felt quite pleased and happy, just as if her brother were still alive. And she went back merrily into the house to dinner.

The bird flew away, sat himself on a goldsmith's house, and began to sing :

> " My mother, she killed me ;
> My father, he ate me ;
> My sister, little Margery,
> Gathered up all my bones,
> Tied them in a silk handkerchief,
> And laid them under the Juniper-tree :
> Kywitt ! Kywitt ! what a beautiful bird am I ! "

The goldsmith sat in his workshop, making a gold chain, but he heard the bird, which sat on his roof, and sang, and he thought it very beautiful. He stood up, and as he went over the door-step he lost one slipper. But he went right into the middle of the street, with one slipper and one sock on ; he had on his leather apron ; in one hand he carried the gold chain, and in the other the pincers, while the sun shone brightly up the street. There he stood, and looked at the bird.

" Bird," said he, " how beautifully you can sing ! Sing me that song again."

" No," said the bird, " I do not sing twice for nothing. Give me that gold chain, and I will sing it again."

"There," said the goldsmith; "you shall have the gold chain—now sing me that song once more."

Then the bird came and took the gold chain in his right claw, and went and sat before the goldsmith, and sang:

> My mother, she killed me;
> My father, he ate me;
> My sister, little Margery,
> Gathered up all my bones,
> Tied them in a silk handkerchief,
> And laid them under the Juniper-tree:
> Kywitt! Kywitt! what a beautiful bird am I!

Afterwards he flew away to a shoemaker's, and set himself on his roof, and sang:

> My mother, she killed me;
> My father, he ate me;
> My sister, little Margery,
> Gathered up all my bones,
> Tied them in a silk handkerchief,
> And laid them under the Juniper-tree:
> Kywitt! Kywitt! what a beautiful bird am I!

When the shoemaker heard it, he ran out of his door in his shirt-sleeves, looked towards his roof, and had to hold his hand over his eyes, so that the sun should not dazzle him.

"Bird," said he, "how beautifully you can sing!" And he called in at his door, "Wife, just come out; there is a bird here which can sing so beautifully." Then he called his daughter and his workpeople, both boys and girls; they all came into the street, looked at the bird, and saw how handsome he was; for he had bright red and green feathers, and his neck shone like real gold, and his eyes twinkled in his head like stars.

"Bird," said the shoemaker, "now sing me that song again."

"No," replied the bird, "I do not sing twice for nothing; you must give me something."

" Wife," said the man, " go to the garret : on the highest shelf there stands a pair of red shoes—bring them here."

The wife went and fetched the shoes.

" There," said the man, " now sing me that song again."

Then the bird came and took the shoes in his left claw and flew back on the roof, and sang :

> My mother, she killed me ;
> My father, he ate me ;
> My sister, little Margery,
> Gathered up all my bones,
> Tied them in a silk handkerchief,
> And laid them under the Juniper-tree :
> Kywitt ! Kywitt ! what a beautiful bird am I !

And when he had finished, he flew away, with the chain in his right claw and the shoes in his left. He flew far away to a mill, and the mill went " Clipper, clapper, clipper, clapper, clipper, clapper." And in the mill there sat twenty millers, who chopped a stone, and chopped, " Hick, hack, hick, hack, hick, hack " ; and the mill went, " Clipper, clapper, clipper, clapper, clipper, clapper."

The bird flew up, and sat in a lime-tree that grew before the mill, and sang :

> My mother, she killed me ;

then one man stopped ;

> My father, he ate me ;

then two more stopped and listened ;

> My sister, little Margery,

then four more stopped ;

> Gathered up all my bones,
> Tied them in a silk handkerchief,

now only eight more were chopping,

                    Laid them under
now only five,
                    the Juniper-tree.
now only one.

        Kywitt! Kywitt! what a beautiful bird am I!

Then the last man stopped too, and heard the last word.
"Bird," said he, "how beautifully you sing! Please to sing me that song once more."

"No," answered the bird, "I do not sing twice for nothing; give me the millstone, and I will sing it again."

"Yes," said he, "if it belonged to me only, you should have it."

"Yes," cried all the others, "if he sings it again, he shall have it."

Then the bird came down, and all the twenty millers took poles, and lifted the stone up. The bird stuck his neck through the hole in the millstone, and put it on like a collar, and flew back to the tree, and sang:

> My mother, she killed me;
> My father, he ate me;
> My sister, little Margery,
> Gathered up all my bones,
> Tied them in a silk handkerchief,
> And laid them under the Juniper-tree:
> Kywitt! Kywitt! what a beautiful bird am I!

And when he had done singing, he opened his wings, and though he had in his right claw the chain, in his left the shoes, and round his neck the millstone, he flew far away to his father's house.

In the room sat the father, the mother, and little Margery at dinner; and the father said, "Oh, how happy I am! altogether joyful."

"For me," said the mother, "I feel quite frightened, as if a dreadful storm was coming."

But Margery sat, and cried and cried.

Then there came the bird flying, and as he perched himself on the roof, "Oh," said the father, "I feel so happy, and the sun shines out of doors so beautifully! It is just as if I were going to see an old friend."

"No," said the wife; "I am so frightened, my teeth chatter, and it feels as if there was a fire in my veins"; and she tore open her dress. But Margery sat in a corner, and cried, holding her apron before her eyes, till the apron was quite wet through.

The bird perched upon the Juniper-tree, and sang:

> My mother, she killed me;

Then the mother stopped up her ears, and shut her eyes tight, and did not want to see or hear; but there was a roaring in her ears like the loudest thunder, and her eyes burned and flashed like lightning—

> My father, he ate me;

"Oh, wife," said the man, "look at that beautiful bird!—he sings so splendidly. And the sun shines so warm, and there is a smell like real cinnamon!"

> My sister, little Margery,

Then Margery laid her head on her knee, and sobbed out loud; but the man said, "I shall go out—I must look at the bird quite close."

"Oh, do not go," said the wife; "it seems to me as if the whole house shook, and was in flames."

But the man went out and watched the bird, which still went on singing:

> Gathered up all my bones,
> Tied them in a silk handkerchief,
> And laid them under the Juniper-tree:
> Kywitt! Kywitt! what a beautiful bird am I!

After that, the bird let the gold chain fall, and it fell

right on to the man's neck, fitting exactly round it.   He went in and said, "See what a beautiful bird that is—it has given me such a splendid gold chain!"

But the wife was frightened, and fell flat down on the' floor, and her cap dropped off her head.

Then the bird sang again :

> My mother, she killed me ;

"Oh, that I were a thousand feet under the earth, so that I might not hear!"

> My father, he ate me,

Then she fell down, as if she was dead.

> My sister, little Margery,

"Oh!" said Margery, "I will go out too, and see if the bird will give me anything."

> Gathered up all my bones,
> Tied them in a silk handkerchief,

And the shoes were thrown down.

> And laid them under the Juniper-tree :
> Kywitt! Kywitt! what a beautiful bird am I !

Then Margery was very joyful ; she put on the new red shoes, and danced and jumped about.   "Oh," said she, "I was so unhappy when I came out, and now I am so happy!   That is a wonderful bird ; he has given me a pair of red shoes."

"For me," cried the wife, and jumped up, and her hair stood on end like flames of fire, "I feel as if the world were come to an end ; I will go out—perhaps I shall feel easier."

But as she went out of the door—smash !—the bird threw the millstone on her head, and she was crushed to pieces.

The father and Margery heard it, and rushed out to see what had happened : there was a great flame and smoke rising up from the place, and when that was gone, there stood the little brother all alive again—as if he had never died. He took his father and Margery by the hand, and they were all three quite happy, and went into the house to dinner.

CLEVER ALICE

Once upon a time there was a man who had a daughter, who was called "Clever Alice"; and when she was grown up, her father said, "We must see about her marrying."

"Yes," replied her mother, "whenever a young man shall appear who is worthy of her."

At last a certain youth, by name Hans, came from a distance to make a proposal of marriage; but he required one condition, that the Clever Alice should be very prudent.

"Oh," said her father, "no fear of that! she has got a head full of brains"; and the mother added, "Ah, she can see the wind blow up the street, and hear the flies cough!"

"Very well," replied Hans; "but remember, if she is not very prudent, I will not take her." Soon afterwards they sat down to dinner, and her mother said, "Alice, go down into the cellar and draw some beer."

So Clever Alice took the jug down from the wall, and went into the cellar, jerking the lid up and down on her way, to pass away the time. As soon as she got downstairs, she drew a stool and placed it before the cask, in order that she might not have to stoop, for she thought stooping might in some way injure her back, and give it an undesirable bend. Then she placed the can before her and turned the tap, and while the beer was

375

running, as she did not wish her eyes to be idle, she looked about upon the wall above and below. Presently she perceived, after much peeping into this corner and that corner, a hatchet, which the bricklayers had left behind, sticking out of the ceiling right above her head. At the sight of this Clever Alice began to cry, saying, "Oh! if I marry Hans, and we have a child, and he grows up, and we send him into the cellar to draw beer, the hatchet will fall upon his head and kill him"; and so she sat there weeping with all her might over the impending misfortune.

Meanwhile the good folks upstairs were waiting for the beer, but as Clever Alice did not come, her mother told the maid to go and see what she was stopping for. The maid went down into the cellar, and found Alice sitting before the cask crying heartily, and she asked, "Alice, what are you weeping about?"

"Ah," she replied, "have I not cause? If I marry Hans, and we have a child, and he grow up, and we send him here to draw beer, that hatchet will fall upon his head and kill him."

"Oh," said the maid, "what a clever Alice we have!" And, sitting down, she began to weep, too, for the misfortune that was to happen.

After a while, when the servant did not return, the good folks above began to feel very thirsty; so the husband told the boy to go down into the cellar, and see what had become of Alice and the maid. The boy went down, and there sat Clever Alice and the maid both crying, so he asked the reason; and Alice told him the same tale, of the hatchet that was to fall on her child, if she married Hans, and if they had a child. When she had finished, the boy exclaimed, "What a clever Alice we have!" and fell weeping and howling with the others.

Upstairs they were still waiting, and the husband said, when the boy did not return, "Do you go down, wife, into the cellar and see why Alice stays so long." So she went down, and finding all three sitting there crying, asked the reason, and Alice told her about the hatchet which must inevitably fall upon the head of her son. Then the mother likewise exclaimed, " Oh, what a clever Alice we have !" and, sitting down, began to weep as much as any of the rest.

Meanwhile the husband waited for his wife's return ; but at last he felt so very thirsty, that he said, " I must go myself down into the cellar and see what is keeping our Alice." As soon as he entered the cellar, there he found the four sitting and crying together, and when he heard the reason, he also exclaimed, " Oh, what a clever Alice we have !" and sat down to cry with the whole strength of his lungs.

At this time the bridegroom above sat waiting, but when nobody returned, he thought they must be waiting for him, and so he went down to see what was the matter. When he entered, there sat the five crying and groaning, each one in a louder key than his neighbour.

" What misfortune has happened ?" he asked.

" Ah, dear Hans !" cried Alice, " if you and I should marry one another, and have a child, and he grow up, and we, perhaps, send him down to this cellar to tap the beer, the hatchet which has been left sticking up there may fall on his head, and so kill him ; and do you not think this is enough to weep about ?"

" Now," said Hans, " more prudence than this is not necessary for my housekeeping ; because you are such a clever Alice, I will have you for my wife." And, taking her hand, he led her home, and celebrated the wedding directly.

After they had been married a little while, Hans said one morning, " Wife, I will go out to work and earn some money ; do you go into the field and gather some corn wherewith to make bread."

"Yes," she answered, "I will do so, dear Hans." And when he was gone, she cooked herself a nice mess of pottage to take with her. As she came to the field she said to herself, "What shall I do? Shall I cut first, or eat first? Ay, I will eat first!" Then she ate up the contents of her pot, and when it was finished, she thought to herself, "Now, shall I reap first or sleep first? Well, I think I will have a nap!" and so she laid herself down amongst the corn, and went to sleep.

Meanwhile Hans returned home, but Alice did not come, and so he said, "Oh, what a prudent Alice I have! She is so industrious that she does not even come home to eat anything." By-and-by, however, evening came on, and still she did not return; so Hans went out to see how much she had reaped; but, behold, nothing at all, and there lay Alice fast asleep among the corn! So home he ran very fast, and brought a net with little bells hanging on it, which he threw over her head while she still slept on. When he had done this, he went back again and shut to the house-door, and, seating himself on his stool, began working very industriously.

At last, when it was nearly dark, the Clever Alice awoke, and as soon as she stood up, the net fell all over her hair, and the bells jingled at every step she took. This quite frightened her, and she began to doubt whether she were really Clever Alice, and said to herself, "Am I she, or am I not?" This was a question she could not answer, and she stood still a long while considering about it. At last she thought she would go home and ask whether she were really herself—supposing somebody would be able to tell her. When she came to the house-door it was shut; so she tapped at the window, and asked, "Hans, is Alice within?" "Yes," he replied, "she is." At which answer she became really terrified, and exclaiming, "Ah, heaven, then I am not Alice!" she ran up to another house, intending to ask the same

question.   But as soon as the folks within heard the
jingling of the bells in her net, they refused to open
their doors, and nobody would receive her.   So she ran
straight away from the village, and no one has ever seen
her since.

THE END